BURROW

BURROW

MANZU ISLAM

PEEPAL TREE

First published in Great Britain in 2004
Peepal Tree Press
17 King's Avenue
Leeds LS6 1QS
England

ISBN 1 900715 90 2

Peepal Tree gratefully acknowledges Arts Council support

For

Ines Aguirre

PROLOGUE

It all began with crocuses.

Each spring, for the last seven years, Tapan has been going to Hyde Park to see crocuses. He wanders at random, takes it slowly, stopping every so often for a closer look. He hunches over the clumps, brushes his eyes over the spread of colours. He compares the present blooms with those of previous years, and continues until he reaches the Serpentine.

He finds this ritual absurd because he is not into flowers and doesn't care much for crocuses. Yet he comes here each year because crocuses petaled his earliest vision of England.

Long before he came to England, when he was growing up in Bangladesh, his grandfather gave him a book. He called him to the shade of the veranda in the afternoon. He was slumped on a canvas recliner, eyes half closed, puffing a hooka. Straightening his back slightly he took the book from his lap and handed it to Tapan. 'My boy,' he said. 'You can see England in this book. The most beautiful land on earth.'

He dutifully read the book to please his grandfather. The author, a Bangladeshi man of romantic temper, while giving vent to his passion for all things English, had composed a charming narrative of his brief stay in London. He forgot much of the book but the crocuses remained.

On his seventh year in England he goes to Hyde Park once more. It is a bright spring day. He gets off at Marble Arch tube station, walks along Bayswater Road, and enters the park through Victoria Gate. As usual he hasn't set a precise course, but he knows that somehow he will reach the Serpentine.

He walks for a long time among the soft spring grasses, oblivious to his childhood vision of England blooming here in a mosaic of lilac, purple, yellow and white. He comes back, following the routes he has taken earlier, tries others that go straight between the trees, or diagonally across the grass that dips at a slight incline. He quickens his pace, almost breaks into a run to reach the next landmark, but still does not find his way to the Serpentine. He feels he is circling in a maze.

Exhausted, he sits leaning against the smooth trunk of a tall tree. Just to his right is a purple patch of crocuses. He turns his head to look at them, chooses the brightest one, and presses the tip of his finger against its spongy flesh. A wind slightly ruffles the grasses. He zips his jacket up and pulls his woolly cap down.

Recently he has been dreaming of something that he doesn't quite remember. But this morning was different. A bang on his door woke him up and he caught the dream before it could flee to the other side of his memory.

He is sure that the season of his dream is autumn. He is by the sea. Trees are shedding their leaves. Suddenly a yellow leaf falls on his face. He does not flinch but picks the leaf up and feels its moisture in his hand. What connection does the leaf have with him? He doesn't know – perhaps it's not even important to know. All he knows is that the dream goes through him as though he is with an old friend in a familiar garden.

Nothing ruffles his dream: neither the roar of the wind nor the silence of the depths. But the yellow leaf whispering to the conch by the sea is different. Every time he hears the whispering leaf he is carried away as if by a lullaby across the seas. To an unknown land. No one notices his departure except his grandfather. He is happy, the tassel of his fez dangling in the wind. He smiles as he waves goodbye to Tapan. 'See the crocuses for me, but take care not to touch them,' he says. 'It'll please me, my boy, you seeing the crocuses for me.'

He arrives on a barren shore littered with the debris of lost time: muskets, gallows, steam engines, indigo, spices, torn muslin, and diamond encrusted crowns. Yet he expects his dream to bloom, as if on his arrival the bone dry land will receive long awaited rain. He is happy for himself and for his grandfather. But when it rains the whole day it leaves the conch full of water, right to its brim. So the whisper of the leaf turns back upon itself like the cry of Echo in the desolation of the forest.

He is ambling along the empty shore. Suddenly through the thicket of mist a horseman gallops towards him. He has a sword, unsheathed, in his armoured hand. The horseman's face is covered by the visor of his jousting helmet, like a dark veil of death. The leaf, trembling somewhere between himself and the horseman, and unable to whisper to the conch, floats in the air. The horseman, with his spurred feet firmly in the stirrup and pulling the reigns tightly, gallops in to slice the leaf. His grandfather turns his back and walks away. Even the conch cannot mourn for the mutilation of the leaf. Hemmed in by the debris of lost time he lies flat on the sand. Then a sudden gust of wind brings the sliced leaf and drops it on his naked face. The horseman, with a pull on the reins, rides away, his job done.

Split in half, the leaf caresses his face, telling him the story it would have whispered to the conch if it hadn't rained that day. To begin with, it tells him what he has always known, that he is indeed an intruder on the land of the horseman. And yet, hadn't the horseman, a long time ago, set sail, with murderous conquest in his heart, for the land from where he came? Even in his dreams he is puzzled by this curious symmetry: he came here because the horseman went there. But unlike the horseman's lumbering tracks through trails of blood, he came lightly, as if on the homing flight of a migratory bird.

Somehow, and always, he reaches a steeply sloping pathway that carries him headlong, as if he is shooting down a slide. Then he invariably comes up against the horseman. As expected, the horseman has already turned into the gatekeeper. He doesn't see the expression on the gatekeeper's face, nor does he hear him say a word. Rooted deep in his land, his bulk as stolid as the trunk of an oak tree, he is entirely given to the power of smell. When he attempts to sneak past, the gatekeeper smells him out and bars his way with his bulk. Seeing his desperate plight, his grandfather pleads for him, 'Please, honourable custodian. Please, let my grandson enter your beautiful land. I've been a most loyal servant of your people. Look, I've brought you the duck curry. Remember how much you used to like it. Please.' The gatekeeper not only ignores his grandfather but chases him away.

Exhausted by his repeated attempts to get through, he sits down in the shadow cast by the gatekeeper, whose girth matches his height.

He passes the time by waiting, expecting the gatekeeper to put on a face, until he hears the rustle of feet gliding through the mist. With swaying lanterns they are carrying a coffin towards the passage that leads to the gate at the end of the mist. On an impulse, he rushes towards them and asks, 'Whose body are you carrying?'

They do not answer him, they are faceless and tongueless, as they approach the archway with the rhythmic sway of their lanterns. As though he has known of the approach of the body for sometime, and without a word being exchanged, the gatekeeper lets them pass.

Once more he hears the hooves, and when he looks back, he sees the horseman galloping towards him, the unsheathed sword in his hand. His grandfather is there too, observing the scene from behind the dunes, sobbing, but he does not come to claim the body: he is too ashamed of having an illegal immigrant as his grandson.

It is still bright in Hyde Park. A dog barks and comes to sniff at him and Tapan jumps up, shakes the dream out of himself. Frightened, the dog runs away as if it has seen a ghost.

Free at last, he walks through many more patches of crocuses, looking at their colours: how beautiful they look in this late afternoon, against the soft spring sun. He feels happy and finally, as he has done so many times before, he reaches the Serpentine.

CHAPTER 1

Nothing could be simpler. All Tapan had to do was to find two witnesses willing to tag along with them to the registry office. Once the ceremony was over, it was just a matter of waiting. The woman at the law centre told him, 'If there is no complication you'll be through the process in a year.'

He knew that the woman in round glasses did not believe his story. She had seen it all too often before to swallow any soppy shit about love. 'Don't drag love into this sordid affair,' she seemed to be saying as she puckered her brow and looked beyond him. 'I know you're only interested in the marriage certificate. You want to legalise your stay in our country. Don't you?'

Of course, there was no love. But what could be the complication? In fact it was Adela who suggested that they get married, pretend to be a happy couple until he got his residency. 'Perhaps we can fall in love when you're a full British citizen,' Adela joked as they came out of the registry office.

Perhaps it was the marriage that poisoned the promise of love. Once they had concluded the transaction and become husband and wife on paper their fate was sealed. He needed to stay in England and she needed to betray England. In the following months, these things came between them, though there were no wild rows, hysterical scenes, or bitter accusations.

Even in their most tender moments, at the point of absolute surrender, when Adela gave him her green eyes without any reserve and he reciprocated, they became aware of their sordid transaction. If they went through with the act of love it was done with such abstraction, as if they were extracting pleasure from mechanical bodies. Worse still, like a whore and a gigolo.

Afterwards, they didn't talk, carefully avoided each other. While Adela went for her long shower, he stayed staring at the television. Yet, there was a time when they felt at ease, if not happy, in each other's company. He was Tapan Ali, a foreign student from Bangladesh, and she was Adela Richardson, a local English student. Both of them were final year students at a provincial English university. She studied Economics, he Philosophy.

When they first met, Tapan was part of a dopey bohemian circle on the campus, hovering around various international solidarity groups without any real conviction. He enjoyed women's company but did not have a girlfriend. His real passion lay in consuming Western ideas: Spinoza's geometric wisdom kept him trembling with joy the whole night, and if he needed love, Diotima's discourse on Eros from Plato's *Symposium* was more than enough for him. Besides, deep down he was still keeping time with his old Bengali clock. His upbringing hadn't prepared him for free-floating erotic encounters. His instincts for finding a mate were switched off, because the people of his culture didn't need them. They could always rely on an arranged marriage to take care of love.

Adela Richardson came from a well-to-do, middle-class family from the home counties. Her passion in life was betrayal: she wanted to betray her family, her class, her race, her nation and her history. The more she betrayed, the more she felt she had found herself.

When Adela led Tapan to the dance floor, she had no idea that she would end up marrying him. She had organised a late-night event to raise money for one of her many international solidarities. Was it for the Anti-Apartheid campaign, or for the Polisarios in the Sahara?

Under the dim light there was food and drink and throbbing music. Tapan didn't take the floor like the others, who were dancing either in couples, or in groups of friends, or just moving solo. He was standing at the back, slightly awkward, drinking beer and smoking cigarettes. Adela, always the compassionate one, spotted him, and dragged him to the floor. It was a slow, deep, reggae number. Facing each other, but keeping a good distance between them, they danced. He didn't know how to move and keep the beat. He wasn't used to dancing. She knew the moves but looked inelegant, as if the smooth co-ordination demanded by the rooted pulse of the music was beyond her body. Suddenly she put her arms around him and pressed against him. He felt unnerved at the bodily contact and could hardly move his rigid limbs.

Many drinks later, his senses dull, when she took him to the floor for the second time, he was able to respond to her. She whispered in her ear. 'You're as brown as chocolate. Yummy – I like licking chocolate.' He didn't understand what she was saying but he offered his lips. And they kissed.

That night he ended up in her flat. Adela laughed. 'You're twenty-five and still a virgin. Am I corrupting you?' She promised him that, like Elisa, she would be his sentimental educator. She kept her promise. The next morning he walked the rectangular squares of the campus, as if in a dream, thinking: was it love?

They never confronted this word but they became friends who from time to time slept together. He confided in her and she listened. He relied on her generosity, her empathy. She liked him the way she liked other foreigners. Dark faces. She didn't ask for much; she was happy to give. The only thing she wanted was the recognition that she was different from the rest of her kind.

No, she had a soft spot for him. She liked the way he looked at her as if through the colour of her skin, through the blond roots of her dark hair, and through the green of her eyes. Yes, through the bodily surface to the beautiful self inside. She felt safe around him, liked the way he walked, his long thin body, his crazy hair, and his silly smile. Above all, with him around, she felt so different from her origins, and felt it so effortlessly that she felt permanently changed. It made her happy. But she didn't call it love.

In the spring term of his final year a telegram came from Bangladesh. His grandfather was dead. He didn't know the complexities of his grandfather's finances. Apparently he had left a large debt. He could well believe that because it had cost a lot to support his study in England for the last five years. The first two years went into polishing his English and completing his A levels

13

at Hackney College in London. The last three at this provincial university. Whatever the truth about his grandfather's finances, the money stopped coming from Bangladesh. He could borrow from friends, work on the sly. That way he could somehow see the year through. But at the end of it, that is, by the summer of '77, he would have to return to Bangladesh. He had no other option.

He thought none of this at the time he received the telegram. He locked himself in his room, opened his grandfather's letters. In the main they were formal letters: how was his health? How was his accountancy study coming along? Had he got used to potatoes and kippers? Oh yes, in his first letter he asked whether he had been to Hyde Park to see the crocuses. In the last few letters he mentioned that he was looking for a wife for Tapan. As soon as he returned home after his studies he would be married. A beautiful wife and a good family.

During his five years in England he had grown distant from his grandfather. Even come to despise him. And there was the lie that he was studying accountancy. Often he would imagine his grandfather saying in a stern voice: 'Accounts, my boy. Not only is it a sure big earner but much more. Forget about wasting your time on this no-good philosophy business. Otherwise, you'll go nutty thinking Either/Or, and doing Nichtung. If you want to harness the power of Western mind, get hold of their double-entry book-keeping. You'll find there the secret art of empire.' In those moments Tapan would laugh at the old fool and savour his sweet revenge. Perhaps, like Adela, he was also driven by his need to betray.

Now he wasn't laughing. He felt guilty for lying to him and sad. He sobbed over the letters. His grandfather was all he had.

As usual it was Adela who came to comfort him, took him for a walk by the lake. That night there was so much intensity when they rubbed their skin against each other, he thought it must be love.

He was resigned to the inevitable. He would have to go back to Bangladesh. He could do nothing to alter this, but Adela said there was a way: he could marry a British citizen, and this would sort out his residency problem without much difficulty. But who would marry him? 'Why,' said Adela. 'I'll marry you. No strings attached. You'd have no obligation towards me.'

'Marriage is serious business, Adela,' he said. 'We shouldn't take it so lightly.'

'I don't believe in marriage, Tapan. I'd never get married for real. It's only to fuck the system, isn't it? You get your problem sorted without any cost to either of us. Nothing could be simpler.'

He didn't argue with her for he wanted to stay in England. He had nobody and nothing in Bangladesh to go back to. Here he had his friends. Besides, the kind of life he wanted to live was only possible in England. He wanted economic independence, anonymity and no responsibility for anybody or anything.

He got married to Adela and, their studies finished, they moved to North London in the summer of '77.

'Since we've got to pretend, let's pretend that it's real,' said Adela as she rolled the walls yellow. She wanted to give her new home in North London a bright look for both of them.

'Of course we've to pretend that it's real. Otherwise, we'll be found out by the Immigration,' said Tapan as he painted the ceiling white from the middle rung of the ladder. He wouldn't have minded the old way the interior looked but he was happy to go along with Adela. Besides, a newly decorated home, with its carefully considered colour scheme harmoniously blending with the arrangement of furniture and paintings, would make a good impression. It would signal their commitment – the effusion of love that so spontaneously ought to be theirs as a newly married couple – and their desperate need to carve out a protective zone from the chaos outside. Especially for their little ones to come. It would be foolish to take any chances with the ever vigilant immigration officials.

Adela didn't respond; she got on with the task with the same unfaltering rhythm as before: sliding the roller almost vertically up the wall, bringing it down, then going horizontal, adding a few short, sharp jabs, and finishing it off with a long arc of a flourish. When she bent down to gather more paint from the tray on the floor, some strands of her dark hair with blond roots strayed onto her face.

Out of the corner of his eye, under the harsh light of the

shadeless bulb, Tapan saw a woman straining her back at the most ancient of labours – the task of building her nest. She wasn't pretending: it was a labour of absolute conviction. How could she do this without the promise of love? All they had between them was a pretence, a deception coolly calculated so that he would get to stay in England. Seeing Adela straighten her back, he took his eyes back to his brush strokes on the ceiling.

Resuming her painting Adela said, 'If we believe that it's real, we don't have to pretend.'

'You know it's pretence, Adela,' he said. 'Remember, you don't believe in marriage.'

'Don't pretend that you don't understand. Of course, I didn't mean the bloody ritual. And the legal shit. You can be so silly sometimes, Tapan.'

'But I like you, I respect you. And I've always admired you. That's no pretence, Adela. But it's as real as it gets with me.'

'I know that, Tapan. But I mean the feelings that make people do stupid things like getting married. Can we believe that feeling is real with us?'

When Tapan climbed down the ladder, Adela continued to paint. He put his arms around her and planted a kiss on the back of her head. She turned around to face him with the roller still in her hand. It didn't matter that the paint was dripping on the floor because they saw something new in each other's eyes. Although they didn't want to spoil the moment by giving this feeling a name – not now, not ever – they liked what they saw. Almost simultaneously they gave their lips to each other the way they had their eyes.

With her good economics degree Adela could have gone for a well-paid job in the City. Instead, she joined the economic regeneration unit of the local council. While Adela went out to work, Tapan stayed at home. Until he got clearance from the Home Office he did not have the right to work.

Each morning he waited for the dog from next door to bark and for the postman to curse. He collected the post as soon as it was pushed through the door. As yet there had been no news from the Home Office. He was slightly anxious but not unduly concerned. He got on with tidying up the house, went to the local library to read the newspaper, did some shopping in the afternoon. By the time Adela returned home in the early evening he had done the cooking. While Adela told him about her day at the office over a glass of wine, he set the table. Over dinner Adela continued with her anecdotes, telling him of the intrigues between her colleagues, of her new assignments, of the horrible man from the housing department leering at her and, always, of the terrible traffic. Afterwards, they did the washing up together, watched the TV, read books and went to bed. If one of them was in the mood the other obliged and they made love. Some evenings Kofi turned up after dinner and they smoked dope and listened to music. Most weekends they met up with Eva and Kishor to have dinner together, gossip long into the night, and smoke dope. If they went to a demo – CND or Anti-Apartheid – Kofi and Danzel joined them. Occasionally they went to see a film or a play. As time went by they seemed to have forgotten the ignoble origin of their marriage, felt contented the way most couples do in the routine of their domestic life.

Then one morning the letter from the Home Office arrived: they were to go for interviews together and separately.

The interview together went well, the questionings were unintrusive and polite; they went over their old story of suddenly falling in love and of their desperate desire never to be separated. The case officer seemed impressed by Adela's job, by Tapan's education, and of their home so near to his favourite football team. He even chatted with Tapan about Arsenal's new signings and form this season and wished them good luck. But the separate interviews were very different. Both of them were called at the same time: Tapan was led to a cubicle halfway down the corridor, and Adela further along.

'Would you be so kind as to tell me,' the officer asked Tapan, with a straight face, 'the middle names of your parents-in-law.'

Tapan stayed quiet, scratched his head, and bit his lips.

'Right now I can't remember.'

'I see. By any chance do you know their denomination?'

'No.'

'Your wife, Mrs…'

'Mrs Adela Ali.'

'How old are Mrs Adela Ali's nephews?' The officer asked with the same straight face as before. 'Sorry, forgive my mistake. They're your nephews too. How old are they?'

'I don't remember.'

'Do you know the name of the school your wife went to?'

'I don't know.'

'Isn't the country you come from...' the officer hesitated, 'One of the poorest on earth?'

'Yes.'

'Don't get me wrong, Mr Ali. I understand your situation,' the officer said, in a voice of concern. 'Life would be so much easier for you here. Wouldn't it?'

'Maybe. But I didn't marry Adela for that.'

'Good. Why did you marry then?'

He wanted to go over the old story of falling in love and their dreams of life together but remained silent as the officer lifted his brows and waited for the answer. Lying didn't come easily to Tapan at the best of times. Now he seemed incapable of even the most inept of lies. When the officer cleared his throat with a muffled cough and looked at his watch, Tapan said, 'Because we like each other.' He paused, looked rather abstractedly at the blue globe on the table, and added, 'Adela is a good woman.'

'Of course. Of course,' said the officer. 'I understand.'

When Tapan returned to the waiting room, Adela wasn't there. He sat down, glanced at the glum, tense faces of people sitting in rows, and waiting their turns to be slaughtered in the cubicles. Mostly brown and black faces like his. He wondered what tales they were rehearsing in their minds. Would they be candid about their appalling miseries and calamities and beg to be let in? Or, would they invent some fancy tales of love?

When the man next to him asked for the time, Tapan pointed to the large clock on the wall and got up. He shuffled across the room and stood against the large glass window. From there he could see only the massive flank of another identical building and another identical window in which stood a figure, perhaps looking out as vacantly and as lost as himself. He wanted a cigarette desperately. Then Adela walked in looking withdrawn and they hurried out of the building. They said nothing to each other on their way home in the tube, or during the walk from the station.

Now, while he put the kettle on, she went for a shower. Adela took showers as if crises could be washed away in torrents of water. The tea was lukewarm by the time she returned to the kitchen in her bath robe. She picked up her cup and sat on a stool slightly behind him and at an angle, so that he couldn't see her face. Taking a sip she said, 'You don't want to know what they asked me?'

'What's the point, Adela. It couldn't have been good.'

'No. It wasn't good. But they can't deport you as long as we stay married. And feel it for real.'

'How can we feel it for real, Adela? We got into this shit so I could fool the buggers to let me stay in this country. You could do a good turn for a wretch like me and betray your family into the bargain. That's all there was to it.'

For a long while Adela stayed quiet, sipped tea and swung one of her legs like a pendulum. At last she said, 'I can't deny what you've just said. But when you put things like that it sounds so horrible.'

'These are facts, Adela,' he said. 'We've got to face up to them.'

'But if we feel it for real, we can put it right. Can't we?'

'We can play-act, masquerade, Adela.' His voice was raised and trembling. 'We can cheat the whole goddamn world with our mimicry. But we can't invent real feeling.'

'If I'd become Muslim, would it have been more real?'

'What a daft thing to say. Where on earth did you get that idea?'

'It's what the immigration officer asked me.' Adela said this so quietly that Tapan didn't hear her clearly.

'What?'

'The immigration officer asked me if I became a Muslim when we got married.'

'Oh I see. What did you say?'

'What could I say? You've never asked me to become a Muslim.'

'Let's get one thing clear, Adela,' he said. 'Even if I were marrying for real, I wouldn't ask my wife to become a Muslim. You don't know anything about me.'

19

Adela got up and went to bed; he stayed up staring at the TV. No, they didn't know much about each other. If they'd been truly in love they would have talked silly things about the schools they'd gone to, bored each other with sugary dribbles over their little nephews and nieces, and perhaps even learnt the middle names of their parents. And, of course, she might have understood why it wasn't important for him to have her convert to Islam.

They tried to get on with life as best as possible, but things were becoming more difficult. They had several visits from the Home Office: officers going through their rooms, wardrobe, sleeping arrangements to pick up the slightest sign of a bogus marriage. Each visit left them unsettled, added one more unbearable strain to their relationship, so that whatever attachment or companionship there had been between them began to fade. More and more, they felt soiled by their sordid contract, exchanged without the slightest moral consideration, solely for the profit they stood to gain.

No matter how hard Adela tried to imagine her marriage signature as a pure altruistic gift, with no expectation of return, she felt used. Although Tapan had much less reason to feel used, he couldn't let go of the nagging feeling that he was merely an unfortunate object of her pity and charity. Besides, he was the means through which she wanted to complete her betrayal. It seemed they were doomed.

And nearly a year after their marriage, the Home Office still had not concluded its investigation. Recently, there had been strange movements at odd hours in the house opposite. They didn't know for sure what was really going on but both of them, separately, and without having talked about it, felt that perhaps a surveillance team had moved in.

Then the Home Office got in touch with Adela's parents.

CHAPTER 2

Adela was preparing to leave for the office when the telephone rang. Still half-asleep in bed, Tapan opened his eyes and saw her picking up the receiver. Her lips quivered in a strange mingling of surprise, joy and terror. He heard her say, 'Mum.' She asked the caller to wait a minute, put the receiver back on the cradle, went downstairs and closed the door behind her.

It was the first intrusion of family into their lives. Although Adela had never spoken of it explicitly, knowing what he knew, Tapan sensed that this was bad news. It was there in the way she said 'Mum' into the cold, plastic mouth of the receiver. But why this secrecy? What was it Adela didn't want him to hear? Her mother's hysterical ravings about her dreadful deed with a wretched Paki? Perhaps she didn't want him to witness her defensive, almost childlike responses to her mother's assaults. Or was she gloating over her triumph, her betrayal of everything that her parents stood for? Yes, yes, I share my bed with a dirty, devious scrounger of a Paki.

He came down when she'd finished. Her face was red and there were tears in her eyes. 'What's happened, Adela?' he asked.

She turned her face away from him, wiped her tears and said, 'You don't want to know.' Then she gathered her handbag and left for work.

He didn't feel like staying home that day. Luckily it was Kofi's day off, and about midday he set off for Kofi's place, twenty minutes' walk, in Stamford Hill. It was early summer – the summer of '78 – and the sun was out after the persistent rain of the last few days. Kofi was pleased to see him but said, 'What's wrong with you, Brother? You don't look right to me.'

21

'Nothing special really. Just things are getting a bit heavy, you know.'

'That's badness, Brother,' Kofi said. 'Come in. Let's get us sorted.'

It was when he was doing his A levels at Hackney College that Tapan had met Kofi, who'd come from Ghana to join his parents. There he'd also met Danzel, whose parents came the Windrush way from the West Indies, though he was Hackney-born and never set foot out of London. They were good friends and when they donned their brown duffel coats and round metallic glasses and walked down Kingsland High Street, they appeared to be members of an exclusive club, but unlike the other two, Tapan wasn't a British citizen.

'I'm making the old stew, Brother,' Kofi said. 'Fancy number one hot?'

'Yeah.'

Tapan loved Kofi's number one hot, which was twice as hot as his hot curry, and a perfect accompaniment to a spliff.

'Roll a joint, Brother,' Kofi now said, 'while I make us a number one.'

Kofi's bedsit looked dark even on the brightest day. He never opened his curtains and he wasn't keen on bright lights either. A dim light in the corner was all there was in his room, creating a twilight zone in which the hues were so faint that they looked like scrubbed watercolours. When Tapan once asked Kofi about this dimness and he said: 'Brother, it's to catch time.'

Kofi's number one was as hot and good as ever. While they ate, Kofi put some music on, very low. It was Gregory Isaacs – the cool-ruler of the universe – taming the tempest of turbulent Kingston. After the meal, on their second joint, Kofi asked him, 'So, Brother, what's bothering you?'

'Well,' said Tapan, 'this bloody immigration thing is getting on my nerves. I should've gone back to Bangladesh.'

'Easy, Brother. Easy,' Kofi said. 'They want to see how much shit you can take. Don't let them get the better of you. Play it cool like Gandhi.'

'But it's messing me up, Kofi. It's even introducing bad feelings between me and Adela. I should've gone back to Bangladesh.'

'There's time, Brother, time,' Kofi said. 'You can go back when you get your citizenship. Don't let the fuckers beat you.' After a long puff on the spliff, he added, 'And don't you mess around with Adela. She's a good woman.'

Later Kofi suggested they go out for a walk, as they used to do when they were green in London. Kofi loved architecture. Often they went to central London to see the grand buildings along the river. Kofi walked around them enchanted, now coming close to see the details of carvings, now standing right back for the long perspective, and always taking note of the arches, columns, cornices and the traceries on the windows.

Tapan didn't care much about buildings, he was more interested in the way Kofi loved them, responded to them. One day Kofi had been looking and loving the buildings in his usual way, when suddenly his mood had altered.

'Look at the fine works, Brother. Beautiful,' he said. 'But what do you see?'

'They're very impressive looking.'

'Look, Brother, look. Carefully. What d'you really, really see?'

'I don't understand what you're getting at, Kofi.'

'Don't they poke your eyes, Brother, with the muscles of empire?'

'What?'

'Yeah, Brother. You're looking at the body-builders of empire. Real heavy stuff. Bad business.'

'But they are beautiful. Aren't they, Kofi?'

'Yeah, Brother. Beautiful. I love them. But deep down they're real wickedness.'

The clouds, gathering when they went out, broke as they reached the bus stop, so instead of going to see the buildings by the river, they went to Centerprise to play a game of chess.

It was early evening, and Centerprise was full of chess players, book readers and local revolutionaries of all shades of colours and doctrines, and a good number of casual interlopers brought in, like them, by the sudden rain. There were no empty seats left. So what to do? Perhaps they could call on Eva and Kishor.

Before that Tapan phoned Adela.

'How are you, Adela? We must talk, you know.'

23

'Not now, Tapan,' she said. 'I've just got back from work and have to go out again. I'm in a hurry.'

'When will you be back?' he asked. 'Shall I cook for you?'

'I don't know when I'll be back. No need to cook. And don't wait up for me.'

Hoods up on their duffel coats, they went out in the rain again. At the bus stop they bumped into Danzel, who was on his way home from work. 'How you doing, my main man?' he said to Tapan, who just shrugged his shoulders. 'Is it that bad?' said Danzel. 'Don't let the Babylon system get you down, Brother. Stay cool.'

When the bus came Danzel said he would join them later at Eva's and Kishor's. At Finsbury Park, Kofi told Tapan to go ahead. He had to score some dope, from a dealer nearby.

'We're going to have a mighty session tonight. One of them master-blaster, Brother,' Kofi said with a grin.

Eva and Kishor were Tapan's university friends. Kishor, a high-caste Hindu, had come to England from Kenya. Eva, a mestiza political refugee, had fled the death squads in Colombia.

Looking at Tapan's gloomy face, Eva was about to say something witty to cheer him up, but seeing his eyes, locked as if in a crypt, she swallowed her words, and looked over his head at the blue ceramic bells dangling from the ceiling.

'Let's see what we can do about that grim face of yours,' said Kishor. 'How about a joint, my Bangladeshi Brother?'

Tapan nodded his head slightly.

As Kishor heated the resin, letting loose the oily aroma of Afghan Black into the unvented air of the room, he said: 'Beware! Beware! The Mujahideen are coming.'

While Kishor rolled the joint, Eva went to make tea in the kitchen. Handing the joint to Tapan, Kishor put on a tape: it was LKJ chanting in ragamuffin rage: *Inglan is a bitch* over the top of a heavy bass-line riff and depth-charge drum beats. It made Tapan ease up a bit and he smiled as he took the tea from Eva. She wanted to ask about Adela, but sensing that something was wrong, and not wishing to spoil the moment, she didn't.

'You're lucky, Compañero,' Eva said. 'Kishor has cooked beef today.'

Kishor laughed out raucously, as he always did, to draw attention to his beef-eating ways. As usual, Eva couldn't resist commenting cynically, 'Attention. Imperialism is shaking. Our Hindu comrade is eating beef.'

Undaunted, Kishor half closed his eyes, put his chin up, and held the pose as if he didn't intend to drop it until he got his due recognition. Tapan began studying the dangling ceramic bells and Eva got up to change the music.

Feeling stranded, Kishor blurted out the punchline: 'Beef!' Eva tossed her head; she'd had enough of this stupid joke.

No one knew how it started but it had become an in-joke among the members of the dopey circle at university. One of them just had to mention *Beef* and the rest would give themselves belly-aches, laughing.

Now Tapan swallowed his usual chuckle with a long drag on the joint. Eva put on Joe Arrano's salsa Colombiana. She resumed her seat opposite Tapan and began to mouth the lyrics and move her head to the rhythm. Then she looked Tapan straight in the eyes and asked, 'Is Adela joining us tonight?'

'I don't know,' he said. 'But Kofi and Danzel are coming.'

Eva sprang to her feet saying that there weren't enough tomatoes for a salad for four, sent Kishor to the kitchen to cook an extra pot of rice and went out to buy some tomatoes from the open-all-hours Oriental store down the road.

Tapan rang to see if Adela was back home, but she wasn't. Perhaps it was for the best because he didn't know what to say to her.

Tapan joined Kishor in the kitchen. 'Relationship botheration, eh?' Kishor said. 'Join the camp, mate.'

Eva's and Kishor's relationship was regularly difficult, but that had to do with the complexities between lovers. Before Tapan could point out that his difficulties with Adela weren't anything like theirs, Kishor was telling him that the political situation in Eva's country had changed.

'She wants to go back as soon as possible.'

'Are you going with her, then?'

'Shit, Man. No. I admit England could be a bitch sometimes, but we know her.'

25

'So, you don't love her any more?'

'Of course, I love her,' said Kishor. 'But England is home –
isn't it? I just can't leave. Whatever the difficulties, I've to fight it
out here.'

'So love is not enough.'

While Kishor searched his mind to say something that would
make sense, they heard the front door open. As usual, the grocer
had short-changed Eva, but she came back laughing.

'He's real sweet. He calls me Madam Latina,' she said. 'Funny.
He told me I was practically one of his people.'

'He's a bloody con artist. Don't you be taken in by him,' said
Kishor.

Eva ignored him and began to lay the tomatoes on the chopping board.

'What people does he mean?' Tapan asked.

'Not Colon's Indios,' she said. 'But real Indians from India
proper.'

Kishor laughed with such childish innocence that Eva mel-
lowed towards him, giving him the bright brown bubbles of her
eyes. Seizing the moment, Kishor slipped in his silly *Beef* joke. Eva
wasn't annoyed this time; she leaned back her head, laughing.
'Tonto,' she said. Now they were back again: a couple in love.

When Kofi and Danzel arrived, they all sat down to eat. Kishor
was happy because everyone complimented him on his excellent
beef curry. Afterwards, Eva proposed that they should go to the
pub down the road. Friday was jazz night. No one was particularly keen to go out but they didn't want to disappoint Eva, so,
after a joint, they went to the pub. Before they left Tapan called
Adela once more. She wasn't home.

In the pub, they sat in an alcove that protected them from the
buzz of activities around the musicians, who were already in full
flow. Danzel bought a round of Guinness for everyone, except
Kofi, who never drank any alcohol. He had coke.

After the second round, Eva tried to cajole them to jive to a jazz
number with a frantic swing. Having failed, she took to the floor
alone. Danzel, pointing to the musicians, sucked his teeth and
said, 'Rass. Me jus' kyaan believe it. White them playing jazz.'

Nobody paid him much attention, except Kishor, who gave

him a reproachful look. Surprisingly, Danzel didn't accuse him of being a 'bloodclaat coconut' as he usually did when he was in his ghetto talk mode, and instead turned thoughtful and recited fragments of Langston Hughes: 'Jazz – tom tom being in the negro soul…the tom tom of the revolt against…white world.'

Kofi said, 'Really!' and took to the floor. While Eva messed around, keeping time with her snapping fingers, he shimmied, rooted to the spot. He moved a few notches down from the tempo of the music, creating a virtual rhythm of his own, as though his own body was an instrument, providing a counterpoint.

Back in Eva's and Kishor's flat, Tapan phoned Adela again. It was past midnight and she still wasn't home. Kishor was rolling his Afghan Black, Kofi and Danzel their home-grown grass. Eva put on Joao Gilberto – so cool and bohemian – playing Bossa Nova.

Then between Burning Spear rooting deep into the earth and Dexter Gordon saxing the midnight into an abstract melancholy, they smoked on, all except Eva. She never smoked dope – it was anti-revolutionary escapism – though she would happily roll joints for the group.

Suddenly Danzel asked, 'Who wants to leave this Babylon and go back home?'

Kofi said he was serious this time, he would be back home by the end of the year. Danzel said he would go back with Kofi – they had already worked out a good plan. Tapan wanted to stay in England and Kishor wouldn't go anywhere else. Eva said, 'You lot are junkies for England, Compañeros. None of you would ever go back.'

'We're immigrants, Comrade,' said Kishor in a tone of crude sarcasm. 'We love England.'

Now Eva was really cross; she sat quiet, studying the blue ceramic bells and when Kishor put a record of flamenco guitar on the player, she went to bed. The rest smoked on, letting the flamenco guitar creep into them almost imperceptibly, and then, when they least expected it, rush back to thrust its matador's sword right through their hearts. Then there was Billy Holiday singing 'April in Paris' in a voice so sad and sensuous that it made them laugh and cry all at once. Finally, they settled for Bismilla Khan playing shehnai with Allarakha on the tabla.

From corner to corner the room was full of smoke; suddenly Bismilla Khan was blowing so fast and furious, dropping notes like a heavy downpour of rain, that poor Allarakha, despite the dexterity of his fingers, was finding it hard to keep pace.

They would have let Bismilla Khan go on for the whole night if Eva hadn't got up to complain.

Tapan tried one last time to call Adela. She still wasn't home, and since he wasn't keen to go back to the empty house, Kofi invited him to stay at his place.

As Kofi took off his shirt to sleep, Tapan caught sight of his amulet and remarked: 'Surely, Kofi, you can't take that old mumbo-jumbo about the amulet seriously?'

He was recalling what Kofi had told him about the amulet the first time he'd noticed it – that when he was leaving for England he'd gone to see the griot – known as the machine of ancient memories in his village – and he'd given Kofi the amulet and told him that the ancestors had harnessed and sealed the whistle of birds in its wooden body. If the passion of birds was stirred in the body of the wearer – as it must when the desire for flight and escape reached their limits – the amulet's power would be released like the wind of harmattan. When that happened the wearer was pulled beyond the force of gravity. But this, the griot had cautioned Kofi, was a very dangerous thing to do.

Enigmatic as ever the memory machine wouldn't confirm this, but Kofi was sure that many of the ancestors had released the secrets of the amulets, especially while limbo dancing in the triangular Belsens of the Atlantic, and whistled their way into the air. And then back home.

Kofi fingered the amulet and said, 'Easy, Brother, easy. Most of the times I don't. For example, when I look at my watch, put on the light or take a train, I don't.'

'And isn't that the world we live in?'

'Certainly, Brother. That's why I don't believe in the amulet most of the time.'

'When do you believe in it then?'

'To be frank with you, I don't believe in it at all. But sometimes I feel it.'

'I don't get it, Kofi. What do you mean?'

'Listen, Brother, if I can put words to the feeling, then it wouldn't be feeling any more. Right?'

'I still can't get my head around it, Kofi.'

'You will, Brother. When you get the feeling yourself.'

Tapan stayed silent for a while, thinking, but when he wanted to ask Kofi further questions, his friend had already fallen asleep. Finally, alone in the room without shadows, he thought about what he had been avoiding the whole day: perhaps he should move out of Adela's home before their relationship became more complicated, before real bitterness set in.

CHAPTER 3

Tapan knew that terrible things were happening in East London, but what could he do about them?

He didn't belong to a political group, nor was he part of a community. He attended CND marches and Anti-Apartheid rallies in the broad avenues of central London, and the festive Rock against Racism concerts that took place in well-kept parks. They were, he would admit, more like outings to him than arenas of political involvement. Besides, though he was a Paki like them and suffered his share of Paki-bashing, he'd had nothing to do with the Bangladeshis of the East End: they were almost as alien to him as the Cypriots of Green Lane.

But on his way home from Kofi's place, a young woman with cropped hair had pursued him until he bought a copy of the *Morning Star*. On the bus he flicked through the paper, made a mental note of the article on the second page, and came back to it when the bus halted in a traffic jam. Apart from telling of the general harassment of the Bangladeshi community, it catalogued a series of violent assaults and murders. Recently, there had been more ominous developments: the National Front had laid siege to the heart of the community in Brick Lane. During the week this siege simmered and on Sundays it exploded into battles. The National Front would gather at the corner of Brick Lane, selling their newspaper *Bulldog*, and the Bangladeshi community, supported by anti-racist groups, would try to prevent them. Below the article there was a little ad urging people to come down to Brick Lane the following Sunday.

As the bus finally arrived in Manor House, Tapan folded the paper in the long pocket of his duffel coat, and got off. It was a damp and overcast Saturday. He was slightly nervous as he unlocked the front door and walked in. At first he thought Adela wasn't back home yet. It was silent and the curtains were drawn. His half-empty cup of tea still lay on the glass-top table where he had left it.

It was only when he was halfway up the stairs that he heard the shower. He paused, and then continued up, heading for the bathroom. He would slip in quietly – as he had often done – and greet her through the pale blue shower curtain, ask her about yesterday's phone call, about last night. At the point of turning the handle on the door, its cold aluminium tingled the tips of his fingers. He was invading the privacy of a woman having her shower. He had no right to do so; it would be an act of violation.

He wasn't sure whether Adela had heard him. If she had, she didn't give him any sign; the shower went on with the same torrent as before. He came down, put the kettle on, and waited in front of the television. She didn't come down in her bathrobe, pouring on him the perfume of her fresh skin mingled with eucalyptus, as she usually did after a shower. Instead, she went to the bedroom, slipped into the green dungarees that made her look pale and misshapen, and then came down. He wondered why she had put them on. She hadn't worn them for ages, ever since he'd told her how terrible she looked in them. He turned the TV off and asked her if she wanted a tea. She didn't.

He didn't ask her about the phone call or where she'd been last night. Nor did she ask him anything, though she told him that the strange activities in the house opposite were to do with squatters. The police had been there only an hour ago to secure the place for the owner – apparently an Asian, big in real estate. She went upstairs and read a book, made several phone calls, while he watched football on the TV downstairs, sprawled on the sofa and slept. In the late afternoon she came down – as quiet and unobtrusive as before – to make tea and toast. He pretended not to have noticed her. After she went up the stairs again, he went to the kitchen to cook. Usually they went shopping on Saturdays, but since they hadn't bothered, there wasn't much to cook. He rustled up a curry with the leftover vegetables and waited for her to come down, which she did, in the late evening.

She gave him a can of lager and opened one herself. Facing a print of Cézanne's *Portrait of the Artist's Wife* on the wall, they ate in silence, passing things to each other with exaggerated politeness. Both of them glanced at the print several times, but neither was sure whether it was simply to bear the silence between them, or to see something in it. If the latter was the case, neither had the slightest idea what they had seen.

After dinner, they did the washing up together. Back in the living room, each on their separate sofas, they sat as if they were strangers in a darkened theatre, absorbed in their separate ways by the unfolding tragedy on the screen. At last Adela said, 'Now that there's no pretence any more, we must find a way of bearing it.'

'Do you want me to move out?'

'Well. You can stay until your papers come through,' she said. 'I imagine that should be pretty soon.'

He didn't say anything; he just meekly squashed his eyes to convey something – what, he wasn't sure. Agreement? Gratitude? Resignation? Or, just sadness? She went up to the bedroom, he made his bed on the sofa. It was the first time they'd slept separately in the same house since they got married.

He had a restless night, his mind spinning. What could he do or say that would make it up to Adela? Should he pretend that he had just realised how much he loved her, and confess it with such a display of sincerity that she would shed all her misgivings about him, making both of them sob until they wiped each other's tears, carried away, as if the most beautiful thing had just happened to them? How low could he get? At least she deserved some honesty from him. But what could he do? Should he just call it quits and go back to Bangladesh?

If his parents had been alive, it would have been natural for him to go back; perhaps he would never have come to England in the first place. Strange that he hadn't thought about his parents for years. He had no memory of his mother. She had died giving birth to him in her mother's hut at the edge of the great swamp. Sometimes he dreamed of his mother, of the folds of her sari, really. Now he sees himself in the hut in which he was born, lying beside his mother.

As always the old cobra emerges from the dense undergrowth

that surrounds the hut. He is not scared of the cobra; it is not known to have harmed anyone. Thunder and lightning wake him and he hears the cobra as it passes, slithering, as though the last thing it wants is to disturb anyone's sleep, past the mud hut with its corrugated roof, across the plain dotted with tall trees, towards the great swamp. For reasons known only to itself, the old cobra always keeps to a precise time, between the waning of the moon and the cry of the jackal. Soon after hearing the hiss of the cobra and the pattering of the rain, he falls asleep.

Only later, when an intense desire to see the cobra makes him grope under the pillow, through the folds of his mother's sari, is he scared. No one has ever seen the cobra. All that is known of it is the hiss of its passing in the rain. When there is no rain, and the night sky is full of stars, you become aware of it simply by opening your ears to the inaudible murmurs beyond the clamour of the world.

It is not really a dream about his mother, but about the folds of her sari, and only of that brief moment when he looked for the cobra. When he was child, he had loved to fold himself in the sari his grandmother told him had been his mother's. In those moments he felt protected. Even now, at rare moments, he wishes he still had the innocence of feeling that way.

Although his father lived until Tapan was eight years old, he didn't see much of him. He lived with his maternal grandmother in the hut at the edge of the great swamp. His father visited him occasionally and brought him books with pictures in them. His father and his paternal grandfather didn't see eye to eye. Indeed, their relationship had so broken down that he didn't know he had a grandfather until his father's death. Although he'd heard that his father's death was to do with his political activities, he never knew exactly how he died. He neither saw his dead body nor attended his funeral. He never dreamed about his father, but often fantasised that he was alive, and that he comes face to face with him in the street of a strange city. Although his father does not recognise him, walks past him, and disappears into the crowd, he feels happy because he knows that his father is still alive.

Tapan didn't know when he had fallen asleep, but he was woken up by violent retching sounds coming from upstairs.

Adela was vomiting in the bathroom. He went up and stood outside the door and asked if she needed help. She said he shouldn't worry; it was nothing serious really, only a mild case of food poisoning. No – he shouldn't call a doctor. She went to bed and he made tea and toast and took them up to her. She thanked him and said that she would be going out a bit later, but didn't say where.

When she went out, he looked at the little ad in *The Morning Star* again. He wasn't sure what made up his mind, but he was on the bus – on his way to East London.

Brick Lane was crowded though most of the people in it had nothing to do with either of the sides of the barricade. They were mainly punters on their way to or returning from the Sunday market. It was where Brick Lane joined Bethnal Green Road that the battle line was drawn: from the Bethnal Green Road side the National Front threatened to break into Brick Lane amidst the flutter of Union Jacks, and from the Brick Lane side a small group of Bangladeshi youths, supported by anti-racist groups, tried to block them. In between them there was a large number of police officers.

He joined the Brick Lane side, stood alone, feeling the discomfort of a stranger in an intimate gathering. He didn't know anyone there: the anti-racist contingent – mostly white – seemed to belong to various political or religious groups, and the handful of Bangladeshis seemed to know each other well. Once he settled down a bit, and added his straining, uncertain voice to the slogans, he noticed two people, odd and awkward individuals like himself. Later he would come to know them as Brother Josef K – a Jewish East Ender, and Comrade Moo Ya – a Chinese from Limehouse. Huddled together as in a self-protective shoal, the Bangladeshi presence was mainly composed of young men, but among them was a woman with a megaphone. Although a small figure, she was orchestrating the whole dynamics of the barricade – its slogans, its joining of arms, its push forward, and its resolve to carry on. Her name was Nilufar Mia.

Although he had exchanged nervous smiles with Brother Josef K and Comrade Moo Ya, he didn't speak to anyone on the picket line until a young Bangladeshi man offered him a cigarette. His

name was Sundar. Since Tapan was in a giving-up phase, he –
despite his desire to accept it as a way of establishing some sort of
contact – refused it with a polite smile. Undaunted, and with an
innocent smile, Sundar then offered him a paan from a small
silver box. Tapan hadn't had a paan for a long time, so his eyes lit
up, and he took it with a broad smile. Pleased that his gift had been
accepted, Sundar lit his cigarette and said, 'Bhaio, you're a tough
fighter. No?'

Tapan was lost for words over Sundar's familiarity, his intimacy, as if they were friends of many years. He merely gave him
a nervous smile and slipped the paan into his mouth. He didn't
know that folded in the paan cone there was – along with the betel
nuts – some strong chewing tobacco. For a novice that could be
a tango with the devil.

In the affray of the picket, amongst the jostling crowd and the
slogans hurled at the neo-Nazi mob just a few yards ahead, Tapan
chewed on the paan. He felt the caustic juice sipping down his
gullet, but didn't think much of it until he began to spin and
levitate higher and higher. Recently, the idea of becoming a bird
had slipped into his mind, but he never thought of it as something
that might really happen to him, the way it was happening to him
now: He was becoming a bird – not just any bird, but a giant fish-
eagle with a huge beak and talons.

Suddenly he leapt through the barricade and flew up, spreading his wings in the sky. He swooped down on the racist mob and
began to cause panic, blitzing them with his beak and talons.
Seeing this, the police moved in to arrest him. For a moment
everyone froze and looked on with astonishment until Sundar –
throwing away his half-smoked cigarette – rushed in to rescue
him. A small group followed him, amongst whom was Nilufar
Mia – Sundar's cousin. Now the racist group, already looking
fierce with their cropped heads and bovver boots, re-doubled the
threats of death as they fluttered their union jacks. The people
manning the barricade, undaunted, moved forward to meet
them. The policemen holding Tapan got distracted. Taking this
opportunity, Sundar and the others snatched Tapan from their
hands.

35

Tapan had already passed out. Four people carried him back, face up, Nilufar holding his head. The sky was overcast and there was a light rain in the air. Nilufar couldn't see his eyes then, but the rain falling on his closed eyelids, down the curve of his face, evoked an immense sadness in her.

For a moment Nilufar closed her eyes. She could hear the wind carrying the sound of an evening raga from the far distance. It could easily have been mistaken for a deep, nocturnal mood played on a sharod. But that wasn't it. What she really heard was the wail of women at dusk, waiting – as they have always done during wars – to receive the dead bodies of their sons. When Nilufar opened her eyes and looked at his face, she wanted to cry for him. When she looked at the curve of his lips she wanted to kiss them. Her dreams that night were not of sadness but of desire. Remembering the dreams in the morning, she wasn't ashamed. Rather she was surprised that she was capable of such emotions, that she was feeling something she had vowed never to feel again.

They took him to Sundar's flat, only a few yards down the Lane. While Nilufar washed his face with cold water, Sundar went to call Doctor Karamat Ali from downstairs. Since there was no need for the others to wait, Nilufar had sent them back to the picket line. Now she was alone with Tapan, who opened his eyes before the doctor arrived. He saw her face arched over his, so close that he could feel her breath brushing his skin. Lowering her face further, her fringe dangling across her cheeks, she said, 'Don't worry, you will be fine.' He tried to nod his head but there was no need for an answer. Strange that it should happen this way, but as soon as he saw her eyes looking at him with that rare tenderness, he felt healed. But more than that he felt she was answering his summons to be touched. Perhaps it was the other way around. At last he said, 'I'm fine. Thank you.' Just then Sundar came in with Doctor Karamat Ali.

For the next two weeks Adela and Tapan kept out of each other's way as much as possible. Adela went away for a long weekend with friends he didn't know, went out to dinner with colleagues, took mysterious phone calls upstairs, and vomited in the mornings. For his part, Tapan began to spend more and more time in East London, helping Sundar, Nilufar and their defence group as they made banners, printed leaflets, distributed them from house to house, had meetings with various Bangladeshi groups in different estates, and gossiped for long hours between serious planning and discussion in Toynbee Hall or the Montefiore Centre. Some nights he slept in Sundar's flat. And, there was Nilufar's enchanting presence – the way she flung a strip of her hair over her face, and the lustrous black of her eyes. Yet, since that brief moment in Sundar's flat, they hadn't spent a moment alone, hadn't exchanged any intimate words, and besides, he was a bit intimidated by her. She seemed to carry herself in heavy armour, as if on a permanent war footing.

He was concerned about Adela's vomiting, but she convinced him that she had been to see her doctor, and that it was no more than a spell of indigestion – apparently a condition that ran in her family. But seriously, she said, they needed to talk, and resolve this dreadful situation, because it couldn't have been doing any good to either of them.

'I think the investigation is over and done with,' Adela said to Tapan as if it was a matter of fact. 'The Home Office won't bother us any more.'

'Yeah?' He responded in a strangled voice.

'You're safe now. Just a few more days and you'll get your papers through,' said Adela.

'Do you think so?'

'Yeah, I'm sure of it.'

'Thanks for everything, Adela. I don't know how I can repay you.'

'Well, in fact, there's something that you can do. I mean, it's not right that we continue to share the same house.'

'You want me to move out?'

'Obviously, you can stay until you find a place.'

Sundar said of course he could move in with him – immediately if he wanted – and soon he would fix him with a job at Spice Land, where the staff were provided with accommodation upstairs. Within a few days Sundar came for him in his Mini. There was no dramatic scene: Adela was relieved when he packed his bags and went away. When she shut the door on him, she had no desire to see him again. Now she was happy to go her own way in search of other intimacies that would perhaps take her to the elusive harmony of her dreams. Perhaps it would be the same for him. But what could she do with the secrets and the traces that he left behind?

As he drove away in Sundar's car, heading for East London, wind blowing in his face, Sundar telling him how much he was looking forward to sharing his bed-sit with him, and how useful he would be to the community, Tapan was so elated that he didn't think about the consequences of his decision.

CHAPTER 4

It wasn't like Nilufar to stay in bed so late in the morning, even though it was her day off. Pollen had got to her this year; she had been sneezing since that walk through the park, and was perhaps running a slight temperature. So much was happening in this summer of '78; she was in the middle of it, and it had taken its toll.

She thought of phoning her sister, Shapna, to ask her to bring something from the chemist, but at the point of lifting the receiver, she decided against it. All she wanted was to curl up in her bed, with the shades and silence of her room, and abandon herself to thoughts of her mother's music. She made herself a hot chocolate, and when she lay in the bed, her head slightly raised on the pillow, her eyes caught on the photograph. She saw it every day, but usually didn't linger on it, didn't allow its trapped sensations and memories to burst out of the frame and take her with them. Now, her eyes wouldn't budge until she was pulled into its rectangular surface and became the girl in the picture.

The girl in the picture, wearing a lilac silk kameez, was Nilufar – then only nine years old. It was her third summer in England and the sun shone that day as if they were in another country, far away – perhaps in the tropics. Her father, unusually, took the whole day off, and they went to Kew Gardens for a picnic. Every so often, looking up at the blue, cloudless sky, her father kept chanting, as if it was a mantra: 'Look, something wonderful to behold. The fortunes of our foreheads have never been so kind.' After a while, everyone in the party had stopped paying him attention, except her mother, who still made the effort to say, 'Almost like Bangladesh, na?'

39

Her mother was so determined to make it a grand occasion that she had been preparing for days. The night before the picnic she cooked bhoona lamb, tandoori drumsticks, aubergine and potato bhaji, puries, and pilao rice with the finest Tilda bashmati. Although Nilufar was only nine then, she stayed up late, hung around her mother, asking for chores. Her mother smiled lovingly at her, gave her cloves of garlic to peel and said, 'Someday, my daughter will make a good wife to some lucky man.' Nilufar was so absorbed in her task that she didn't say, 'No, I'm not going to marry anyone. Never,' as little girls of her age usually do. Between peeling cloves of garlic and, once that was finished, peeling potatoes, or doing nothing in particular, she listened to her mother. Her mother sometimes stirred deep in the cooking pots, at other times rocked over the curve of the cutter, finely chopping this or that vegetable, but she always managed to make music out of them.

Now, so many years later, it occurred to Nilufar that her mother's music must have been her secret escape route, that the rhythms she drew from her mundane chores took her beyond the four walls of her inner courtyard, beyond the monotony of her life. Not to forget that, when alone, her mother sometimes hummed Koranic verses with the melodies of the wind. Languidly that night, her mother would scoop a spoon of gravy, and ask Nilufar to taste it to see if it was salty enough, or if a bit more chilli was needed. That night, between the ritual of cooking and the rhythm that streamed from her mother's actions, they were so happy together, her mother and herself.

When her father came back from his late shift in the factory, he was cross with her mother for cooking so much.

'It's not a marriage party, Begum,' he said. 'It's only a picnic.'

'What do you mean?' her mother said.

'Picnic is an English custom, you know. Portable tinty-minty things like sandwiches or boiled eggs are sufficient.'

'Are you going crazy or what? You know, these things don't agree with our taste,' her mother said.

'Have you considered what the English will think? When they see us taking such mountain-high stuff, and curry and all, they're sure to think of us as a funny-wunny lot.'

'So, what you saying?' her mother said. 'Should we eat disagreeable things to please them?'

'You're impossible, Begum,' her father said. 'You're not thinking of using your bare hand to eat in public places – are you?'

Her mother didn't bother to respond, she just smiled mischievously and served Surat Mia his dinner.

Next morning Nilufar got up early – at the hour cocks would have been crowing, had there been crowing-cocks in this city. She whispered into the ears of her six-year-old sister, 'Remember, oh Shapna, remember; what day is it?' Shapna woke up without her usual getting-up-for-school complaints. When their bodies rustled and their whispers reached next door, their four-year-old brother Kaisar got up too. He came to sit on Nilufar's lap. It felt like Eid day. So, as befitting such a day, and without any prompting from the grown-ups, they had showers, put on nice, clean clothes, and were ready long before uncle Halim, accompanied by his family, rang the bell.

From Whitechapel they took the tube to Kew Gardens with the heaps of food stuffed in plastic containers of all manners and sizes. At Aldgate East an old Bengali man, who had just got on the train, made his way towards her father. He had a smile on his face and said, 'Surat Mia, are you going for picnic? I pray for you, may Allah grant a fine day for your family.' Her father smiled back with gratitude. Lingering a moment, as if to savour the happiness that would be theirs for the rest of the day, the old man moved away to the far corner of the compartment, though there were seats nearer. At the time Nilufar was so excited by the promise of the occasion that she didn't reflect on the way the old man acted. Now it became clear to her that perhaps he hadn't wanted to intrude into the circle of dreams that bound the family that day.

Once the tube moved beyond Aldgate East, her father began to feel uneasy, as though they were entering a hostile, foreign territory. The fretful gestures of white passengers, their noses tingling from the waft of spicy aroma, made him even more nervous. He withdrew, making himself a sombre relief of stone. From then on he adopted an exaggerated aloofness, as though the family carrying the heaps of spicy food had nothing to do with him. Soon, Uncle Halim adopted the same posture. Auntie

Halim and Nilufar's mother, on the other hand, despite wearing veils, in between chewing paan leaves with rude noises, carried on gossiping in high-pitched tones. For them the train compartment seemed merely the inner courtyard of their homes.

Only when the picnic party got off at Kew Gardens did Surat Mia manage to ease himself into a lighter mood. 'Ah, wonderful,' he said once again. 'The fortunes of our foreheads have never been so kind.'

In Kew Gardens, they set off down the long, open avenue lined with tall trees, then looped and meandered through the bushes, shrubs and flower beds. They continued until they found a secluded patch of grass under the low, spreading branches of a tree with thick foliage. While her mother and Auntie Halim spread the rugs and unloaded the picnic, Nilufar – eager to explore – went running towards the river. Shapna and Cousin Rima were keeping pace with her, but poor Kaisar was lagging behind. Nilufar stopped, waited for him and continued towards the river holding his hand.

By the time they came back from their explorations, the picnic was laid on out on the rugs. Feeling awkward again, Surat Mia maintained his distance, leaning against the trunk of the tree and puffing at his cigarette. First her mother served the kids, then she served her father and Uncle Halim. Noticing that he wasn't given a spoon, her father said, 'Don't tell me, Begum. You haven't brought any spoon?'

'Why? I didn't know you turning English under your skin,' her mother said, looking quizzically at her father. 'You want to eat like a sahib with them spoon and knife?'

Reluctantly, Surat Mia and Uncle Halim went back with their plates to the trunk of the tree, hoping, perhaps, its enormous girth would veil their shame. As they began to eat with their fingers, a white family strayed into their spot, and both brothers froze like a pair of naughty boys caught in some nefarious act. Luckily, as soon as they saw the spectacle of brown bodies hunched over their strange feast, the white family hurried away. For the rest of the picnic, no white family dared to breach their little spot under the tree.

Her father, though, didn't relax until the eating was over, and

42

then only when Nilufar brought him a paan. 'Honestly, na? What a weather!' Her father said again. 'The good fortune of our foreheads has never been so kind.'

Her father wasn't the kind of person to ask her questions, but now he asked her if she knew what kind of tree it was. Nilufar looked up to study the shapes of the leaves and said that it was an oak. Just to confirm her knowledge she then examined the plaque nailed to the trunk – which her father couldn't read because, like the prophet, he remained unlettered – and said, 'Yes, oak it is, Abba.'

Surat Mia put his hand on Nilufar's head, caressed it lovingly, and said, 'My daughter doesn't lack anything, she has head full of brains. May Allah grant you more power of thought.' He added, 'One day you'll know, my good daughter, all the names of the plants, trees and flowers of this land. And that day this land will be yours.' No sooner had he said this than he looked away into the distance, as if behind the clear blue sky, beyond his range of vision, clouds were already gathering. He couldn't help thinking that on that day of possession – despite their blood-bond and love – Nilufar would be lost to him. Surat Mia shook his head to clear his mind of such despairing thoughts and again – proud and happy – looked lovingly at Nilufar. Although Nilufar wasn't sure what her father was on about, she felt the pride and the love with which he spoke and that made her curl up in his lap.

Once the picnic was over, and after a siesta under the shade of the oak, they set off to explore again. Following no particular direction, they went through field after field of green with flowers and shrubs and trees that were native to England and other cold and temperate zones. Each time they passed a species that Nilufar happened to know from her schoolwork, she called out its name – birch, poplar, chestnut, fir, oak, elm, cedar – and explained, 'This must be willow, Abba, look at its weeping leaves.' Surat Mia was amazed at Nilufar's precocious mastery of the natural works of England, which for him were simply flowers, shrubs and trees without names. Inside the giant green-houses things were very different. He became animated over the tropical ferns, trees, and flowers that blossomed in the heat of the glasshouses. When he saw a small clump of sugar canes, he told the children what variety they were. He became dreamy-eyed remembering the sugar canes that surrounded his mother's house with their long swaying leaves; how as children they chewed the succulent fibres of mature canes; how they played hide and seek amongst their densely packed columns on moonlit nights; how jackals howled from the undergrowth on dark nights. He showered similar stories on the children at the sight of mango, banana and papaya trees.

Her father was very happy, but Uncle Halim had to be the spoilsport.

'Surat Bhai,' he said, 'we mustn't forget how these things got here.'

'What do you mean, Halim?'

'You must know how the Feringeewallahs went snooping around the world with their magnifying glasses – you know, like that pipe-smoking chapee from Baker Street. Ha, Surat Bhai, they went around naming our things like they invented them.'

'How should I know these things, Halim?'

'Oh, Surat Bhai, what can I say! You must agree, yes, their greed is almost as boundless as Allah's bounty!'

'I don't know, Halim. Are you sure you're not talking bombastic?'

'Listen, Surat Bhai, you can't deny that after naming, they pocketed our things like they were inheritances from their forefathers.'

'Why bother with bringing up these old things, Halim?'

'Because they ate our bodies and souls like hogs, Surat Bhai. Most amusing/bemusing affair – na?'

'But the more we talk about these things, the more botheration they bring – na?'

'Maybe. But that's how these things came here, Surat Bhai. Whiteman's canes and Whiteman's coolies, all the same. Na?'

'Um,' her father said pensively. 'Now that we're here in England, these things can be ours again.'

It was in another glasshouse, given over to a meticulous simulacra of a tropical pond, with lotuses floating by the red hibiscus, where Uncle Halim took the photograph at which Nilufar was now looking.

They were so close and happy then. Shapna and Nilufar, wearing identical salwar and kameez, were crouching in front, looking at the lotuses. Just behind, Kaisar was holding onto his mother, and her father – despite the stiffness of his posture – couldn't quite hide the pleasure of the moment bubbling over his face. Now, looking at the photograph, Nilufar felt so sad that she couldn't hold back her tears. Who could have foreseen that one day she would be separated from her family?

If she hadn't gone to university, none of this would have happened. Perhaps the Most Venerable Pir-Sahib was right when he tried to stop her from going to university. Perhaps her father should have listened to him. Instead, her father avoided the Most Venerable Pir-Sahib until Nilufar was well settled on her course. He had thought that Nilufar, with her good education, would bring him a well-to-do son-in-law. He had no idea that his dutiful daughter would come out of university wearing a strange set of spectacles that led her to see things a female should never see.

When Nilufar finished her studies and came back home, her father could hardly hide his pride at having a BA and a fully qualified teacher in the family. He kept inviting relatives and friends just to show off his daughter's achievement. Nilufar found these occasions embarrassing, but played along because they made her father so happy.

Once settled back in East London, Nilufar kept herself busy working for a local school, and generally tried to be helpful to her community. If someone needed an interpreter to see a doctor or a lawyer, she would happily accompany them; if someone needed help filling in their social security forms, they had only to ask her. But her father was getting more and more worried by what he came to see as the foreignness of her ideas and her feringhee style. He stopped looking her in the eyes and then stopped talking to her, as though she didn't exist. Her mother, desperate to defuse the situation, brought up the subject of marriage. No excuse and no explanation. Nilufar simply said 'No', very slowly and clearly. Her mother knew Nilufar well enough not to raise the issue again. Everybody waited for the inevitable parting of the ways to take place.

So, indeed, they did, one misty morning. Nilufar began gathering her things as though embarking on a long exile. Her mother sobbed, pulling the veil of her sari diagonally over her face; from the stairs, Shapna and Kaisar looked on with tearful eyes, but her father stayed as silent as a stone in the gloom of the sitting room. When the taxi arrived, it took Nilufar to stay with some university friends in Islington. Within a few months she was back in Tower Hamlets, in a flat of her own in Henriques Street. Later, Shapna had told Nilufar that she'd gone around imagining that somehow it wasn't happening, that the clock would turn back to a time when they were all happy together.

If Kaisar hadn't come to Nilufar's to borrow money, Shapna wouldn't have known that her sister was ill. Nilufar didn't like giving Kaisar any money; she knew about his drug addiction. Yet, when he begged her, told her how hungry he was, she usually gave in. She wished she had time to cook for him, persuade him to move in with her – that way she could take care of him, get him off his habit. When he came around to borrow money, she mentioned this idea to him, but without conviction.

She had been so busy. As if her regular job at the school wasn't demanding enough, she volunteered to work in the supplementary circuit, so that the Bangladeshi kids would have a decent chance of making the grades; and then there was her women's group to run. Lately, of course, there'd been the work for the defence group – especially since the group has decided to patrol the streets and housing estates during the night. Although, as a woman, she wasn't expected to go out on patrol, Nilufar insisted on serving her share of the rota.

'Slow down, Appa.' Shapna insisted. 'At this rate, you'll go under in no time.' Every time Nilufar heard Shapna talk like this, just as their mother had done, she would just nod evasively. Shapna was so exasperated by her sister's lack of care for herself, her manic drive to right all wrongs, that she often came very close to saying something really cruel to snap her out of it. But Shapna loved her sister so much that she could never bring herself to say anything hurtful to her.

When Kaisar phoned Shapna to tell her that Nilufar was ill, she phoned Nilufar, sounding very cross, 'How come you don't tell me anything these days, Appa. I get so worried about you.' Trying to sound much better than she was, Nilufar told her that it was nothing serious – only hay fever – so common this year. But nothing was going to stop Shapna from coming – as soon as she had cooked something nice, and on the way she would pick up some medicine from the chemist.

Nilufar was thinking that when Shapna arrived, they should talk about Kaisar. His drugs habit was getting serious; they had to do something about it. Not long ago everybody thought Kaisar had so much promise – so well-behaved and intelligent. How had it all gone wrong?

She remembered how he, her baby brother, used to follow her around the house, sit on her lap, and she would read him stories. Stories about a giant chocolate factory, or Alice going through the mirror. He would ask, 'Can a boy also go through the mirror?' At those times, their mother, who couldn't read, would quietly slip into the room. She would hover around, sweeping the floor, dusting, or arranging the clothes in the drawers, but they were mere pretexts for observing these intimate moments between an elder sister and her little brother. She would feel that everything was fine in her little world, that the pain of immigration was worth it, that her children would grow up with so much possibility, and that they would be happy. They would be there for each other, supporting each other in good and bad times. She would go out of the room as quietly as she had come in, and bring back glasses of hot milk and home-made sweets. Taking a sip of milk, Kaisar would say, 'Nilu Appa said boys can also go through the mirrors.' Nilufar would laugh, resting her chin on the mop of his thick, black hair. Their mother would be baffled, but she would smile and bless them, 'May Allah look after you.'

When Nilufar went to university, Kaisar – though he was fourteen by then – still retained his childish innocence. He didn't feel embarrassed – as would most boys of his age – about going around with his big sister, didn't feel the need to hide his pride in her. Nilufar was happy that Kaisar came with the rest of the family to take her to the university. They hired a minibus from the community hall. Uncle Halim drove, her father beside him, and the rest of the family occupied the rows of seats at the back.

Kaisar had been looking out of the window at the autumnal colours of the English countryside, its rolling hills and stone-curved villages surrounded by trees and the ancient churches with their steeples. When they were on a straight stretch of road lined with yellowing beeches, he suddenly said he didn't like the city, would rather live in the countryside when he grew up. Hearing that, Uncle Halim told him that the countryside wasn't for brown fellows like him, that the whites wouldn't want him there. Kaisar was quiet for a while but said – as if after a long reflection – that the whites wouldn't mind him, because he wouldn't make the place stinky by cooking dry fishes like the Bangladeshis, or by spitting pan-red saliva all over the place. Uncle Halim gave a loud, mocking laugh, but Nilufar looked at him with eyes that told him that he could live wherever he wanted. This was his country by birthright.

During her first two years at university, Kaisar visited her often. He loved the green pastures and the lake and the attention of her friends. He was full of ambition: he would come here to study one day – perhaps he would study geology because he wanted to know about the rocks that harboured the primal time of our planet. But it wasn't to happen. He stopped coming to the campus to visit Nilufar during her third year, left school without any grades, and became part of a gang. Soon he was doing drugs and petty crimes – carried away, like a hummingbird, by the nectar of the street.

When Nilufar came back from university, Kaisar stopped doing drugs, started an evening course to get the grades, and even got a part-time job at a restaurant. But, soon after Nilufar left home, Kaisar went back to drugs, and after a few months he also left home. As far as Surat Mia was concerned, they ceased to exist; now he had only Shapna, who – despite being raised in England – continued to play the dutiful daughter: prayed five times a day, agreed to an arranged marriage and went around wearing a black veil.

In fact, Surat Mia didn't have to convince Shapna to do any of these things; she had decided that this was the right path for her, so convinced was she by the teachings of the Most Venerable Pir-Sahib.

Even Nilufar – despite the memories of bitter struggle, despite coming to face each other across an impenetrable barrier – thought that the Most Venerable Pir-Sahib was the most serene looking man she had seen. Nilufar didn't know how and when he had come to England, but he loomed large in her childhood landscape – even though she had only seen him twice, and briefly.

When she was ten years old, severely affected by asthma at the beginning of winter, she went to see him for the first time. Her mother accompanied her on the twenty-minute walk it took to reach his flat in Myrdle Street. Although Nilufar knew about the Most Venerable Pir-Sahib's importance in the Bangladeshi community in East London and his miraculous powers she wasn't sure what to expect.

When Monu Mia the blind – Pir-Sahib's assistant – led Nilufar into Pir-Sahib's chamber, she found him seated on the floral circle of a thick Persian rug. Nilufar was taken aback, frightened, but also captivated by his enormous size – as though, should he decide to stand up, he would touch the ceiling. He was leaning back on a round white pillow, his long white beard arching onto his chest. To his right there was a hooka with its long pipe, to his left a bronze spittoon, and in front a silver plate piled with paan cones. He was like a giant bird with white plumage from head to toe: immaculate white socks on his feet, a pair of starched white pyjamas covering his legs, a finely pressed white silk askan draped over his shoulders. He was crowned with a white Kashmiri cap. Head bowed, Nilufar stood in front of him for what seemed like an eternity, her legs trembling. He didn't seem to notice her presence; he was absorbed in his own world – now chewing a paan, now taking a puff on the pipe. The room smelt of sweet tobacco, mingled with roses.

At last Pir-Sahib turned his smooth, polished marble of a face towards her, and looked at her with his clear eyes, as if looking through a window of hyaline glass. He then gently nodded his beard; and Nilufar understood this to be the signal for her to sit down. Since women weren't allowed in his presence, not even hidden in their yashmak veils, her mother spoke from the adjacent room. She begged Pir-Sahib to bless Nilufar so that she would be cured of her asthma.

Suddenly Pir-Sahib turned to his left to spit paan-juice saliva into the bronze spittoon. Taking this as a signal, Monu Mia the blind came running with a glass of water. Now sitting upright, his feet tucked under his buttocks, Pir-Sahib intoned a long Arabic verse and blew softly into the glass. Arching over her with a grin, Monu Mia the blind urged her to drink. It was when she emptied the glass that the Most Venerable Pir-Sahib put his right hand on her head. She had seen the hand holding the pipe; it looked so smooth, as though it had never touched anything harsh in its life. She didn't know what was happening, but as soon as the hand rested on her head, she felt as though the hand had melted and cascaded down her hair in a cold stream of water. She was scared that her mother would be cross with her if she had found out that she had wet her pants, so she kept it a secret. Serene as ever, the Most Venerable Pir-Sahib closed his eyes and leaned back on the pillow, but Monu Mia the blind screwed his nose at the smell of urine.

Following that visit, Nilufar was cured of her asthma. Then she had accepted the miracle as if it was the most natural thing to have happened, because she had the blessings of the Most Venerable Pir-Sahib. But her second visit was very different.

It was six years later, at the age of sixteen, when she was preparing for her O levels, that the second visit took place. She wasn't very keen on the idea, but her father persuaded her otherwise. 'Thanks to Allah, I know you lack nothing, my daughter,' Surat Mia said. 'But one could always do with some extra bit of help – na? You must admit the Most Venerable one has one or two trickery in his bag. He's certainly very close to Allah.'

She was now old enough to need a veil to be in his presence. Her mother took her to Newham, but that year all the veils were black. She wanted Nilufar to have a white veil, so she stayed up late to make one.

Spring was early that year: cherries and crocuses had already blossomed by early March, and clumps of daffodils were beginning to appear in the green patches along the roads. One early afternoon on a Friday, after the midday prayers, after they had eaten together, she was ready to set off with her father. Kaisar giggled, seeing her in the veil. 'You look like a ghost, Appa. Can you see anything in it?' Nilufar made some gruff, funny noises and lifted her hands like a zombie. Kaisar cowered in mock horror, but Shapna looked at her longingly. As he always did while he was in public with her mother, her father – stiff as a steel lamppost – walked way ahead of Nilufar. Only once did he stop for her to catch up with him so that he could tell her, 'These yellow flowers, they're daffodils – na?' He was pleased to have finally called an English flower by its name. That night, after hearing of it from Nilufar, her mother – smiling behind her sari – told her father, 'Oh Ma, such knowledge! You are now practically an English man.'

At first Nilufar felt weird walking the familiar streets in a veil; she felt exposed rather than sheltered from other eyes. She thought she must look like a robotic cone. Yet, once she reached Whitechapel Road, and was used to the shaded world of the veil, she began to take pleasure in it. Of course, she could do nothing about other people's attention, and their fantasies running wild about the figure under the veil, but she could pretend to be anyone she liked. Besides, she could look at people straight on without any embarrassment, scrutinise them intimately without being suspected of doing so. She was beginning to like this perfect voyeur's machine.

The Most Venerable one hadn't changed a bit; he looked his same old serene self. As before, as soon as he spat out the paan-red saliva into the spittoon, Monu Mia the blind brought in a glass of water. This time she didn't wet her pants. Yes, his right hand was as soft as ever, but unlike the previous time it didn't melt into a cascade of showers.

As the Most Venerable Pir-Sahib was a busy man with a large clientele, they weren't supposed to linger, but someone had cancelled at the last minute. The Most Venerable Pir-Sahib invited her father to a paan. Leaning on the round pillow, chewing paan and puffing the hooka, he began a casual sermon. He spoke quietly and deliberately, pronouncing each word with meticulous precision. Nilufar was astonished by how the articulation of his jaws didn't disrupt the faint smile on his lips.

'You see, order is the key to the universe. Allah in his supreme wisdom has placed everything in its proper place. If you alter a tiny bit, the whole thing will fall apart. What the scientist fellows are propagating is full of fundamental flaws and mistaken notions. Not to say arrogance. A single verse of the Koran will debunk them a thousand times. But let us consider what they are saying. I strongly advise people to close their eyes and ears and skin to their wicked knowledge. If I had my way I would burn their books. But Allah has chosen some of us for the difficult task of reminding people of His supreme order against all sorts of deviations and confusions. So, painful though it is for us, we have to soil our eyes with the wicked knowledge of the scientists so that we can demonstrate their fallacies. But you have to be very vigilant.

'You know some of our very wise men have been seduced by the satanic knowledge of the scientists. I don't have to remind you of the sad cases of Ibn-Sina, Al-Kindi, Al-Razi, Ibn-Rushd and some of their fellow travellers down the ages. It was right that they were severely punished by the custodians of order – our prudent emirs and sultans. I wish there were presidents and prime ministers like them these days. But above all we have to be thankful to Al-Ghazzali for showing once and for all the mistaken ways of the scientifically minded. As I was saying, let us consider for a moment what the scientists are saying. You will see that even their mistaken and arrogant ideas confirm the immaculate order that Allah has created.

'For example, take their conception of the solar system. Ho, ho, the Sun in the middle – what a ridiculous idea! But let us, for argument's sake, accept that for the time being. Ho, ho, the Sun in the middle: Mercury, Venus, Earth and Mars circling the inner orbit; then Jupiter, Saturn, Uranus, Neptune and Pluto in the outer orbit. In turn, some of these planets have their own satellites, like Earth has the moon, orbiting them. Apart from these, there are thousands of asteroids and meteoroids moving, orbiting and shooting all over the place. Now imagine that solar systems like ours are repeated innumerable times in the universe, all moving and orbiting. My question is: how they do not collide against each other? Because Allah has ordered everything in a manner that each has its own place. So all planets, asteroids and what-not have their assigned routes. They wouldn't deviate until

Allah – fed up with the wickedness of the human kind – would call on Israfil to blow the trumpet of doomsday. So you can see, scientific notions, mistaken and arrogant though they are, couldn't help but prove the order that the supreme wisdom of Allah has created.

'Everything has a fixed place: cows have their place, humans have theirs. Allah in his scheme of things hasn't given the cow the faculty of knowledge. You must understand that the purpose of cows, apart from the other tasks to which we might employ them, is to show us their muscles and their meat. Their passion is to attract us to their flesh and beg us: "Oh we're so good to eat, cut our throats in this very instance and eat us." I hear one German, no doubt he was very mad. What was his name? Nich, Fretch or Cha? I think it was Nich because he was of the lowest order. You know, he actually pontificated that us humans became cows. He also had the audacity to entertain the notion of war against Allah. But Allah had His retribution and made his brains go jelly. So he ended up the cow that he wanted to be. The same thing happened to Nimrod. I don't want to remind you of his arrogance. But Allah sent a tiny gnat; it entered his skull and bored through his brain.

'We mustn't forget that among us humans too there is order and assigned places. We are the sun, women the moon. We live under light, expose our face to the elements, toil to earn bread and manage the statecraft. Woman, the secondary being – made from the ribs of the first man – is placed in the shadow. They are given the task of multiplying the species and the maintenance of the household. You see, if we disrupt this order, we bring the day when Israfil will blow his trumpet so much closer. Now do you see the order of Allah?

'Perhaps one last example is in order. You must agree that there is no confusion between land and water. Correspondingly, there is no confusion between the creatures that Allah has put in there. You see, Allah's order is founded on clarity and absolute separation. If you like, the difference between a tiger and a fish. Allah has made the fish to inhabit water and the tiger to inhabit land. So there is no confusion between land and water. With the grace of Allah, I hope everything is clear now.'

Surat Mia looked baffled and scratched his head. He said, 'You know I'm an ignorant man, the Most Venerable one. I know nothing of such high thoughts. I don't know any German/ Urman, either correct or incorrect in their heads, except. . . oh what's his name? Eatlal or Phitlar? You know that mighty killer of Jews. I don't register in my uncultivated mind much of your subtle argumentation. But what I say is that you, the Most Venerable one, must be saying the correct thing. That's enough for me.'

At first he didn't notice it. From underneath, against the front of the veil, Nilufar stuck her index finger out. It stood out like a little tent. Seeing that he hadn't noticed her, she moved her little tent from side to side. Finally the Most Venerable Pir-Sahib noticed her and asked:

'What is it, my child?'

Almost choking on her words, very faintly she said, 'How about frogs?'

'What?'

'Frogs,' Nilufar said, much louder this time.

'What about frogs, my child?'

'Don't they live both in water and on land?'

Like a stunned animal, the Most Venerable one kept absolute silence for a while, and then he puffed his hooka rapidly, smoke clouding the room. He didn't look at Nilufar again, but turned to her father, his voice losing some of its immaculate clarity. 'Now you see the danger, Surat Mia,' he said. 'English schooling plants confusion in their brains, and they ask the most impertinent questions. Girls shouldn't be educated. Reading Koran is fine. Perhaps a bit of reading and writing so that they can instruct their children. But their constitution is not fit to absorb much more than that. I'm always telling you people, but you wouldn't listen. Girls shouldn't be educated, especially in English schools. Such impertinence! Allah have mercy on the poor child.'

Since that visit Nilufar hadn't seen the Most Venerable one, but the bad feelings between them continued to simmer, and reached a new level when she returned from university. In the meantime, he kept on preaching against girls' education, and perfected a sermon that he delivered whenever the opportunity arose. Frequent visitors to his chamber got to know the sermon by heart. 'Shaitan has so many crafty ways to lead us astray. He is the master of stratagem,' he would begin. 'I do not want to overstress the point but you must know that females are the weakest links of our culture. Naturally Shaitan works through them to undermine the righteous way.

'You must know that by sending our girls to school we make it easier for Shaitan to capture their souls. And they might end up committing all kinds of abomination like copulating without marriage, or lying in the sun wearing hardly any clothes. If you want to see your daughters producing half-castes, or silly-billing in bikini, then very well, do as you please. If not, think twice before sending your daughters to school.'

Up until Nilufar came back from university, the Most Venerable one reserved his sermon for the visitors to his chamber. Now – facing Nilufar's vigorous opposition – he circulated leaflets, sent his followers around to homes, to schools, to marriage parties, to cafes and restaurants, and held rallies and marches. For him the nightmare came true when he heard that Nilufar had founded the women's group. From then on he spent hours leaning on his pillow, and between chewing paan and smoking hooka, allowed himself the pleasure of imagining that he had the power of fatwa to condemn her to death: 'My righteous brothers, you who have gathered in Brick Lane, be the instrument of Allah's judgement. Cast your stone at that abomination.'

Frustrated, he circulated leaflets denouncing the women's group as a gathering of satanic rituals and whores. But the Most Venerable one had his successes. There were many young women who, though born in London, knowing nothing apart from English, who had even attended universities and colleges, yet flocked to his Koranic school. They became enraptured by his message of purity. Their zeal baffled the older Bangladeshis, even those who lived a pious life, and regularly prayed and fasted. Although never an active militant, Shapna quietly followed the Most Venerable Pir-Sahib's teachings, gave up her studies, and went around in a veil. For her, the veil wasn't a female voyeur's paradise.

Yet, it wasn't until Shapna's marriage that reality finally dawned on Nilufar that they had taken such different directions at the forking path.

As she had already walked out on her family, Nilufar didn't know what was happening. It was Sundar who told her that Shapna was getting married.

Nilufar went to see her in Whitechapel Street, where she worked at the Little Bangala nursery. When Shapna saw Nilufar she knew exactly why she was there. She asked someone to take her place for a while and led Nilufar to the empty staff room at the back. She made two cups of tea and they sat down together on an old misshapen settee. On a musty afternoon that seemed to have gathered all the gloom of the English climate, Nilufar kept looking at her sister, but Shapna wouldn't meet her eyes – she kept hers lowered, fixed on a glossy magazine on the floor. She couldn't reciprocate the look of complicity the two sisters had always shared. She didn't feel a victim by accepting an arranged marriage, as Nilufar wanted her to feel.

'Are they pushing you into it? I heard he's coming from Bangladesh. God, you haven't even seen him,' said Nilufar, breathlessly, as if she was choking on the words. 'You know, you can say no, Shapna. I'll help you.'

Shapna stayed quiet, still looking at the magazine on the floor.

'You got it wrong, Appa. No one is forcing me,' said Shapna at last. 'I want it this way. Is there any shame in doing things like our mothers?'

Nilufar didn't say any more, because the gulf between herself and her sister was clear now. Nothing meaningful on this subject could now be said between them. Nilufar put the cup abruptly on the table, and headed towards the door. Each step of the way she wanted to turn around, and say something to Shapna, at least wish her good luck on her marriage, but she felt awkward. At the door Shapna said, 'Look after yourself, Appa. You're getting so thin. Khuda-hafez.' Still Nilufar didn't look back; she quickened her steps to go outside, because she didn't want Shapna to see her tears.

Now Shapna had arrived at Nilufar's with a lunch carrier full of curries, and Chumki – her daughter – in the pushchair. While Shapna went to the kitchen to warm up the curries and boil some rice, Nilufar played with Chumki. Then she remembered that she had recently bought a book for Chumki that was still lying on her desk. She put the book on Chumki's lap, and helped her turn the pages. It was a book with pictures of animals in it. When Shapna came back from the kitchen, she found Nilufar swaying an arm from the base of her nose as if it was the trunk of an elephant and trumpeting, to Chumki's amusement. Shapna stood there, watching. She felt pity for Nilufar, for living all alone with no one to comfort her. For a moment Shapna felt for Nilufar the way their mother would have felt for her, and imagined what she would have said: 'Poor Nilufar. Allah, what sadness must have been written in her destiny.'

Of course, she missed her family, but Nilufar didn't feel sad for herself; she rather liked being alone – enjoyed her domestic lassitude and her solitude among the shadows and silence of her room. Besides, she had found again the feeling she thought she had lost. On that day, after that strange event at the picket line, after they carried Tapan to Sundar's flat, it came to her so suddenly that she hadn't had the time to put her usual defences up, and before she knew it, she was already looking at him with that feeling. Still they carried on as if nothing had happened, but something was happening even though they hadn't spoken of it, or exchanged the surreptitious glances that couples do at the beginning of a romance. Every time Tapan was around, among the crowds on the picket line or at the marches, or planning the course of events with the defence group, she felt he was there in a different way from the rest of her friends and comrades. She felt a tingling on the edges of her jaws, a desire to let her defences down, and go before him totally disarmed and naked. Did he feel the same way about her? She was sure that he did – you can't be wrong about this thing, can you? Now that Tapan was coming to live in East London, they would have a better chance of telling each other how they really felt about each other – and could give in to the feeling.

CHAPTER 5

'Something special to welcome you, Bhaio,' said Sundar. He was preparing lamb with satkora cooking-lemon and whistling in the bittersweet aroma that filled the flat. Sundar's was a tiny one-bedroom flat right in the middle of Brick Lane. He insisted that Tapan take his bedroom while he slept in the lounge that, apart from serving as a diner, lent itself as the meeting room for the defence group. But Tapan wouldn't hear of it and, after a tussle, Sundar conceded, but promised Tapan that he would soon fix him with a job and a room of his own. While Sundar got on with the cooking, Tapan went for a shower.

It was true that he was leaving North London and the kind of life that he had lived since he had come to England, but it really surprised Tapan that his arrival in East London should feel as momentous as his arrival in England from Bangladesh had done. Most absurdly of all, it felt like coming home, when eight years ago, as he left Bangladesh, and as his grandfather – the tassel of his fez dangling in the wind – lifted his ivory-headed stick at the airport to send him away, he had felt the pain of a final goodbye. For some reason he had always associated that moment with the smell of palm bread.

He wasn't sure what the trigger was now; the bittersweet aroma of Sundar's cooking had nothing to do with palm bread. Perhaps, it was the buzzing of the shower, and the sense that he had just concluded yet another momentous departure that had sparked it off. He remembered having palm bread for breakfast on the morning he left for England; during the flight he had lingered on the flavour until the airline lunch had spoiled it. But now he wasn't thinking of that breakfast. Beyond that palm bread lay another, from further back in time. This one was inseparable from memories of wild ducks.

It was the end of a long journey. He had gone to visit his grandmother – his mother's mother – in the dry season. From there he was returning to his grandfather – that's his father's father. On that journey he had been escorted by Bisu Bhai – his grandmother's farm keeper.

It was a long journey on foot and they were supposed to arrive the night before, but it must have been about nine the following morning when they reached his grandfather's village. Sunlight came through the branches of bamboo, and the dew had already begun to melt. Worried the whole night, his grandfather had sent out search parties with torchlights to the swamp, to the banks of the river, to the cane fields. In the morning, he was waiting on the plain where, behind the dense bush of rattan and tamarind, the railway line turned north. Despite the sleepless night and his anxiety, he was wearing a striped suit and a red fez with its dangling tassel. Even then it made Tapan laugh, seeing how out of place his grandfather looked among bare-chested peasants wearing lungis. Although his grandfather didn't say anything to Bisu Bhai, he looked hard at him with his red eyes, and stamped his ivory-headed stick on the ground.

His grandfather walked stiffly, holding his hand. All he said to him was, 'You need a good bathing, my boy.' No sooner had Tapan reached the outer gate of the house, than he smelt the palm bread, but he had to wait to taste it until he'd had a bath in the pond. Although by then the early mist had lifted, the water hadn't warmed yet. As he went hesitantly into the calm water, as it broke into ripples, he felt a slight shiver. He had a quick dip. When he surfaced he saw a kingfisher perched on an overhanging branch. He wanted to see the kingfisher catch a fish, but it stayed still on the branch, and though from time to time it fretted and wagged its tail, it never dived.

When Tapan came back from the pond he found his grandfather waiting for him at the inner bungalow with breakfast. It was there on a soft red rug with blue flowers that his grandfather served him palm bread. It was somewhere in the course of breakfast that his grandfather told him that he was taking him to the town house. 'Country is no place for a young man to grow up. You need to know the world and its ways.' Perhaps Tapan nodded to show that he was listening, but he wasn't listening, as the palm breads had already taken him down their coiling flavours.

In the afternoon, after he'd had a light lunch and a nap, his grandfather took him out on a hunt. As they walked through rice fields, sugar cane fields and mustard fields, his grandfather kept pointing out, 'See this yellow field,' he said. 'Right up to the bush in the distance. This is mine. One day it is going to be yours, my boy.'

Now the whole idea sounded so absurd to him that he almost laughed out loud. Yet, at that time he had allowed his eyes to linger on the land that his grandfather pointed out to him, had run his hand dreamily over the swaying rice plants, and felt powerful imagining himself as the owner of it all. He was so grateful to his grandfather that he wanted to hug him, but seeing him walking stiff in his suit, a Sola hat on his head, wellingtons reaching his thighs, and an ivory-headed stick in his hand, he didn't dare to express any emotion. On the narrow pathway they walked single file, he just behind his grandfather, but ahead of the servant boy who carried the double-barrelled shotgun. In front were the dogs, whining, running about and wagging their tails. On the way, the peasants, mostly sharecroppers of his grandfather, got off the path to make way for them. Stooping their heads low, they gave his grandfather their salaams, and he acknowledged them with a nod of his Sola hat, though sometimes – seemingly at random – he stopped to inquire how the crops were coming along.

At the time, Tapan didn't think much of these exchanges. However, that evening, as he was waiting to be called for dinner in the outer bungalow, Bisu Bhai said something that really shocked him. Dragging on a coconut hooka, fire glowing on his face, Bisu Bhai told him how the peasants hated his grandfather.

'Don't put that face on like you've seen one of them low-down lady-ghosts. How do you expect them to be? Loving him like their own fatherji? Let me tell you one or two correct things – achya? I suppose even you're not so silly that you don't see that it's the peasants who put in all the back-breaking work. Na?

60

'From the time the muezzin calls for morning prayer to the time when the birds return to their nests, rain or sun, they work the land with their bare hands. You must know that they provide all the seeds and fertiliser. Not to mention reaping and harvesting. What Big Sahib does? You don't need Vatya Das's funny funny ideas to see it. Achya? But Big Sahib gets the half of the harvest.

'But this is nothing compared to the British time. He used to get two-thirds. I've eaten Big Sahib's salt, I don't want to badmouth him. But the whole district knows that he was a big friend of the British during the Raj.

'I don't know how to say it. Something very shameful, you understand. Let me think correctly, achya? One day I came here on an urgent business. When I arrived I saw a mighty this and that going on. Big Sahib had invited one of them English magistrates. Would you believe, he shook hands with him! After that he took him out on a duck hunt. Oh Allah, the things I've seen! No less than fifty ducks they shot that day. Plenty of roasts and curries they made. Big Sahib smiling and fussing over the magistrate, serving him like a poor boy-servant. Oh the shame of it! You understand me correctly, ha?'

The day of the hunt, after Tapan and his grandfather had crossed the plains on foot, they came to the river. There they took the boat, but the servant boy stayed by the shore with the dogs. As the boat began moving, his grandfather showed him the gun. 'Look at it, my boy. Such fine workmanship. You don't get things like this any more. You see, the British knew how to do things well.'

Handing the gun to Tapan, his grandfather became misty-eyed, as if overcome by distant memories. 'You see, it was a present from an English magistrate. Hunt Sahib was his name,' he said. 'He gave it to me as a token of my service. Such a fine piece, ha, my boy? I treasure it more than anything else. One day it will be your inheritance. I hope you'll look after it well.'

As the boat approached the other bank, where wild ducks fed in the shallow lagoon, Tapan slid his index finger over the smooth metallic barrels, and dreamt of owning the gun one day. He thought, perhaps, sometime in the future, like his grandfather, he would go hunting with this gun.

Now he wondered what his friends in East London – especially Masuk Ali – would say if he told them about his grandfather. No doubt Masuk Ali would say, 'It can't be true, Soul Brother. You're kidding, innit? Your old gran a rat like that fuckin' Poltu Khan?' Yes, yes, he would say, his grandfather was a traitor. An ass-licker of the British Raj.

Yet, on that day – despite the haughty aloofness – he felt close to his grandfather. When the boat reached the lagoon, they got off and waded through the shallow water towards the small islands of sand. The sky was blue and merged with the plain in the distance. Apart from the gentle waves breaking onto the tall reeds by the bank, there was silence. Head down, almost crawling, they approached the ducks from behind a dune. His grandfather took a shot at a flock, and then another in the air. Tapan felt as if the sound of the gun had broken the sky to pieces like a fragile piece of glass, and it shattered on the plain. But the birds – so many of them – ducks and storks and herons – flew up screaming to form a sky of their own. His grandfather was very pleased to have killed ten ducks. He said that Hunt Sahib was such a good shot that he had killed twenty-five in one go.

Once the ducks had landed again, his grandfather put the gun on Tapan's shoulder, and held it steady for him. He was scared to pull the trigger but on his grandfather's insistence he did. The gun kicked him back and the shot went up into the empty sky. Folding the barrels to clean them of the empty shells, his grandfather said, 'Killing with a gun or with a slingshot is the difference between the British and us. You have to know the ways of the gun, my boy.'

In the inner courtyard, on an open fire, cooking went on late into the night. The smell of roasting duck fat, mingling with spices, reached distant parts of the large compound. It made Tapan very hungry. Yet, after his conversation with Bisu Bhai, when he was called to dinner in the inner bungalow, he couldn't eat. Under a hanging flambeau, in front of the fire, his grandfather sat in the middle of a huge carpet circled by dishes full of ducks, cooked in all manner of roasts, kebabs and curries. His grandfather was asking him which of the dishes he would try first, which of the pieces he would prefer. All Tapan was thinking about was what

Bisu Bhai had said about his grandfather, that he was hated by the peasants, that he served duck to the English magistrate like a servant. He said he was feeling sickly and had a tummy ache. He left his grandfather sitting alone on the carpet. Next morning he said goodbye to Bisu Bhai, who returned to his grandmother's village, and he left for the town with his grandfather.

There they lived in a dark house with tiny windows. He was doing well at school but felt alone. Each morning he went for a walk with his grandfather by the riverbank. On the way he passed the red municipal building, the red courthouse, the red magistrate's office, the red railway station, the red police station, the red government school and the red collector's office, where his grandfather worked as an accounts clerk. 'See these buildings, my boy. British sahibs built them,' his grandfather would say. 'They stand for order and rational method among chaos. I wish the Britishers were still here. No, the mob went mad about kicking the British out. What we have now? First the no good Pakistan, then the no good Bangladesh. All the same, my boy. Disorder and chaos.'

His grandfather had long been dreaming about it and planning, but he waited to tell Tapan about it until he finished his higher secondary education. One afternoon he called him to the shade of the veranda, where he was slumped on a canvass recliner, eyes half closed, puffing a hooka. He didn't move, didn't turn to look at him, but simply said, 'I'm sending you to England, my boy. You'll be studying accountancy.'

For months he instructed Tapan in British etiquette, made him wear a three-piece suit during hot summer days, and initiated him into the British diet. Sweating profusely in his three-piece, Tapan didn't dare go out. He would stay locked up in his room, fanning desperately to cool himself down, but his grandfather would insist: 'Go out in your three-piece, my boy. Walk the streets, head held high. That way you get the feel of being a real sahib.'

As soon as he went out, the street boys followed him chanting, 'Ho, ho, there goes a monkey-sahib. Ho, ho, him getting cooked in his clothes.' He would walk fast, almost strutting to lose them, but even turning away from his street and merging with the crowds on Station Road, he didn't feel any more comfortable. He wouldn't look up to meet anyone's eyes. Head down and pouring with sweat he would do a quick turn around the central market and return home, where the street boys would be waiting for him.

Yet, this was nothing compared to what his grandfather put him through with regard to food. For months he stopped giving him rice and curry – except on the morning of his flight for England, when he was allowed a Bengali meal with palm bread for pudding. During the months of dietary training, he wasn't even allowed to use pickles or green chillies to break the monotony of his diet. God only knows where his grandfather got his information, but he was convinced that things like rice and spices weren't available in England. So he had better get used to boiled potatoes, boiled vegetables and boiled meat. 'Moreover,' his grandfather would say, 'to act like a proper sahib, my boy, you have to eat like a sahib.'

So, day after day, and for months, leading up to his departure for England, Tapan gagged on boiled potatoes and sweated in his three-piece suit. On the plane, all he could think about was eating spicy food and being free of that damn three-piece. Perhaps it was then that he dreamt of betraying his grandfather.

Sundar, worried that Tapan was taking so long in the bathroom, knocked on the door. ' Are you all right, Bhaio?' he said. 'The meal is nearly ready.' Sundar hadn't told Tapan that he had invited Nilufar to have dinner with them.

As they sat in the lounge, on the old, musty sofa, plates on their laps, Sundar asked, 'How do you like it – is it tip-top, Bhaio?' Tapan said that the lamb with satkora cooking-lemon was excellent; Nilufar agreed. Sundar then raised his glass of mango juice and said, 'Welcome to East London, Bhaio. Welcome to our city.'

Sundar knew well that Tapan had given up, yet he offered him a cigarette, which he declined as usual with a polite smile. Nilufar looked up as if to ask, 'How about me? Why don't you offer me a fag too?' But Sundar had this thing about women and cigarettes; he had always felt unnerved at the sight of a Bengali woman with a fag between her lips. Somehow it never failed to remind him of their betrayals, and conjure up for him their smoky road to European ways. If Nilufar hadn't been feeling unusually mellow

– and vulnerable in her feelings towards Tapan – she would have picked a quarrel with Sundar, but now she merely slumped back on the sofa and twirled a wisp of her hair.

Sundar rushed to the kitchen and came back with cones of paan on a plate. Hoping that it would make up for denying her a cigarette, he offered the first paan to Nilufar, who took it with a tacit recognition of the gesture. As they chewed paan, Tapan and Nilufar at last looked at each other, and she gave him the lustrous black of her eyes – the way she had done after that incident at the picket line. He took it as a rare gift that didn't demand any reciprocation, yet felt compelled to lose himself in it. He was disturbed to feel the same way he had felt when he walked the rectangular squares of the campus after spending that first night with Adela.

CHAPTER 6

The summer of '78 was nearly over and Tapan was still waiting for a decision. He had arranged for his post to be redirected from Adela's to Sundar's address, but nothing came from the Home Office. He had reason enough to be anxious – but how could be disbelieve Adela? She wasn't the kind of person to deceive him, tell him a lie that everything was in order, while biding her time to take her revenge on him. He put the delay down to fussy red tape – so common these days at all levels of the state system.

Sundar fixed him up with a job at a large Bangladeshi grocer's shop; he kept an eye on the stock and managed the till. Although the pay wasn't good, it really was the best job for someone like him, someone without legitimate documents. If he had worked in a sweatshop it would have been much harder, and in a restaurant the hours would have been longer. Sundar, true to his promise, also arranged for him to move into a flat in Bethnal Green. In those days, the area was infested with racist menace and the flat was damp and grotty, but he didn't have to pay any rent. He had simply to look after the place until the family who lived there returned from their long holiday in Bangladesh. Everything seemed to be working out and he was contented.

Although by then Brick Lane had become more secure, sporadic attacks were still taking place all over East London. Not a day went by without some Bangladeshis being knifed in the streets, kicked like softballs, taunted and chased by racist groups. The families on the housing estates were still living in terror: bombs and shit through their letterboxes, bricks through the windows, and the gangs waiting – always waiting like hyenas at the street corners. So the defence group extended their patrols to the housing estates and the streets.

The group had decided that it was too risky for Tapan to go out on patrol. If he was caught by the police, that would be the end of his bid to stay in England. Besides, he hadn't had training like the others, and he was too clumsy and scared of physical conflict. His job was to stay by the phone in Sundar's flat and log the locations of incidents on a map.

One day though, on a routine patrol, he tagged along with the group. They set off from Brick Lane; Masuk Ali was doing the advance reconnaissance – skipping away and disappearing for a while, then coming back with information about what lay ahead. It was a quiet night and after a few streets, they eased themselves into a jovial mood. Even Masuk Ali stopped doing his reconnaissance; he stayed with the group to join in with the fun. Someone had started an old joke – about a Bangladeshi and the Western loo. Everybody took turns to carry the joke forward, and sometimes several of them spoke together as if repeating a well-drilled chorus.

The Bangladeshi man in the joke is new to London. Nature calls and he needs to go. He takes a look at the strange loo and postpones, but after a while he can't hold it any more. So he goes in to do his business. He doesn't sit on the loo, but squats on it after his own country fashion. Since he doesn't know how to use the flush, he waits and waits for his waste to disappear. But it doesn't. So, what to do? He puts the lid down and goes out for a while. When he comes back he finds that it is still there, floating. Oh Allah, what to do? He can't leave it there. Oh, the shame of it! He scoops it and bundles it in layers of newspapers. Then he goes to the nearby park and buries it there. A policeman comes by and asks him, 'What you doing here, this time of the night?' The Bangladeshi man says, 'I'm planting my roots, sir.'

After a few more jokes and laughter all around, they joined in singing a light-hearted harvest song from Bangladesh. Suddenly they saw a police patrol car almost on them. Sundar whistled and they had to scatter fast; Nilufar and Tapan ended up together. Flat against the dark slime of a wall, they pressed against each other, holding their breath and merging together. Once the police car had disappeared, they could no longer resist the force that pulled their bodies right into each other, and their lips touched. That was the first time they kissed.

Soon they re-grouped and resumed the patrol again. Sensing that this could, after all, be a dangerous night, Masuk Ali walked beside Tapan. 'Soul Brother, if we meet a situation, you just run. If you can't run, then make sure that you stay by my side. No funny business. Okay, Soul Brother?'

Near Whitechapel station, the patrol met a gang writing 'Kill Pakis' and spraying swastikas with red spray paint. When the patrol went to confront them, Tapan, instead of running away – as he should have done – followed them, but stayed aloof from the scuffle. All of a sudden he felt a blow land on his face, and before he had the time to react, a knife was homing in on him. Luckily, Masuk Ali flew in just in time to kick away the knife. He pressed the attacker to the ground, twisted his wrist until it cracked, and then lifted the knife right over his heart. If Nilufar hadn't stopped him, he would have killed the skinhead. Afterwards, at the debriefing, Sundar gave Masuk Ali a serious telling-off for losing his discipline. 'That fuckin' git was on Soul Brother real bad. Innit,' said Masuk Ali. 'I can't just stand there, sucking my thumb.'

Tapan went along with several more patrols, and each time he and Nilufar deliberately fell behind, or strayed sideways. In those moments, they held hands, talked a little, and invariably, just before turning a corner and rejoining the group, they kissed.

It wasn't easy for them to spend time together, to form a solitary circle of two and recklessly give in to each other's impulses the way lovers do. Nilufar's flat was out of bounds. Too many eyes were on it: distant relatives, her parents' acquaintances and friends, mothers of her school kids, and the people she helped. She was a well-known figure in the community and they all kept an eye on her flat. As if a young woman living on her own wasn't scandalous enough, if a man had so much as entered her flat, it would have caused collective shame. So, Nilufar didn't dare invite him home. Since Tapan's flat – situated at the edge of Bethnal Green – wasn't at the hub of the Bangladeshi community in '78, it was a relatively safe place for them to meet. But the flat was too smelly and damp and dilapidated for a lovers' tryst.

One day they planned to meet each other at St. Katharine Docks. They weren't into playing games, yet each arrived separately at the rendezvous and acted as if they didn't know each other. He came on time, but Nilufar was already there, looking at the masts in the marina and smoking a cigarette. He passed her by, keeping his distance, careful not to draw her attention, but looking at her all the time. Of course, she'd seen him as soon as he crossed the drawbridge to come to the other side of the marina, but she let him glide past as if he was a stranger, whom she couldn't look at directly without appearing too forward or rude.

Flicking the ash from the cigarette, she laughed to herself, thinking how extraordinary it was that they should be playing the same game without having discussed it previously. It was fun to continue with it. She was intrigued by the strange man with a crazy mop of hair, a duffel coat and a pair of round, metallic glasses, glancing at her obliquely from the distance. What had he found so interesting in her? Had he fallen in love with her at first sight? No, he couldn't possibly be so ridiculous. Besides, she hadn't given her eyes to him yet. It was all very mysterious, this strange man, who seemed so sad, so lost in the labyrinth of a treacherous city. She wanted to caress that face, press it against her breasts, and if that mouth wanted to bite her nipples, she would let it. Oh, that strange man, already she was becoming breathless with his salty odour! How obscene to think of a stranger like this! Stubbing the butt of her cigarette on the ground, she moved on towards the tables under green umbrellas. She ordered a coffee and lit another cigarette.

Who was this woman? It was unusual to see an Asian woman so solitary, wandering on her own, so self-absorbed in her own dreams, and smoking in such a carefree way. Her thin, small frame in blue jeans and white anorak, made her look rather boyish. He was intrigued by the way she moved, her straight back, the thick fold of her silky black hair resting on the curve of her nape. More than that, it was the sheer force of her presence, as if she was a bundle of energy about to explode into fireworks, that attracted his attention.

How to approach this enigma of a woman sitting all alone and smoking under the green umbrella? If he hadn't given up smoking, he could have approached her with the pretext of asking for a light. He must find a way to be near her. If necessary, he would throw caution to the winds and risk public humiliation, because he could no longer resist that mysterious summons of the senses. So he became unusually bold and asked her if he could join her. She nodded her head, but without looking up at him. He sat down on a chair to her right and, after a long awkward silence, said, 'Such a beautiful day.' She turned to him, seemingly surprised. 'What?' Before he knew it, he was swallowed up by the lustrous black of her eyes and it was all over. He couldn't play the game any more. 'Nilu,' he said. 'You look so beautiful.'

Nilufar blew a ring of smoke and laughed over her triumph. 'Tapan,' she said, 'you're such a pushover.' Then she kissed him. The waitress brought in the coffee. Looking at the cups, Tapan said, 'Why have you ordered two cups? Who were you expecting?'

As soon as she said, 'You, of course,' she bit her lips, realising that she too had just given the game away. They laughed and had their coffees under the green umbrella. Afterwards, they walked along the river, holding hands. Near the *Girl with a Dolphin*, leaping out from the fountain into the sky, they stopped. Taking a step back for the right perspective, Nilufar cocked her head and saw something deeply affecting in the sculpture, then she snuggled into him. He lifted her face, trying to see what she saw, but her eyes were already misty with longing, and they kissed.

Slowly they climbed the stairs onto Tower Bridge and looked out over London. In the late summer sun, the city of stone, glass and steel didn't seem like Kofi's muscles of empire, but more as if it was about to leap into the sky like the *Girl with a Dolphin*. Looking east, up the river, Nilufar proposed that they go to see the Old Royal Observatory in Greenwich. Tapan agreed. So they climbed down the way they had come and took the boat from the pier at the Tower of London.

In the courtyard of the Old Observatory they became like little children, skipping and jumping across the brass strip that marks the prime meridian. If Tapan leapt from the Western to the Eastern hemisphere, Nilufar skipped the other way. Dodging two little Chinese girls, perhaps twins, who were doing the same, they came face to face, straddling across the hemispheres, and kissed. 'What are we now?' Tapan asked.

'A queer lot of English-Binglish,' said Nilufar, laughing. 'That's what we are, Tapan.'

Inside the museum, while Nilufar attentively followed the chronicles of John Harrison's austere labour on his H-series timekeepers, Tapan used the exhibits as a pretext to better observe her changing moods: her wonderment, her puzzlement, her curiosity and her joy of discovery. He didn't mean to spy on her, but merely wanted to get past a few more layers of her armour, and come closer to her.

It was late afternoon when they came out of the Observatory; the mauve of the evening hadn't yet set in. How to spend the time until it was dark? Sometimes they held hands, sometimes hooked into each other's arms, and from time to time, for no apparent reason, Nilufar snuggled into him as they wandered through the parks, stopping to gaze at the gift shops – at one of which Nilufar bought a papier-mâché starfish for Chumki.

They had no plans, but ended up in a Chinese restaurant, where they had Peking duck and egg fried rice and bottles of Thai lager. When they paid the bill and got up to go, they knew what they wanted to happen next, and it happened without a word being spoken between them. Luckily they found a room in the first hotel they called at, a room with muted wallpaper and two tiny beds with blue floral patterned quilts. They put the beds together, but the ridge between the beds annoyed them.

'Do you still love her?' Nilufar asked.

'Who do you mean, Nilu?'

'Adela, your wife.'

'Let's not talk about her now,' said Tapan. ' Let's concentrate on us now. Only the two of us. And nothing else.'

'Yes, you're right. Let's concentrate on us alone,' said Nilufar. 'But I'm curious to know how you felt for her.'

'You're not jealous, are you?' Tapan said. 'Listen, it's all over between me and Adela.'

'Good. But you must have loved her once.'

'Please, Nilu. Please, drop the subject. Please.'

Silence at last and the fragrance from the dried flowers in a bowl. Pulling the blue quilt over her head, Nilufar stayed quiet, wondering what madness had prompted her to spoil their first night together by asking stupid questions. Why not give in to the moment and take off the mask? So, she took off the mask and let her body erupt from deep within into pure force. Tapan was already waiting – and he moved to mimic her in every way as they became the wasp and the orchid.

CHAPTER 7

It was late autumn; someone had phoned the Home Office. The informer told the case officer that not only had Tapan's marriage to Adela collapsed, but that it was bogus to begin with. The case officer had no reason to doubt the informer because the person seemed reliable; certainly he or she – whoever it might have been – seemed in a very good position to know the truth. Tapan received a letter from the Home Office, forwarded by Adela, informing him that his stay in the country was now illegal and requiring him to report to his nearest police station.

Now he knew he had two options: either submit himself to the Immigration and be deported, or do a runner. When he asked Nilufar what he should do, she looked at him for a long time, her eyes gathering mist, but she wasn't able to say anything. What could she say? Of course, it would be sensible for him to go back to Bangladesh, because a life on the run would be worse than that of a prisoner condemned to a life sentence. Even if a prisoner was locked up somewhere like Alcatraz, he could at least go by his own name – call himself Al Capone if he liked. Tapan would be nameless; he wouldn't exist as far as the world was concerned. No doubt, it would be a life of endless drudgery and he would never be able to surface from the black hole.

Yet, how she wished that he could stay! She'd thought she would never get the feeling again, the feeling she lost when Walter had to leave. Damn it, what was she to think, because Tapan made her feel so happy again, and at times almost crazy? She found herself humming to those silly, soppy songs on the radio, even dancing like an imbecile schoolgirl. She didn't want to lose him, but if he wanted to go back she would understand.

He had until the next day to decide. Nilufar told him to phone her as soon as he made up his mind, because, whatever the decision, there was much to prepare. He went back to his flat in Bethnal Green, collected a few of his belongings in a rucksack, and went to sleep.

He couldn't remember much of what he dreamt in the night, but he woke with a sense of clarity. He opened the curtains and the late autumn sun only sharpened this feeling. Even the old sailor from upstairs singing opera didn't disturb him any more. Suddenly he remembered that he had danced under a shower of crocuses in his dream and – a migratory bird on a homing flight – had crossed oceans, deserts, mountains, and endless plains of grass to reach his destination.

Any time of the day would have been a bad time for something like this. Perhaps he should have waited until after dark, then, if he avoided the shops with neon signs and kept his head down as he passed the lampposts, slinking along like a stray cat, he could pretend that he was invisible. He had reason enough not to feel at ease, yet, as if without a care in the world, he risked the streets in broad daylight.

He didn't take the lift to go down. It wasn't so much that he was anxious to avoid meeting anyone close up, more that he was afraid that the bloody stench might cloud his moment of clarity. Not that the stairs were free of their share of piss and puke, but going down the stairs he could use the motion of his limbs to keep his clarity from slipping away. Slinging the rucksack over his shoulder, he slid down the stairs, and out into the courtyard. But as soon as he set his feet on the dead-end alleyway and looked ahead between rows of tall, old apartments of a bygone modernist utopia, he felt unsure of his decision.

Shouldn't he have waited until it was dark? In broad daylight, he might give the impression that he was on the run. But, then, he was on the run. Luckily, the alleyway was empty and he hurried along to reach the frantic traffic of men and machines on the main street. Once there he hoped to get lost in the surrounding bustle, but his nerves were losing him fast in the rumbles down in his guts. He had walked this way so many times but never felt like this before, even though he could never shake off the dread of falling victim to a racist ambush again. He had never strayed from the right side of the law, not for cutting any self-righteous pose, but simply because of the way he was. Now he was a criminal, a fugitive. Why hold it back? Say it loud, say the shame of our time: an illegal immigrant.

He was planning to go to Sundar's flat, and from there phone Nilufar. When he looked up at the main road to plot his direction, he hesitated again and felt like turning back. Before he could give it a second thought, someone had already surprised him from behind. It was Poltu Khan, the smart guy who ran a travel agency. But that was only a front; his real business was fixing things for illegals. He could do anything. If you needed a shady passport, a bogus marriage certificate, dodgy admissions or crooked employment, he was the man for you. He was an informer too. People said the authorities turned a blind eye to his little scam – because he paid them off in kind. When the authorities weren't getting anywhere with their fishing trips and they came breathing down his neck – which had happened often enough – he gave them some illegal immigrants.

'Hey, Tapan Ali, what's on your mind, man?' said Poltu Khan, as if he knew his troubles.

'Nothing really. I thought I should've brought the umbrella,' said Tapan. 'It might rain.'

'You should know better, eh. In England it always rains,' said Poltu Khan. 'But you see there are two types of people in this world: one type carries umbrella, and the other doesn't. You don't look like an umbrella-carrying type to me. Am I right?'

'Well, usually I don't. But I'm going somewhere important, and don't want to arrive with my clothes wet.'

'Is that so? Sure, if it's that important, you don't want to arrive looking like a wet dog,' said Poltu Khan. 'But take it from me, it won't rain for some time.'

'Right, if you say so, Mr. Khan... I'm off then.'

'Are you going far?'

'I'll check out a friend in Wapping first, then to my appointment.'

'Well, what do you know. I'm going that way myself,' said Poltu Khan. 'Let's go.'

Now that he was on the run as an illegal, the last thing Tapan wanted was to spend time with Poltu Khan. The man had a knowing grin, and Tapan felt that he had figured out what he was up to. Would the bastard grass on him? He felt a knot in his stomach, but gave nothing away. He wasn't a gambling man, never staking his lot on a mere dice throw, but this unexpected meeting with Poltu Khan had made the decision for him. Now there was no turning back.

From Bethnal Green Road they turned into Brick Lane. Poltu Khan offered to treat him to tea and sweets at Alauddin cafe, but Tapan declined. Between the milling crowd in the Lane, they continued to walk together. Poltu Khan waved his hand to greet the many he knew; Tapan kept his head down to avoid any eye contact.

'Bloody sods,' Poltu Khan mumbled, though without betraying his customary impassive facade. Tapan pretended not to have heard him. Poltu Khan then took a packet of Dunhill from the side pocket of his sleek, black jacket, offered one to Tapan, who took it with a nod of thanks, and put one between his own lips. He produced an expensive silver lighter and offered the flame to Tapan.

'What a pathetic lot, aren't they, Tapan Ali?'

'I don't follow you, Mr. Khan.'

Poltu Khan blew smoke, pointing his nose to the sky, then he looked at Tapan with surprise. 'You're an educated man, Tapan Ali. You should know how they're like – our country brothers. I bet they talk bad behind my back. But every time they need fixing, they come running to me. I can't stand the sight of them, but I'm a kind man. I fix them, all right.'

Tapan couldn't help thinking, 'I'd like to smash your head in, you motherfucking rat.' They passed Sundar's flat, but now he couldn't possibly stop there. He had to play along with Poltu Khan that he was going to Wapping. Poltu Khan continued to greet people until they reached Whitechapel Road, where their paths diverged. Tapan, almost on automatic trigger, wheeled to the right. But before he could get away, Poltu Khan took a step in his direction and gave Tapan his business card.

'You're an educated man, Tapan Ali. You never know when you might be in a spot of bother – and I'd like to help you. I could fix things for you. See you soon, right?'

'Yeah,' mumbled Tapan under his breath. Still on edge, he moved briskly away from Poltu Khan, as if he had just escaped the jaws of a born-again T-Rex. He hadn't planned to go this way, but throwing away the butt-end of the Dunhill, on an impulse he turned left onto Leman Street. He still had the feeling that Poltu Khan was shadowing him because it was his business to know about illegals.

He looked behind but saw only a young couple walking, absorbed in each other, like a single organism. He felt like another cigarette. It had been quite a while since he'd given up smoking, but the tension of the moment had made him accept Poltu Khan's Dunhill. He cursed himself for that fatal slip. Now he felt hooked again. He rushed into a news agents at the corner of Leman and Prescot Street and bought a packet of hand-rolling tobacco – his old brand, Golden Virginia – and a pack of green Rizla and a box of matches. As soon as he was out of the shop, and while walking, he rolled a cigarette. It surprised him that he hadn't lost the knack; it rolled nice and thin with tobacco evenly distributed along its length. Feeling much calmer, he continued ahead, across Cable Street and through Dock Street, towards the riverfront. At the end of Dock Street he turned right into East Smithfield and then, taking the steep stairs down, he entered St. Katharine Docks.

On most late autumn weekdays, there were few tourists at the Docks. Tapan liked the place at such times; its emptiness offering pleasant feelings of solitude. And how pleasant the Docks had felt when he was last there, playing that game with Nilufar, when they had enclosed themselves in a circle of their own.

Today, though, the unexpected sun had brought in many people. This suited him fine because the last thing he wanted was to draw attention to himself. He wandered around, mingling with the casual innocence of a tourist. When, at the approach of a small boat, the brightly painted drawbridges went up, he joined the milling crowd to see it squeeze into the harbour. Today, though, he wasn't there for the scene.

He went to the cafe and ordered a cake and a cappuccino. He wished he could sit outside by the water, with the sun on his face. There were many empty tables under the green umbrellas, where he had sat with Nilufar. But today the eyes drove him inside. When the waitress, a young woman with a bright, bubbly manner, came to take his order, he thought she looked at him twice, as if she had seen something unusual. What does an illegal immigrant look like? Was he already showing the tell-tell marks of a criminal type: arms elongating, forehead turning low and narrow, ears enlarging, and jaws jutting out alarmingly with large canine teeth?

Well, you couldn't entirely blame her. He knew that he didn't look all that together; that might've given her the wrong impression. He relaxed somewhat when it occurred to him that there was probably no nosey-parker Sir Galton measuring him up – perhaps from behind a broadsheet – with his telephoto eyes. No doubt Sir Galton would've been very pleased with his Oriental find: 'By jove, he's the type. Fancy finding him right here in England!' But then, hadn't the old bugger started that goddamn cloning business in the first place? Right now, how could he be certain that there weren't a whole lot of Sir Galton clones carrying on his dirty work, with the same attention to detail?

Halfway into his coffee, the young waitress came to ask him if everything was to his satisfaction. He thought this was odd: in an up-market restaurant, yes, but this kind of customer service was unusual in a joint like this. When the waitress looked back at him a second time, he'd had enough. Besides, the inside of the cafe was strictly non-smoking and he was dying for a fag. He left payment for the bill on the table and rushed out.

It was late in the afternoon and the clouds, whose unexpected partings had earlier allowed the sun to slip through, were closing in fast. He moved briskly towards Tower Bridge, rolled a fag and realised how quickly he was falling back into his old addiction. He walked along the steep wall by the river, glancing occasionally at the murky flow between the banks. As he passed *Girl with a Dolphin* leaping from the fountain into the sky, he thought of Nilufar. He paused and leant over the embankment and looked at the water slapping down below. He approached a hotel, determined to phone Nilufar from the lobby, but seeing a thick-set and very stern-looking man in uniform keeping guard at the doorway, he lost his nerve. He backed off with his head down and headed towards Tower Bridge. There, instead of crossing the bridge, he went through the low arch of the tunnel to arrive on the promenade by the southern facade of the Tower. The prom-enade, lined with autumnal trees, was nearly empty. He sat on a bench, his back to the grey, crenellated towers and ominous turrets, facing the river.

He sat there for a long time. It was getting dark and he heard the deep harsh cries of the ravens in the Tower, felt a chill in his bones. From the trees that lined the promenade leaves were falling. As he was getting up, a yellow leaf brushed his face as it fell to the ground. He turned the lapel up on his thin cotton jacket and went back the way he had come.

Now he took the stairs to the bridge, heading south along the western catwalk, but he didn't feel the excitement he usually felt on this bridge of tall gothic towers marooned on the skyline. Nor did he feel the slightest urge to look at the river, or the city of lights on its banks. The city did not leap into the sky like the *Girl with a Dolphin*, as it had done when he had come here with Nilufar.

When he paused to lick the paper on his roll-up, a man who was leaning against the railings asked Tapan for a light. Tapan flinched as the man pressed on him very close. Regaining his composure a little, he lit a match, first to offer to the stranger and then to light his own.

'Much obliged,' said the man.

'If you want to keep the box, you're welcome to it,' said Tapan. 'I can get one from the station.'

'Kind of you, but no. I'm going to the station myself.'

Tapan didn't care for company, especially not this stranger's, but the man had already locked onto him and was matching his steps. He was a white man, middle-aged, careless in appearance but clean. Taking a drag on his cigarette, the man asked him abruptly.

'If you don't mind me asking – where are you from?'

Tapan was taken aback. Why was he asking a question like this? Was he on his trail? But he didn't look the type.

'Well, around here – from that side of the river,' said Tapan. 'I mean, East London.'

'Is that so? But you don't sound Cockney to me.'

'How does a Cockney sound then?'

'Of course, you're from East London, malum,' said the man. 'Don't get me wrong, I don't want to pry into your affairs. All I wanted to know was your origin.'

'You don't need me to tell you that, do you?'

'You see – if I'm not mistaken – I'm also from your part of the world,' said the man. 'You see. Way back, during the Raj. My father was with the forces; I was born there.'

'I don't get it,' said Tapan. 'What part of the world are you talking about?'

'Hindustan, of course,' said the man.

Tapan couldn't be bothered to tell the man he was actually from Bangladesh; he'd let the man assume whatever he wanted. Now the man fell silent. This suited Tapan fine; he didn't have to respond to his stupid gibber. As he puffed on his roll-up and turned right into Tooley Street, he quickened a gear. The guy was still tagging along. After a while he started again, but this time as if he was talking to himself.

'My father was a bandmaster. On Sundays he used to lead marches through the towns, throwing his baton high in the air. Good show. Natives used to love it. Pardon me, I didn't mean you.

'So did I. We lived in the regimental quarters. Mainly mofussil. I was ten when – what do you call it – oh yes, Swaraj came. Rest you know, achah, malum? Back to England. At first it was difficult. I hated Gandhi, wished him dead. That native took my country, I believed then. At least that's what my father told me.

'Very difficult, you know. England was a strange place. I missed the smell, the heat. But, above all, the rivers. Gradually, I was forgetting all that. Then when the Pakis started to come here – I don't understand why you bother. England, a godforsaken place, if you want to know. Why leave all that sunshine and such nice places?

'Anyway, when the Pakis started to come. No offence, I didn't mean you. I was pissed off like everybody else. I thought you lot had what you wanted – Swaraj I mean. Why come here to muck things up for us? Anyway, when your people started to burn all those spices. And, of course, all those fruits and vegetables in Halal shops, my old sense of smell and things I loved started to come back. Yes, the rivers. I miss them very much. You see, that's why I go to Tower Bridge, to see the river.

'But it's not the same, is it? It makes me more sad – and very angry. It's a pity that I never got to know you people. In the barracks all I saw was nappy-wallahs and methar-wallahs. Those fellows came and went. Never spoke. I thought all Indians were some sort of wallahs.'

While they walked, Tapan continued to smoke, occasionally gritting his teeth, but determined to keep his mouth shut. When they drew near London Bridge Station, the man said he lived around the corner.

'Pity. I never knew a real Indian. If you don't mind, I'd like to know you,' said the man. 'Any assistance, just ask.'

'Thanks.'

'I really mean it. Any assistance. Bill Smith the name,' said the man. 'But they call me Bombay Bill around here. Look out for me on Tower Bridge. If not, the Black Beggar round the corner. So long, my friend.'

'Yeah,' Tapan mumbled under his breath as he turned his back on the man. He was glad to have shaken Bombay Bill off his back. He could fry in hell for all he cared. The old sod was a nut case. Fancy churning up mother Ganges – of all places – from the bowels of the old girl Thames. Who does he think he is: Serpent Vasuki, the churner of the ocean of creation? No time for all that now; he must phone Nilufar.

He found an empty phone box, went in and dialled the number. No answer. He tried again. Still no answer. Getting desperate, he rang Sundar. No luck there either. He didn't want to walk back the way he came; didn't want to bump into Bombay Bill again. Now he would have to make a long, circuitous journey by tube to get to Aldgate East, then to Sundar's flat in Brick Lane. On the tube, he thought of Bombay Bill and had the strange feeling that this wasn't the end of it, that he would meet him again.

CHAPTER 8

Later that night, Sundar and Nilufar took Tapan to the Isle of Dogs. There, on the fifteenth floor of a tower block, he would begin his life in hiding. On the way in the car, driving through the mist of the approaching winter, Sundar told him that he needed to lie low for a few days, and after that he would be able to do some work, move around a bit, but cautiously as there was always the danger of getting caught in a fishing raid. Not to forget, of course, the treachery of the informers.

'But don't worry, Bhaio,' Sundar continued. 'We're putting you at the centre of a giant maze. They wouldn't find you in a million years. Allah willing, of course.'

Inside the flat, while Nilufar went to the kitchen to put the kettle on, Sundar and Tapan went to the sitting room. Seeing Tapan roll a cigarette, Sundar chuckled like the silly cartoon dog that he so much loved to watch on television. 'Bhaio. I know you're not cut out for the frugal style of Gandhiji. It's about time that you kicked that austerity business. It doesn't suit you, Bhaio.'

Blowing a puff of smoke, Tapan nearly laughed, but instead the cold made him shiver. Sundar got up, slotted some coins into the meter box and turned the gas fire on. It was amazing that after so many years in England, and after so many words of reassurance that *he would get used to it in time*, his body stubbornly retained a tropical antipathy to all things cold.

Now he put his feet in front of the fire and stooped a little to warm his hands. Sundar did the same. 'Doing the illegal thing is a serious business, Bhaio,' said Sundar. 'Have you thought of the consequences? Yes, you'll be living in a giant maze, but the buggers will never stop hunting you. So the bottom line is that you won't be able to surface again. Maybe now and then to take a gulp of air like a fish. Fancy, Bhaio, you becoming a fish!'

Looking at the fire, Tapan listened to Sundar without really listening. He finished one cigarette, then lit another, but kept his silence. He had nothing to say – what could he have said, anyway? He knew that somehow it had to happen like this; that how it had started was of no consequence now, but it couldn't have been otherwise. It was as if a *malin génie* had stitched him up in a tangle of time without his having the slightest inkling of it, as if he was a sleepwalker on a path laid out for him with the meticulous precision of a draftsman's sketch. He had to walk down its straight line, between symmetrical rows of conifers – strange, how they never rustle in the wind – silently, step by step down into this hole.

Yes, this was his destiny. *Que sera, sera*, he puffed and blew the smoke away, emptying his lungs, and giving himself up atrociously to the warmth of the fire, and imagining himself, not as a fish, as Sundar would have it, but as a mole burrowing a labyrinthine passage down in the belly of the metropolis.

When Nilufar brought in the tea, he gave her a warm, cheerful smile. She was surprised by his change of mood, but relieved that he was bearing up so well. 'I fear Poltu Khan the most,' she said. 'He's such a rat.'

'At least with Poltu Khan you know where you stand,' said Sundar. 'But there are worse types. You'd never know that they are informing on you.'

Sundar opened his silver box and gave Tapan and Nilufar cones of paan, and took one himself. When Tapan began to chew on the paan with tobacco leaves, Sundar said, 'Bhaio, fancy that! You're becoming a genuine paan man.'

Nilufar helped Tapan to make his bed. Holding the sheet at the other end, she looked at him as if to say how she wished she was staying with him, holding him tightly so that nothing could harm him. But she couldn't possibly stay now, because she didn't want to upset Sundar. Sundar wasn't against her relationship with Tapan. On the contrary, he was very pleased about it and hoped that it would work out for them. But the idea that she might share Tapan's bed – for that matter, anyone else's bed – before marriage was too alien for him.

'I don't want to leave you alone,' she said. 'But you know how it is. Let the situation settle a bit, then we'll find a way.'

'Don't worry, Nilu. I understand that,' he said.

Just before they left, they told Tapan that they would be back the next day, bringing the rest of his things from his old flat, and some shopping. 'Fancy some hilsa fish, Bhaio?' Sundar asked. Tapan liked the idea, but didn't say anything. Until they returned, though, he would have to manage with a bottle of milk and some crumpets, but there were plenty of tea bags and sugar and loose coins for the gas meter. Sundar and Nilufar were on their way to the lift when Sundar dashed back, and gave Tapan his box of paan, saying, 'I hate to see a genuine paan man go without.' Then he paused to add, 'Be careful, Bhaio. You don't know who the informers are.'

Tapan closed the door, sat down by the fire, smoked a cigarette, and chewed a paan. Then he went to bed.

Just before he fell into deep sleep he heard hurried footsteps and people greeting each other in low whispers in the corridor, but someone was climbing up step-by-step, stair-by-stair to the fifteenth floor. So delicate that it could well have been a dream. He had no idea why Adela didn't bother to take the lift; he could never understand her passion for making things difficult for herself. But why of all people was Adela opening the door and coming into his room? Perhaps she was doing it so that she could wake the whole neighbourhood up by crying rape as she had done so many years ago, hearing the boom boom of the caves and seeing a native, as dark as Krishna, tearing at her undergarments with the ferocious lust of a beast. He could never work out her moods. But there she was, hardly making any noise, except her breathing ruffling the sheets, except the rustle of her silk undergarments as she took them off. She wasn't supposed to be here, let alone playing this game in which their skin touched to light up the sky with the colours of the rainbow. He was surprised by Adela's indirection, as if her coyness had made her adopt the visual tricks of a Bollywood melodrama, where something like the probing of a bee into a chrysanthemum was made to suggest the coupling of hero and heroine. Tapan preferred the bizarre coupling of the wasp and the orchid as the noblest image for the meeting of human bodies. But this wasn't his game; all the moves were Adela's, hers alone.

At first he hadn't noticed that Nilufar had tiptoed her way to the door, pressing her right ear so close that the tiniest of their moans and groans wouldn't escape her. She wasn't there to create a scene, she was simply there. When he became aware of her, of her brown face with black, black eyes mocking him, mocking his lust for rubbing his skin against the white mistress, mocking his intense desire to mimic the pale masters of the empire and choke himself to death in the perfume of his bed, it was too late. All it took was a moment, and Adela and he had already given themselves to the empire of the senses, where the usual calculations of probity and reason ceased to matter any more. Neither of them wanted to keep the boat moored, so they let it go down the rapids, where the mind doesn't think but is moved by the surges of the body. Adela, my love, how could I not desire you? When you give yourself to me and I to you, we always do so beyond the history of our skin, beyond the time of the empire.

Suddenly he heard Nilufar's laughter mocking his excuses for having it off with a white woman. But you got to believe me, Nilu, it isn't like that. When Adela and I look at each other, as I do with you, it is always something I can never explain, something so strong that it would make me plunge into the mouth of a volcano. I thought you of all people, Nilu, my Nilu, would understand this. It is true that your skin that I find so pretty matches mine, that your black eyes burn me to ashes and I don't even want to rise up like a phoenix, that the curve of your lips drives me crazy and I end up listening to the sound of the sea, but I look at you beyond the time of your skin, the same way I look at Adela. Perhaps I'm kidding myself because this wretched time of the skin has lasted so long, it has damaged us. I know it isn't easy to go beyond it, especially for a weak one like me. But what can I do, Nilu? Don't be so jealous, Nilu – can't I love both of you equally? Anyway, when Adela comes to me in the night, I just cannot refuse her.

Adela didn't come to speak, she hushed him with her finger on

85

his lips, because there was no need for words. All he needed was to listen to their footsteps as they went out for a walk by the lake in the campus where they were students together. She put her finger in his mouth; he bit hard but she didn't complain, not even a muffled cry of pain. He wanted to please her, the way Nilufar let him please her, but as always Adela came to give. She told him that he shouldn't move, that if sleep wanted to take him, let it take him. Yes, he should try to sleep – so many things happening lately. He must be so tired, the least she could do was to help him sleep. She was firm yet so gentle as she lowered herself against his skin, her breasts caressing him inch by inch, almost nerve by nerve, going down and down on him until she took him in her mouth, and once more he was walking by the lake. And suddenly he had to take a dip in the lake, and Adela was encouraging him with her mouth, but all he could see was her hair spreading over him like the wings of a peacock. When he surfaced from the lake, he was wet but he didn't mind that because he was so happy, and under such a hot sun his clothes would soon be dry, leaving, perhaps, only the faint, lingering smell of a chrysanthemum.

In the morning he got up remembering Adela. For a moment, it crossed his mind that it was Adela who had informed the Home Office. She knew the truth, and she had the motive. But then he convinced himself that Adela couldn't be the person who had given him away, because – despite what had happened between them – she couldn't deny the feelings they still had for each other.

CHAPTER 9

The gloom of winter was already there, but Tapan wasn't bothered. He made teas, rolled his cigarettes and ate crumpets. These things he did at regular intervals throughout the day, each time concluding the cycle with a paan from the silver box that Sundar had left him. He had nothing to do but wait for Nilufar and Sundar to visit him in the afternoon.

As soon as she finished her day at school, Nilufar left for Sundar's flat. On the way, she stopped by Shapna's to drop off the papier-mâché starfish she had bought for Chumki in Greenwich. Shapna insisted that she stayed for tea. Chumki was happy with her starfish, waving it up and down as she ran around the room. Usually Nilufar forgot time when she played with Chumki, but now she was looking at her watch every few minutes. When Shapna brought in the tea and Bombay-toasts, she asked, 'Why you so anxious, Appa? You're not thinking of him?'

'You don't understand these things, Shapna. I love him.'

'You bet I don't understand, Appa. Why you had to get involved with someone crazy like him? What prospect does he have?'

'You see, there you go again. It's a waste of time talking to you. I don't need anyone's prospect. I can look after myself.'

'Are you sure you're not just feeling sorry for him, Appa? You're always trying to save someone, aren't you?'

Nilufar stayed silent for a while, took sips of tea and decided that she didn't want to continue this discussion. Since Shapna's marriage, she had come to accept the gulf between herself and her sister, though they still cared for each other deeply. But they avoided many subjects and rarely talked about anything meaningful.

'How's Shahid?'

'He's doing fine. He's opening his second restaurant. But I don't see him much.'

'What do you mean, Shapna?'

'He never comes home before I get to sleep. When he gets up, he's off to his restaurant again.'

'How do you feel about it?'

'I don't mind it. I get on with my things. You know, looking after Chumki, cooking and cleaning. I do my prayers and read the Koran.'

'Are you happy, Shapna?'

'Why do you ask these silly things, Appa? I do my duty, that's all.'

'Sorry, Shapna. Sorry.'

'Really, Appa, I don't mind that he's not here. I'm happy to be on my own.'

'What's wrong, Shapna?'

'I don't know how to say it, Appa.' Shapna broke into a sob. 'I think he's seeing loose women.'

Nilufar held Shapna, just as she had held her when they were children, when Shapna used to wake up screaming from her nightmares. Seeing her mother cry, Chumki stopped playing and started to cry herself. Hurriedly wiping her face, Shapna picked up Chumki, and began to walk around the room, humming a lullaby. Soon Chumki fell asleep.

'You're getting so thin, Appa. You're not eating properly, are you?' Shapna said at the door. 'Promise me that you'll come here every day to eat. I'll cook the things you like.'

As soon as Nilufar arrived at Sundar's flat, they set off together to Bethnal Green to pick up Tapan's things, then they returned to Brick Lane to do some shopping. They bought rice, spices, vegetables, meat, and, of course, hilsa fish.

It was five in the afternoon, and already dark, when they reached Tapan's flat in the Isle of Dogs. Sundar parked the car in a side street next to the estate. Only when they reached the perimeter wall, did they notice the men. They were leaning against a van that was parked in the approach to the tower block where Tapan was hiding. Hunched below the parapet, Nilufar and Sundar went around the tower block to where, under the porch light, they could see the men more clearly. They were white men, official looking; they seemed to be waiting for someone to come out of the tower. Although, Nilufar and Sundar didn't recognise them, it occurred to them that they might be from the Immigration. Perhaps they were waiting for the police to arrive before they raided the tower block.

Half an hour or so later, they saw two more white men come out of the tower with someone whose head was covered by a blanket. They put this person in the van and then the four white men drove away. Who was the person under the blanket? Sundar said it couldn't have been Tapan, because no one except them knew that he was hiding there. Nilufar wondered how he could be so sure. After all, the informers had their way of finding out these things.

But they couldn't rush in to find out whether the person under the blanket had been Tapan. If Tapan was still safe, they didn't want to give him away by being followed. They waited for another half an hour to make sure that no Immigration, no police, and no informers were there. Finally, they were ready to approach the tower block when Sundar suddenly pulled Nilufar behind the parapet again. A car had parked in the same spot as the van. The man who came out of the car was Poltu Khan. Now there was no doubt that the Immigration had been there to pick up illegals.

They waited for another twenty minutes until they saw Poltu Khan come out of the tower block and drive away. They followed him to his house. Nilufar stayed in the car as Sundar got out and approached him.

'What a surprise, Sundar Mia. Good to see you,' said Poltu Khan. 'What can I do for you?'

'Don't play games with me,' said Sundar. 'Where have you been?'

'Come, come, Sundar Mia. Why you look so upset?'

'But where have you been?'

'You know me, Sundar Mia. I like going for a drive. Take some fresh air.'

'Don't fuck around with me. I know your business,' said Sundar. 'Who have you grassed now?'

'That's character assassination, Sundar Mia. You people always think the worst of me.'

Sundar didn't want to have any more to do with Poltu Khan; a few phone calls would be enough to find who the person under the blanket was. He was almost back in his car when he heard Poltu Khan shouting, 'If you want to know the truth, Sundar Mia, I have been out helping a friend.'

In the car Sundar said he thought that Poltu Khan needed to be taught a lesson. He would set Masuk Ali and the boys onto him. By now it was nearly midnight when they got back to the Isle of Dogs. This time they saw a police car waiting on the approach to the tower block. No way they could go and see Tapan now. They would try again tomorrow. After dropping Nilufar at her flat, Sundar went to a public telephone box. He found out through his sources that the person under the blanket wasn't Tapan. He knew that Nilufar wouldn't sleep the whole night for worrying about it, so he phoned her to give her the good news.

When Nilufar and Sundar hadn't arrived by eight o'clock, Tapan was getting worried. He had no idea what was happening outside. He went to lie on the bed for a while, then sat on the chair by the gas fire, and then walked – rolling and lighting cigarettes. He repeated the walk, God knows how many times, always following the same narrow circle between the armchair and the blue sofa at the end of the red, floral carpet. At one point, he almost stumbled on the armchair as he began to feel dizzy, but as he steadied himself it occurred to him that perhaps the flat was under surveillance. No, he was convinced of it, though he had no idea how the fuckers might have got the hunch that he was holed up here, right in this shithole. Who knows, perhaps at this very moment they were training their eyes on him from the opposite block of flats. He took a long drag from his cigarette, then blew out the smoke with relief, because it all made sense to him now. How could he have doubted Nilufar and Sundar? They wouldn't abandon him for anything; surely they hadn't shown up because they didn't want to take the risk of being followed.

Rounding the room once more, he stopped before the front window. Carefully then, with a slight movement of his fingers, he created a tiny chink between the folds of the filthy curtains. He stooped a little in the darkness, closed his left eye, put the right one to the chink and, almost touching the cool of the glass, tried to look across at the flats opposite. But the mist got in the way. Nothing could be seen except for the muted outline of lights in barely distinguishable windows. Reassured by the protective envelope of the mist, he allowed himself a smile: Good, it serves the buggers right. Damn good show, man; now even that tight-upper-lipped-twit, that so called fog specialist par excellence – what's his name? – yes, that Sherlock Holmes, even he couldn't check me out now from the other side.

Exhausted, he sat chewing the last paan that Sundar had left for him. It calmed him down. He wasn't bothered that he had finished the packet of crumpets; he could always fall asleep imagining the sensations of all the tastes he loved the most. So, he let himself be dragged to the dance floor by slender Bashmati – ah the perfumed courtesan, jiving rapturously with spluttering condiments, and if he was driven to frenzy by incendiary chillies, he was soothed by their mellower consorts: cumin, coriander, cinnamon and turmeric. Everything was perfect. Time went by.

Nilufar hardly slept that night. She tossed and turned, thinking of Tapan, of his being cooped up alone in the Isle of Dogs, and of his hunger. He must be feeling abandoned.

Living alone, Nilufar didn't cook much; if she cooked at all, she cooked a simple dish and made it last for several days. Often she would just make do with takeaways. But today she got up early to cook the hilsa fish that they had bought the day before. She cooked it the way Tapan liked: steamed with mustard paste and green chillies.

She was glad that it was Saturday and she didn't have to go to work, though there was the supplementary lesson for Bangladeshi kids and she couldn't possibly miss that. Besides, she had promised the old lady next door she would take her to the hospital, and there was an urgent racial harassment case to follow up with the police. Luckily everything went smoothly and she finished doing all these things by twelve. She phoned Sundar to hurry him up, but he had some urgent defence group business to sort out, and wouldn't be able to get away before half past one.

Nilufar wrapped the steamed hilsa fish in tin foil to keep it warm, and went to see Shapna. She was worried about Shapna; she hadn't seen her cry like that for a long time. On the way she bought some chocolate for Chumki from the corner shop. It was Shahid who opened the door.

Nilufar was surprised to see Shapna in such a happy mood. She was about to go out with Shahid wearing her veil. Now she took the veil off and began to fuss over her sister.

'You must have some lunch, Appa,' she said. 'We've some rice and curry left.'

Nilufar said that she wasn't hungry; besides, she was going out to a late lunch and, before Shahid had the chance to interrogate her, she asked them where they were going.

Shapna hesitated, and looked away from her sister.

'We're taking Chumki to see the Most Venerable Pir-Sahib. It was very kind of the Most Venerable one to see us at such a short notice.'

'What's wrong with Chumki? asked Nilufar, sounding worried.

'Nothing wrong with Chumki,' said Shahid. 'We just want a tabiz to protect her from evil eyes.'

Every time Nilufar heard about the Most Venerable Pir-Sahib, rage rose in her and she would imagine herself pulling his beard out hair by hair. He was one of the subjects that she couldn't talk about with Shapna. She asked instead about Kaisar. Shapna hadn't seen him for the last few days either.

'I heard he's even mugging people these days', said Shahid.

'I don't believe it,' said Shapna. 'Kaisar isn't like that.'

'What's he like then?' said Shahid. 'A bloody druggy. His sort will do anything to get a fix.'

'Let's not talk about it any more,' said Shapna.

'Yeah. Let's seal our bloody mouths,' said Shahid. 'Your brother is a bloody saint – yeah?'

'There's no need for this,' said Shapna.

'Let me tell you one or two correct things, yeah?' said Shahid. 'You sisters have bloody spoiled him. What he needs is a strong hand. I say, a few good beatings will sort him out.'

Shapna didn't say anything, but her earlier happiness had completely disappeared. Nilufar headed for the door saying that she had to get back to her flat. Shahid offered her a lift, but Nilufar said she would rather walk. Shapna put her black veil on again and they all went out together. Before getting into the car, Shapna said, 'Amma is coming tomorrow. She wants to see you very much. Please come round.'

Sundar arrived at Nilufar's flat at around two and they immediately set off to see Tapan.

The night before, Tapan had fallen asleep quickly, but woke again after an hour or so. He could hear a faint tapping through the walls, as though somewhere in the building someone was burrowing with their paws. He pressed his ears to the floor. The vibrations were getting louder. Who was it, and why so desperate to break into his shelter? He crawled on all fours, checked the doors and windows. Damn it, the curtain wasn't thick enough; a glow shone through the window. It wasn't easy, but somehow he managed to hang a thick blanket from the curtain rail. It was much better now, darker – and much safer. Then the blanket fell to the ground with a thud, bringing down the curtain rail with it. Now he was totally exposed in front of the curtainless window. He went around the flat, desperately looking for a hammer, screws or nails – anything to fix the curtain rail. He was breathing so heavily that for a moment he thought there was someone else in the room, just behind him – all worked up for the kill. But what could he do about the curtain? As if things weren't already bad enough, there were footsteps now, whispers forming into a tightened cluster, and coming nearer. Perhaps, it was Poltu Khan prowling the building, trying to locate his shelter.

He needed to do something about the curtain, but couldn't find any tools. All he could find was some cutlery in the kitchen and a wooden chopping board. He put the grips of the curtain rail back into their holes above the window frames and inserted the spoons round them as pegs. But he needed to hammer the spoons into the holes to secure the rail, especially if it was to carry the weight of the blanket. He was about to hammer with the chopping board, then realised that the noise would only draw more attention to himself. So, what to do? Wrapping a towel around his hand, he pushed the spoons in as hard as possible. He didn't care that his hand was hurting; he had to secure the curtain. Luckily the curtain stayed, but he couldn't take the risk of hanging the blanket.

He went back to bed but the glow from the window was still bothering him. Besides, the footsteps and whispers were still there outside. He should have known that Poltu Khan wasn't the type to give up so easily. He must find a more secure place. So, he moved to the small storeroom at the back with his pillow and quilt. It felt much safer there, between its narrow walls, among the piles of junk, because there wasn't a window to let in light. There, it was silent at last.

He got up late in the morning, feeling calm and unusually light. He rolled a cigarette, went to the back window, parted the curtain and looked out. From the highest floor of this tall municipal tower, situated in the serpentine arc of the Isle of Dogs, his eyes travelled down the Thames. He was happy to find the sun shimmering on the water. Fluttering in the river was the white reflection of the Maritime museum, Georgian hub of Greenwich. There, in the cool shadow of the Old Observatory lay the brass strip that marked itself as the centre of time and the world. He remembered how happy he was jumping and skipping, and finally straddling the brass strip with Nilufar. And the kiss that had miraculously brought the hemispheres together.

Straining his eyes to look further into the distance, he remembered that he had seen a pair of old binoculars in the kitchen, hanging among broken umbrellas and strings of garlic. He found them and returned to the window. Almost breathless with the anticipation of a rare discovery, he focused on the Old Observatory. But even with his vision magnified eight-fold, he couldn't see the brass strip marking the centre, only the white buildings – their imperial opulence enlarged. Panning at random he lingered on the river. For a while it amused him to observe the frenetic rush of the powerboats as they whipped up waves from the calm surface of the water. But then the monotony of it all began to get on his nerves.

Suddenly a gull glided into his vision. It circled the air with its wings of white snow, dipped downwards while parting its yellow bill, then swerved whimsically in the direction of the Old Observatory. Fascinated, he followed the bird with the steady pan of his binoculars. He was determined not to lose anything, not even the tiniest of its loops. Ah, look at the bird, how it cuts the air from east to west as if it has rubbed out the brass strip with the swish of its wings.

Then – God only knows what got into him – he put the binoculars down and spread his arms. First he fluttered them gently, then with furious flaps he tried to soar into the sky. Trying a few more times, he gave up, as if surprised that he hadn't mustered either the suppleness or the power of the wings of the gull. Sadly, he sensed that it was not an easy task to be a bird. Perhaps, if he could burrow deep enough, he could reach the airy depths of things. Surely then – without even fluttering his wings – he could shed the heavy mass of his body and take to the air. What a strange idea. How can a body burrow deep into the earth and yet fly in the sky? Mumbo-jumbo rubbish! Of course it was – that's if you still go nutso about that gravitational bird shit – or was it a rotten apple? – that plopped on Sir Isaac's head.

Still looking at the sky, Tapan found himself whistling a song he'd heard sung by a man of *suf* from Sind. It concerned the seemingly contradictory passages of the two illustrious brethren of the song-maker who, despite taking opposite routes, arrived at the same place. It wasn't a miracle but the most natural thing in the world.

Rumi flew up the heights of perfection
like an eagle in the twinkling
of an eye; Attar reached the same place
by creeping like an ant.

Now, Tapan sniffed the air, his snout picking up particles of danger from miles away. He closed the curtain and withdrew into the dim shade of the room.

When Nilufar and Sundar reached the tower block, they were as cautious as before. They paused by the perimeter wall and surveyed the vicinity of the tower block; they saw nothing untoward – just a few boys playing football in the concrete courtyard.

Nilufar said, 'Shouldn't we have waited until dark?'

'Why?' said Sundar.

'If we're being followed, we'd give him away.'

'But no one except us knows that he's here.'

'Suppose they've found out.'

'Well. In this case, they don't need to follow us.'

They were surprised to see Tapan calm and composed. He cheerfully opened the door for them, didn't even ask why they hadn't come yesterday. Sundar tried to explain but he stopped him.

'I knew you couldn't come, because you didn't want to take the risk of being followed,' said Tapan. 'Have you got a paan, Sundar? I'm dying for one.'

While Tapan sat down with Sundar to have the paan, Nilufar unpacked the shopping. Then she boiled a pot of rice to go with the hilsa fish. Only when the steam of rice reached him in the sitting room did Tapan realise how hungry he was. He felt, too, a strange sensation, because the steam of rice was taking him back to a journey he had made many years before he had come to England. He remembered waking up early in the morning with the cocks crowing in the coop, and the muezzin calling for prayers. He, still tucked in his bed, heard his grandmother praying – the nasal monotony of her Arabic verses – and fell back to sleep again, as if caught in a hum of bees. But he had to get up because the journey was long; it always took the whole day to walk from his grandmother's to his grandfather's village.

When Nilufar called him for lunch, he uncoiled himself with a start from that journey, from that other steam of rice.

CHAPTER 10

He didn't care about how much time was passing, hardly bothered with the digital blips of a quartz timer, or with the tick-tock of an old metronome. For all he cared, time could drop down dead as a dodo, or better still, like a good old Indian. As it was, nearly a month had passed since he'd moved to the fifteenth floor of this tower block in the Isle of Dogs. Tomorrow he would be moving to Limehouse, to another safe house. He remembered Sundar telling him, 'You'll be living in an invisible city, Bhaio. But it's our city.'

'What do you mean, Sundar?' he'd asked naively.

'What can I say, Bhaio. It's like a city under the city.'

'You mean, an underground city?'

'Yes, Bhaio, yes. There are houses, tower blocks, estates, and neighbourhoods scattered all over Tower Hamlets,' said Sundar. 'But the beauty of it, Bhaio, lies in the passageway.'

'What passageway? asked Tapan.

'You'll see it, Bhaio. A secret passageway that links all these scattered places and brings them together. That's what makes it into our city.'

Leaning back in the chair, lighting a cigarette, Tapan was wondering how to pass his last day in the Isle of Dogs. Unlike recent days, Nilufar and Sundar weren't able to come to see him that evening. Then it occurred to him that he could always abandon himself to tracing that distant memory of rice. For years he hadn't wanted to remember his past, his left-behind days in Bangladesh. All he wanted was to fashion a new memory out of his time in England. But he could do little to resist when that steam of rice had reached him on his third day in the Isle of Dogs, after he had been starving for two days. If Nilufar hadn't interrupted him that time by calling him to lunch, he would have been carried away by that memory. Now he had the whole day and night to give himself to it.

He couldn't quite remember the reason for undertaking it, but of the journey itself he was certain, because it was his first journey on foot from his grandmother's to his grandfather's village. Before that he had made the same journey on boats during rainy seasons, and on palanquins during dry seasons.

On that morning, muttering prayers, his grandmother came right up to the tall palm tree by the outer pond to say good-bye. He had turned the sharp bend to the left of the pond – Bisu Bhai beside him – and submerged in the sea of tall green jute stalks. In the early morning haze it was almost dark in the jute fields, and droplets of dew were hanging from the leaves. He was getting wet, lashed from both sides, as they moved through the narrow path. From the distance he could hear the harsh cries of ospreys breaking the silence. Once the ripples of those cries died down there was a lull – an interlude of intense silence – before other animals and men woke up. How not to remember that in that silence he had searched for the expression that his grandmother's face had offered him when she waved good-bye. Was she smiling? How could he be certain of it since the pleats of skin on her face, and her toothless gums, had always made her look as if she were smiling? But now, flicking the lengthening ash from his cigarette, Tapan liked to think that it was a smile, and not an expression of the ravages of old age. He needed that smile to lighten his soul so that he could come a bit closer to acquiring the senses of a mole that he needed to continue with his burrowing game. How strange that the smile of a grandmother should resemble that of a mole.

When he and Bisu Bhai emerged from the jute fields, the sun was already shining bright and the droplets of dew on the leaves were evaporating. Treading the narrow path between the yellowish green of young rice plants, they reached the raised mud road, lined with jham-berry and tall palm trees. Further on they arrived at the bamboo bridge that joined the banks of a small river. Across the bridge was the market, spread out on a large dry field and strewn with low thatched huts and fig trees. At its centre, in common with most country markets in those parts, stood a giant banyan tree. Under the banyan, in a circular formation, barbers set their stalls by hanging mirrors from the trunk. Bisu Bhai thought he needed a shave to make himself presentable at Tapan's grandfather's house. Even though Bisu Bhai was no more than farm keeper, he felt that he represented the honour of Tapan's grandmother's house every time he visited his grandfather's house.

Bisu Bhai went straight for Vatya Das, the old barber, who was awaiting his first customer of the day with his familiar red cape on his shoulders. He looked, as always – with his enigmatic, sculptured face with sunken cheeks and bright piercing eyes – strangely ethereal and yet all too solid. He wasn't a stranger to Tapan, for he came each year, on the eve of Eid, to his grandmother's house, where he gave all the male members the standard bowl-cut for a few pounds of rice.

Bisu Bhai, after greeting him warmly, sat on the squat, wooden stool. Vatya Das sat in front of him, on a stool raised slightly above. They shared a bidi and smalltalk, then Vatya Das began to shave Bisu Bhai. Pretending to be oblivious to their conversation, Tapan stood leaning against the banyan and played with its hanging roots. As he worked, the old barber hummed the mournful ballad of Khudhiram Basu – a martyr in the anti-colonial war. While the nationalist leaders talked non-violence, he lobbed a bomb at the elephant carrying the colonial GG; and the British hanged him for it.

Oh mother, give me my leave for once, I want to go on a walkabout.

Suddenly Vatya Das stopped his humming and looked at Tapan. 'It's a long journey for a little man like you, Tapan Bapu,' he said. 'But I see you've a pair of good skinny legs. They'll take you far.'

From the way Vatya Das talked that day under the banyan, Tapan sensed that the barber had made a connection between Khudhiram Basu's walkabout on the British gallows and his own journey, but could never fathom what that connection might be. For years he wanted to ask Vatya Das about it, but he never got the chance.

Now, he was beginning to sense a connection and was assailed by the question: would his journey take him, like Khudhiram Basu, to the gallows, to loops of silence under the English sky? He was far from ready to face up to this terrible question; he had a lot to live for.

Then it dawned on him that, more than Khudhiram Basu, it was Vatya Das, the barber who shaved Bisu Bhai, with whom he had the most intimate relationship. How could he have missed that connection before, especially considering that for a long twenty years Vatya Das had lived the life of a mole? Yes, they were both moles, Vatya Das and himself.

Tapan had heard amazing tales about Vatya Das, a frequent visitor to his grandmother's house. Finally one day, while the barber was cutting his hair on the eve of yet another Eid, Tapan couldn't hold onto it any longer. He asked, 'Is it true Vatya Da?'

'What you talking about, Tapan Bapu?'

'Did you really live underground for twenty years, Vatya Da? Fooling and fighting the British?'

Pretending to be taken by surprise, Vatya Das shook his head and smiled and told him that they were simply old barber's tales.

'Where did you hear such things, Tapan Bapu? Don't you know that we barbers belong to the lowest rung of the species, that we issued from the feet of Brahma? Naturally we feel a certain kinship with creatures that move beneath the earth. That's all, Tapan Bapu, just an old barber's tale.'

The rest of the villagers, except the landowners, weren't so reticent. Late in the cool afternoons, or under the starry night sky, and in between chewing paan and sharing chillums of tobacco, they would tell Vatya Das tales with relish, how Vatya Das could turn into a grasshopper at the approach of the law, or melt among the dense hyacinths of the lake. How ridiculous to think that a man of such powers could be caught, and yet once – during the early years of his life when, as a young landless peasant, he led a rebellion against the landlords – he had served some time in prison. Nobody believed that the police had trapped him, but that he was caught because he wanted to be caught.

As had happened during those days, he – like many other militants against the British Raj – was sent to the penal colony on

Andaman Island. On his return to the village, he – instead of keeping out of trouble – continued to fight the British empire and the landlords with the power of the wind that he brought from the sea. Although the police records, based on seemingly solid information, said that he had come back a communist, the villagers didn't care for such strange explanations.

There were so many stories, but the one that they most loved to tell was the story in which Vatya Das – a diminutive, skin-and-bone man – was supposed to have cut down a giant magistrate of Empress Victoria into two equal parts, with a single blow of his machete.

Although there were no eyewitnesses to the event, people told of it with such conviction, and with such care for visual, auditory, and tactile details that it was as if they were still bodily there. Always at the beginning they would tell how they felt the wind twisting turbulently as it touched the ground. Since they weren't bragging folks, they didn't mind admitting how scared they were, and how much they wanted to look away and hide. But once they dared to look up, they couldn't take their eyes off Vatya Das, because he was landing vertically from the sky with a machete in his hand. After that they felt compelled to follow him.

Suddenly, everything was calm, as if the twister never came, but the sky had turned red. Some even remembered seeing wild ducks against the red sky. Holding the machete upright, but now and then swaying it like a snake, Vatya Das headed towards the club. As everybody knew, the magistrate, at that precise moment – just after his game – would have been in the changing room. From there he would take the short walk to the lawned garden walled with English ivy, where, in the company of other colonial officials, he would have his tea.

In the event, he never made it to tea as Vatya Das, with a dancing move, cornered him in the changing room. Even those villagers who were born many years after the event, would solemnly swear that they had seen Vatya Das standing a long time facing the magistrate, looking straight into his blue colonial eyes, as no one had dared to do before. To the nodding agreement of all, as if it was a sacred text, they would add that the magistrate said not a word, he was dumb as a baby. But just before the fatal blow,

Vatya Das, holding the machete high, had apparently broken his silence and said most politely, 'Excuse me, Magistrate Sahib. I'll do what I'm about to do not because I'm a patriot, not even because you are a white man, but because you are a machine of the empire. Do you follow what I'm saying, Magistrate Sahib?'

Now Tapan took a puff of his cigarette, put a paan cone in his mouth, and laughed out loud, thinking of Vatya Das as an anti-colonial Luddite.

Whether Vatya Das cut the human machine of the empire into two or not was never firmly established. However, that didn't prevent the colonial administration from declaring him to be a miscreant and a public enemy and setting up a special task force for arresting him. From then on Vatya Das lived the life of a mole and escaped capture for twenty long years. What was more, despite the high intensity surveillance of the colonial police, Vatya Das never left the village during all that time. Indeed, while he moved invisibly in his various disguises, he continued to organise the peasants against the landlords and the British. At first, however, he only came out cloaked in the dark of the night; for the rest of the time he stayed in his burrow, which he'd dug in the middle of the wild mango grove. Since it was common knowledge that the mango grove was haunted by the phantoms of the wild, no one dared approach it. This suited Vatya Das – the friend of the phantoms – well.

Yet another tale that the villagers loved to tell concerned an unfortunate English officer – not the one whom Vatya Das might or might not have cut into two. This one was from the nearby district town, new to his colonial post, who – to the astonishment of all parties concerned – insisted on investigating the mango grove. As no native policeman would accompany him, he went on his own. Nobody knows what happened to him, but he came running out of the grove, raving about seeing his own likeness hanging from a tree, and grimacing into a mirror and singing: *I'm a jolly good Ganga Din boy*. After this event, to no one's surprise, the poor officer went around saying that his proper name was Ganga Din, and that he was a native gentleman from Kiplingpur.

As time went by, Vatya Das – in various disguises – started to make appearances during the light of day. Never did he wish to fool the villagers and no one was fooled. From the moment he stepped into the sun in the disguise of a travelling dentist, they knew who he was. Although they never quite trusted him with their teeth, they kept their mouths shut. But there were some who wouldn't leave him alone; they would pester him to do a dentistry trick so that they could grow gold teeth. He soon gave up dentistry, and pursued all manners of other disguises. Although these disguises allowed him to do his political work in the village, he wouldn't stay overground when the police came.

One day, however, something very strange happened. As was the routine in those days, a colonial police unit, commanded by a white officer, came to raid the village looking for Vatya Das. On that day, instead of burrowing into his den in the mango grove, he came out in the guise of a barber. He had done a good job in shaving off his long curly hair, radical bushy beard, and his thick, joined-together eyebrows. But the villagers recognised him immediately by his piercing eyes. When they saw Vatya Das in the guise of a barber approaching the white officer – who was resting under the landlord's bakul tree by the pond – they were afraid for him. But, neither the white officer nor his native subordinates, despite possessing his photograph, recognised him. Vatya Das offered to shave the officer free, who accepted without giving it a second thought, and lay back in his easy chair. Vatya Das gave the officer a professional shave, and after that a massage of such exquisite touches that he fell asleep under the bakul tree. Everybody was so impressed that they said that he was a natural at the barbering job. Since the old barber had died sometime ago without leaving an heir, the villagers at once took to Vatya Das as their new barber, even though he wasn't born of the barber caste. That was the first time anyone knew of a barber who wasn't a barber, but Vatya Das was happy because at last he had become a genuine member of Mahatma Gandhi's children of God.

Usually Tapan met Vatya Das when he came to cut his hair before Eid. However, one day he bumped into him in a different part of the village. It was a hot afternoon. He'd been alone in his grandmother's house. He'd done everything, even caught grasshoppers from the creeper bushes, and still he was bored. So, he set off for the lake with his fishing rod.

He hadn't gone far into the jute fields when Vatya Das suddenly appeared from behind a dense screen of stalks. Perhaps because he wasn't used to seeing him except while having his hair cut, Tapan was startled – as if he had seen a ghost. Realising his unease, Vatya Das told him that he was on his way to the market to set up his saloon for the evening and this path was simply the shortest way. Now at ease, Tapan was walking beside the barber. When they emerged from the jute fields and arrived on the mud road, Tapan was intrigued to see that Vatya Das didn't walk on the road. Instead, he was keeping parallel with Tapan, threading through the rough jagged roots, waterlogged fields and upturned lumps of earth and nettle bushes of that rough terrain.

'Vatya Da, why don't you walk on the road?'

Vatya Das stayed quiet for a while, scratched his head, then answered.

'It'll take long to explain, Tapan Bapu. But let us say that pleasures like these soften your resolve both physically and mentally. One develops petit bourgeois tendencies.'

'But what kind of pleasure is it to walk on a mud road? It doesn't make any sense, Vatya Da,' said Tapan. 'You're not walking on a paved road or riding a bike or being pulled along in a rikshaw, are you?'

'It starts with little pleasures like these. Slowly, slowly your mind and body weaken, and before you know it, you're lured away from the correct path. Moreover, you see, Tapan Bapu, what you may consider to be mere silly hardships, in fact, remind you of the difficult vocation you have undertaken – prepare you for the hazards of a revolutionary life.'

Tapan was puzzled; he couldn't make any sense of what Vatya Das was saying.

'You mean, Vatya Da, walking on jagged roots is part of revolutionary training?'

'Yes, but as I was saying, a lot more besides, Tapan Bapu.'

Together they walked on until the road forked, where Tapan expected Vatya Das to take the road that went to the market, and he the one to the lake. To his surprise, Vatya Das continued to walk alongside him. Soon they reached the lake, calm in the afternoon. With Vatya Das beside him, Tapan sat on the roots of an ancient tamarind tree and flung his line. While Tapan was preparing the bait for the second time, Vatya Das brought out his coconut hooka and filled the chillum with scented tobacco leaves. Tapan wasn't going question this but Vatya Das, feeling guilty about his inconsistencies, himself brought up the matter of tobacco. He told Tapan that he was well aware that the pleasure of smoking was a stain on his revolutionary spirit of renunciation, but this was one indulgence in his life he couldn't quite give up. There were times, he told Tapan, when he would go without food for a whole week and, standing still as a stork on one leg, he would chant to renounce his habit. But to no avail.

'Nobody is without some flaws,' said Vatya Das.

Then he lit the charcoal of his hooka and began to take long puffs. He offered the hooka to Tapan, saying he wasn't trying to corrupt him, but since young boys like him did it on the sly, he might as well share a smoke with him. After a moment of hesitation, Tapan took the hooka and smoked.

Seeing Vatya Das lying next to him that afternoon by the lake, his body withered by old age and years of scrupulous renunciation, Tapan had felt an intense sadness. Somehow he knew that Vatya Das would be dying soon. He couldn't help thinking: 'Who will mourn for you, Vatya Da? I suppose as a communist you don't care for such things, but memories, surely you leave behind memories.'

Now, hiding in this tower block, Tapan shivered, sensing that Vatya Das's underground war against the Raj wasn't that different from his own burrowing. That afternoon by the lake, Tapan had wanted to ask: 'Vatya Da, you have renounced everything – you've never had a house to live in, you never married, never eaten any good food; you have only a torn dhoti and your barber's tools. But what for, what have you achieved?' He didn't ask these questions, but if he had, and if Vatya Das's modesty hadn't come in the way, would he perhaps have said: 'Why, haven't I brought freedom? I would be the first to admit that it's a sham freedom. Full of mimicking masters. But it's something – no?'

While he looked out over the lake, Vatya Das, handing him the hooka once more, began telling him stories. He told him of his voyage to Andaman, how on a dark night, a cargo boat had brought him to the penal colony. The passage through the sea was rough; they were all locked in chains and vomiting. It was only when he sensed a bond with other inmates that his nightmare of being in hell began to pass. He woke up very early the next morning in his prison shack to a chorus of hisses. When he opened his eyes he saw hundreds of snakes hanging from the ceiling. The inmate next to him held his hand and told him, 'Nothing to be afraid of, comrade. Okay, you can get a poisonous bite. But it's not such a big deal. Death comes very quickly. Don't tell me, comrade, that you're afraid of dying?'

It didn't take him long to accept death, and once he had done so, he not only stopped being scared, but found a new sense of elation. As time went by on the island, he plunged himself – with renewed vigour – into practising the art of renunciation. So did the other comrades. It made little difference to them that their condition was already bad: hardly any shelter from the elements, no proper food, and the snakes and the leeches. Most of them were suffering from malaria, tuberculosis and malnutrition.

Many strange things happened on the island, but none stranger than the fact that some comrades, especially those who came from the towns, from the well-to-do families, actually envied Vatya Das. Looking at him with green in their eyes, they told him how lucky he was for being so poor and so low in caste. Whereas it had taken them years to master the rudiments of the art of deprivation, Vatya Das had acquired it naturally in the course of his lowly existence. He, without conscious effort, had done without even green chilli and salt while eating rice, or slept in the open on the pavement with the mosquitoes swarming on his naked flesh, or passed winter nights without a blanket. But there was still further to go, and Vatya Das, along with mastering the esoteric logic of dialectics – which he recited like holy mantra – learned how to stay without food and water for days, how to walk on burning coals, and how to expel sexual passion from his mind and body. Tapan was puzzled; scratching his head, he asked:

'You seem like the acetic shadus, but you are a revolutionary. How do you differ from them, Vatya Da?'

Smiling a little, Vatya Das sat up; he lit his chillum and took a puff. 'Not a lot. We aspire to the same renunciation of earthly pleasures and desires, but unlike the shadus, we are materialists,' he said. 'We don't want to escape the cycle of birth and re-birth, nor do we want to unite with the divine. We actually denounce all these. We prepare ourselves to be strong enough to stand up to the powerful.'

Tapan looked again at the withered body, his loins wrapped around with a torn dhoti. There was the image of a man who had nothing. Where was the sign of power? It wasn't that Vatya Das didn't make any sense, but the young Tapan couldn't quite appreciate his vocation; it all seemed futile to him.

Between listening to Vatya Das and sharing his hooka that afternoon, and the tenderness that welled in him, time went by so quickly that before he realised it, it was dark. In the distance, lights were already flickering in the lake. Tapan was a bit scared because he knew the lights signalled the dances of the demonic spirits that reigned over the water. But with Vatya Das – who would surely have thought him a wimp in believing such nonsense – he put on a brave face. However, despite this, the thought of having to cross the jute fields on his own in the dark made him emit a fearful odour. Vatya Das sniffed it from the air with his sensitive snout.

'Don't you worry, Tapan Bapu, I would escort you across the jute fields. But let us share a smoke first.'

Betraying a slight hint of passion, Vatya Das filled the chillum with fresh tobacco leaves, put in new pieces of charcoal and offered the hooka to Tapan.

'Tapan Bapu. Do me the honour of lighting this hooka, special Kambira tobacco from the north, you know,' he said. 'I will remember you as someone who will remember me one day. I wish I could come back that day to share a hooka with you. But, you see, I'm a materialist. So, there's no returning for me.'

Now, in this tower block in London, with a burning cigarette in his hand, Tapan was thinking: 'You're sharing a smoke with me, all right, Vatya Da. I smoke while I remember you, and I smell the air with your snout of a mole.'

That evening by the lake, feeling the event as a confirmation of the bond between them, he took the hooka from Vatya Das. While the lake whispered in the wind and the demonic lights danced their wild dances in the dark, Tapan, leaning against the tamarind tree, smoked the hooka. Fearful though that moment was, Tapan felt safe because his Vatya Da was with him. When they set off after the smoke, Vatya Das for once stuck to the road, and Tapan had to walk briskly to stay with him. Suddenly Vatya Das cleared his throat to signal a change of direction, paused a moment to allow Tapan to find his bearings, then sloped down from the road to enter the jute fields. There the darkness was absolute. Vatya Das told Tapan to hold onto him, which he did by placing a hand on his bare shoulder, and so the two of them made their way. Despite the lanes being full of sudden curves and sharp angles, they never strayed into the plantation. Only occasionally did Tapan feel a stalk gently brushing against his arms. He was not surprised by this extraordinary feat, yet overcome with curiosity, he asked, 'How do you do it, Vatya Da? How can you see in the dark?'

'You see, Tapan Bapu, underground you have to live differently. So you adapt your body, reorganise your organs, so to speak.'

'I don't follow you properly, Vatya Da.'

'I don't see very well, but then the power of sight is not very useful underground, is it?' said Vatya Das. 'Do you know about animals that live underground, Tapan Bapu?'

'Yes, I've heard about them, Vatya Da. Aren't they almost blind?'

'Like me, you mean! Yet, you see Tapan Bapu, they never stop moving. They construct complex routes, most amazing mazes, never get lost, always find their food – not to mention that they never get caught by their enemies. Isn't that something, Tapan Bapu?'

'Yes, but how can we be like them, Vatya Da? We are not made that way.'

'In a way, you're right, Tapan Bapu. But those animal powers are buried under our skin. With sufficient care and training we can bring them out, make our noses see the dimmest things in the world, and our skin detect the heat of a colour from miles away, and our ears pick up the direction of the slightest breeze. You will know these things one day, Tapan Bapu, you will know.'

That night Vatya Das led him through the dark as if he saw things with his nose. Or was it his skin? Or was it his ears? Or all of them? Although Tapan couldn't be sure, he had no doubt that Vatya Das saw everything as sharply as a falcon did.

Then it occurred to Tapan that Vatya Das, apart from the sensitivity of his organs, had marked out his territory so well that he had become one with the path he trod. That night, between the dark mass of the jute fields, Vatya Das fell asleep, and yet he led Tapan to his grandmother's house. Earlier in that journey Vatya Das told Tapan how he slept during those years he was working underground against the British. Obviously, there wasn't much time for sleep, because there was so much to do. Moreover, when he wasn't in his burrow, he had to keep on moving. So, after a while, when his organs had mapped out the territory over which he moved, he could fall asleep while walking. He would set off from one village, negotiate the difficult turns and the zigzag paths in his sleep, and still arrive at his destination some miles away. So, still tuned to the old ways, Vatya Das, while sleeping, had guided Tapan safely through that night. But as soon as they crossed the jute fields and approached the outer courtyard by the pond, where Uncle Hamid was looking out for him with a lantern, Vatya Das woke up.

'We've arrived, Tapan Bapu,' he said.

Often he would fantasise about meeting Vatya Das again: he would imagine how meaningful their encounter would be, how much he would learn from him, and how deep a bond he would build with him. But that was the last time he saw him alive. As soon as he saw Uncle Hamid rushing towards them with a lantern, Vatya Das turned around and disappeared into the dark mass of the jute fields. It was when Tapan came to visit his grandmother's house the following year, and while he was washing his feet in the pond before entering the inner courtyard, that Uncle Hamid told him the news. He said, 'The old barber, you know, the one with funny funny ideas. Yes, the one who cut down the British officer into two, is dead.'

Early the next morning Tapan set off for the temple ground by the river where they burnt the dead. When he reached the place, the dead body was already laid under a pile of wood. The air was full of kerosene fumes. No burning ghee, no perfume of sandalwood for him. Nor was there any phurohit to preside over the ceremony, nor any relatives to mourn. Perhaps that's the way he would have wanted it, something small and low key. The gathering consisted entirely of the barbers who shared the banyan with him in the market, except for three comrades from the olden days. Perhaps not wishing to send him to the elements only on the fumes of kerosene, perhaps overcome by tender memories, the comrades carried with them the scented flowers of dawn. One by one, they sprinkled petals of jasmine, khatalia and bakul on the funeral mound. Suddenly one of them began singing the ballad of Khudiram Basu – *Oh mother, give me my leave for once, I want to go walkabout –* while another, with a torch in his hand, circled the funeral mound three times. He paused at each of the four corners for few seconds until the fire was lit. Crouching in the distance, Tapan stayed behind the outer parapet of the temple, from where he was hardly visible to the men by the pyre. Suddenly Vatya Das's body sprang up from underneath the burning piles of wood and stood erect among the flames as if taking off vertically towards the distant stars. 'What were you trying to do, Vatya Da?' Tapan asked himself. 'Wanted to be a rocket man, or just a phoenix man, eh?'

Because he had never seen a burning body in the open before, Tapan was taken aback by the way Vatya Das shot up from the fire. For a moment, in his confusion, he had the dreadful feeling that they were burning him alive. But as if expecting it, the three comrades promptly pulled him down with bamboo, while the barbers beat drums and circled around the fire. A few scented flowers weren't enough; without ghee and sandalwood the burning scent of raw flesh quickly filled the air. Soon the barbers stopped circling the fire. The comrades held hands, but instead of chanting mantra, they sang the *Internationale*, and of the heroic deeds of Vatya Das.

Hear hear, oh brothers, here lies the slayer
of the British. A thorn in the flesh of the masters
and mighty.
You know him, oh brothers, as a cutter of hair
but he was the lowest of the low
a man lower than a man, an untouchable
oh brothers, but how he climbs

110

up and up, higher than
the clouds.

Here, here, oh brothers, here lies
a shadu who wasn't a shadu
and a barber who wasn't
a barber.

When Tapan saw the burnt flakes in the air, he thought, 'Vatya Da, you're finally flying, and you're doing that with some style.' Once the fire was out, the comrades gathered the ashes in an earthen pot and, accompanied by the drumming of the barbers, spread them in the river, over the rice paddies, sugar canes, and jute fields – which were then bare after the harvest.

Now cooped up in the dark, and again feeling rather cold because he'd had to turn the heating off as the meter was running low and he had no more coins, Tapan said to himself, 'I do remember you Vatya Da, I do remember you; how could I forget a mole who could fly. But then, you knew that I would remember you, didn't you?' Almost unconsciously and forgetting the materialism of Vatya Das, he then intoned a passage from *Isa Upanishad*:

'May life go to immortal life, and body go to ashes. OM. O my soul, remember past strivings, remember! O my soul, remember past strivings, remember!'

No sooner had he done this than he sensed the piercing eyes of Vatya Das rebuking him: 'If you can't remember me without making my soul immortal, Tapan Bapu, then don't remember me at all. And, please spare me your pathetic nostalgia – don't make me live in the metaphysical mumbo-jumbo of OM.'

Tapan was so carried away by the memories of rice, of Vatya Das and the journey that he hadn't realised that it was already five in the afternoon. No wonder he was feeling so hungry. Suddenly it occurred to him that all those years ago, at the onset of that journey, the vapour of rice came to him overlaid with another flavour.

For a moment, he was there again; his grandmother had woken him up for the journey and he'd gone to the inner pond to brush his teeth. While he was brushing his teeth his nose picked up, apart from the vapour of red aman rice, the smell of frying bitter gourds. Now the memory of those bitter gourds was making Tapan ravenous with hunger. He rushed to the kitchen, pulled open the fridge door, and shoved his hand into the vegetable box. Yes, the bitter gourds were there, wrapped in brown paper, just the way Nilufar had left them on her last visit. He knew the recipe well enough to begin immediately.

He deftly cut the bitter gourds into wafer-thin slices without lifting the knifepoint off the chopping board. Despite his rush to get on with it, he didn't forget the details and soaked them in salted water. While the salt was drawing the bitterness from the gourds, he cooked the rice. But he must give the process a few hours until no more than a tinge of bitterness was left. He thought of eating something to relieve his hunger, until the bitter gourds were ready for frying. He toasted a slice of bread, spread butter and blackberry jam on it, but halted the process just before taking a bite. He didn't want to lessen the intensity of his hunger, rather to increase it by prolonging it until the fried bitter gourds were ready to offer him that elusive sensation of contentment. Almost elated by the decision, he threw the toast into the bin, and lit a cigarette. He went back to the living room, sat in the chair by the fire, but that only reminded him it was cold. He got up, circled the room, wandered into the kitchen, looked at the bitter gourds and came to a halt before the back window.

Cautiously, he parted the curtains to look outside. Darkness, made dense by fog, had fallen on the Thames. Yet the lights by the river, though somewhat dimmed, were still throwing up an amber glow by the sheer force of their numbers. However, his hunger didn't allow him to stay still for long. So he moved away from the window, walked again the narrow passage between the bed and the sofa, around the chairs by the fire and the table, and stopped by the front window. He didn't dare get too close to it because someone might be watching him. His hunger hadn't eased the slightest bit, but he was determined to hold on until the bitter gourds were ready for frying. Almost automatically he lit yet another cigarette, went back to the kitchen, drank a glass of water, and again looked at the bitter gourds. Although they would still be far too bitter, he nearly gave in to the temptation of frying them immediately. But he resisted because he wanted them to turn out, no matter how long it took, just the way they were that morning years ago. He tried to put on the radio that Nilufar and Sundar had brought for him, but it wasn't working.

Perhaps a headstand would help to sustain him. He crouched on the floor, placed his head in a triangle with his hands on the carpet and then, balancing on the crown of his head, lifted himself upside-down, feet pointing to the ceiling. At first he could feel the blood swelling his face, and his ears slightly buzzing, but soon his mind became aligned with the stillness of his limbs and torso. Feeling much better he wandered into the kitchen and, against his better judgement, decided not to delay any longer. While he fried the bitter gourds with a pinch of turmeric, a few green chillies and some finely diced cloves of garlic, he hummed to himself the ballad of Khudhiram Basu. After that he served himself a mound of rice on a large transparent plate and placed the fried bitter gourds on it. He didn't want to rush it. He took the plate to the kitchen table, settled himself on a chair, and looked expectantly at the fried bitter gourds.

He looked at the plate for a long time, postponing the moment of disappointment, because no matter how good it tasted it could never reproduce the elusive sensation of those bitter gourds that morning when he set off from his grandmother's village. Finally, he took a pinch of fried bitter gourds, mixed it with a handful of rice and the fat end of a green chilli, producing a ball. No sooner had he flicked the ball into his mouth than he spat it out, scattering grains of rice all over the lino. It was as vile as the spilled guts of a fish. He felt nauseated, made a run for the toilet, poured out a bluish slime into the loo.

He didn't feel like eating any longer; the hunger had disappeared. With no coins left to turn on the heating, he decided to go back to bed. Once in bed he remembered Vatya Das again, his mastery of the art of hunger, which he hoped to use against the power of the British. In the event, he never got to use it – at least not the way Mahatma did. Yet, many were of the opinion that it wasn't all in vain. During his last days, when years of renunciation had finally caught up with him, Vatya Das couldn't work as a barber any more. Since he didn't have a son to look after him, and hadn't saved a single coin, he lay in his hut without food. At first the barbers from the market had brought him food, but they had soon stopped coming. The rest of the villagers, as they passed his hut, would look up, sigh and say: 'Oh, his time has come.'

It was not a matter of ill will that the villagers hadn't brought him any food, but a recognition of the writing of destiny. Eventually people forgot him, as if he was already dead. Months and months went by, but he was still alive. No one was surprised. Everyone in the village took it for granted that Vatya Das, after years of arduous practice, had mastered the art of gathering nutrients from the air. When he died one afternoon of that winter season, it was said that a tornado suddenly rose from the eastern flank of the village, the spot where Vatya Das had his small, wattle-walled hut. It whipped up such a ferocious swirl that it seemed the conch of doomsday had been blown, but miraculously it left everything the way it was, except an old nim tree, which it lifted towards the heavens.

Tapan straightened his back against the headboard of his bed, and sniffed as if gathering nutrients from the air, but it only made him feel hungry again. So he slid back under the duvet and tried to fall asleep. But he was only halfway through the journey that he – prompted by the vapour of rice – had begun to remember. No way could he fall asleep without completing the journey.

Once Bisu Bhai had his shave under the Banyan in the market, they left Vatya Das. They took the straight public road that led to the edges of low-lying, water-logged fields, where the yellowish green of young rice plants stretched for miles. Bisu Bhai, now looking clean and smelling of shaving lather, led the way. Balancing precariously on the narrow ridges between the paddy fields, Tapan followed him, still thinking of Vatya Das. At the end of the flat expanse of paddies lay the raised mound of earth on which the rail track ran. Bisu Bhai walked on one of the rails, Tapan on the other, holding hands to keep balance. Soon they met up with a traveller, who was making his way to the nearest town, some twenty miles away. He looked both nervous and excited because it was his first visit to the town.

'If you're going to the town, why aren't you taking the train?' Bisu Bhai asked the man.

'Oh, I'm wanting to save the money to see a talky-film. It's my mind's desire since my boy-body turned man-body – understand, what I mean?' said the man. 'One more thing, on the way I'm also wanting to pay a visit to the house of my mother's sister. My mother is sending her a pot of thick cream milk and some catfish curry. They're my auntie's favourites, you know.'

'What film are you desiring to see?' asked Bisu Bhai.

'I don't know really. Oh I'm much shamed to say.'

'You mean, you want to see them ladies dancing, achya?' said Bisu Bhai. 'Some story line with love affairs, eh? You like them pale ladies from Karachi, wearing trousers? Oh what bottoms they have, honestly.'

'I don't know. I'm much ashamed,' stuttered the man.

Bisu Bhai, who considered himself an expert on towny things, advised the man how to get to the cinema hall, how to buy a ticket, how not to be conned by the black marketeers, and where to eat the cheapest meal. He also told him that the best place to sleep free was on the veranda of the red courtroom that the British had built.

From the rail track they climbed down to take the mud road that, between bamboo and betel-palm trees, wove through the villages. While walking next to Bisu Bhai, and thinking about the courtroom where the man would be sleeping that night, Tapan asked, 'Why did the British built everything red? Courtrooms, police stations, railway stations, officers' quarters?' Bisu Bhai, despite being an unlettered man, who hardly ever left the village – except for occasional visits to the town with Uncle Hamid, when he used to sneak out to see films – claimed to know many things. When he heard Tapan's question, he looked puzzled, chewed his teeth, and then turned serious.

'Ha, very interesting, them British. Ha, nobody liked red like them. Certainly, too much red,' said Bisu Bhai.

'But why, Bisu Bhai?' asked Tapan.

'It's blood, you know. The colour of blood.'

'But why?' Tapan asked again.

'It's a very cunning business, you know,' said Bisu Bhai. 'Them British thought the red would make us people run to our latrines with shitting fright. Some wrongdoing against them, and there would be blood. Now, you understand me correctly, ha?'

115

'I'm not sure, Bisu Bhai.'

'You foolish boy. You haven't seen them British, have you?'

'No.'

'Let me think correctly, achya. Them left before you were born.'

'Why?'

'Oh, there were too many botherations for them,' said Bisu Bhai.

'What kind of botheration?'

'You know, Subus Basu fighting them in Burma. Master Da looting their arms in Chittagong. And, ha, Vatya Das cutting the officer into two, and spreading funny funny ideas.'

'What happened then?'

'You see, the whole thing was getting too much botheration for the British. So, they cooked up this no good Pakistani/Hindustani mess for us. And then buggered off like a cowardly dog with its tail between its legs.'

'Sorry, Bisu Bhai,' said Tapan. 'I still don't understand why they painted everything red.'

'Oh, Allah, such foolishness. But consider for a moment the colour of the British,' said Bisu Bhai.

'They're very handsome-looking people, the British. Aren't they Bisu Bhai?'

'Ha, ha. But you're not understanding things correctly. You see they've no colour. You can see through them like water.'

'How can that be possible, Bisu Bhai?'

'Have you ever seen a low-down lady-ghost? The kind who waits by the latrine holes to frighten people, and always wearing white?'

'No,' said Tapan.

'I thought so,' said Bisu Bhai. 'But the point is the British look like she. Do you know why?'

'No.'

'Achya, they don't have much blood. If you don't have any blood, what do you think about all the time, ha?'

'Blood.'

'Good. Very good. Now tell me, what the lady-ghost by the latrine does when she gets a man?'

'She breaks his neck and drinks his blood.'

116

'You're learning fast, aren't you? Now you understand correctly why them British built everything red – ha?'

As they walked on with their umbrellas unfurled because the sun was already up in the sky, Tapan was still thinking about what Bisu Bhai had said.

'Have you seen an Englishman, Bisu Bhai?'

'What do you mean, seen, eh? I've seen plenty real close, you know.'

'Have you?' said Tapan, excitedly.

'I don't want to brag, but once I nearly touched one.'

'Yeah?'

'You see, I was serving him a glass of sherbet. Let me think correctly. Ha, it was a hot day and he was mighty thirsty. Before I could put the glass on the table, he took it from me in a double hurry. To my utter fright, his skin nearly brushed mine.'

'So, you haven't actually touched one.'

'Allah saved me then. But you know what happened?'

'What, Bisu Bhai?'

'Your Uncle Hamid shook hands with the Englishman.'

'Is that true?'

'Ha, ha. After that your Uncle Hamid had plenty of troubles. He washed his hand no less than ten times. He wouldn't even eat his food with his hands for days. Oh, the funny sight of seeing a man eating with a spoon.'

'It isn't funny, Bisu Bhai.'

'Not funny! Even your grandmother teased him no end: *Hamid Bapa, you're turning English or what?*'

'I don't believe grandmother saying things like that.'

'You don't know your grandmother like I do. Oh, I remember something real good now.'

'What?'

'You haven't met the old Bhatacharya – the brahmin. Some fellow he was. He died the year of partition.'

'What's about him, Bisu Bhai?'

'When the Englishman came to shake his hand, he jumped up into the bakul tree. He was much afraid that the Englishman would pollute him by touching him. Then he saw that the Englishman was walking all over his shadow, under the same

117

bakul tree. He jumped off in great panic. Do you know how many times he bathed in the pond to purify himself? '

'No.'

'No less then seven times. Ha, I've seen plenty British.'

'But Bisu Bhai, I've read in my school books that the English were such great lords. They even had some funny notions about us. Did you know that they thought of us as no better than those monkeys with their red ugly bottoms? How come the brahmin felt polluted by the English? Surely, the English aren't untouchables?'

'Them thinking of us like red monkey bottoms! Achya, really? It can't be true. Are you reading your schoolbooks correctly or what? Anyway, that Bhatacharya brahmin didn't care for such things, you know. For him it was a matter of cooking. He thought that the creator, when he was cooking our ancestors, forgot to cook the English properly. In fact, he threw the English down from heaven totally uncooked. And that brahmin, you know, wouldn't touch uncooked meat for anything in the world. He thought the English bodies, being uncooked meat, were number one untouchables. You understand me correctly, ha?'

Now lying in bed, Tapan laughed to himself as he thought of Bisu Bhai and his strange stories about the English. If that story about the Brahmin was right – which he doubted – that Bhatacharya would have proved a serious embarrassment to the anti-racists.

On that journey again. His grandfather's house was still a long way off. When it was past midday and the heat was rising from the furrows of ploughed lands, they stopped by a village market. From a tea stall they bought sugary tea and ate the rice breads that Bisu Bhai carried in a bundle of muslin. Casually pouring the milk for their tea in an arc from high up, the man from the tea stall asked Bisu Bhai whether he was stopping on his way to the shrine of Pir-Baba. Surely he knew that tomorrow would be the celebration of the birth of Pir-Baba – the sufi mystic who died some three hundred years ago – and there would be a fair. Bisu Bhai said that he wasn't going because he was escorting the boy to his grandfather's house.

Once out of the market, they went north. After a while, they met up with a group of Bauls who climbed onto the road from

118

somewhere across the fields. Months ago they had set off from the coastal district in the far south and were heading for the Pir-Baba's shrine. Soon they met other groups of Bauls coming from distant parts of the country, clad in saffron and ochre cloths, their hair matted down to their loins and carrying doog-doogi drums, cymbals tied to their fingers, and one-string ektaras and two-string dootaras slung across their shoulders. When the time came for them to veer off at the turning that led towards Tapan's grandfather's village, Bisu Bhai, as if in a dream, continued to follow the Bauls. It was late in the afternoon when they reached the shrine. Bisu Bhai said he would pay a quick respect to Pir-Baba and then they would set off immediately; that way there would still be time to complete the journey before midnight.

Already the throngs of Bauls, who had been congregating for the past day, were tapping their doog-doogi drums and tinkling their cymbals. The lead singers, with wild red eyes, were plucking their one-string ektaras or two-string dootaras and feeling the range of their voices with long, undulating notes. They had been smoking ganja for quite some time in their small clay chillums. Forgetting the journey they had to make, Bisu Bhai, with Tapan next to him, sat down by a group. And time went by.

Now lying in bed, in this tower block in the Isle of Dogs, Tapan was struggling to stay awake, but the Bauls – the nomads of the green plains and the deltas – were taking him along on a different plane. Where did they come from, where were they going? What a stupid question. Everybody knows that a Baul wanders aimlessly like the wind that carries his music far on this flat, monotonous plane. Not caring to arrive, not going anywhere in particular, the Bauls circulate endlessly to the end of time. Of course, one cannot ignore the shrines; if the Bauls can be said to have any aims, it is to stop by the shrines, but only momentarily, and always to begin new journeys along secret pathways across the vast stretches of the sub-continent. The stops at the shrines, nodes on an elaborate but almost invisible network, afford them the rare luxury of staying still for a while and meeting up with their brother Bauls from distant parts of the country and beyond.

Years later, sharing a chillum of ganja with Bisu Bhai – who although not a proper Baul, was a fellow traveller – Tapan learnt

119

more about their secret wanderings. No trains, buses and highways for them: their routes always diverged from the straight path. Nor did they care for national borders. Indeed, their wanderings and their melodies had created a secret map of the sub-continent. Of course, the national authorities had no knowledge of it: how naively they slept thinking that the borders were secure.

But thinking back now, Tapan began to feel that it was not during the course of their long journeys, but in the static space of their gatherings that the Bauls really travelled. He remembered sitting among the Bauls, the chillum circulating. He, though too young to partake in the smoking, felt dizzy through the sheer density of the cloud of hemp that hung in the air. Suddenly the lead Bauls stood up, strummed their one-string ektaras and plucked melodies from two-string dootaras, waved their long matted locks, whirled around and began to sing. After a while, the players of doog-doogi drums and cymbals, still seated on the ground, joined in. Hours went by as the Bauls sang of their journeys in quest of love, separating from the unnamed and never-seen beloved, longing erotically to join her, but always separating and making endless journeys to find her. But it was not so much the content of their songs, rather it was the strange intensity of their voices that rose vertically to meet up with the stars, and their feet dancing to the secret rhythms from the womb of the earth, that gave their bodies the speed that matched that of light. Yes, the Bauls really travel faster when they aren't travelling at all.

Now, almost on the verge of surrendering to sleep, Tapan shook himself to wake himself up. He thought about attempting to fly like a gull again. If only he could muster the intensities of the Bauls, perhaps shouting wildly and jerking his head to the demonic rhythm that went beyond the music, he could flap his arms as though they were wings, and fly like a gull. But he had none of the Bauls' intensity, nor Vatya Das's power of renunciation to make himself light enough to take off into the air. Poor Tapan. He was really too heavy for that sort of thing; so he fell asleep.

CHAPTER 11

Late in the night, the cold biting harder than the last time, Tapan was on the move again. As usual Sundar drove him, Nilufar beside him in the front seat. He was hunched up in the back, his flat cap pulled down until it reached his eyebrows. Neither the posture nor the cap was meant to be a disguise, but already the wariness of the mole was becoming a habit with him. Now, taking the reverse direction to the earlier route, they went north from the Isle of Dogs, and then turned west along the river. Although the flat itself couldn't be distinguished from the one in the Isle of Dogs, Limehouse was something else. He was moving from the outer zones of our city towards its centre. Sundar said, 'We're approaching towards Bangla Town. How do you feel, Bhaio?'

Inside the flat, Sundar opened a map of Tower Hamlets and ran his fingers over the lines drawn with red ink. 'These are our streets,' he said. He then pointed out the asterisks on the map, glowing in orange at regular intervals covering most of the borough: at least one for each street and each housing block. When Tapan bent down to look at them he saw that each of the asterisks was numbered. Sundar laughed at his puzzled look and explained that each of the numbers stood for a contact point. Whenever he needed help, all he had to do was knock on the door of any of the houses on the map. At the back of the map, Sundar had arranged the numbers in order, pairing them with a house number and a name. Folding the map, he handed it to Tapan, and said:

'From now on Bhaio, you can move freely anywhere you like within this map. Of course, you have to take care not to arouse any suspicion. If you need to go out, it is best during the night. Ho, ho, Bhaio, you would be like that batty fella – Count Dracula. Anyway, never get into a situation where you need to show papers, or might be asked to reveal your identity. I know you don't care much for driving. You're some mighty walker, Bhaio. Like them Aussie Bushman fellas. This good, very good because the coppers are always fishing for papers when you drive. Usually they don't bother you much in the street. But sometimes when they see a Paki face, they get suspicious. Like crazies they check you out for illegals. Take care not to walk like an illegal, Bhaio. Don't walk bent down like you carrying a sackful of fear. Or shame. Always upright, Bhaio.'

He wasn't really listening to what Sundar was saying, because he was travelling elsewhere along the coiling holes of his smoke. It was Sundar who really launched him this time. He was off as soon as he heard of the good Count. He had nothing against blood sucking, though personally it didn't interest him much – at least not now – perhaps if circumstances were different, he wouldn't have minded having those big teeth and sucking some beautiful women. He remembered how Adela used to get turned on by that bloodsucker. How about Nilufar? Well, he hadn't seen one of those films with her yet. However, what really got him going was that bat thing. Yes, he wanted to have his wings and fly his nocturnal flights. Fly and fly. Not going for some pretty neck, eager to be sucked. Not even for the most delicious jackfruit across the sea, but elsewhere, no matter where, always elsewhere.

He could have gone on flying, but came back down to earth with the Aussie Bushman fellas. He didn't know much about the Bushmen – some kind of Bauls maybe: both were wanderers and musical map makers. But, how could he lay his feet on the earth's surface and join in harmony with the elusive substances that lay deep in its innermost strata? He didn't have the music that a Baul carries in his locks of tangled hair, or a bushman in the soles of his feet. If he tried hard enough, perhaps he could learn to sing like a Baul, or even tune into some of the Bushman's songlines, but singing was one thing and becoming-music was another. To be a walker like a Baul or a Bushman one had to become one with the music: limb by limb in harmony with the rumbles of the earth, swish of the wind, hiss of the fire and the silence of the sky.

'What are you thinking, Bhaio?' asked Sundar.

'Nothing really,' said Tapan.

'Yeah! Anyway, you need a job, Bhaio.'

'Yes, I was thinking the same.'

'Good. But times are bad, Bhaio. Even the Greek or the Jewish factories are getting risky these days. And our restaurants are not as safe as they used to be. Too many fishing raids. So, I was thinking of Dr. Karamat Ali.'

'No. Not that weirdo doctor. He's a shit bag. I don't trust him,' said Nilufar.

'Yes, yes, I agree. But the fellow is trying to turn a new leaf. You know, he wants to do philanthropic work now,' said Sundar.

'Scum like him don't change.'

'Don't be so harsh on the fellow, Nilufar. You know, the fellow is a bit fed up with his doctory and his grocery shop. He wants to do something challenging. So he has the idea of setting up an English newspaper.'

'That stingy scum is opening a newspaper? Can't believe it. Besides, he can't put two sentences together even in Bengali,' said Nilufar.

'May be. But the job is safe. No paperwork involved. What do you think, Bhaio?'

'I don't mind any job, really,' said Tapan.

'Good. I admit the Doctor is a stingy bugger, but he is not a rat.'

'What do I have to do, Sundar?'

'Mainly you'll correct his English. And he might ask you to do one or two articles. Thirty pounds a week. Cash in hand. It's not bad, is it, Bhaio?'

Although it was Dr. Karamat Ali who had treated Tapan when he fainted at the picket line, he didn't know him well. But in East London you didn't have to know him personally to know of him, because his stinginess was legendary. Everybody knew that he was so mean that he even kept his own children half-starved. Often he was heard shouting: 'Oh Allah, why have I such bad luck! These children are such big eaters. They'll ruin me.'

He cheated the workers in his grocery shop of their pay on all sorts of phoney excuses. When there was a big flood in Bangladesh two years ago, everybody contributed something to the relief fund, but Dr. Karamat Ali didn't give a penny.

' You wouldn't believe how my workers are cheating me. Honestly, they are turning me into a naked beggar,' he said, when he was asked to make a donation. 'Oh Allah, what can I say about my doctory business. No one consults me these days. Even the proper English doctors are becoming high-minded and seeing the illegals without asking any questions. On top of it, they are doing it free. Oh Allah, they've ruined me.'

No one knew how he dared to call himself a doctor, because he'd never attended a medical school, and certainly wasn't a registered member of the profession in the UK. When people asked him about his qualifications he would evade the question with a breathless display of his detailed knowledge of anatomy in what sounded like Latin, the complex aetiology of disease, and the subtle art of reading a symptom. He would always conclude by reciting the Hippocratic oath, as if that confirmed his position as a good orthodox doctor.

But he had a good business brain. He specialised in illegal cases and door-to-door service. When someone without legitimate papers, or without a national health number needed to see a doctor, Karamat Ali promoted himself as the right man. He had also done abortions on the side, but his genius had found its ideal expression when he went around the Bangladeshi houses throughout Tower Hamlets and announced: 'Dr. Ali calling – an expert physician of many years of experience. Do not mistake me for a mumbo-jumbo man. I have no time for the ayurvedic types, herbalists, homeopaths, faith healers, bringers of jinn or witch doctors. I'm not in the cheating business. You are looking at a scientifically trained allopathic physician. If you are so unlucky as to suffer from aches and pains, colds and flu, bad stomachs, funny feelings in the mind etc., etc., I'm here to help. For only £5 you will receive a full, scientific investigation. And the price includes comprehensive advice on treatment and drugs. I do not like to blow my own trumpet, but the truth needs to be told. I have fathomed the origin of many deadly diseases and prescribed the proper course of their elimination.'

Despite access to free medical treatment in Britain, many Bangladeshi people were accustomed to use Karamat Ali's door-to-door service for minor illnesses, though he did face a stiff competition from the herbalists and the bringers of jinn and the like.

Nilufar still wasn't convinced that it was a good idea for Tapan to get involved with Dr. Karamat Ali, but Sundar knew how to exploit her weak spots. 'You know, his wife and children left him. The poor Doctor is very lonely now. So he wants to busy himself with philanthropic work.'

Nilufar looked doubtful, but said nothing.

'So, that's settled then, Bhaio. I'll take you to see the Doctor in a couple of days.'

'That will be fine, Sundar.'

'Oh, yes, Bhaio. I'd nearly forgotten,' said Sundar. 'Your friend Kofi has been asking about you. He wants to come and see you.'

'Yeah! I'd love to see him.'

'Right. I'll bring him along the next time.'

As Sundar was getting up to leave, Tapan said he was desperate for some fresh air, but Sundar couldn't accompany him just then. He needed to get back to a debriefing meeting of the defence group. Nilufar said she would go with Tapan.

'How will you get back?' asked Sundar.

'Don't worry about me. I'll take a taxi,' said Nilufar.

All three of them went out together. Sundar waited for a while to make sure that Tapan was safe on the road.

Tapan felt nervous out in the open again. On the East India Dock Road, he held Nilufar tightly, as if she could shield him from the unexpected dangers. For a while they walked through the mist in silence, but slowly he was becoming more relaxed. By the time they reached West India Dock Road, he unfastened his arms from Nilufar, and began to roll some cigarettes. He gave the first one to Nilufar knowing that, since she couldn't smoke in front of Sundar, she was probably desperate for one. Still silent, they dragged on their cigarettes, and continued through the mist.

They were in what had been an old Chinese area, and Tapan stood by a lamppost and sniffed the air. There was no smell of opium, only the lingering smell of soya and sesame oil. Sadly, there weren't as many Chinese restaurants as there once had been, and those that remained had closed hours ago. Now it was hard to believe that once upon a time, here, on these ordinary streets lined with shops, council blocks and terraced houses, lay the dens of opium-eaters. From these exuded, like the 'great stink', the dread of yellow-goings-on. But this was not the only story.

Ah, how not to remember comrade Moo Ya – with his round glasses and beret – how he used to close his eyes when he smiled. He was always there on the picket line throughout the battle of Brick Lane in the summer of '78. He was the only Chinese there, but he was one of the few who followed Sundar to rescue Tapan from the police. Later he came to see Tapan in Sundar's flat, where he was convalescing, with a container full of noodles. He laughed, closing his eyes, 'I bet you're thinking it's from my family takeaway – ya? Chinese people number 23, number 47 – ya? You people like it hot – ya? I cook it Sichuan style – plenty hot –ya?'

Tapan liked the dish so much that he made Moo teach him how to cook it. Afterwards, when he left Adela and moved in with Sundar, and subsequently when he lived alone in his own flat, from time to time – giving the old curry a miss – he would cook noodles, Comrade Moo Ya style.

One day he even invited Moo and served the dish.

'I hope you won't be disappointed, Moo,' said Tapan. Sundar, who was sitting next to Moo, jovially slapped his shoulder and cried out, 'Comrade Moo, how do you like the noodles – Comrade Moo Ya style?'

Moo found it so funny that he said 'Ya' and laughed and laughed and kept his eyes closed for a whole five minutes.

'I wish I were a Chinese stereotype – ya?' said Moo after the meal. 'Then I could teach you fellows something really useful. Kung Fu – you know the sort of things – ya? You could pulp the racist bastards, real good – ya?'

Sundar told him that he had done his bit for the struggle by giving it *noodles – Comrade Moo Ya style*. Everybody laughed again, including Moo, who as usual closed his eyes.

In those days, Tapan hadn't thought much about the legendary dens and the dark holes. Now he wished the whole place was full of them and he knew their secrets. One day, after a quiet period at the picket, Moo had taken him to his flat in Limehouse Causeway. He told Tapan that his people had mastered the art of living in cities they had made their own, no matter where and how far they went from their native land. The secret of it, he said, was invisibility. Pouring green tea into two tiny white porcelain cups, he took his round glasses off and smiled gently, but this time without closing his eyes.

'You can't miss Chinatown – ya?' said Moo. 'But how many Chinese have you met? Apart from me, none – ya?'

'I don't get your point, Moo,' said Tapan.

'My community tells me I'm too mixed up. My head is not right. Maybe my head is not right – ya? Otherwise you would never meet me. You can't miss Chinatown but the rest of our people you don't hear or see – ya?'

'Sure, one can't miss Chinatown,' said Tapan. 'Surely, Moo, it gives your people too much visibility – no?' said Tapan.

'Chinatown is a facade only. Built to divert attention – ya?' said Moo. 'So they don't come looking for us. Places where we really are. We stay hiding, out of sight. Dark places – ya? That's how we build invisible cities, our real cities, ya – Comrade?'

Tapan wondered where Moo was now – good Comrade Moo Ya. Last time he'd heard of him he was going to south London, to somewhere where there were no Chinese. Moo had said he couldn't take that stupid invisibility thing any more; he needed to get out. 'Comrade,' he said, 'it doesn't make any sense – ya? Why travel so far carrying your Canton on you back. I'm fed up being a tortoise, Comrade – ya?'

How curious that while Moo was fleeing the invisible city, he was trying to inhabit it. Tapan couldn't help laughing at the irony. Now, more than anything, he needed dens and underground passages; how else could he be a mole?

Suddenly a police car emerged from the fog and halted in front of them. It was too late to hide, and running would have made matters worse, so they held their breath and waited for the inevitable. Luckily the police were looking for someone else; had they seen a nignog running away? Nilufar gritted her teeth but stayed quiet. Before they left the police gave them a quizzical look and said, 'Just closed your shop then, Mr. Patel? Bet you're coining it in.'

Wandering along the warehouses where the East India Company stored cotton, saltpetre, and spices brought from Bengal, they reached the Limehouse Marina. Holding hands, they leaned forward against the railing and looked at the mist-covered river, as if they were trying to look beyond its immense darkness. For a long time they stood there, motionless, until Nilufar snuggled into him, and he felt her pulse echoing the secret music of the breeze and the waves. He felt he was beginning to give himself to her in a way that he hadn't done before.

A motor boat started up and they saw its searchlight struggling against the mist. As the boat approached the Marina they moved back and, hurrying to the right, crouched behind the parapet. They heard the voice of the same policeman they'd met earlier. He was shouting through a loudspeaker, 'Hey Patel, are you there? We'd like to have a word with you.'

Tapan froze like stunned prey, but Nilufar nudged him on. Crawling they moved behind the pub on the bank; through the smell of beer in the air. Now they couldn't see the boat but seemed that it had just moored. Perhaps the chase had begun, but they were already on the stairs that led away from the river. They looked down and saw some figures approaching with a torch, but they were too far away to hear what the figures were saying. Not looking back, they broke into a run, and only after turning a bend in the road did they settle for a brisk walk. It took a few more streets before they could ease down to their normal pace. Then Tapan rolled a cigarette. As soon as he lit it, Nilufar wanted a puff. He handed it to her and rolled another.

As they approached Stepney Green station, a car came to halt at a curve, some fifty metres away. Someone got out of the car, but in the mist it wasn't easy to see who it was. But Tapan picked up the familiar perfume. Yes, it was Poltu Khan. They hid behind the station and kept their eyes on him. Nilufar said, 'I think he's trailing you.'

'I know, but I don't understand what he's waiting for. Why hasn't he given me away already?'

'Maybe he doesn't know exactly where you are. Or perhaps he has some other plan for you.'

'He knows. I'm sure of that, Nilu. But I can't work out his motives.'

'A scum like him is after only one thing.'

'What's that?'

'Profit.'

'Maybe, but look at him, Nilu.'

Now Nilufar turned her gaze more intently on Poltu Khan. He was moving between opaque stretches of mist and patches of light. Nilufar almost bit her lips as she noticed the way he moved and the frame of his body. He and Tapan looked so alike. Besides, he appeared so lost that Nilufar didn't know what to make of it. Why was he following Tapan so obsessively?

'What do you see, Nilu?'

'Just a scumbag.'

Poltu Khan drove off and they crossed the road.

When they approached the tower block, Tapan was still walking briskly to get to his flat, but Nilufar stopped him. She wanted to wait and observe for a while. They went into a telephone box at an angle to the front of the flat and pretended to make a call, their ears alert so that nothing would escape them. Minutes went by, but Nilufar still wasn't sure. He, though, whispered softly that it was safe to go in. When Nilufar asked him how he knew, Tapan said, 'I don't know, Nilu, but I can see things with my ears. People are deep in their sleep now. Hardly any movement except someone turning in her bed. No one is at our door.'

Nilufar looked at him with amazement. Regaining her composure she nearly asked him how he knew that it was a she who was turning in her bed, but stopped because she sensed what was happening. She touched him and found the same smooth, naked skin that humans wear, the same old face with his usual high cheekbones and the stubble – jaws flat as any speaker of words – but she could feel that he had changed. Somewhere from beneath the surface of his skin, using his body as a camouflage, a mole was already beginning to feel its way around its territory.

It was early morning when they finally got back into the flat.

Nilufar unpacked the box in which she had collected the few possessions that Tapan had left behind at the Isle of Dogs, and arranged them so they looked as though they had always belonged there. Tapan was leaning against the door and looking curiously at Nilufar, who was then placing his old typewriter on the table. Just behind the table was the window, covered with a musty but rich damask curtain. It looked so out of place in this very modest council flat that Tapan was beginning to wonder about its origin.

Perhaps the tenant of the flat had worked for one of the posh hotels in the city – as many Bengalis did after jumping ship at Tilbury – and the curtain was one of its discards. Perhaps the tenant was highly ambitious; he had set up a restaurant of his own, and the curtain ended up in his flat when the venture collapsed.

Suddenly a sharp click interrupted his thoughts. Nilufar had punched a key on the typewriter and turned sideways to cast a glance at him out of the corner of her left eye. What precisely she wanted to express he wasn't sure, but her desire for a kiss was unmistakable. He approached her, held her hand and gave her a kiss. She responded likewise, but didn't linger long, because there was still much to do. She went to the kitchen to give the cooker a quick clean. He toyed with the typewriter that he hadn't touched since he'd finished his university studies. For a moment the idea of writing flashed through his mind: how amazing it would be to feel the faltering rhythm of his fingers again as they criss-crossed the keyboard to capture the loops of his thoughts. Who knows, perhaps he might even experience one of those rare moments when his fingers didn't trail behind his thoughts like a camera obscura chasing a ghost in the dark. No, then his fingers would be free to copulate with the cold metal of the keyboard, giving birth to his thoughts in well-formed patterns. He should let his fingers play and play with the metal, and let himself slide through the body of words. Once on the other side of words, he could easily fly like the good Count and touch the pulse of the earth like a Bushman.

If Nilufar had known what he was thinking, she would have given him a bewildered look, then puckered her lips with biting irony. All the writing he'd be doing would be odd scribbles for that damn Doctor. No doubt the Doctor would ask him to write a load of crap: sound moral advice for the youth and a positive image of the community for the English. Who knows, perhaps the bugger had political ambitions. Now that he had made his dosh, he'd want to build himself up as a philanthropic type. Perhaps he even fancied himself as the first Paki mayor, riding in the black limo and sporting the heavy metal of his office around his neck.

Hearing Nilufar enter the room Tapan swallowed his thoughts and turned to face her. She was on her way to the bedroom, but paused to say that she'd had to throw away his mattress, quilt and pillow covers because they were too worn and filthy. She produced a new, deep-blue cotton set which was still wrapped in cellophane. Since she hadn't bothered to explain where it came from, he took it to be her present. He went over to give her another kiss.

'I hope you like the colour,' she said. She tore off the cellophane and the smell of new cotton somewhat lifted the mustiness of the room. Each holding a corner of the sheet, they began to make the bed together.

Suddenly, he felt what he'd been feeling at Limehouse Marina earlier in the night. He put the light off. 'Why? You don't want to see my skin?' asked Nilufar. He didn't say anything, but lightly touched her face with his palm.

He never told her so, but her presence always made him feel safe; he could wander at his ease in a familiar landscape, among the shrubs and plants that he had tended. Now it wasn't this Nilufar that he wanted, but the Nilufar of the eyes so dark it looked as if the light came to die there. How often, between serious discussions, and in the midst of the tension of the picket line had he caught himself casting a sly glance at her. Strangely, he couldn't remember what precisely he looked at. Perhaps like the light he became trapped in her eyes.

She had always been a bit shy and not very adventurous when it came to the rituals of sex, but she gave herself to him without any reserve. He pleased himself giving her pleasure. Afterwards there would be a smile on his face as he pulled the sheet over their naked bodies, and she tucked her head into his chest. The strangest thing was that he didn't feel awkward calling it love.

Perhaps it was a bit unusual for him to put off the light, because

131

he loved to see her face tensing up with pleasure, and her eyes suddenly releasing all that trapped light. But why hadn't he wanted to see her skin? Perhaps he wanted to protect his own eyes lest they betrayed his secret longing for Adela. But when Nilufar felt the palm of his hand on her face, she felt something she hadn't felt before.

So much is invested in the eyes, in the order of things in which a particular face, a particular pigment of the skin could make all the difference to whether you are loved or hated, or lived out your life as a master or a slave. Perhaps that's why he had darkened the room, so that the surface of the skin, on which so much had been written, wouldn't come between them. When she felt his palm on her face, she felt it going through her as if he were trying to touch some elusive substance inside her. Trembling, she grabbed his hand and broke into a sob and opened the porous membrane of her skin so wide that she almost enveloped him. Then he put his face between her breasts and turned sideways to press his left ear to listen to her. Her body spoke to him from inside, not the pumping of the heart and the lungs or the rumbles of the stomach, but the murmur of the great flow of the ocean that went between her veins, and together they became sound and wove the secret harmony that a mole weaves with the earth, or an eagle with a thermal.

He hadn't come to the end yet. Nor had she. Now that they were shedding their faces, the writing on their skins, they had to gather speed to go further. He could always rely on his nose to go off on its own and sniff out the deepest odour there was on earth, beneath it and above it. It was at such moments – when he switched off his little *cogito* – that he could see as Vatya Das saw between the jute fields in the night, or find his way like a mole in its burrow. At first he rubbed her lips with the tip of his nose. Between the strong odour of spices and herbs he could smell the muddy smell of fresh water fishes and the tubers that looked like turnips. But the strong smell of desire on her tongue was something else. Now she was beginning to burrow inside him. Sliding his nose down and up again on her breast he could smell the tang of sweat mingling with lavender. Everything was happening very fast now; she was becoming a nose and a smell like him. Finally down the valley, only pausing to circle the navel, he entered the forest and the wet ground underneath. There he danced like Nataraj around the circle of fire until light broke through the fold of the curtain.

Still in bed, and leaning against the headboard, he rolled a cigarette. Nilufar reached for her packet of Silk Cut from her handbag on the side of the bed. They smoked in silence, but he felt something was wrong.

Looking withdrawn, and blowing a dense cloud of smoke, Nilufar said, 'You were thinking of Adela. Weren't you?'

He rustled in the bed, dragged quickly on his cigarette, puckered his lips, but didn't say anything.

'Weren't you?'

'I don't have to answer this.'

'Why? Because you're afraid of the truth?'

'Listen. I don't ask you about Walter. Do I?'

'But I don't think of Walter when we make love.'

'I told you, Adela's past history. It's you I care about now.'

'Don't try to change the subject, Tapan.'

'Would you give that jealousy thing a rest. So what if I was thinking of Adela?'

'I see. So, you don't deny it.'

'Look. I care about you – and you know that. So give it a rest, please.'

'So, what are you saying? I've to share you with Adela?'

'You know I'm not saying that. You're just jealous, Nilu.'

'Don't give me that bullshit. You can have your bloody memsahib. What do I care?'

Nilufar got dressed and stormed out of the flat. He stayed in the bed, smoked cigarettes and chewed paan until well past midday.

CHAPTER 12

From Tapan's shelter in Limehouse, Nilufar took the long stretch of Commercial Road. It was a cold and murky morning. She was already regretting the row, and the way she'd walked out on him. Now she told herself that it was only natural that he should still have some feelings for Adela. Hadn't she felt that way about Walter? She wondered what would have happened if Walter hadn't gone back to South Africa. What, indeed, her parents, her relatives, and her community would have made of it if she had brought that tall African man home. She had stopped thinking of Walter since she met Tapan. Couldn't Tapan do the same – especially when they made love?

She couldn't quite admit to herself that she was jealous, but Adela bothered her. However, she was even more worried about the way Tapan had been acting lately: his strange intuitions and wild ideas. He seemed to be going off somewhere she couldn't follow. She was afraid that if he continued like this he might loose all bearings and end up doing something really crazy. She felt guilty for encouraging him to go illegal, because she wanted to cling onto him. At times, she even got carried away imagining them having a place of their own and growing old together. Always together.

For his sake, it would be better if he went back to Bangladesh. Of course, she would miss him, remember him in the way she remembered Walter, but she would learn to live with it.

Suddenly she felt as if she was lost among the dunes of the Sahara without a drop of water. Not even a tiny patch of moisture trapped in her handkerchief. All she wanted now was to drown herself in the music of her mother.

Near Watney Market someone approached her. She took a while to get her bearings and acknowledge Brother Josef K. She was surprised by Brother Josef K's boldness. He usually slunk away, head down, and never said *hello* to her. In fact, Josef was the quietest man she knew. One really had to open one's ears like a prairie dog to hear him.

He'd been there from the beginning at the barricades that summer when the battle of Brick Lane raged, but he never joined in with the slogans. Yet, suddenly he would shout out so loudly that even the skinheads would be stunned. *You bastards!* No one knew much about him except that he was a Jew who lived alone in Hessel Street, and that he had a shop where he repaired watches, radios and gramophones. During the early days of the barricade, people often asked him: Josef what? He just shrugged his shoulders, or rubbed his enormous head fringed with white curls, but didn't answer. If pressed hard he gave a nervous smile, as if apologising for his memory loss. So people started to call him Brother Josef X until some smart aleck re-named him Brother Josef K. The name stuck because Josef gave such a broad smile on hearing it that everyone assumed he approved of it.

Now Brother Josef K asked, 'What's happened to Brother Tapan Ali?'

Nilufar stayed silent for a long time, then said, 'Well.'

'You don't have to say anything. I understand,' said Josef.

'It's been ages. How you keeping?'

'Fine. If you see Brother Tapan Ali tell him that I'm thinking of him,' said Josef.

And head down, Brother Josef K hurried along and disappeared among the crowd of the market. Nilufar was desperate for a cigarette, but she couldn't risk smoking in the street, so she went into an English cafe that served the market traders. She sat in a corner, away from the window. She ordered a tea and looked warily around to see if there were any Bangladeshi customers in the cafe. Finding none, she lit a cigarette.

From the market Nilufar bought a toy fire-engine for Chumki, and resumed her walk along Commercial Road. Soon she came face to face with Haji Falu Mia, her uncle – her mother's sister's husband – and Sundar's father. Although he conducted himself with his usual dignity, his head high, his posture erect, he looked rather frail. Nilufar lowered her eyes and gave him a salaam.

'My niece. How's she doing? How come you don't come to see your old uncle?'

'I've been a bit busy, uncle.'

'Oh, Allah, what's the world coming to! You young people have no time for us elders any more.'

'It's not true, uncle.'

'Listen my niece. You know you're breaking your father's and mother's hearts.'

Nilufar kept her head down, twirled her hair, but didn't say anything.

'Oh, Allah, your mother crying so much. And your father. I thought I'd never see a man fall so low. He locks himself up at home for the shame of it. He doesn't even come to the mosque.'

'I know, uncle. But what can I do?'

'Just go back home. Young woman like you living on her own is not right. And listen to your father a bit.'

Nilufar shrugged her shoulders, and was about to make her goodbye salaam, when Haji Falu Mia asked:

'Have you seen our Tapan Ali, lately?'

'No.'

'He doesn't come to see me any more. I wonder where he's disappeared to.'

'I don't know, uncle.'

'He's a crazy fellow. But, you know, I miss him. He was very fond of stories from olden days. He made me tell so many old stories. If you see him, tell him I'm looking for him. I've a few more stories to tell.'

'If I see him, I will uncle,' said Nilufar.

Shapna was pleased to see Nilufar early. She wasn't expecting her until late afternoon. Nilufar gave Chumki her present and she ran to the sitting room to try it out. Nilufar followed her. She was surprised to see Uncle Halim in the sitting room.

'Oh, my niece. I haven't seen you for ages. Oh, Allah, how thin you have become.'

'How is auntie?' asked Nilufar.

'She's fine. But I'm more worried about your father and mother.'

'They are fine, aren't they?'

'How can they be fine? First you left home, then your brother Kaisar. Everywhere I go I hear bad things about Kaisar. Your mother is worried sick about him.'

'What's happened to Kaisar?'

'I don't know. Your mother was crying so much. So I said I'd look around for him. I've been going everywhere this morning looking for him, but nobody has seen him. All they tell me is the bad things he is doing.'

'I'm also worried about him, Uncle. I haven't seen him lately either,' said Nilufar.

'You, my niece, you look after everyone in the world except your own family. It's a very funny business, na?'

Nilufar didn't say anything; she was looking at Chumki making hooting noises and sliding the fire-engine across the floor.

Uncle Halim got up saying that he needed to check a few more places for Kaisar. At the door, he turned around to say, 'I've been thinking a bit lately, you know. Kaisar's generation has different memories than your father's and mine. Na?'

'I suppose so,' said Nilufar.

'You see, we came because there wasn't much to eat back home. So we go mad seeing so much meat in England. We behave like skinny dogs whaw-whawing for a piece. If they give us a little leftover, we wag our tails for days. We go around saying: "Aren't we lucky. So lucky to eat meat." And if we have a few bobs, we eat so much meat that we pop our hearts before we are thirty. Accha, you understand what I'm saying?'

'You shouldn't be so hard on your generation, Uncle,' said Nilufar.

'I'm just telling the truth, na? But these fellows like Kaisar, who are born here in England, are a different lot. They want everything that English fellows have. They go mighty mad with just leftovers. I tell you, they are no immigrants, they are wholly different types. Na?'

When Uncle Halim left, Shapna told Nilufar that she was

more worried than ever about Kaisar. Nilufar agreed that they must do something about him before it was too late. As she prepared food in the kitchen, Shapna told Nilufar that their father was leaving for Bangladesh in few days time.

'We're also moving?'

'Where?'

'Bromley. Shahid is buying a big house there.'

'That's nice.'

'I'm not sure about it. Anyway, Appa, what are you going to do?'

Nilufar was searching her mind for something to say, when the bell rang. 'It must be Amma,' said Shapna as she went to open the door.

Hasina Bibi came in with containers full of fried carp and duck curry. As soon as she saw Nilufar, she said, 'Oh, Allah. My firstborn, look at you. You're getting so thin and dark. You, my daughter, you look after everyone in the world but who looks after you.'

'Don't worry, Amma. I'm fine.'

'You know, your father is going to Bangladesh for a while.'

'Why, Amma?'

'What can I say, my daughter. All he does is stay in his room all day and smoke. He doesn't talk to me, not even to your Uncle Halim. Such a stubborn fool he is, full of shame. What to do with him? So we are sending him back to Bangladesh for a while. I hope he comes back with his head corrected.'

'Has he seen a doctor?' asked Nilufar.

'He needs no doctor. He just needs his foolishness sorted,' said Hasina Bibi. 'Anyway, my daughter, come home everyday while your father is away. I'll cook something good to eat. Accha?'

After that Hasina Bibi wailed over Kaisar. Then she put Chumki on her lap and said, 'You have the face of the full moon, my grandchild. A king will marry you when you grow up.' Nilufar smiled, Shapna looked away.

Chumki looked tired and she was beginning to whinge. Shapna hurriedly brought a plate of rice for her with dhal and pieces of chicken. Hasina Bibi made the rice into little balls and tried to feed Chumki. But Chumki refused to eat. So, what to do?

Her grandmother began to sing the epic story of the Brothers Falconers in a monotonous rhythm with nasal intonation. Chumki opened her mouth and began to gobble the balls of rice like a duck. Both Shapna and Nilufar came to sit by their mother.

'Thanks to the storytellers, who told the stories like their fathers on monsoon nights, who in turn also told the stories like their fathers on monsoon nights, and so on from the time we began to live on this plain by the river. Now I tell the stories of the Brothers Falconers, like my mother did at dusk, who in turn also told the stories like her mother at dusk. Now I, Hasina Bibi, tell it to my grandchild, to the face of the full moon, under a bright electric light in a tall house in London town.

'Forgive me, the storytellers, for telling the story in London town. Salaam to you for granting me the right to tell it to my grandchild. So, the story of the two Brothers Falconers. Once upon a time, in the dust of the dry season. All night dreaming; they don't wait for the cocks to crow. For the falcon wakes them up with the full moon still in the sky. Brother Big is a singer and Brother Small is a dancer. First Brother Big sings sweet to the falcon, then Brother Small dances around the falcon, who's sitting like a monk. They sing and dance until the falcon flaps his wings.

'Hunt the hunt, the falcon will hunt. Brothers Falconers, giblets and livers they give to the falcon. Flowers they throw on the courtyard and the conch they blow as they prepare to go. People turn in their beds. Oh the Brothers Falconers, good hunt they will hunt. And we are going to eat waterfowls more than before.

'Brother Big takes the falcon on his shoulder and walks into the dew, Brother Small following behind. How am I, Hasina Bibi, to tell the tales of the Brothers Falconers in London town? Brothers Falconers walk the plain, paddies and grass; mustard a lot, but yellow they do not see. Fog of the dawn too thick; grasshoppers jump on their feet. Thank you storytellers, thank you for granting me the right to tell the story. To whom else, but to my grandchild, to my full moon, Chumki Bibi.

'Sand dunes of the big river, far far until the sky dips into the trees. Waterfowls they will hunt, falcon swooping down on them from the sky. At sunrise, they see the yellow; the sun hangs in the middle. Still they walk. Brother Small takes the falcon but he screams. Brother Big takes him back on his shoulder, crossing a small river on a bamboo bridge.

'Sun dips to the west; they look for a place for the eating of the day. Find they find a cotton tree not far from the path where were their feet. Red flowers look at the blue; they find a shade cool as the pool. Sorry, the storytellers, sorry the mothers, for not telling the story as it was told before. I have to tell it to my full moon, to Chumki Bibi in London town. Before they sit, they let the falcon go to fly his fly and hunt his food.

'Rice bread and molasses they eat, red petals falling from the tree. Storytellers, storytellers, grant it to my grandchild. Chumki Bibi her name, a full moon in London town. Grant that one day she is a storyteller. Brother Falconers lie in the breeze, Brother Big singing soft, Brother Small falling asleep.

'Falcon flying and swooping, screaming and ripping the sky and creating havoc among the parrots. At first Brother Small thinks he is dreaming, full of bad spirits and things. Falcon flapping its wings on his face wakes him to the parrots greening the sky. Brother Big doesn't get up, sleeps full of blue and cold. Brother Small shakes him, shakes the way he shakes a lychee tree, but he doesn't open his eyelids. Oh he slept on the hole of the black snake, oh he bit him blue. Brother Small wails for Brother Big, dead as a wood. Dead as a wood, covered in the red petals of the cotton tree. But what Brother Small could do? Waiting, sun going down, then a man comes in a bullock cart full of sugar cane. He takes pity on Brother Small, lays Brother Big among his sugar cane. By night he takes him to the old snake man by the riverbank. Snake man shakes his head, nothing could he do. Brother Big was as dead as a wood. So sadness, sadness, never sadder than this. One dead so young, handsome as a prince. Bless my grandchild, Chumki Bibi, bless that she grows old as old as the old witch. Forgive me, the storytellers, forgive Hasina Bibi, telling the tales in London town.

'Hearing the howling of Brother Small, snake man takes pity. He walks around scratching his head. One thing he can do is to take him to the queen of snakes down below in the kingdom of snakes. He sprinkles magic water on the falcon to make him see the way to the kingdom of snakes. To Brother Small he gives an amulet to save him from the dangers of the way.

'Late into the night Brother Small makes a raft of banana logs. He puts Brother Big on it, wrapped in a maroon shawl, and sets sail with the falcon flying above. Falcon guides the raft until a whirlpool takes them down, down to the gates of a strange city. From the mist rise two black snakes high as the sky, their hoods large enough to shade a city. Oh, they coil at Brother Small. Fangs they open to strike him, but the amulet stops them. To the queen they take him.

'Brother Small begs the queen for the life of Brother Big. She is bored, her eyes almost closing; she hisses softly and poison from her fangs drips on a golden goblet. An ancient snake, counsellor to the queen, whispers: Drink from the goblet and please the queen. The queen snake, the mighty power of the unseen, she can give back the life, as she took it. Dipping the amulet into the goblet, Brother Small drinks a large swig. Sweet as nectar it tastes, light as a feather he feels.

'Suddenly he taps his feet, ringing his anklets like drops of rain. From her coil on the coral throne, the queen opens her eyes on the marble floor. First to the right, then to the left, tac tac tata dum, sare gama pada nicha, he dances. He dances and dances, circles the throne, legs bent, thumping the floor. With hands and the body and the face and the eyes he dances. Still on her throne, the queen uncoils to stand on her tail, she spreads her hood as wide as the ceiling and sways her head. Like a spinning top Brother Small dances, his anklets breathless as the wind, feet bleeding on the floor. Sliding from the throne, the snake queen takes the floor. She dances, all the snakes dance, right through the night they dance.'

Her grandmother was getting into the rhythm to conclude the story, but she stopped as she realised that Chumki had fallen asleep. Nilufar and Shapna looked disappointed; they wished their mother had ended the story. In their childhood their mother had often told them the story of the Brothers Falconers, but they hadn't heard it for a long time. They felt like small girls again listening to their mother.

Shapna took Chumki to bed. Afterwards, when Nilufar and Shapna were in the kitchen warming the food, the telephone rang. Shapna went running to answer it. It was Uncle Halim. He had found Kaisar in the local hospital; he had been admitted with a stab wound. Shapna didn't say anything in front of her mother. She went to the kitchen to whisper the news to Nilufar.

Nilufar put on her coat to leave for the hospital. Her mother sensed that something was wrong and asked, 'Where are you going, my daughter, without eating?'

Nilufar told her that something urgent regarding her school had come up; she had to leave immediately. Her mother looked at her quizzically.

CHAPTER 13

Tapan could not stop his mind from going over the previous day's events. He and Nilufar were so close together and they made love so beautifully. So, why was he thinking of Adela? He should have known that women had their ways of knowing these things. Yes, he could understand why Nilufar had felt so jealous of Adela and why she had stormed out. How could he convince Nilufar that it was her, only her that he wanted now.

In the late afternoon he heard the bell ring. He wasn't expecting anyone. It was in the evening he'd arranged with Sundar to go and see Dr. Karamat Ali. Besides, the way the bell rang didn't sound familiar. Who could be at the door? Had Poltu Khan finally decided that his time was up? Was it an immigration officer with police back-up coming to take him away?

He trembled like a mole at the approaching tremor of an enemy at the entrance to its tunnel. He flared his nose, took in quick breaths with it, but couldn't tell who was at the door. This time, his nose failed him. He waited but the bell wouldn't stop; then he heard banging on the door. Why were they so insistent? It seemed as if they wouldn't hesitate to break open the door. What could he do? He crawled to the kitchen to see if he could get away through the window. Perhaps there was a pipe he could use to climb down. No such luck. He sat on the chair in the kitchen facing the table. As the banging continued, he kept jerking his head, as if at a certain rhythm and momentum he would discover the power of the mole and burrow his way down through the building, down into sewers beneath. For a while he didn't realise that the banging had stopped.

He stayed still for a while before getting up. He tiptoed to the front door and carefully placed his right ear against it. All he could hear was the faint cry of a baby in the distance. He paused before the stained mirror in the corridor. He was surprised to see himself in his hunched up posture. Why was he walking like an illegal immigrant even when he was alone? Was he hiding from himself, from his own ignoble self? He straightened up, corrected his posture, but it felt so uncomfortable, so unnatural. What else could he do but walk hunched up, past the stained mirror into that other, infinite and translucent mirror mimicking his every gesture? Look, Madam/Sir, there goes an illegal immigrant.

He rolled a cigarette, made a paan cone with tobacco leaves. He took a few quick drags, then, chewing the paan, as always he calmed down. He thought of cooking something nice for Sundar. All he found in the kitchen was some dry fish, muli and green beans. He wasn't sure whether it would be a good idea to cook dry fish in this block. The smell might be too much for the neighbours. While he was dithering about what to do, the bell rang again. This time it sounded familiar. Since he wasn't expecting Sundar until early evening, he thought it was Nilufar.

Sundar was at the door. 'I had a meeting cancelled. So I came early, Bhaio,' he said. 'I thought we could sit down for a good gossip time. You know, for some old adda.'

'That would be nice, Sundar.'

While making a tea for Sundar he asked, 'Would people complain if I cooked dry fish, Sundar?'

'What do you mean, Bhaio?'

'Would the English people mind?'

'Of course, they'd mind, Bhaio. They'd say: Oh no, the curse of "Great-Stink" is on us again.'

'So I shouldn't cook dry fish, then.'

'Don't be silly, Bhaio. Of course, you should cook dry fish. Who cares who minds. The "Great-Stink" is here to stay.'

'But I don't want to upset anyone, Sundar.'

'Listen, Bhaio. Very few English people are left around here.

Most of them fled to Essex. And those who remain are well used to dry fish.'

'So, it's okay, then?'

'Bhaio, I told you that you're entering our city. It's not just fancy talk, you know.'

Between small talk, smoking cigarettes and chewing paan, Tapan cooked the dry fish.

'We've sorted that bloody rat, Bhaio,' said Sundar.

'What do you mean, Sundar?'

'Well. Poltu Khan was asking for it, wasn't he?'

'You didn't kill him?'

'I wish we had killed that bloody rat. But unfortunately no. Only a few cuts and bruises. And a few teeth,' said Sundar.

'Was it wise, Sundar? Besides, he's not the only informer around here.'

'Yeah, Bhaio, you're right. There are worse types than him. But it will send them a message.'

'Did he say anything, Sundar?'

'Well. He kept on saying that we got it wrong. Apparently some other informers were trying to give away one of his friends. So, he said, he was hanging around. You know, around places like the Isle of Dogs and Limehouse to protect his friend.'

'Did you believe him, Sundar?'

'Don't be silly, Bhaio. Of course, we didn't believe him. When he said that, Masuk Ali gave his face a bloody kick. I think it was then that he lost some of his teeth.'

'I wonder why he would say something like that.'

'He's a stupid rat – that's why. It was really ridiculous, Bhaio. When we got through to him he actually admitted that he had been snooping around for the Immigration. He even admitted that he led the Immigration to some unfortunate illegals in the Isle of Dogs and Limehouse. He said he had to do it to create a diversion to protect his friend. But the funny thing was...' Sundar stopped abruptly.

'What, Sundar?'

'It's too ridiculous, Bhaio. He said the friend was you. Yeah, he said he was protecting you.'

'Do you believe him, Sundar?'

'Of course, not. That bloody rat would say anything to protect his skin.'

They ate the dry fish curry in the evening. Sundar said he loved it. Afterwards they had tea, smoked cigarettes and chewed paan.

'How is your father?' asked Tapan.

'He looks alright to me. But the old goat thinks he's going to die soon.'

'I'm sorry that I haven't been to see him lately. He used to tell me stories from the olden days.'

'He never tells me any story. All he does is pester me to take his dead body to Bangladesh when he dies. Anyway, he's been asking about you a lot, Bhaio. I suppose he gets lonely.'

Tapan was about to ask Sundar whether he would take him to see his father, but Sundar had changed the subject.

'Oh, yeah. I've forgotten to tell you. Nilufar had some bad news about Kaisar.'

'What's happened?'

'Well, you know. He's into drugs and street crimes. Now he's ended up in hospital with a knife wound.'

'Is it bad?

'No. It's not that serious, but he needs looking after. So, when he's released from hospital Nilufar is taking him to her place.'

'I didn't know any of it.'

'Don't worry about it, Bhaio. You know what Nilufar's like. She feels responsible for everyone, wants to save everyone. She blames herself for what happened to Kaisar. So, she set her mind to look after him.'

'I see.'

'Listen, Bhaio. I know you and Nilufar get on well together. So, why don't you marry her?'

'I can't Sundar. You know Adela.'

'I thought you and Adela are finished.'

'Yes, we are. But the thing is we're still technically married.'

'That's a bloody mess, Bhaio. So, what are you going to do?'

'Obviously in my present situation I can't initiate divorce proceedings myself.'

'Listen. Go and see Adela. Ask her to divorce you. Then we'll take it from there.'

'I'll think about it, Sundar.'

'Don't think, Bhaio. Do it immediately. You see, if you marry Nilufar it solves all the problem.'

'What do you mean, Sundar?'

'Simple really. You know that Nilufar is a full British citizen. So, by marrying her you solve your immigration problem. And Nilufar gets the chance of patching things up with her father.'

'You know, I'd do anything for Nilu. But I've been through that route before with Adela. As you know, it didn't work. In fact, it was a disaster. Besides, the Home Office wouldn't believe me the second time round.'

'I admit it would be difficult to convince the Home Office that it's genuine this time. But this is the only option, Bhaio. For your sake and for Nilufar's sake. So, get your act together, Bhaio.'

They still had some time to kill before leaving to see Dr. Karamat Ali, so they had one more round of tea, cigarettes and paan. Turning sombre, Sundar said he had dreamt about his mother the night before. He was going to visit the cemetery tomorrow; he would tend her grave, clear it of weeds and offer his prayers.

Tapan had never heard Sundar mention his mother before, and when he asked Sundar to tell him about her, he said it was a long story. Staying silent for a while, as if he was trying to remember his own mother, whom he had never seen except in dreams, Tapan said, 'I don't mind how long it is, Sundar. I'd love to hear about your mother.' Sundar dragged on his cigarette, shook his head, then he began telling his mother's story.

'My mother's folks were peasants, Bhaio. Poor sharecroppers. They grew jute and indigo for the British. As you know, Bhaio, they stopped growing indigo after the big rebellion. But their lives didn't change much after partition. I don't know much about her ancestors. Peasants do not have that kind of memory. You see, Bhaio, they had nothing – no land, no money, no title to leave behind. Perhaps only a cow or a plough. Even the ground on which they built their huts didn't belong to them. So they didn't need that kind of memory.

'Only the landlords could trace their ancestry, Bhaio. Well-to-do farmers who had their own lands – like my father's family –

had some memories of their bloodlines. All my mother's folks knew was that they had always been sharecroppers and lived at the bend of the river. This is, of course, not to say that they didn't have memories. Often they sang of the days when they fought the British and the landlords against the three-quarter sharecropping system. They remember floods, droughts, hurricanes, and the famine during the war. Of her personal life, Bhaio, I don't know much. All I know was that she got married to my father when she was sixteen. My aunty said that she was a pretty one, that she was good at finding wild roots during the famine time, and that she didn't cry – as was the custom – on her marriage day. I don't know her proper name, perhaps she didn't have one. In the village she was simply known as Falu Mia, the Londonee's wife.

'Anyway, Bhaio. It was in the early 50s – my father then well over forty, living in England since 1937– that he came to marry my mother. My mother didn't talk about these things, but my aunty said that everybody knew that he had a white wife in England. No one, though, made any fuss about it. He lived in England for fifteen years. He came back as a sahib, wearing suit, and plenty of money to splash around. He bought the landlord's property and his big house. Bhaio, he came back as a big man. My mother's folks felt privileged that he wanted to marry one of their daughters. Of course, my mother didn't talk to me about any of these things, Bhaio.

'You know my father, Bhaio, he ain't much of a talking man either. I don't know what you got in you, Bhaio, he seems to talk to you. Anyway, my aunty told me that he saw my mother husking rice for the landlord when he went to buy his property. Apparently, he said something in English but no one understood him. He married my mother within weeks. It is said that he had forty goats slaughtered and invited the whole village for the occasion. Afterwards he stayed in the village for six months or so. When I was born he was already back in England and he never went back to Bangladesh again.

'I was born in 1953, Bhaio. I only saw my father when I came to England with my mother in 1975. People say many things about why he didn't go back to Bangladesh again. So many stories, Bhaio. But my aunty tells me that he was found out.

'Oh, the shame of it, Bhaio. One afternoon my father was sitting on the veranda of the landlord's house that he had bought. He was entertaining the village elders with his exploits in England. There were sighs of admiration and expressions of wonder. Then the schoolteacher brought him an English newspaper. He found out that my father was not only incapable of reading any English but he was a complete illiterate. The shame of it, Bhaio. But worse was to come. No one knew for sure how it was found out. My aunty says it was the landlord who used his channels in London. Anyway, they found out that he washed whiteman's dirty plates and married a very low-down whitewoman. He left in the middle of the night and never returned.

'As you know, Bhaio, these days he always makes me promise that I will take his body back to Bangladesh when he dies. What's got into the head of the old fool, I don't understand. We buried our mother here. You see the funny tricks of destiny, Bhaio? Anyway, the old man cried his heart out when my mother died. I don't know why – he hardly knew her. Ammajan – that's how I used to call my mother – died within two years of coming to England. She was barely forty, Bhaio. But the old goat seems to live on and on. When he brought us here, my mother and me, he put us up in a different house. He still lived with his white wife. Her name was Sally or something. We didn't see him much. Ammajan didn't like England much. She didn't like the landlord's house either where she and I lived all those years. Don't get me wrong, Bhaio, the old fool ain't a bad man. He sent my mother and me money every month. But my mother lived like any other peasant woman, husking rice, milking cows, making dung fuel for cooking and things like that. Ask Aunty – she knows more. You know Nilufar's mother, don't you? I'm sorry that you haven't met her. Such a nice woman. She and my mother are sisters, you know.

'When Uncle Surat Mia – that's Nilufar's father – such a sad person, Bhaio – if you marry Nilufar, it will make him happy – anyway, when Uncle Surat Mia was going to Bangladesh to get himself a wife, my father recommended my mother's sister. Like most Bangladeshis of his generation he harboured the idea of returning to Bangladesh. Like a big shot, you know. But Uncle

Surat Ali is a wise man. As soon as he realized that it wasn't going to happen, he brought his family over. Unlike some people, he didn't have a white woman on the side. What else can I say about my mother, Bhaio? She died like most peasant women do. Leaving behind not many memories. But she was all I had. I can't say much about my father. I hardly know him. Perhaps, you know more about him than I do. At least he talks to you, tells you his stories. Perhaps one day you could tell me things about him, Bhaio.'

It was time to go out to see Dr. Karamat Ali. In the car Sundar told Tapan that the Doctor was calling his newspaper *The Good News*. It would be a weekly newspaper with the Doctor serving as editor, reporter and designer. He would also be in charge of sales, publicity and distribution.

'It'll be a scissors job mainly, Bhaio,' said Sundar laughing. 'Cut and paste.'

'So, what do I do?'

'Well. The Doctor fancies himself writing editorials in good English. But he can't write any English. Here you come in. He would jot down his thoughts in Bengali – which he writes poorly. Your job is to arrange them properly and translate them into English. You would do the same if he decides to play the reporter on community matters. Apart from these, he might ask you to write columns on special interests.'

Tapan wasn't really listening because he was trying to see his old haunts through the dark night – made worse by the fog. Tapan felt unusually light. He wasn't hunching, but walking tall and erect, as he had seen Sundar's father – Haji Falu Mia – walk. Before they knocked at the door, Sundar cautioned Tapan that the Doctor wasn't much of a listening man. He was more like a runaway train when it came to talking.

'The bloody Doctor will talk himself into a silly parrot. We just have to bear it, Bhaio,' said Sundar.

The Doctor was waiting for them in the sitting room; the table was laden with Bombay mix, rushgulla, jilapi and halvah in fine porcelain dishes.

'Come, come, Mr. Tapan. I'm much honoured to have such a learned person as yourself in my humble abode,' said the Doctor, all excited.

'Some mighty fine display of this and that goodies you got here, Doctor Sahib. You shouldn't have gone to such great expenses on our account. It must have been a great drain on your finances,' said Sundar, winking at Tapan on the sly. 'What have we done to deserve such generosity, Doctor Sahib?'

'Na. Don't mention it, Sundar Mia. I'm not deserving of such high compliments. I say expenses. You see, Sundar Mia, my philosophy is that one mustn't hesitate to incur expenses. Certainly where expenses are deserved.'

'We really appreciate your generosity, Doctor Sahib.'

'You've brought to my abode a learned person, Sundar Mia. A BA from an English university. Very high class, Mr. Tapan. Very good, very good. Not many people appreciate a learned person these days. But I'm an oldfashion type. I esteem learning more than anything else in the world. You see, I'm a man of science myself.'

'Your science has served us well, Doctor Sahib. We're much honoured to be in your presence,' said Sundar.

'Don't mention it, Sundar Mia. The honour is mine. Have some refreshment, gentlemen, before we converse further.'

'Some mighty fine sweets you've here, Doctor Sahib. I must compliment you on your fine selection,' said Sundar.

'Excellent. Excellent. Help yourself, Mr. Tapan. Eat exceedingly well.'

'Where did you get these sweets from, Doctor Sahib?'

'Ah, Sundar Mia, glad that you've asked. I went to see the chef at Ambala myself. You see, he and his wife are my patients.'

'Do you remember treating me when I fainted? I never got to thank you for it. It was really kind of you, Doctor Ali.'

'Don't mention it, Mr. Tapan. It was an honour to treat a learned person such as yourself,' said the Doctor. 'Oh yes, I'd almost forgotten it, Mr. Tapan. Forgive me, please. You get my medical services free of charge as part of your contract, Mr. Tapan. What do you think of it?' said the Doctor.

'Very kind of you, Doctor Ali,' said Tapan.

'Don't mention it, Mr. Tapan. You see, I look after my employees,' said the Doctor. 'Sorry, sorry. What nonsense I talk. Please forgive me, Mr. Tapan. We will be more like collaborators and partners. Na, Mr. Tapan?'

For some reason the Doctor got up and left the sitting room.

While he was gone, Sundar said, 'If you humour the Doctor, Bhaio, it pleases him. He's a mean bugger, but foolishly vain.'

'He wasn't too bad, Sundar.'

'So far we're lucky that he hasn't gone off into one of his long-winded anecdotes. When he mentioned the chef at Ambala I thought, here we go again.'

The Doctor came back. 'Sorry, sorry. I never got to tell you about the chef at Ambala. Pardon my bad manners.'

'We don't mind, Doctor Sahib. Perhaps it could wait for another time.'

'I'm not going to hear of it, Sundar Mia. You've brought to my place a learned person, and I have to treat him right. As I was saying – I went to see the chef at Ambala.'

'Is he the one with the pretty young wife?' asked Sundar.

'More like a mad wife, if you want know the truth. Anyway, I went to see the chef and told him that I was having special guests. He said he'd prepare the sweets himself. Such a fine fellow, you know. I don't understand, Mr. Tapan, how come some people are so mean minded.'

'I don't follow you, Doctor Ali. Who do you mean?' asked Tapan.

'Some very uneducated types. You see, they think the chef fellow is a Hindu. For them all good mistywallas are Hindus. For God's sake, the man is a Haji. Very keen on jihad, you know. You should see him aroused to passion. He walks up and down with his sword, speaking nothing but Arabic. He makes his finest sweet then. But his wife gets worried. She calls me. I investigate him very properly, following the strict rigour of my scientific method. Then I prescribe something to eliminate his turbulence.'

'So, you cured his illness, then?'

'It's not that simple, Sundar Mia. It's a very tricky case, you know. Anyway, after my medication the fellow calms down so much that he sits down like a baby. His wife feeds him milk with a spoon. I'm sure you know these things, Mr. Tapan.'

'I've no idea what you're on about, Doctor Ali.'

'You are into writery thing, aren't you, Mr. Tapan?'

'Nothing serious, Doctor Ali.'

'It doesn't matter, Mr. Tapan. If you've dabbled into arty things, you'd know such turbulence.'

'I'm not sure about that, Doctor Ali,' said Tapan.

'Anyway, his wife gets upset when she sees him having the next jihad temperament. She calls to complain. Very unbalanced woman, you see. I tell the chef that it is not he, but his wife who is in need of my treatment. What to say, Mr. Tapan – a very sad case, very sad. The chef fellow practically wets his pants in fright before her. Such tamasha, Mr. Tapan, such tamasha. He doesn't dare to mention it to her.'

'Maybe he loves too much his pretty young wife, Doctor Sahib.'

'You don't know her, Sundar Mia. Such an unbalanced woman. Anyway, as I was saying, she calls me to complain. She says, "Doctor Sahib, what funny business. On top of your payment we give you the leftover sweets. I've even given you a full boal fish for present. The only thing I asked for is the elimination of the causes. Permanent extinction of his temperament. I can't have him chasing his kitchen staff with a sword. What shame, Doctor Sahib! The other day he nearly cut off one of his staff's ear with his sword. Poor boy, he cried so much. You promise me permanent elimination, Doctor Sahib, but every time it comes back. There he goes off on his next jihad. What am I to do, Doctor Sahib?" Such an unbalanced woman.'

'But if she calls a physician, you can't blame her if she expects a cure, can you, Doctor Sahib?' said Sundar.

'You don't understand such matters, Sundar Mia. It would be criminal to eliminate such temperament permanently. You understand these things, Mr. Tapan, don't you?'

'I'm not so sure, Doctor Ali.'

'Anyway, the thing is, his artistry, his genius for making fine sweets comes from such temperaments. You can say he's a poet among meestywallas. So I don't eliminate permanently his cause but merely manage it so that he can go on with his fine creation.'

'I can see the fine results, Doctor Sahib,' said Sundar tasting a meesty-sweet.

'Yes, yes. But what his wife does? Such an unbalanced woman!'

She calls the damn herbalists to apply their totally unscientific craft. You know, making magic portions out of weeds and stuff. Other day she even called the Bringer of Jinn. Such nonsense. Anyway, no one could do anything for him. You see, they don't understand the mysterious nature of artistic temperament. So she runs to me again.'

'You've done a fine job on him, Doctor Sahib. These meesty-sweets are top class.'

'Yes. Excellent, Sundar Mia, his sweets are excellent. But I wish I could offer you some home cooking. Nothing beats home cooking, right?'

'So, what's happened, Doctor Ali?' asked Tapan.

'You see, my wife-bibi was fed up with too much nakedness in England. She couldn't take all them young ladies parading themselves half-naked on television. She wouldn't go to parks in summer because she might see ladies exposing their bottoms to the sun.'

'You're a forward-looking man – aren't you, Doctor Sahib?' said Sundar.

'Yes, yes. I must admit I've been a bit partial to these things, but I've never betrayed my wife-bibi. You see, I only look at them ladies with my artistic eyes. You understand these things, Mr. Tapan, don't you?'

'I'm not so sure, Doctor Ali,' said Tapan.

'Anyway. One more thing. You see, my wife-bibi has been rather upset with my management style of our finances. Very unfortunate, very unfortunate. She left for her father's house in Bangladesh. Now I'm having to rely on my utterly bad cooking and takeaways from Miraj cafe. And I'm grateful to that kind chef at Ambala – he always passes on to me any leftover sweets for free.'

'So sorry to hear about it, Doctor Ali.'

'Thank you, Mr. Tapan.'

'So, what are you going to do now, Doctor Sahib?'.

'I'm not leaving any inheritance to my children. That's for sure. For all the hard labour I did for them, what do I get? They despise me, Sundar Mia, they despise me. Would you believe that they are actually ashamed of their own father. I blame the English climate for it. You know the soil sometimes does play tricks on your brain, especially if your organs are not suited for that soil. It's not some abal-tabal-nonsense talk, but a properly scientific idea, you know. Anyway, so I thought why not? From now on I will dedicate my life to public services. Why not? Only doing good.'

The Doctor was about to go on, but Sundar, seizing the opportunity of his slight pause, intervened.

'Yes, yes very fine sweets, Doctor Sahib, but let's talk about the paper. It's already very late. We need to get back soon.'

'Yes, certainly. Thanks, Sundar Mia, for bringing up the subject. Welcome to *The Good News*, Mr. Tapan. I hope the arrangements are to your satisfaction.'

'Thanks for offering me the job.'

'Don't mention it, Mr. Tapan. I like to do my bit for an educated man. You can completely rely on my discretion. No one will know your status. Your secrets are safe with me.'

'It's kind of you, Doctor Ali.'

'I hope Sundar Mia has filled you in about the details.'

'Yes.'

'For the first edition I want you to write a special column. You can write anything you like, Mr. Tapan. Stories with human interest. And why not? Topics containing high thoughts. You shouldn't be afraid of dealing with controversial matters. You see, I believe in complete press freedom.'

'I will do my best, Doctor Ali.'

'Good. Now we need to sort out the technicalities.'

'What are these, Doctor Ali? I don't follow you,' said Tapan.

'Obviously you can't use your own name, Mr. Tapan. We must take every care not to divulge your identity. So we need to invent a new name for you. What do you think, Mr. Tapan?'

'You're absolutely right, Doctor Ali.'

'Good. How about Ali's Diary?'

'It's not a new name, Doctor Sahib. Bhaio is called Ali and you're also called Ali,' said Sundar.

'You're absolutely right Sundar Mia. But here lies the beauty of the trick. They would be utterly confused. They wouldn't know which Ali is doing the writing.'

'I see one problem, though, Doctor Sahib.'

'What could that be, Sundar Mia?'

'Since you are the editor and called Ali, people might get confused. They might think you are the actual writer of the column. Do you see the problem, Doctor Sahib?'

'I don't see any problem, Sundar Mia. I say it's for the best.'

'I don't understand, Doctor Sahib.'

'It's very simple Sundar Mia. If people think that it is I who is the actual author of the column, then Mr. Tapan's identity will be all the more protected. Isn't it a class one move, Sundar Mia?'

Sundar shrugged his shoulders, but didn't say anything. But the Doctor hadn't finished yet.

'I'm sure, Mr. Tapan, you have your own writing method. But I was thinking that a first person approach would be the most suitable for the columns I have in mind. You know, columns containing high thoughts and written from the point of view of an elevated personage.'

'But why it has to be in the first person, Doctor Sahib?' asked Sundar.

'I'm only a man of science, but correct me if I'm wrong, Mr. Tapan. The first person approach engages the reader more – na? They feel that the story is coming from the intimate experience of the person. Don't get me wrong, Mr. Tapan, I don't want to interfere with your method of writing. But I take my editorial duty very seriously. Only after a long deliberation that I've decided that you write the column in the first person.'

'I don't really mind, Doctor Ali. I'll write whatever way you want me to.'

'Good. I know it will be good working with you, Mr. Tapan. A man of science and a man of letters working together. Ah, I'm already feeling good about my philanthropic activities.'

When Sundar and Tapan got up, the Doctor put three dirty ten pound notes into Tapan's hand. In the car Sundar laughed.

'You know what the bugger's trying to do, Bhaio?'

'I don't care about these things, Sundar.'

'I knew the bugger had some ulterior motives. But I never thought he would want to pass off your writing as his own. What can you do, Bhaio? A job is a job. You can't be choosy in your position.'

156

CHAPTER 14

It was almost a week since Tapan had visited Doctor Karamat Ali. He had not yet written his column for the Doctor, but was determined to make a start. He didn't know what to write and as he sat hunched up over the typewriter, time went by as he rolled and smoked cigarettes, and chewed paan after paan. From time to time he touched the cold keyboard, but his mind yielded nothing. He got up, closed the curtain, and wandered around the flat.

He had already passed the glass showcase in the sitting room several times on these wanderings. Although he had paused before the painting depicting the black stone of Mecca that hung over it, he hadn't been drawn to the showcase itself. Now, for no particular reason, he pulled at one of the panels, and found – to his surprise – that it was not locked. Perhaps the owner of the flat – in the haste of his departure to Bangladesh – had forgotten to lock it. He felt as if he was intruding into his secret world. Yet, squatting before the showcase, its doors wide open, he couldn't resist the temptation of exploring its disordered, cobwebbed contents. Soon it became apparent to him there were no figurines – either of humans, or of animals. At first he thought that the man followed a strict, austere interpretation of the Islamic codes concerning representation. But he found this hard to believe since, among the Bangladeshi Muslims of his generation, this kind of rigidity was rare.

As he went through the shelves he discovered the contents were much more ordered than he thought. On the top shelf, there were sets of blue and white plates decorated with Arabic calligraphy and polished stones – mostly amber and green in colour. On the second, there were all kinds of clay pots and pans, almost half red, the rest black. On the next, besides crystal glasses of all shapes, there were brass containers with elaborate floral etching and inlays. On the last but one shelf, there was a delicate china tea set painted with twisted trees, climbing plants and silent lakes. When he looked closer at the set, he saw – in between the foliage – a flock of birds. Had the owner noticed the birds, or just pretended that they weren't there? Perhaps he thought that the birds were so small, so delicate, and so stylised that they could pass as a part of the foliage. Perhaps, he had somehow convinced himself that even his omniscient god would be fooled by them. Such was the cunning of his country-people! Yet, the birds couldn't be ignored.

Tapan took one of the saucers out of the case and, after polishing its surface with his lungi, looked at the tiny birds again. Almost unconsciously he began to purse his lips and empty his lungs, but he could not whistle like a bird. The more he tried, the more he produced a harsh vibrating noise like the grating of a rusty machine. He thought he even heard a raven opening its throat from the eaves to mock his pathetic attempt. Perhaps it was one of the ravens from the Tower of London that guarded the Koh-i-noor.

Finally, he looked at the lowest of the shelves, which was nearly empty except for a bundle of paper gathered together with a rubber band. He found, between the papers, a number of photographs. Apart from some recent snapshots of a family on an outing, there were some old ones in black and white. He presumed that the old man in the family group was the owner of the flat. He looked sombre and wore a long coat and an Afghan cap. Now he realised that the owner had nothing against figural representation. Otherwise, he wouldn't have allowed his image to be captured by a camera. Although everything in the family photographs evoked winter, the day must have been a clear one, because – despite the leafless trees covered in snow – there was no fog, no mist, and no cloud to obscure the vision. Standing next to the man was a woman, who had wrapped herself in a shawl over her long coat and sari. She looked much younger and prettier than the man. It was obvious that the woman was his wife. The children, a boy and a girl, looked somewhere between ten and twelve. When Tapan looked at the children more closely, he realised how lucky they were to have their mother's good looks and none of the ugliness of their father. The man, it seemed, had increased his value in the marriage market in Bangladesh by emigrating to England. He had, no doubt, styled himself as a big man about London town.

There were three black and white photographs. One showed three young men, trying to look confidently relaxed, against the railings of a stranger's house in London. He thought it must have been one of those houses Nilufar had pointed out to him when they went out for a walk on his first night in Limehouse. When he looked closely at the faces of the men, he realised that the one in the middle – with a cigarette dangling from his lips, wearing a smart double-breasted suit and a porkpie hat – was the owner in his younger days. If Tapan was still uncertain about the owner's former profession, the other two black and white photographs left him in no doubt at all. He had been a sailor.

The second picture wasn't really a photograph but a reproduction of a pencil drawing. Perhaps it had been cut from a newspaper or a magazine. It showed the boiler room of a ship. In it, there were oddly distributed figures, half-naked and brown – and comically with their turbans on – feeding coal into the burning mouths of a boiler. Perhaps our man had worked in a similar boiler room and the reproduction captured some of his old memories. From the looks of these men Tapan almost feared for them, because their tortured expressions made him feel that they were about to end it all by throwing themselves into the fires of hell.

The last of the black and white prints showed a merchant ship sinking with its hull tilting diagonally towards the sky, and white surf breaking on its half-submerged deck. Although there was no caption underneath, Tapan was sure that the picture depicted one of the ships sunk by the German U-boats during the Second World War. Perhaps our man worked on a similar boat. Who knows whether he counted himself lucky, but he had survived –

unlike those thousands of others from the Indian empire who, serving the *Mother Country* in the merchant navy, had perished in the cold water of the Atlantic – had survived to live with a dreadful memory. Looking at this print, Tapan wondered if the man had nightmares about those days – or just over the Paki-bashers on the corner, always waiting with knives in their hands.

Once more Tapan sat before the typewriter. Then, it occurred to him that the story he had drawn from the photographs wasn't new to him. He had heard a similar story before – but from whom? Of course, it was Haji Falu Mia who had told it to him. Tapan leaned back in his chair, closed his eyes, and tried to imagine Haji Falu Mia walking – his posture erect and head high – down Brick Lane. Suddenly all the stories that Haji Falu Mia had told him came flooding back; and there were the stories that Sundar had told him about his father. Already he could sense the contrasts and the subtle variations between them. He realised that he had found the subject matter for his column. He was about to begin his story about Haji Falu Mia – or rather transcribe his conversations with him – when he had to stop. Sundar had arrived with Kofi.

Kofi hugged Tapan and said, 'How you been, Brother?'

'I'm fine, Kofi. How are things in North London?'

'Lots have happened, Brother. I tell you in a minute.'

While Kofi and Tapan went to the sitting room, Sundar went to the kitchen to make tea. Tilting his head backwards, as if to achieve the right perspective, Kofi looked at Tapan.

'Look at you, Brother,' said Kofi. 'You turning into Brother Mole, eh?'

'Well. In my position I have to keep a low profile, you know.'

'Yeah, Brother,' said Kofi. 'Listen. Everyone has been worried sick about you.'

'Sorry, Kofi. I know I should have been in touch. You know what it's like.'

'Don't worry, Brother. You just dig and stay safe – yeah?'

'How's everybody, Kofi?'

'Well. Eva has gone back to her country. Poor Kishor was totally smashed up. He moved back with his parents in South London. And Danzel, you know, the same old self.'

'How about you, Kofi?'

'You know me, Brother. I've a real good plan now. This time I'm really going home.'

'Yeah, I heard it before, Kofi.'

'If you hear this plan, Brother, you'll know I'm serious this time. I'll tell you about it sometime.'

'Yeah, you do that Kofi. But for me there is no going back. I'm here to stay in England.'

'Don't get me wrong, Brother. I understand what you mean. Do you remember what Eva said about us?'

'Yeah. We're junkies for England.'

Sundar brought in the tea and some samosas that he had bought on the way. Everyone was in a good mood, and as they took tea and ate samosas, then another round of tea, and smoking cigarette, the talk flowed. Kofi wasn't very keen on paan, but Tapan and Sundar took a cone every time they lit a cigarette. Sundar was pleased to see Tapan laughing again.

'Listen. I need to tell you something, Brother,' said Kofi, arranging his round glasses and turning serious.

'What is it, Kofi?'

'Well, I don't know how to put it, Brother. So, let me come to it straight away. Yeah? Adela has a child. So have you, Brother.'

'What?' Tapan felt as if the ground beneath his feet had shifted.

'A little boy, Brother. Looks just like you.'

Tapan stayed silent for a while, bit his nails, rolled a cigarette and then mumbled as if he hadn't quite got the drift of what Kofi was saying.

'You're not kidding – are you, Kofi?'

'Listen, that's why I'm here, Brother. You're a daddy man now.'

Now the shock of the news was getting mixed up with anger. Tapan dragged at his cigarette in fury, smoke enveloping him. He felt like throwing acid at Adela's face. Kofi kept scratching his chin and Sundar fixed his eyes on a red stain on the beige carpet.

'Has Adela sent you?' said Tapan suddenly.

'Well. She was feeling kinda bad how to break the news to you. You know how these things are like. The more you delay the more difficult it becomes. Right? So she kept phoning me to help her out. But I'm here for myself too. I wanted you to know about your son, Brother.'

'Thanks, Kofi, for coming. I really don't want to know about it. That's Adela's bloody business. Nothing to do with me.'

'Don't be rash, Bhaio,' said Sundar, lifting his eyes from the stain. 'I know it's a mess. But a child is a child. You can't deny your own son.'

'I just don't want to hear about it – okay, Sundar?'

'Beautiful little boy, Brother,' said Kofi. 'Adela said if you want, you can go and see him anytime. By the way, he's called Tipu Ali.'

'I can't be bothered, Kofi. It has nothing to do with me. For all I care, Adela and her child can go to hell.' Tapan stormed out of the sitting room and shut himself in the bedroom.

After a while, giving Tapan a chance to calm down a bit, Kofi came to the bedroom to bid him goodbye.

'Think it over, Brother,' he said. 'See you soon – yeah? And go with the power of the mole.'

Tapan stayed slumped on the bed for a long time after Kofi and Sundar had left. He felt angry with Adela for keeping it a secret from him, for having his child without even asking him. How did it happen? Then he realised how stupid and naïve he had been, that he should have realised that Adela was already pregnant when he left her.

In time, Tapan began to feel calmer, but didn't know what to do. He felt desperate to see Nilufar, to talk things over with her. He hadn't seen her since that terrible moment when she'd stormed out on him. It wasn't easy to arrange to see her though. She had brought Kaisar to her flat from the hospital. She was nursing him and was very reluctant to leave him alone. But Tapan insisted. 'I must see you, Nilu.'

'Can't it wait for few days. Listen, right now Kaisar needs me.'

'I understand, but it's urgent, Nilu.'

Nilufar had asked Shapna to watch over Kaisar so that she could get away for a few hours. She told Tapan she would meet him on Tower Bridge at seven in the evening. When Shapna arrived at Nilufar's flat, she was waiting by the door to go out.

'You're not going to see that crazy man, Appa – are you?'

'I don't want to talk about it now. I'm in a hurry.'

'You know, Appa. Our community people are talking.'

'Let them talk. What can I do, Shapna?'

'Listen, Appa. If you're serious about him, then marry him,' said Shapna. 'Apart from anything else, it will please our father.'

'What's wrong with you lot. All you can think about is bloody marriage,' and Nilufar left in a huff.

Tapan took a bus from Limehouse; it felt strange to be travelling alone again. He was trying not looking like an illegal immigrant, but the more he tried, the more he slouched. Bit by bit he rolled into himself like a porcupine. When he got off the bus, there at the corner of Leman Street was Poltu Khan. He looked as sleek as usual in his black suit, and smelt of the same old sickeningly sweet perfume, but his thin lips were swollen, he had cuts and bruises all over his face, and some of his front teeth were missing. Now that Tapan had a good look at him, he didn't look sleek at all, but rather forlorn and lost.

'Tapan Ali, my man. How you been?' said Poltu Khan, extending his hand. Tapan didn't take his hand; he accelerated and walked past him. But Poltu Khan kept following him.

'What got into you, man? You don't treat an old friend like this. Let's have a cigarette at least,' said Poltu Khan as he trotted to catch up with Tapan. He offered Tapan one of his Dunhills.

'Thank you, Mr. Khan. I'd rather stick to my rolls.'

'Yeah, you do that. I've the impression that you got it all wrong about me.'

'I know you're an important person, Mr. Khan. But I don't spend my days thinking about you.'

'But I do, Tapan Ali. I do, my man.'

'You do whatever you please, Mr. Khan. But let me alone.'

'Listen. I know people who are doing their best not to let you be alone.'

'What do you mean, Mr. Khan?'

'You know, a person in your position. Yeah, Tapan Ali? Too many vultures are after your carcass.'

'I know, Mr. Khan. I know you have been tracking me. So, why wait? Get your pound of flesh and get it over with. But please leave me alone.'

'Come, come, Tapan Ali. All I want to do is to protect you.'

'Why would you want to protect me?'

'I have my reasons. Let's meet one day, I'll tell you.'

'I don't want to meet you, Mr. Khan. Do what you need to do, but please don't bother me again.'

Tapan turned and quickened his pace. When he saw that Poltu Khan was still following him, he felt panic and almost broke into a run to get away. At the next corner, when he looked back he couldn't see Poltu Khan any more. This only increased his tension. He thought Poltu Khan must have popped into one of the small shops that lined the street to use the phone. He must be calling the Immigration or the police. What to do? He ran and jumped onto a red double-decker, and after two stops changed buses again, got off and meandered through alleyways, until finally feeling confident that he had lost Poltu Khan, he arrived by Tower Bridge. By then he was running twenty minutes late.

Nilufar had said she would wait for him at the south end of the Bridge. It was a clear night. So much light gleamed on the Thames that it was difficult to imagine that darkness could flow through it. He was walking at his ease, along the western catwalk. When he was about halfway along, he thought he could see an outline leaning against the railings. He thought it was Nilufar – perhaps anxious about his delay, she was looking at the lights to take her mind off it. He rushed towards the figure, but when he was about to call out, the figure turned.

'Ah, it's you,' said Bombay Bill.

It took Tapan a while to recognise him. He nodded his head and carried on. He didn't want to stop and listen to his annoying babble, he needed to find Nilufar. When Bombay Bill turned to follow him, Tapan stopped.

'I'm in a hurry, Mr. Bill. I can't stop now.'

'I understand. Malum. Don't you think that the river looks pretty today? But it's never as pretty as the Ganges, is it?'

'Yeah, Mr. Bill. I must be off now.'

Then, just to detain him a bit longer, Bombay Bill asked for a light. Reluctantly Tapan did so. Blowing the first smoke, Bombay

Bill said, 'Trust me, I can help you. You don't believe me, do you?'

Tapan just shrugged his shoulders and began walking again. Bombay Bill called out, 'I really mean it, you know. Come and see me when you're ready. Malum?'

Tapan walked to the end of the bridge, but Nilufar was nowhere to be seen. He got off the bridge, circled its approach several times, waited, and then wandered around the nearby lanes. Finally Nilufar approached him. 'What took you so long?'

'It's a long story, Nilu. I'll tell you in a minute. But why you weren't on the bridge?'

'I was on the bridge. But I had to get off.'

'Why?'

'Well. There was an old guy up there. A bloody racist pig. He was giving me a load of crap about Pakis. So, I had to get off.'

'Did he tell you who he was?'

'That was really weird. He said his mates call him Bombay Bill.'

'Yeah. I came across him too.'

Nilufar looked distant and tired. Although they walked holding hands, looking for a suitable pub, they didn't feel completely at ease with each other, and when they decided on a pub and entered it, at first they didn't feel comfortable there either – they felt all the white punters were looking at them. But once they saw a group of black men laughing and drinking, they felt safe. Nilufar had a gin and tonic and Tapan a pint of Guinness. They took a quiet table in an alcove. Tapan rolled a cigarette, Nilufar lit her Silk Cut.

'What was so urgent?' she asked.

'You know, Kofi came to see me. Adela has a boy.'

Nilufar stayed silent for a while, took a sip of her gin and tonic, smoked her Silk Cut.

'Is it yours?'

'I think so.'

'That's bloody mess. So what you plan to do about it?'

'I don't know, Nilu. That's why I wanted to see you.'

'Listen. I can't tell you what to do. You can go and play bloody happy family with Adela, for all I care.'

'Don't be like this, Nilu. Nothing has changed between us. I don't want anything to do with Adela and her child.'

'Don't be dumb, Tapan. You can't just run away. Of course you have to go and see your child and sort things out with Adela.'

'I've nothing to sort with Adela.'

'Don't deny things, Tapan. I know you have unresolved business with Adela. Besides, you're still married to her on paper.'

'So, I should go and see her then?'

'Grow up, will you? Don't ask me what to do.'

Tapan got up to buy another round.

'So how do you feel about the child?' she asked when he came back.

'I don't know. It feels unreal to me.'

'So, when are you going to talk to Adela?'

'I don't know. I have nothing to say to her. I'll just give her a piece of my mind, and bye.'

Nilufar sat back in her chair and looked into the distance. Twirling her hair she said, 'I'm worried about you, Tapan.'

'Why, Nilu?'

'This illegal thing is not doing any good to you. You can't live the rest of your life like this. I'm really worried about your wild fantasies. Your strange ideas and intuitions.'

'I thought you wanted me to stay in England.'

'Of course I want you to stay. But not like this. You really frighten me sometimes. I can't follow the things you do and say any more. I understand this mole business to an extent. But you are becoming obsessive. We must explore other options if you want to stay.'

'What can we do, Nilu?'

'First you have to ask yourself why you want to stay.'

'I don't know, Nilu. I just want to stay. I've nothing to go back to Bangladesh for. It might sound funny, but – despite all the difficulties – I feel at home here. Besides, I love you.'

'Don't give me that bullshit. You wanted to stay before we met. That's why you married Adela – didn't you?'

'I can't deny what you're saying. But I love you now.'

'Listen. Apart from us, you must find some good reason to stay here.'

'I don't know, Nilu. I just want to stay. Isn't it enough reason?'

'It's bloody self-indulgence. Do you know why the immigrants come to this bloody country? Do you know why other illegal immigrants put up with all the shit?'

'I'm not an idiot, Nilu. But each person has his or her own reason to want to stay here.'

'We're not talking about anybody, Tapan. We're talking about immigrants and illegal immigrants. It's not for some fancy reason they want to stay here. They're willing to do any nasty, back-breaking work so that they can feed themselves and their kids. And they want a better future for their kids.'

'Don't lecture me, Nilu. I know these things. But is it wrong that I can't imagine myself being anywhere else other than in England? And that I love you and want to stay with you?'

'Damn it. If you haven't noticed, I love you too and want you to stay. But this illegal thing needs to end.'

'How?'

'There's only one option really. You know, I don't give a damn about marriage. But for our sake I'm prepared to go through with it. Even if we're married it won't be easy. The Home Office will be very reluctant to believe that it's genuine the second time round. But if we love each other, want to stay together, I think we can eventually convince them.'

'I'm not so sure about it, Nilu. Look what it did to me and Adela. It spoiled everything.'

'Do you have any other option?'

'No. Anyway, how do we go about it, then?'

'First you have to go and see Adela. Ask her to divorce you. You stay hiding for a while. Then we get married and take it from there.'

'I'm still a bit worried, Nilu. You know, making the same mistake twice.'

'If you don't feel anything special for me, then, of course, you'd be making the same mistake. You know what I mean?'

'Of course, I feel special for you. I love you – yeah?'

'Okay,' said Nilufar. 'Listen. I won't be able to see you much for the next few weeks. I need to look after Kaisar. If I let it slip this time, he will end up in a jail. Or dead in some gutter. I hope you understand.'

'Yeah, I do, Nilu. Right. So, I'll go and see Adela.'

When they came out of the pub, they kissed each other, walked hand in hand, and on Tower Bridge Nilufar snuggled into him. Although they were slightly worried about bumping into Bombay Bill again, they stood against the railings and watched the lights playing on the river. Suddenly they felt the way they felt at Limehouse Marina and listened to the secret music of the breeze and the waves. He held Nilufar tightly and kissed her silky hair; she burrowed deep into him.

CHAPTER 15

When Tapan came back to his shelter in Limehouse after meeting Nilufar, he felt so light, so happy and lucid that he sat down to piece together his conversations with Haji Falu Mia. He played the ventriloquist's dummy, mimicking the words that the Haji had spoken so effortlessly that after a while he forgot that they were not his words.

Please forgive me if I can't tell you exactly how old I am. You see, I was born in a village where no one kept any written records. Only in the towns and in the cities were there registry offices. Even there only the high-class people, who kept company with the British, had their names written on paper. No one, except them, followed the ways of the clock and kept time with it.

My mother used to tell me that I was born in the year of the great flood. But, as you know, there have been so many great floods. So I didn't know when I was born for sure. Mind you, this is not something that bothers me. But to do business in the world that the British brought to us you had to have a clock time written against your name.

I didn't know that anyone would be interested in my story. You see, I haven't done anything special. Never been involved in any heroic action, never pursued any noble cause. Nor am I a high-class per-

169

son. I'm a simple immigrant. All I did was live a life like many of the immigrants of my generation. But if you insist on hearing my story, I will tell it.

I was born in a swampy region. It was a part of British India then. You will be surprised to hear that the people in my village had never seen a Whiteman. On a flat, flat land we lived isolated, miles from anywhere. We could cast our eyes further and further over our flat land until it touched the sky. We felt that we were the only ones who lived on this earth. After the rain, after the monsoon down-pour, we became an island. In the dry season there would be muddy fields and plains of dust. We had no proper road linking us to the outside world. It is very funny that I should travel so much and see so much of the world. It is destiny, you know. Allah knows everything.

We were farmers, but unlike most people in the village - who were landless sharecroppers - we had a few acres of land of our own to cultivate; and our own ploughs and bullocks. We had a house of two huts and a kitchen. After the rainy season when the land became flooded we didn't do much except fishing in the swamp and setting traps for wild ducks. In that season we also visited our relatives who lived across the great swamp. When the floodwater subsided we worked the land. You must know that even we chil-dren had to do our fair share. Way before dawn we would get up to work with our elder brothers, cous-ins, fathers and uncles. I suppose you know that we lived in a big blood-clan family then. I think twenty-five of us lived together between two huts.

From dawn to dusk we worked the land. We ploughed, seeded, reaped and drained water. We grew rice, mustard, jute and sweet potatoes. It might sound to you a very hard and poor life, especially for the children. But we were better off than most people in the village. And I was happy.

I was growing up to be a farmer like my father and his father. But one day - as destiny would have it - a man who had disappeared years ago returned to the village. He was to change my life.

You see, after he had disappeared from the village, he became a sailor. I used to go to a tea stall at the market where he told his tales of adventure well into the night. I listened to him with my mouth open. He told us of the cities he had seen, of the power of the sea, and of the strange manners and customs of various people. He also told us of the untold riches that could be made from exploring foreign parts. He even said that he made enough money to buy the landlord's house. Everyone was astonished, but I believed him. He said he wasn't staying long, because he couldn't ignore the call of foreign places. You see, he only came back out of his nostalgia for the swamp. I was determined to go with him.

For days I had organised things in secret. Before the man left we had arranged to meet in two days' time at the railway station of our district town. It was in the middle of monsoon; that night it was raining particularly heavily. I don't remember what hour it was, but everybody was fast asleep in our hut. When I put my straw hat on and lit the lantern to go out, my mother woke up. She asked me where I was going. I said I needed to go to the toilet, which was in the bush, behind the hut. That was the last thing I said to my mother. A lie. You see, my life has been one big lie. I deserved all the suffering that I received in life. I broke my poor Ammajan's heart. I didn't even know when she died. Allah, forgive me.

On that night I sneaked out and went to the cowshed. I led two of the bullocks out into the night and onto the boat, which was moored under the fig tree just in front of the hut. As the bullocks knew me well, they didn't make any noise. Once I secured the bullocks on the boat I pushed it further into the water and jumped on board. I punted, then rowed through the twists and the turns of the swamp in the rain. At times I felt like turning back but the idea of the sea and foreign cities drove me on. In the early morning I reached my destination. I sold the bullocks and set off again.

Much later, when I established contact with my

home again, I learnt that my Ammajan wailed for days
and waited by the swamp for any news of me. The
following day the whole village spread out across
the swamp in their boats looking for me. But once I
had unloaded the bullocks, the boat became much
lighter, and the clear water allowed me to row
faster. By the afternoon of the following day I was
at the ghat of our district town. I sold the boat
there, and looked for the railway station, where I
had arranged to meet the man. You know, the sailor.

Sure, he was waiting for me at the station. That
was the first time that I had seen a train. I was
amazed but it was nothing compared to so many amazing things that I have seen since then. The next day
we took the train to Calcutta. What can I say about
Calcutta? I felt I was in a different planet. Everything was moving so fast that I had to hold on to
myself not to be swept along. Anyway, I wasn't there
for the sights, but to get a job on a ship. As he
promised, the man took me to Kidderpore Docks, and
introduced me to a ghat serang. I was much surprised
that the serang was from my home district. He was
kind to offer me a job, but I had to promise to pay
him my wages for the next six months. This is how I
became a lashkar – it was 1935.

Like other lashkars, I worked in the boiler room.
At first I was a donkey-wallah: greasing, oiling and
polishing the machines. Then I became a fireman-
wallah: feeding the furnaces with coal. I was a hard
worker. I have been to Singapore, Shanghai,
Mombassa, Rotterdam, New York and many other places.
Unfortunately though, I didn't see much of these
places, because we weren't allowed to leave the ship.
It was our moving prison. You wouldn't believe how
much I prayed that one day it wouldn't be our grave.

You must know that the life on board the ship was
hard. We didn't see much of the white captain and
his white staff. It was the serangs who told us what
to do in our own language. That's why we didn't need
to speak any English, which – I'm afraid to say – I
haven't learnt much. I can ask what I want using it
and express some of my feelings in it. But if you
ask me to engage you in a long conversation, or tell

you a story in English, I'm afraid I can't. Oh no, I'm diverting again. It is the habit of an old man. But I heard some English people say that it is due to the cast of our Oriental mind, that we can't think straight, that we go round and round in loops. Honestly, such fuss they make over nothing!

As I was saying, the life on board the ship was hard. No white man could stand the boiler room. So, we lashkars did all the work there: day and night to keep the ship going. Thumping, pumping machines, and the roar of the fire. Did I tell you about the heat? Oh Allah, it was so hot that not only did we run out of sweat to sweat, but our skins felt like burning in the fire of hell. We were a hardy lot, we took it like old donkeys. White sailors liked to believe that we didn't feel a thing. They thought our brown skins were suckers for heat, that we could absorb any amount. It sounds so funny, doesn't it? Now we can even laugh about it, but it wasn't funny then.

Sometimes, between shifts, I would go out on deck and look at the waves. I never became bored of them. For a long time I would look, and suddenly I would feel that I could see my soul there, in the creases of the waves, being wrapped and unwrapped by a mysterious force. I didn't know why I felt that way, but it made me feel calm afterwards, and gave me the strength to bear the heat of the boiler room. Somehow it also made me forget my longing for my land that I had left.

If dolphins swam ahead of our ship, I loved watching them. When they disappeared from view I would wonder where they had gone. But the albatrosses were something else. When they caught the air and glided in the sky above our ship, I couldn't take my eyes off them. I thought the albatrosses had all the freedom of the world; I wanted to be an albatross and fly across the sea. I know it is silly for a grown man to feel like that, but please don't laugh. You see, when you feel trapped, it is natural for you to wish to become a bird: that you can escape from it all. Do you understand that? Now that I'm a Haji I don't feel that way any more. I leave it all to Allah.

On board the ship I heard the stories about jump-ing ship. So, on my second trip to London I decided to do it. We were anchored at Tilbury docks. Some of my mates on board helped me, and the night before my ship was to return to Calcutta, I sneaked out. I couldn't read any English to know where I was; all I knew was that I had to go west for about two miles or so. You see, some of our countrymen had already set themselves up in communal lodging houses in East London; and there were even some deshi-cafes. I hoped to find shelter there. I walked very sneakily, of course; I was scared. I would look behind and around thinking that the shipping company officials were there in the dark, following me. You must not think that I was an illegal immigrant. You see, then we were British, and had rights to come to the Mother Country. So, I didn't break any immigration law; I was simply coming to my own country. The only law I broke was my contract with the shipping com-pany.

For about an hour I walked, always looking behind and hiding; any footstep made me shiver. I was re-minded of the hide and seek game that we used to play as children in the swamps. When I walked two miles or so I stopped.

I hid behind the wall of a shop until the morn-ing. Later I came to realise that it was a grocery shop belonging to an old Jew. So many strange things have happened. You see, no one knows the mysterious ways of Allah. He was kind, that old Jewish fella. We called him Musa Baba. He warned us about the black-shirt-wallahs. He said only the year before his people had a big fight with them around there. Allah bless the soul of that Jewish fella.

In the morning I went round and round looking for a brown face. Finally I saw one. At first I wasn't sure about him. Although he was brown he looked very British in his suit, long coat and hat. I thought he must have been one of those clerk-babus of the em-pire, and that he might not want to know me. When I gave him my salam he looked at me for a while and then embraced me. You see, like me, he was a jump-ing-ship-man and a peasant before that. He took me to his communal lodging where there were some other people like me. He was a good man; he also took me to the police station to register.

Very few of us at the lodging could read or write any English. So the street names were beyond us. The fact that most English streets looked the same to us didn't help the matter a bit. At first we used to put ribbons on lampposts, hedges and street corners to find our way back to our lodgings. When we got used to the place we – like foxes – could smell our way home. Even taking the bus was a big problem, because we couldn't read the numbers. So, we invented our own system. For instance, number 8 was two eggs, and number 22 was two hooks. You might think of us as illiterate country bumpkins and laugh at us. We don't mind – laugh as much as you want, but we survived.

I worked in the boiler room of a big hotel as a fireman-wallah like I did in the ship. Yes, I also washed plates and floors in hotels. But the longest job I had before the war was as a sweeper in a match factory. Thanks to Allah that back home they knew me only as a washer of the Whiteman's dirty plates, and not as the sweeper of his floor. Otherwise, they would have thought that I'd become an untouchable latrine cleaner. You know, one of them shit-cleaning methor fellas.

Now that I'm a Haji I mustn't speak any lies. Nor should I hide things any more. Allah knows all, may He forgive me. Those days I was very naughty. The match factory was full of young women and they used to love me. Oh, I was very weak. For that I acquired a bad reputation and they called me betty-wallah. What do you call it in English? Lady's man? Yes, yes, that's it. Then in 1939 the war came and I joined the merchant navy. During the Great War it was mostly the lashkars who serviced the merchant navy. Thousands of us died in service. We kept the entire supply line of the war open with our blood. Ships became graves for many of us.

I was mainly doing the North Atlantic route between American Eastern ports and various ports in Britain. In the spring of 1941 we were bringing a

cargo of secret military equipment from New York to
Liverpool. We knew the danger of German U-boat attacks. We were supposed to be escorted by British
war ships, but in the event none came. We were on
our own. I didn't know exactly where, but it was
somewhere in the middle, and we were making slow
progress with our lights off. Suddenly one torpedo
hit us, then another. Those who were in the boiler
room - my lashkar brothers - didn't stand a chance.
Luckily I was off duty at that time, so escaped with
a minor injury only. In the rough sea I floated in a
raft for days, exposed to the elements - cold and
hungry. I was wishing the waves would relieve me of
my misery and take me down to the bottom of the sea.
But - as Allah's wish had it - I was rescued and
brought back to England to a hospital. Once I recovered I thought I'd had enough of the sea. I never
went back again.

The war was still going on furiously and in 1942
I went to work in an ammunition factory. Again most
of the workers were women. But I decided to be good
and not mess around any more. It was then that I met
Maureen. I know people talk bad about her, but she
was a good woman. They said how come she married a
brown fella like me, who couldn't even talk to her
in English, if she wasn't a low down market type?
Let them say whatever they want to say, but Maureen
and I didn't need any words. I was surprised that I
could have feelings for a white woman. You see,
Allah's ways are very mysterious.

You see, Maureen's folks were farmers like us;
they were immigrants too. I don't know history much,
but I think it was the potato famine in Ireland that
drove her folks out. Like many of us, they came to
England to eat. I told you, didn't I, that Maureen
and myself didn't need many words. I had my few
words to express my feelings; Maureen was happy with
that. She would sit by the fire and knit for hours
and tell me long stories. I didn't understand many
parts of them, but I liked to listen to her voice.
She was good to me, she cared for me with everything
she had. May Allah bless her soul.

The war was still going on when we got married in

1944. We had two children – a boy and a girl. They were born very fair. If you look at them you wouldn't know that they aren't proper English, but they still had bad times growing up. People called them half-breeds, polluted types, whore's litter and such things. Later on, when they grew up, their white skin served them well, but they were found out because of their names.

I had my share of trouble with my own people. Well, they said what was done was done, but they insisted that I should at least convert Maureen to Islam. It was my desire too. Everything would have been so nice if she had become a Muslim. But her folks worshipped Hazrat Issa-I-salam and followed the Pope. I tried many ways to convince her to convert, but she wouldn't budge. What could I do? I had to live with it. Some of my people said, as if a low-down whore-type wasn't enough for me, on top of it I had to live with a heathen. I don't know what Allah will make of it, but I couldn't just leave Maureen. You see, I had too much history with her, and too much feelings even though we didn't talk much. I had to be with her until she passed away. May Allah bless her soul. Then I went to Mecca to perform Haj.

After the war it was a good time for us. Maureen looked after the kids and worked part-time as a cleaning lady at a school; I entered the restaurant trade. You see, some of our restaurants were in existence by then. We could feel that the English would go for curry in a big way. I wanted to prepare myself for that moment. I started as a kitchen hand, then a waiter, then back to the kitchen again. I wanted to learn every aspect of the business. We worked hard and saved as much as possible. By the early 50s I had my own restaurant and was doing well. It was then that I met a new immigrant who'd just came from my village. You see, by then many people were leaving their homes in my area and were seeking a better life in England. That man from my village told me that my mother was dead. Oh, the destiny! That changed everything. I started to neglect my work and stay quiet sitting in the dark for hours. I would think of my mother and the hurt that I caused her. Now I'd lost my chance even to say sorry. I also began to remember everything from my childhood. I was going crazy to smell the swamp again. It was Maureen who suggested that I should go for a long break in Bangladesh. She said my soul wouldn't be happy until I'd seen the old place again. So in 1952, after fifteen years in England, I went to the village again.

I don't know what happened to me. It was really crazy. As soon as I arrived in my village I started to act like I was a big man. I suppose I wanted to show that I'd made it good in England and that people should respect me for that. You see, I didn't come back with the things that people usually respected. You know, acquiring a big medical or legal qualification like Bat-at-law. I was the same illiterate peasant as before. But I wanted to show that I made it big in England, so I started to splash money around. It was then that the idea of buying the landlord's property came to me. I knew well that – due to years of laziness and mismanagement – the landlord's family had fallen into hard times. But I was still scared of approaching the big house.

When I finally summoned the courage, I found the landlord in his outer room. He was lying in his easy chair and smoking a hooka with a long pipe. He didn't look at me, let alone ask me to sit down. For a while I listened to his hooka bubbling and looked sneakily at his brooding face. Suddenly, but still keeping his pipe in his mouth, he mumbled as to the nature of my visit. I told him that I wanted to buy his land. All he said was: How dare I consider myself to be such a big man after cleaning Whiteman's shit. I mentioned a price and left. I knew the price I offered was twice the market value, and I knew that in his poor financial state he couldn't refuse me.

After a week, when I went back, the landlord didn't make any appearance. Instead, he sent his servant to talk to me: the landlord had accepted my offer. I was very happy and was looking around the house a bit. Then I saw a young girl husking rice in

178

our country manner: thump thump into a big mortar. I
thought such rhythm and such beauty. I also thought
it would be so nice if she became the lady of this
house. That's how I married my second wife.

But the landlord was a bad man. He needed my
money, but couldn't stomach the idea that a mere
peasant like me should live in his house. Of course,
I didn't want to be found out, but I didn't mind
much when he circulated gossips about my menial jobs
in England. But I couldn't take his nasty talk about
Maureen. Soon people began to whisper that I married
a low-down Whitewoman, who was a market whore. That
was too much for me. So I left and never went back
to Bangladesh. It was six months after I came back
to England that my son in Bangladesh was born. He
has his mother's pretty face, but I didn't see him
until I brought him over here with his mother in
1975.

When I came back in the summer of '52, I worked
even harder in my restaurant business. After her
initial outburst, Maureen pretended that nothing had
happened, and we carried on as before. My white
children were growing up well, but they didn't know
anything about my culture. They even went to church
with their mother. What could I have done? It's
destiny, you know. May Allah forgive me.

I thought my Bangladeshi son wouldn't want to
come to England. But in the early 70s he wrote to me
saying that he wanted to come. At first, I wasn't
very keen for him to come. You see, Paki-bashing was
very strong then. I was beaten up no less than four
times. They kicked and punched me, spat on my face,
urinated on my body. I was a proud man and I had too
much shame. So, I didn't say anything about it to
anybody. Now that I'm a Haji and about to meet my
maker, I don't have any pride any more. That's why
I'm speaking to you all the truth. But Maureen was
something else. She was usually a quiet woman, but
she turned fierce when they threw shit through our
letterbox. She created a big fuss, complained to the
police, and wrote to the MP. She wasn't quiet even
when they petrol-bombed our house. She had spirit,
that woman. One day she even chased some skinhead-

wallahs with a broom. Luckily that lot weren't the
Paki-bashing type. Actually they were anti-racists
themselves. Funny, isn't it?

Anyway, after a few more letters from my son I
gave in. But I couldn't leave his mother on her own,
so I brought both of them over here. England didn't
suit her; the poor woman died very shortly after.
Although I didn't know her much, I was very sad. You
see, she was a part of me, she was my inside memories, the things I felt for my village and the
swamp. I know it is a very strange thing to say, but
when she died I felt as though my mother had just
died. She was a good woman. May Allah bless her
soul. Maureen helped me with the arrangement of
burying her. But as destiny would have it, she herself was dead within few years. Soon after, I sold
my business and went to Mecca for Hajj.

Now I mostly stay at home except for taking walks
to the Brick Lane mosque to pray. Thanks to you good
people for coming to talk to me. May Allah look
after you. I tell Sundar to take my dead body to
Bangladesh to be buried, but he doesn't take me
seriously; he just laughs and says, yes, yes, don't
worry, I'll take you back to Bangladesh. These days
I call Allah's name, but can't keep the idea of the
last journey out of my mind. I don't know why it is
full of my old memories.

I don't know how I get there but the journey
always begins at the edge of the swamp. My son puts
my body wrapped in a shroud in a boat. There is no
one there except him and the boatman. It takes the
whole day to arrive home. My son talks to the boatman but I can't hear what they say. Sometimes the
boatman sings, but I don't hear him. I presume he
sings of the sky and of the water and of the loneliness – the songs that I heard in my childhood while
I navigated my boat through the floating rice
plants. When I catch the boatman's voice stretching
long and vibrating the rice plants I stop. I keep
quiet and stay hidden and listen to his songs.
Funny, isn't it – the things you remember?

At first my son and the boatman row over clear
water, but sometimes, if there is wind, they hoist

the sail. There are lotuses floating here and there. Then the swamp gets more clogged up with hyacinths and becomes maze like. They punt me slowly through the thick reeds where my friends used to hide in our game. Here I used to fish with my rod in the small clearing between hyacinths and set traps to catch wild ducks. Then they take me through the water-logged rice fields and jute fields where I worked, ploughed, reaped and harvested. Finally, the ghat of my house. Not the landlord's house that I bought, but the house of my father's people where we lived together. It is nearly evening. They come to receive me with their lanterns, my nephews and their children, and perhaps one or two of my old friends who are still alive. Blind and with sticks they come to bury me, they bury me in the night next to my father and his father.

CHAPTER 16

On his way to see Adela, during the long bus ride and as he approached the familiar house up the quiet North London cul-de-sac, Tapan told himself that his visit would be a short one. Although he had no intention of losing his temper or starting a row, he didn't want to be friendly towards Adela either. He would simply ask her for the divorce, inquire briefly about her expectation of him as the father of her son, and leave. When Adela opened the door, he looked at her vaguely, and hurried past her into the sitting room. It looked the same as before; the yellow hadn't faded a bit since he and Adela had painted it together. The only difference was the plants that had spread more branches and grown taller. Adela, feeling just as awkward as Tapan, quickly disappeared into the kitchen to make tea. He sat on the green sofa where he had spent so much time watching television, and that had been his bed in the days before he left.

Putting the tray on the table, but without looking at him, Adela said, 'Thanks for coming. I really appreciate this.'

Tapan shrugged his shoulders, lifted his teacup and forcing a tone of anger, said, 'I know I owe you a favour, but I wish you'd had the decency to ask me.'

'Sorry, Tapan. I became so muddled, I didn't know what to do. I hope you'll forgive me.'

'To tell you the truth, I feel pissed off about it. I suppose I'm at your mercy now. You can treat me like shit and get away with it.'

'Sorry. It wasn't easy for me, you know.'

'What was so difficult about it?'

'When we were splitting up, I thought we shouldn't use the child to stay together. I wanted to stay together only for us,' Adela said, looking up and meeting his eyes. Seeing her green eyes, he softened a bit, because they never lied to him, never harboured any malicious intention towards him. As always, he saw care in her eyes, and the traces of the time when – after spending that night with her – he walked the rectangular squares of the campus dreamily thinking that it was love.

'Yes, I agree. But how did it happen?'

'I thought you knew that I was pregnant. It was obvious to everyone else. I was upset, because I felt you didn't want to know. And presumed that you couldn't wait to get out of it.'

'Sorry, Adela. I know I should have known. It was really stupid of me.'

'Well, we can't undo the past. Anyway, I thought I would get rid of it. I even made an appointment at an abortion clinic. But in the end I couldn't go through with it.'

'I'm sorry I wasn't there for you, Adela.'

'It was so hard, you know. I felt so lonely. No one to talk to. Obviously, I wanted to cut all past strings. You know, start with a clean slate, but just couldn't.'

'Why couldn't you do that?'

'Don't get me wrong, Tapan. I've no moral problem with abortion. You know how I fought for women's right to choose. I wasn't even scared of the procedure.'

'What made you decide against it then?'

'I can't explain it, Tapan. Perhaps, there's no explanation. But I suppose, deep down, I wanted to keep a part of you.'

Tapan wanted to meet Adela's green eyes again, commune with her, but didn't dare look up. Adela continued:

'I don't expect anything from you. I just wanted you to know, that's all.'

'Thanks for giving him a Bengali name. Tipu Ali sounds nice to me.'

'I didn't want him to grow up not knowing your part of the story.'

When Adela heard Tipu crying, she ran upstairs. Tapan stayed where he was for a while, then tiptoed up the stairs. The door was open. Adela was at the other side of the room, by the window, her back to the door. She was breastfeeding Tipu. Tapan stayed silent, almost holding his breath, his eyes wide open as he watched Adela and Tipu. How absorbed they seemed with each other: he suckling and she rocking so gently like a wave barely ruffling a lake. He didn't want to intrude on this private moment, so he tiptoed down the stairs and back to his place on the sofa.

Adela came into the room with Tipu. Tapan stood up. 'Do you want to hold him?' she asked.

Tapan didn't say anything; he just extended his hands. He wasn't used to handling babies; he was scared that he might drop Tipu. He looked much darker than Tapan had imagined him to be, and there were unmistakable traces of his grandfather in his face, but he had his mother's green eyes. Tipu pursed his lips, looked at him as if trying to memorise his face. Tapan was taken aback by this; he wasn't sure how to respond.

Adela asked him if he wanted to come along to the supermarket with them. He didn't know what made him agree, but he said he would. Adela fastened Tipu tightly in his baby seat in the back of her Mini; Tapan sat next to Adela. When they arrived at Sainsbury's, Adela settled Tipu in his chair and asked Tapan if he would mind pushing him, while she managed the trolley. Side by side they went through the aisles, as if a happy family of three. Just past the aisle that stocked pasta, dry tomatoes and olive oil, an old lady bent over the pushchair to look at Tipu. Between making faces and silly baby-talk, she said, 'He takes after his father, doesn't he?' Tapan smiled nervously, but Adela said, 'Yes, he does.'

After finishing the shopping they went to a cafe and took a deserted table far away from the till. Tipu fell asleep in his pushchair.

'How are things?' asked Adela.

'Not too bad. Considering my situation. You know, being on the wrong side of the law.'

'I never thought it would come to this.'

'Well. We can't undo the past.'

184

'I don't know what you thought had happened?'

'About what?'

'You know, who informed on you?'

'Listen. I don't want to know about it. Whatever happened, happened. Yeah?'

'But it must have crossed your mind that it could be me.'

'I don't care about it any more, Adela. And if you'd done it, I don't blame you. You had enough reason to feel pissed off with me.'

'You bet I was pissed off with you. But I didn't do it. When we broke up, I wanted to keep it a secret. I also wanted to keep to myself the reason why we got married in the first place. At least until your citizenship papers were through. You have to believe me on this, Tapan.'

'I do believe you, Adela.'

'You know, one day I was bleeding so badly, I got scared. By then I really wanted to keep the baby. I didn't know what to do. In my desperation I called my parents. They took me to the hospital.'

'I'm really sorry that I wasn't there for you, Adela. But you don't have to explain anything.'

'It was terrible, you know. My parents were mocking me: Where is your Paki husband now? Is he shopping for his fourth wife now? I'm sorry, Tapan, I couldn't take it any more. So I lost my control then.'

'I understand; you don't have to explain anything, Adela.'

'I was so stupid. I just blurted out that our marriage was over. And that it wasn't real to begin with.'

'Adela, please. I know, it wasn't your fault. Nobody's fault. It was one of those things.'

'You don't know how horrible it was. The amount of pressure they put on me to have an abortion. My mother going on about half-caste, unnatural and things like that. I told them to get lost. I haven't seen them since.'

'I'm sorry, Adela. But what's done is done. Don't worry about it.'

'I don't know for sure who informed the Home Office. But I've my suspicions. But you've got to believe that it wasn't me.'

'Yes, I do believe you, Adela. Let's not talk about it any more.'

When they returned from shopping, Adela asked him if he wanted to stay for lunch. Tapan was pleased to be asked because he wanted to stay a bit longer with them.

While Adela was preparing the food, Tapan went out to the patio to roll a cigarette. From outside he could see Adela through the window as he circled the small patio with its leafless plants, skeletal in their flowerbeds, along the fences. From time to time, she looked up and smiled at him, then went back to her task. Suddenly she looked so fragile, so alone in her long cotton dress and cardigan, that he felt like rushing in to hold her, comfort her. It was then that he remembered what he had promised Nilufar: that he would ask Adela about the divorce. But how could he do this now? He was about to roll another cigarette when he heard Tipu crying. Since Adela was in the middle of frying the onion for the curry, she couldn't attend to him. Opening the patio door, she asked Tapan if he would go up and see Tipu.

To Tapan's surprise, Tipu stopped crying as he stepped into the room. He picked him up and held him against his chest, his chin on his shoulder. Then he pressed his face against Tipu's head, and stroked his hair – black like his. He felt he had touched a deep, roaring spring so fast that it went through him before he could catch his breath. He thought of it as primitive – this instinctual communion between father and son – but there it was. If he hadn't rushed down the stairs, and come face to face with Adela, her green eyes wide open and bewildered, he would have done something very silly. Perhaps, even ended up crying.

Once the cooking was done, Adela arranged the dishes on the table: bowls of dhal, fried okra, spinach and turnip curry and long-grain rice. Not forgetting the mixed pickle: Patak's, of course. Looking at the pickle in the small terracotta bowl, Tapan remembered what Kishor used to say every time he shared a meal with him: 'Forget your Barganga brand from Bombay. Patak – all British made – is the best. Yeah – beef, Brother?'

'You know, ever since you left I've been trying to reproduce the flavour of your curries. It took me ages to get to know all the spices, and even longer to work out the subtleties of their combination. I don't know if I got them right, perhaps I never will,' said Adela. 'Are they terrible? Be honest with me.'

'They're fine, Adela. In fact, they're excellent. I really mean it.'

After dinner and a cup of tea, and at Adela's suggestion, they went to the park. The onset of spring was in the air; already snowdrops were trembling in the grass, but the trees were still bare. They went around the park with Tipu in his push-chair, but near the duck pond Adela picked him up, and Tapan took charge of the push-chair. Tipu, though, was still too young to appreciate ducks, or the world around him.

'What are you going to do? Are you going back to Bangladesh?'

'I don't know, Adela. See what happens.'

'You'd let me know. Wouldn't you?'

'Of course. But it's very difficult to get in touch. I hope you'll understand.'

'I do. If I can do anything... please let me help you.'

'You take care of Tipu. Don't worry about the rest. I'll be fine.'

'Tipu is my son. He's everything to me. I'll make sure that he doesn't forget you.'

'Thanks.'

Silently they walked to the car. Tapan kissed Tipu on the forehead, but avoided Adela's eyes as she drove away.

CHAPTER 17

'You'll be in good company, Bhaio. There are three bedrooms in
the flat. In the first lives an Ali who works in the kitchen of a
restaurant. In the second lives another Ali who is unemployed.
You are having the third bedroom. Three Alis living together –
isn't that something, Bhaio?' said Sundar as he drove Tapan in his
Mini Metro from Limehouse to his new shelter.

For the last few months he'd got used to the idea of being
alone, the solitary burrowing of a mole. Now, the prospect of
having to share his space with others seemed so unnatural, so full
of dangers.

'Is it safe to share?' he asked.

'Bhaio, you'll be in Shadwell. As you know, this is our territory. Nearly all the houses are ours. So nothing to worry about
from security point of view. In fact, anywhere in Spitalfields,
Stepney, Wapping, Bethnal Green and Mile End is safe. You can
walk as freely as you like in those places. As I've told you, the only
care you have to take is when you cross the main roads. Of course,
there are the usual Paki-bashers to worry about, and not to forget
that there are informers among us. You have to be a bit guarded
about your exact location,' said Sundar.

'How about my flat mates – are they okay?'

'Oh, Bhaio, you'll be in the company of first class Alis. You
know our Masuk Ali, don't you? He's crazy as ever, but no one
knows the alleyways better than him. If you need to go anywhere,
he'll take you. The other Ali is one of our village folks. He's a cook
and a sober type. Works long hours, so you wouldn't see much of

him. You need company, Bhaio. On your own, your mind starts to play tricks on you.'

As soon as Sundar pulled up the car at the landing of a tall tower in Watney Street, Masuk Ali came running, his hands flailing and a broad smile on his face. He must have been waiting for them behind the pillar at the entrance of the tower. He could barely contain his enthusiasm and, almost jumping, he embraced Tapan.

'Welcome Soul Brother. Welcome home.'

Sundar told him to keep his voice down. Lowering his voice to a whisper, Masuk Ali said, 'You worry about nothing, Sundar Bhai. If any fuckin' git comes here to mess around with Soul Brother, I'm going to fuckin' smash his head in.'

Once more animated like a little puppy, he took Tapan's things and they got into the lift to the seventh floor. Tapan was to have the room next to the kitchen. It had windows facing west from which he could see the Tower of London.

Sundar didn't stay long because his father wasn't feeling well. After showing him around the flat, Masuk Ali got busy setting the table.

'Cook Bhai, you know, Abdul Ali. Before he left for work, he cooked something to welcome you.'

'It smells really nice,' said Tapan.

'Yeah, Cook Bhai is a number one cook. All day he cooks nothing but duck shit. You know, with stinky feelings in his guts. If I were him I'd bloody poison that whole lot of fat wankers. But he cooked for you with real good feelings. He'll be mighty pleased if you like it, Soul Brother.'

Once the meal was over, while Tapan chewed a paan and smoked a cigarette, Masuk Ali washed the dishes and sang a song out of tune. Suddenly he shouted out, 'I an' I gonna be cool. Innit, Soul Brother?'

Masuk Ali was born in Bangladesh, but after the death of his mother – when he was twelve – his father brought him over to England. At school he was bullied and beaten up and – like Kaisar – reached sixteen without any grades. He spent years in and out of sweatshops and restaurants, but didn't learn a trade. His father provided him with free food and lodging; he was happy with a few pounds in his pocket.

One day, as he was coming out of Bethnal Green tube station, he was severely beaten up by a group of skinheads. After that he refused to go out for two years. He would imagine that they were always waiting for him at the corner, at the bus stops and in the tube. It became so bad that even the sight of a white face would be enough to cause a full-blown panic attack. Each weekend, his father would arrange an outing.

'How about a boat trip from Westminster to Greenwich? We can walk the centre of the world, and afterwards, we can have a Chinese. Or you choose where to go, my son,' he would say.

Masuk Ali would shrug his shoulders; his father took this as his agreement. Before the outing, Masuk Ali would spend a long time taking a shower and dressing up in his best clothes. Then, at the door he would be paralysed with fear that they were out there waiting for him. He would sweat and shake and look desperately for somewhere to hide. His father had to give him strong valium to make him fall asleep. Afterwards, he would say, 'What's happening to you, Masuk Ali, my son? Not all white people are thinking of harming you. There've been many who've been exceedingly kind to me.'

If one of his friends had arranged to take him to see a film, the same thing would happen.

It was only when his father suddenly died of a heart attack in the spring of '76 that Masuk Ali surfaced again. He started his old routine of working in and out of sweatshops and restaurants, and secretly began taking martial arts lessons. He didn't take much interest in what was happening in Brick Lane in the summer of '78. However, when some of the veterans of the picket line talked of starting a self-defence group, he was only too keen to join.

Tapan needed to take his piece to the Doctor. When he mentioned this to Masuk Ali, he said, 'What you want to see that stingy git for, Soul Brother? He's nothing but pollution. Innit? If I see that wanker I need my face washing a thousand times.'

But when Masuk Ali saw that Tapan was serious, he agreed to accompany him. On the way Tapan pressed on in a higher gear, as if the breeziness of it all would outpace his tension of being on the road until Masuk Ali said, 'Hey, Soul Brother, calm down. Ain't no coyote chasing us,' and he calmed down sufficiently to take note of the route they were taking. It seemed so familiar, as if he had never stopped walking there.

Tapan knew that it was silly to take this long detour, and yet he wanted to walk by Henriques Street. Just as his childhood fantasies of improbable coincidences – to which he had devoted many happy hours – he felt he would come face to face with Nilufar just as he passed her flat. He imagined her standing in front of the door, turning the key but, just before stepping indoors, looking back. Somehow, at that precise moment, he would be there to receive her eyes.

And when they passed Henriques Street, Tapan paused in front of the building where Nilufar had her flat. Although he was desperate to see her, he was actually relieved that his imaginary coincidence hadn't come true. He'd avoided phoning Nilufar for the last two days. He didn't know how to explain why he hadn't raised the matter of the divorce with Adela. In fact, he couldn't explain it to himself.

Adler Street was dark. As they reached St. Bonifatius Haus, they saw two cigarettes – glowing like fireflies – approaching slowly from the northern end. Immediately Tapan's nose flared to catch the smell of danger. He almost dragged Masuk Ali off the pavement and they squatted behind the scrubland that lay to their left. He was pleased that his mole's intuition hadn't failed him, and yet he was scared when he saw Poltu Khan – accompanied by one of his sidekicks – swaggering their way. Gritting his teeth and twitching, Masuk Ali said, 'Do you want me to sort that fuckin' rat out for you. Just give the word, Soul Brother, and I'll pull the rest of his teeth out. You know, like our street dentists. Maybe I'll just cut off one of his ears. Fancy that fuckin' git going around with one ear. That's bound to raise few laughs, innit?'

Tapan had to restrain Masuk Ali as Poltu Khan passed by. Waiting until Poltu Khan had turned the corner, they walked diagonally across the scrub to reach Whitechapel Road. Masuk Ali told him that only two days ago there had been a fishing raid at Boundary Estate. Five people were taken– all young men. He continued, 'Everyone knows that Poltu Khan is a piece of shit. A fuckin' rat. But there are others whole lot worse than him.'

'I know, Masuk Ali.'

'But do you know about Shahid Mia, Soul Brother? You know, Shapna's husband. A Maggi-loving fuckin' tory. Innit. He's grassing people all right.'

'I don't know for sure, but I have my suspicions,' said Tapan.

'I'm mighty sure about him, Soul Brother. And how about that fat lawyer gizza? You know, Mizan Ali. All nice smile and helping people. Take it from me, he's grassing in a big way. Fuckin' rats.'

Doctor Karamat Ali was eagerly waiting for Tapan, but he wasn't very pleased to see Masuk Ali. When Tapan gave him the piece on Haji Falu Mia, he went inside with it. He said he would be back in few minutes with tea, but nearly half an hour passed and he still hadn't come back. Masuk Ali was getting restless; he got up, hopped about the room. Then he opened the door that led to the interior of the house and peered through it. There was no sign of the Doctor.

'The bloody Doc is kinda dodgy in English. He must be having a mighty tough time reading your writing, Soul Brother,' said Masuk Ali. 'I bet he's ripping through few dictionaries to figure it out. He's a shifty customer. I wouldn't be surprised if he nipped out. You know, to ask for help from that teacher gizza next door.'

'But he speaks very good English, Masuk.'

'Yeah, he uses all them bombastic words. He's a showman, innit?'

The Doctor came back with tea and misty-sweets on a tray; he looked rather sombre. 'Good, good. Certainly a piece with human interest,' he said.

'So, it's all right then?'

'Well, Mr. Tapan, to be frank with you, it's not what I was looking for.'

'I thought I could choose any subject I liked.'

'Of course, Mr. Tapan. I'm a complete believer in press freedom.'

'So, what's the problem then?'

'You see, Mr. Tapan, when I asked you to write Ali's Diary in the first person, I had something more elevated in mind. You know, a piece containing high thoughts. Written from the point of view of an important and educated person.'

'You don't like the character in my piece?'

'This is not the issue, Mr. Tapan. People might confuse the character of your piece with me. You see the problem, Mr. Tapan?'

'I thought that was the idea.'

'I'll be frank with you Mr. Tapan. I know I have my faults, but I'm not an illiterate type like your character. Very unfortunate Mr. Tapan, Very unfortunate.'

'So, you think his life story is not worth our effort?'

'Please, don't misunderstand me, Mr. Tapan. I'm not saying that at all. In my philanthropic enterprise all manner of people will have their place.'

'So, you don't want to be confused with him?'

'I admit I've my vices, Mr. Tapan, but I never married a low-down white woman. Are you following me, Mr. Tapan? That kind of confusion will ruin my philanthropic career.'

'What do we do now?'

'Sorry, Mr. Tapan, I can't run the piece, but I'm not asking for my £30 back. If you complete the other tasks that we have agreed upon, your employment is secure. Of course, if it's agreeable to you, Mr. Tapan.'

Tapan stayed quiet and the Doctor took it as his agreement. Looking pleased with himself, the Doctor showed Tapan the prototype of the first issue of *The Good News*. It was mainly composed of bits and pieces of news items, odd stories, and gossip from the entertainment world cut from both Bangladeshi and British newspapers and magazines. But there were some pieces with red ink marks. They were the news items and stories of local interest concerning the Bangladeshi community that the Doctor himself had collected; and his long editorial with high-minded moral advice and exhortations written in Bengali. He wanted Tapan to arrange them properly and translate them into English.

When they left the Doctor's place, Masuk Ali said, 'That fuckin' Doc is bad news, Soul Brother. Innit? If I were you I wouldn't trust him a bit. He's always out to screw you. Fuckin' git.'

On their way back, as they crossed Gunthrope Street, they saw two figures, submerged in the dark, standing motionless at the corner of Brick Lane. Somehow, as always, Tapan sensed the bad news and, stepping sideways with the speed of a matador, he hid in the solid darkness and the damp of Angel Alley. For a moment, he imagined the Ripper laughing through the cobbled pavement. He didn't care for the Ripper who'd gone hunting with a surgeon's knife, yet, how could he not be intrigued by the other Ripper – the invisible one who'd left the detectives dead in their tracks? Tapan wished he could converse with him and learn the secrets of his craft.

Masuk Ali had gone ahead to investigate. He was relieved to find that it was Singh – the community liaison officer – and Jones – the friendly bobby on the beat. After some banter with them, Masuk Ali came back to Angel Alley, but had trouble finding Tapan, who had to whistle to draw his attention. Finding Tapan crouching on the cobble stones, he said, 'Bloody hell, Soul Brother. I passed by here but I didn't see you. What were you trying to do? Go up in smoke like that bloody Ripper?'

Tapan rolled a cigarette and they continued to track their way back to the flat. On the street leading to it, Tapan picked up Poltu Khan's perfume. What was he up to this time? The last time Tapan had met him he looked, with his front teeth missing, so pathetic. Why would he say that he was his friend? Perhaps he was genuine when he claimed that he had been protecting him, but that wasn't his character. He was made to hunt him the way a predator always hunted its prey. Whatever might be happening in Poltu Khan's mind, a mole couldn't take chances. For all he knew, Poltu Khan's expression of care could be a part of his sinister ploy.

When they reached the flat they found Abdul Ali waiting for them at the door. He looked very anxious. He had good reason, because an immigration officer – with a police escort – had been in the building only minutes before. They had gone around floor by floor, flat by flat, asking for a certain Mr. Ali, but there were so many Alis in the block. Almost every flat had its own Ali, and to the Immigration and the police all the Alis – with their small frames and brown faces – looked more or less the same. At one point in their search, they became quite excited, because they were able to differentiate between generations of Alis, and those who had long beards and those who hadn't, but within each group there were so many.

'Bloody hell,' said one of the police officers, 'How are we meant to find our Ali among these Alis? They all look like bloody Pakis to me.'

And, when they insisted on checking passports, it wasn't very productive either, because all the Alis they encountered were legitimate British citizens. In the end they became so exasperated that they left before reaching the flat on the seventh floor.

Although it was obvious, Tapan hadn't thought about names before. Now he laughed to himself, thinking how his name had added a line to the labyrinth. Perhaps they wouldn't be able to find their way to him through the maze of Alis.

Later that night, while Masuk Ali made tea, Abdul Ali asked Tapan to read a letter for him. It was a letter from Bangladesh, from his wife. He felt embarrassed and apologised profusely for asking Tapan to do this delicate favour. But what else could he do since he – unlike his wife – had never attended school. He didn't know how to read or write Bengali, let alone English. The letter, though carefully composed on thick blue paper, didn't contain any personal sentiment. From beginning to end it reported only practical matters: the latest on a long-standing land dispute, a new fence being erected around the orchard, children's health, the birth of a nephew – who has the face of his grandfather – so many going to Hajj this year, and requests for more money to be sent.

Masuk Ali cleared the table and slammed a pack of cards on it. It was a routine between Cook Bhai and himself to play a game before they went to sleep. He asked Tapan whether he would like to join them. Tapan said he couldn't because he needed to get on with the task for the Doctor's *The Good News*.

Tapan – sitting on his bed, bored and yawning – was going through the Doctor's scribbles; he was arranging them into proper narrative form and translating them into English. From the kitchen, occasional laughter and table-thumping broke the silence. Unable to continue with the tiresome task, Tapan decided to leave it until morning; it wouldn't take more than an hour to complete the rest. He went to the bathroom, brushed his teeth and looked at his stubble in the mirror. He was surprised that it had grown into a raggedy beard. He didn't like the way he looked; it gave the impression of someone who had given up on life. But he had so much to live for; he would have a shave soon.

He put his face on the pillow and rolled the quilt over his head, but then he noticed that Abdul Ali and Masuk Ali weren't laughing any more, or thumping the table for a winner. When they had switched to it, he wasn't sure but – like drizzle on a tin roof – they were whispering. He lifted his face off the pillow and rested his head against the back wall. He had to crease his forehead slightly to tune his ears to the right frequency and then he could listen to them clearly. It seemed that they knew that he would be listening, and were speaking for his benefit. It was obvious they had been dealing with the matter for a long time, had by now perfected the scheme. So, they were merely confirming details, not discussing ideas or asking each other questions.

Not too far from the flat – near enough to see through the window – lay the Tower of London with its jagged indentation of stones. Everyone knew that the Koh-i-noor was kept there. Tapan at first thought that what they were talking about was just a fantasy, but Masuk Ali and Abdul Ali clearly knew what kind of fortress it was, about the guards and the high-tech surveillance.

The scheme was simple.

Already they had secured the flat on the ground floor. Finding the cellar had been harder and if the old man hadn't left clues, they would never have found it. Right under the bed where the old man died, under the thick green carpet, was the entrance. Even when you had lifted the carpet it wasn't easy to find it – it was so well disguised with the rest of the cement flooring. Only by lifting one of the legs of the bed could you find the tiny slit to fit the key that opened the hatch. Then, down the ladder, through the vertical shaft you arrived at the base. Years ago, after having visited the Tower, the old man – a distant uncle of Masuk Ali – had begun digging. No one knew what possessed him, but he was determined to liberate the Koh-i-noor. By the time he died he had made a sizeable tunnel, but the Tower was still a long way off.

At his deathbed, the old man, who died childless, had left the flat in the care of Masuk Ali. He also left him a bunch of keys, all looking identical, but one of which opened the hatch to the cellar.

Masuk Ali knew the old man wanted him to continue with his unfinished project.

At first Masuk Ali was worried that Cook Bhai would laugh it off as sheer madness and try to dissuade him. But no sooner had he mentioned it, Cook Bhai was in it, and together they'd continued digging and extending the tunnel towards the Tower. Like the old man, they'd become obsessed with rescuing Koh-i-noor. For them it wasn't just a diamond but an emblem of the history of dispossession.

Every night, after Cook Bhai returned from work, and after they'd had a game of cards, they would put in a few hours, digging and lengthening the tunnel.

Tapan was pleased that finally he was among moles. Perhaps the old man had thought of digging as an exercise of passion in which you found your way through your senses. Perhaps for this reason he hadn't left any directions, any map; there was only the trajectory of his digging. Often Masuk Ali laughed, remembering how clumsy the old man was, how he couldn't tell the difference between north and south, or between east and west. For him a map was full of ghostly signs of non-places, and he had no intention of mastering its secrets. Yet, Masuk Ali was amazed to find that the trajectory of the tunnel did indeed follow the shortest possible route to the Tower.

Suddenly Masuk Ali and Abdul Ali got up and headed for the door. They closed it behind them so gently that – if it hadn't been Tapan – no one would have known that they had left. Once more Tapan put his face against the pillow, hugged it and put the quilt over his head.

Through the shaft, stepping down the ladder, they arrive in the cellar. Surprisingly the space is large; almost like an underground parking lot. It is nearly empty except for two hammocks dangling between two columns in the middle. The rear is full of mud, bricks and stones stacked to the ceiling. A rope with a green bucket, connected to a pulley, runs along it from the tunnel. Small circles of light dance as their heads move; the rest is dark – their helmets have lights on as miners do. Each carries a pickaxe and a shovel. The ground is wet and the air damp, but they do not mind it. Crouching, single file, they proceed through the tunnel, so low that their heads almost touch the ceiling. They take turns to dig while the other fills the bucket on the pulley. Mostly they keep silent, although occasionally Cook Bhai hums a boatman's song. But digging and shovelling is music enough for them.

Each night for hours they toil, crouching and digging like moles. They make some progress. It always makes them happy because each time, at the end of their labour, they feel a bit closer to the Tower. Focusing their headlamps along its length, it pleases them to see the hole running in a straight line of light until there is only darkness. After they've pulled in the fruits of their labour and piled it at the far end of the basement, they lie in the hammocks. Nothing disturbs their thoughts, neither the years it might take, nor whether they will ever reach the Tower.

And if they reached the Tower, what then? How to breach the tight security and the electronic surveillance?

They do not allow themselves to think of these things. They are simply happy with their labour. In the hammocks they light cigarettes and swing sideways in the dark. Sometimes, if they forget to put their headlights out, they see their shadows swinging on the floor. Each on his own but together, they imagine the same thing, as if an invisible signal has passed between them, like the ultrasonic transmission between whales across the seas. With smiles on their faces, they imagine they have rescued Koh-i-noor and brought it back to Brick Lane. So many people are in the street: they are distributing sweets – children dressed up as on an Eid day – strewing petals on the ground, and releasing colourful balloons up into the sky. Still they find it hard to believe that Koh-i-noor is in Brick Lane, in the heart of their Bangla Town in East London, but once they see the white stone catching so much light, they beat kettledrums and begin singing. Still swinging in their hammocks, it doesn't bother them that Koh-i-noor has travelled no more than a mile from the Tower. They feel that not only has it crossed frontiers between cities but also crossed a gulf of time. It is satisfying to think that the time of the Company that stole it, and the time of the Raj who possessed it should come to die here in Brick Lane. Who knows, perhaps at that moment Queen Victoria would be turning in her grave and looking at

Abdul Karim Munchi – her most loyal servant in his white pugri – with accusing eyes, as if she had never known him. As if during all those years her Munchi was only simulating loyalty – serving the ugly queen in god knows what other abject ways – but biding his time to snatch the mountain of light off her crown. Don't forget, we have the memory of elephants.

It must have been five in the morning when Tapan heard the door open and Masuk Ali and Abdul Ali tiptoed in. Finally, it was time to sleep.

CHAPTER 18

It wasn't yet nine o' clock in the morning, and already sewing machines were purring at him in a jarring concert. He knew that in this block, as in so many others in East London, Bangladeshi women drove themselves frantic to complete their quotas – at a third-world rates – for well-known high street labels. Yet, he was getting annoyed with them for disturbing his sleep.

He got up and decided to finish off his work on the Doctor's *The Good News*. At about eleven, Masuk Ali got up, whistling softly, and Abdul Ali opened his door. They looked like people who time their sleep so well that they get up at the most beautiful moment of their dreams, before something unexpectedly goes wrong. Before the horseman gallops in with an unsheathed sword in his hand.

After breakfast, Masuk Ali left to sign on at the dole office. Abdul Ali, coming from the kitchen with a fresh pot of tea and cones of paan on a plate, and looking embarrassed, asked Tapan if he would help him to reply his wife's letter.

Pouring tea for both of them, Abdul Ali began dictating the letter.

Dear Bibi,

I'm pleased to hear all the good news. May Allah bless our nephew. If he takes after father-baba, he must be a very handsome-looking boy. Convey my good wishes to Namyat Bhai on the birth of his son. My village bhai, Kuddus Ali, is coming home in two weeks time. I'll send the new nephew a present with him. Perhaps something warm for the winter.

I'm pleased that the children are well. Feed them plenty of spinach and fish. I'm informed by a deshi bhai that scientists in London believe that fish is good for your brain. That's why you find so many fish and chips shops in London. White sahibs eat fish when they take a walk in the street. Usually they use forks and knives, but you must understand that they use their fingers like our deshi manner to eat fish. I'm not sure, though, of their manner of eating from a newspaper. In this regard our old manner of eating from banana leaves was certainly better. Anyway, the English are a very brainy people. No one beats them in the art of cunning. It is well to remember that it was not by the force of arms that the English won and maintained their empire in our sub-continent, but by the art of their cunning. So do not forget to feed the children plenty of fish.

Since we are on the matter of eating, I must tell you about the curry business. I'm sure that you find it amusing that I should be a cook. Please don't tell the people in the village that I'm nothing but a cooker of curry, otherwise, they are sure to make fun of me for doing such a womanly job. Tell them that I'm a partner in a high-class restaurant. Anyway, as I was saying, it is very strange that I should be a cook, that I, who never entered a kitchen back home, couldn't tell the difference between dhanya and jeera or haldi and saffron, should end up cooking spicy things for the English. But you must understand that the curry we prepare here is not the same as our deshi torkari. Although we use some of the same spices, their manner of preparation, flavour and texture are very different. I'm sure you have never heard of dishes such as Vindaloo, Pal or Madrass. One of our early deshi bhai – a very wise man who knew the secret cravings of English palate – invented them out of his own cunning. We call them English/Banglish dishes. But we don't tell this to the white sahibs. Oh, how they love thinking that they are eating our home cooking. You must know the English sahibs flock to our places day and night to eat the dishes we prepare. Funnily enough, they are demanding that more and more chilli be put in. Hotter the better they like. But we never touch the dishes that we prepare in the restaurant. They don't agree with our taste. So the food that we eat we prepare in our deshi manner. It's a funny business – isn't it? – that I should be a cook.

Regarding the land dispute it is better to come to an understanding with our neighbours. If they are not willing to come to an agreement, ask Namyat Bhai to see a lawyer in town.

Glad to hear that so many are going to Hajj this year. Allah willing, I too intend to go to Hajj next year. Give my salaam to all the elders. I'm fine. Working everyday and saving plenty of money for our future. I'm sending you a money order of the sum of £200.

Khoda Hafiz,
Your husband.

Still feeling embarrassed about having to ask Tapan to write for him, Abdul Ali got up and went to the kitchen. Leaning back in his chair, swallowing the bitter paan juice, Tapan lit a cigarette. He was drifting somewhere else altogether. Propelled by Abdul Ali's letter, he was already tracing the footsteps of our first cook and one of our first travellers to the British Isles.

It was in 1809 and his name was Syed Ali, but the story really begins in 1757 and a Nawab overrun by a small band of pale-faced, queer-looking Feringees in funny trousers, and speaking Bengali in the most terrible accent and corpses left as a feast for foxes and crows in the mango grove at Palashy. When a renegade clerk called Clive emerges as the new lord of Bengal people shrug their shoulders: 'Well, so what! It has nothing to do with us. As long as there is rain, we don't care who is the lord.' That was until they have to give up their traditional crops and plant indigo, jute and a strange leaf called cha from China and weavers had their fingers cut so the muslin wouldn't compete with the rough cotton from England. And things went from bad to worse, especially in the district of Sylhet, when the company sent in their ace tax collector, Robert Lindsay, in 1777.

Apart from collecting land revenues for the Company, Lindsay was always on the look-out for himself. He laid claim to the local lime quarry, and it is said that he even made a song in praise of lime. There was the small matter of the elephants. Six thousand captured and traded during his twelve-year stay in Sylhet. No song for the elephants and their long memories – nor for the tigers he had slaughtered like cattle in abattoirs and sold their skin and bones. He became so rich that he had a castle built in Balcaras in Scotland.

But unknown to Lindsay, fakirs and mystics were having visions of holy war and martyrdom. During the Muharram of 1782, reaching ecstasy through flagellation, they flung themselves into holy war and Lindsay's troops happily obliged their dreams of martydom by shooting them down. And this is where our first cook, Syed Ali's own story really begins. One of the dead fakirs was his father.

Tapan's retrospect was interrupted by Cook Bhai who brought in a fresh pot of tea from the kitchen. He told Tapan he'd made fried green beans and dhal for his lunch, but not to wait for him to eat. He was going to Brick Lane. He'd hang around there, as was his custom during his day off, with his country brothers, exchange news of home, and spend hours over a samosa at Miraj Cafe. Perhaps later he'd watch a Bollywood video with them.

Saying goodbye to the present cook, Tapan's thoughts returned to the first. Nobody suspected him, but Syed Ali grew up dreaming of revenge. He was determined to spill Lindsay's blood even if it meant crossing seven seas. In the summer of 1809 he seized his chance. He got himself a job as a servant to a missionary's son who was returning to England after spending many years in Bengal. At sea, he served his master loyally, amusing him with the stories of fakirs and their miraculous feats. Secretly, though, he contemplated poisoning his young master, or pushing him into the sea. Yet, as the passage continued, he grew fond of the boy, and came to love him as his own little brother. Years later, he would recognise that his heart was too soft for revenge.

From England he made his way to Balcaras in Scotland. On the way he sharpened his determination to plunge his dagger into Lindsay's heart. At Balcaras he found out that each morning, irrespective of the weather and the season, Lindsay went for a ride by the seashore. Syed Ali quickly decided that this was the right place and the moment.

For days he didn't eat anything, slept rough. He didn't realise that autumn could be so cold in Scotland. Despite his meticulous preparation he hadn't brought any warm clothes. Obviously, as he wandered around Balcaras in his cotton pyjamas, long kurta and a pugri, he didn't avoid attention. People pestered him to read their hands, divine their future, prepare a magic potion, or climb a rope to heaven. The young women began to dream of being ravished by him.

News reached Lindsay that Syed Ali was looking for him. Not for a second did it occur to him that he might be there to kill him. All Lindsay was thinking about was curry. He hadn't come back from the Orient addicted to opium, but to spices. In his store-room there were boxes and boxes of dry spices, cared for like precious jewels. But, Lindsay didn't have anyone who knew how to prepare a curry with them. His wife hated spices; they reminded her of the days of boredom and dysentery she had suffered in Sylhet. At his insistence, his cook had a go with them, but he prepared such an atrocious curry that Lindsay threw up after the first spoonful.

Hearing of Syed Ali's presence in town, Lindsay began to daydream about curry more frequently than ever. He would gallop along the seashore, not listening to the waves, but salivating over the flavours of spices in his distant memories. Tapan wondered whether in those moments he thought of the elephants. Six thousand bearers of long memories.

Starved and frozen, Syed Ali could hardly stand up, though seeing the gold and yellow of autumnal leaves, he felt slightly better. He put a yellow leaf in the pocket of his kurta as a token of his determination.

On the appointed day he got up early in the deserted shack where he'd eventually found shelter. He put on a new pair of pyjamas and a kurta and a red pugri that he had brought for the occasion. He offered his morning prayers as usual. Tucking the dagger under his kurta, he went out.

He walked down a street lined with autumnal trees. Everything was still, as if the world was holding its breath, except that occasionally a yellow or gold leaf fell on his pugri. Shivering, he plodded along. The seashore and the beaches were covered in mist. He hardly had the strength to go on, but somehow he managed to reach the spot he had already marked out: along the route that Lindsay always took.

Lindsay was late that day. Syed Ali waited and waited, his limbs frozen like a carcass in cold storage, and when Lindsay finally came, Syed Ali didn't see him through the mist until he was only a step away. Lindsay rode in like a ghost, his head full of dreams of spices. Syed Ali made one last superhuman effort to unsheathe the dagger, but he couldn't get up.

Lindsay wasn't surprised to see him there. He dismounted and gave him a salaam. Then he asked Syed Ali in Bengali if he would be kind enough to cook him a curry. As Syed Ali was too weak and frozen to answer, Lindsay thought he'd agreed to his proposal in his enigmatic oriental way. Lindsay put him on the back of his horse and galloped home with him. When Syed Ali recovered, he became Lindsay's cook.

He would cook curry and Lindsay would eat on his own at his large mahogany table. His wife and his children – suspecting that Syed Ali would poison them – wouldn't come near it. Lindsay, though, not satisfied with eating until he almost choked, would come tiptoeing to the kitchen in the middle of the night to lick the pots in which the spicy dishes had been cooked. In the town the rumour spread that an evil curry spirit had possessed him. Lindsay's wife called in an exorcist, but Lindsay chased him away with his gun.

Tapan wondered what Masuk Ali would have said if he'd told him this story. Perhaps, giving him a bewildered look, he would have said, 'You're pulling my legs, innit? You cooked it up, right? A bloody Whiteman's cooker of curry for our main man! He doesn't fit the bill, Soul Brother.'

But there it was, a cook at the beginning. And he was an Ali.

In the afternoon Abdul Ali came back to the flat with an hilsa fish.

'Cook Bhai gonna cook something bombastic. Cool, innit?'

said Masuk Ali. 'After, we gonna see the cool man himself – the Bringer of Jinn. How about it, Soul Brother?'

'I'm not sure about that, Masuk,' said Tapan. 'I don't believe in that sort of mumbo-jumbo nonsense.'

'What you saying, Soul Brother. He ain't no con artist like the bloody Doc. Him real cool. You have to come and see it for yourself.'

Tapan wasn't very keen on the idea, but he wanted to get out of the flat for a while, so, he said he'd come.

'You won't be disappointed, Soul Brother.' And he shouted out, 'The Bringer is cool, innit, Cook Bhai?'

There was just a hint of fog that night when they set off to Pinchin Street where the Bringer of Jinn lived. Masuk Ali and Cook Bhai were laughing, but Tapan was thinking about Nilufar. He stopped by a telephone box to call her.

'Nilu, is that you? You sound so strange. Are you okay?'

'I'm okay. Just a bit tired,' she said. ' I've been waiting for your call. Why haven't you called me before?'

'I've been thinking of calling, but I thought . . . You know, you're so busy with Kaisar. I didn't want to disturb.'

'Yes, I'm busy with Kaisar. It's a critical time, and I've to be there for him. By the way, have you talked to Adela?'

'Yes, I did.'

'Damn it, Tapan. I thought you would let me know what had happened.'

'It's a bit complicated. I need to see you.'

'I don't get it, Tapan. Have you raised the divorce issue with Adela?'

'Well. As I said, it's a bit complicated. I need to see you to talk things over.'

'Why can't you give me a straight answer. What are you so scared of?'

'Let's meet – yeah? I'll explain.'

'Listen, it's not easy to find free time. I need to keep an eye on Kaisar, make sure that he takes his medicines on time. I don't want him to get back on drugs again. I hope you understand this.'

'I do understand, Nilu. But I need to see you.'

'Call me back tomorrow night. I'll try to arrange something with Shapna.'

As he came out of the phone box, and the three of them walked on, they had no idea that two guys had locked onto them. Only at the turning of Cannon Street did they become aware of their presence. They were smartly dressed in suits and long coats.

Instead of turning left into Cannon Street, Masuk Ali, Tapan and Cook Bhai turned right. When they saw the guys were still following them, they had no doubt about their purpose. What to do? In the kitchen he could pull off the most daring acts, but the streets made Cook Bhai nervous, and the guys trailing them had made him feel like a frightened porcupine. Masuk Ali, though, was in his element; he suggested that they lure the fuckin' gits into the Bringer of Jinn's place, and then set a really wicked Jinn onto them. 'That would teach the wankers a lesson. They won't mess around with us any more. Innit, Soul Brother?'

Even Cook Bhai laughed at that. Suddenly Tapan remembered that in his shoulder bag he had the map of Tower Hamlets that Sundar had given him. On it were the asterisks of glowing orange that marked the contact points: the safe houses in which he could take shelter in an emergency.

In order to put distance between themselves and the guys in suits, they almost ran through Dale Street. On Burslem Street, Tapan knocked on the door of the nearest safe house on the map. He disappeared into the house before the guys following them could reach Burslem Street. Masuk Ali and Abdul Ali kept on walking at their ease. When the guys caught up with them, Masuk Ali smiled and offered them paan from the side pocket of his jacket. Still smiling he said, 'Wanna see Jinn, mates?'

'What the fuck's that? Is not some of your belly dancing, is it?' said one of the guys. Masuk Ali laughed again, Cook Bhai stayed quiet, frightened.

'What's happened to your mate? We'd like to have a word with him. Nothing serious, just a friendly chat.'

'You must be seeing triples, mates. If I were you I'd get a pair of glasses, innit? You sure, you don't wanna come and see Jinn?'

Annoyed, the guys turned back; Masuk Ali and Abdul Ali continued ahead.

The young man who'd opened the door for Tapan didn't ask any questions – neither his name, nor his purpose at this time of the night. He led Tapan through the sitting room – where Boris Karloff was playing Frankenstein's monster in black and white on television – to the kitchen at the back. Next door, in the bedroom, a child woke up crying. Within seconds, a woman – who must have been her mother – got up to console her.

Boris Karloff was still groaning and growling and Tapan was glad when the young man went to put it off. He wasn't very keen on Frankenstein's monster, its pathetic whimper and its senti-mentality – looking for daddy and love. He was human, all too human. Tapan preferred old Count Dracula, the bloodsucker, the flyer without a mirror to encage him.

Her child asleep again, the mother came to the kitchen and asked Tapan if he had eaten dinner. Her husband insisted that he must try the carp curry with turnips. Tapan said he would love to, but he wasn't hungry as he'd just eaten. Looking disappointed, the wife said he must come another time to eat fish curry with them. Or would he prefer pillaw rice with korma? He promised them that one day he would come to share a meal with them. Smiling, the husband said, 'Yes, country brother, you must come. Otherwise, we would mind too much.'

While the husband offered Tapan a cigarette, his wife – without asking – set to prepare a snack. She fried rice crispies with mustard oil and mixed them with chopped green chillies, onion, fresh ginger and coriander leaves. She prepared tea in the deshi manner – boiling milk with sugar and cardamom. From the refrigerator she produced some meesty-sweet and made some fresh cones of paan. She brought all of these for Tapan on a large tray.

He munched a few fried rice crispies and took sips of tea. Both husband and wife, he on the settee and she standing behind, waited on him, ready to serve his needs. The husband said that if he needed to stay the night, he would be most welcome in their home, and his wife nodded her head. Tapan was about to thank them for their offer, but say that he didn't need to stay, when they heard a knock on the door.

The man almost dragged Tapan through their bedroom – where two children were sleeping on a large bed – to the bathroom at the back. Groping in the dark, he lifted the lino, and then the hatch door that led to the passage. He said there was nothing to worry about as the whole neighbourhood was linked up by secret passageways. In only minutes they could surface in another safe house a few streets away. In the dark they waited for the signal to move on, but the wife came back. She tapped on the hatch door through the lino. It was only Masuk Ali and Abdul Ali.

While they were taking their leave of the husband, his wife put the left-over fried rice crispies, meesty-sweets and the cones of paan into three separate plastic bags. At the door she put them into Tapan's hand in a way that he couldn't refuse. Then both of them said, 'Country Brother, you must come and eat with us one day. We will be waiting for you. Take care of yourself, Country Brother.'

Tapan nodded his head and resumed his journey to see the Bringer of Jinn.

Tapan didn't know anything more about the couple who had just given him shelter than what Sundar's map had informed him. They were simply Alis, no: 26. Tapan asked Masuk Ali if he knew anything about them. He was silent for a while, then said abruptly, 'They're our folks, innit?'

When they arrived at the Bringer of Jinn's place, they found Sundar was already there. He should have known better, but Tapan was surprised to see Dr. Karamat Ali – the avowed man of science and a foe of all kinds of quackery and superstition. Strangely, the Doctor didn't look uncomfortable. He was sipping tea and munching biscuits at his ease. Masuk Ali couldn't resist it; he had to say something.

'Hi Doc, fancy seeing you here. Is the Jinn ill or what? I bet he's begging you to do a scientific on him. We can't have sick Jinn, yeah, Doc?'

Karamat Ali looked unruffled, but said, 'Ungrateful creature. Tell me who corrected your head? Without my craft you'd still be going around stark-pagal-mad.'

Masuk Ali was twisting his lips to say something rude but Sundar stopped him.

'Masuk, leave the Doctor sahib alone.'

From the sofa opposite, Syed Alam Noorpuri – the Bringer of

Jinn – felt that he needed to straighten out one or two things about Jinn.

'Jinns do not need our doctory. Scientific or otherwise,' said the Bringer. 'You must know that they're spirit beings. Certainly they have higher status than we do in Allah's creation. Whereas we're made of clay, they're made of fire or air. But like us they can be good or bad. It is true that they do not have a form of their own, but they can assume any form they wish and can live for thousands of years. Of their powers, what can I say? – even a thousand of your Superman, Batman or Incredible Hulk couldn't match a single Jinn. And they possess not only memories of the past but memories of the future.'

Everyone present knew as much – which was why they'd came to see the Bringer – but they pretended to be hearing it for the first time. It gave the Bringer the satisfaction of providing rare knowledge to the uninformed. Consequently, he would be in a better mood when conducting the Jinn. As expected, it worked: the Bringer lifted his chin at an angle to the ceiling and flared his nose. He was even trying to contain a smile of satisfaction about to break loose on his lips. Sundar was pleased that for once Masuk Ali had kept his mouth shut, that he hadn't pointed out to the Bringer that he'd taken his dig at the Doctor the wrong way. Otherwise, the Bringer would have appeared a damn stupid fellow and that would have impaired his capacity of conduction. Masuk Ali, though, could not resist opening his mouth.

'Brother Bringer, how have you become a bringer?'

Sundar sighed in relief because it wasn't a wrong question. In fact, it gave the Bringer further opportunity to harvest pleasure. He brought his chin back to his chest and gave the grin of someone who was very special and wise.

'Good question, Deshi Bhai, good question,' he said. 'Not everyone can be a bringer of Jinn. You see, the craft has to run in the family; it flows through bloodlines. My father was a bringer and so was his father and so on until the first bringer many many years ago. He was granted that privilege by an ancient master who went around riding a white horse, which was really a Jinn in a transmuted form. So, I inherited the spirit of conduction from my family. But you have to cultivate it to become a proper master yourself. You have to learn the correct manner of address, correct procedures and correct verses. It takes many years of devotion and practice. But without the right bloodline and your family granting you the secret codes and names, you can never become a conductor of Jinn.

'You must know that I was a well-known practitioner before I came to England, but I was much afraid that my Jinns, who were very old and pious, might not want to come to see me in England. At first I would summon them using all the right codes, names and procedure, but they wouldn't come until one day I got a visitation from the oldest Jinn. You must know that he's three thousand years old. He came in my dreams and told me that he and his fellow Jinns were very reluctant to come to this ungodly country. It was hard to convince him, but he saw sense in the end – especially when I told him that now that we are here, we have to make England our own country. He understood that without their help we couldn't achieve this purpose, so they began to respond to my summons again.

'Now one of my Jinns – practically a youngster of thousand and half years – even picked up English. Apart from his heavy Paki accent, he speaks a very high class and bombastic style. I do not understand him much. Oh, such good English!' He looked at Tapan.

'Perhaps you, Tapan Ali, since you're a learned fellow from an English university, you could converse with him. Oh, what a bombastic English he speaks! '

From the kitchen the son of the Bringer, Syed Kalam Noorpuri – a budding bringer himself – brought in fresh tea and biscuits for the new guests. Feeling slightly awkward, Tapan put on the table the bags of fried rice crispies, meesty-sweets, and paans that his shelterers had given him. Picking a meesty-sweet with his fingers, Dr. Karamat Ali asked Tapan if he could have a word with him outside, in the garden.

There, the Doctor told him that the first issue of *The Good News* had done well, that he had managed to sell all nine hundred copies. For the coming week he was planning a thousand copies. Moreover, some of the local groceries and sari shops were keen to advertise in it. Then the Doctor began to whisper.

'Please, Mr Tapan, don't tell people of my visit here. People might get the wrong idea. You know, it might harm my scientific credibility.'

'My lips are sealed, Doctor Ali.'

'Good, Mr. Tapan, good. You see, if the herbalists and the witch doctors get to hear of it, they would have a field day. I know I can rely on your discretion. Sundar Mia and I have a long understanding. Abdul Ali the cook is a quiet man; I don't worry about him. And whatever the nature of his craft, the Bringer of Jinn – well, I must admit that at times he and I have been in serious competition for clients – but he is an upright man. Unlike other unscientific fellows and quacks, he has a code of conduct. I'm sure he wouldn't expose me.'

'So, nothing to worry about, Dr. Ali. No one here wants to spoil your scientific credibility.'

'Sure, sure, Mr. Tapan. But I'm most worried about Masuk Ali. Such an unbalanced fellow. I've corrected his head somewhat when he was in a bad way. Not an ounce of gratefulness, Mr. Tapan. Please have a word with him so that he keeps his mouth shut. I know I can rely on you, Mr. Tapan.'

'I'll see what I can do. Masuk Ali is a bit excitable, but his head is not incorrect. He's a very good man, just speaks his mind. Let's see what I can do. But I don't understand why a scientific man like you needs to consult Jinn?'

'Naturally, as you know, Mr. Tapan, I'm very sceptical of any unscientific practice. I've no time for any mumbo-jumbo. But, you see, it's my wife. You know, I need to know one or two things about her. So I thought I would give the old Jinn a try. Unfortunately science cannot harvest the memories of the future. So what to do, Mr. Tapan?'

Before going back into the house the Doctor gave Tapan three ten pound notes for his work on the next issue of *The Good News*. As Tapan was coming in, he met Sundar at the patio door. He was going out for a smoke and Tapan joined him.

'Have you seen Nilu, Bhaio?' asked Sundar.

'No. But I've just talked to her on the phone. On the way here. She seems quite tied up with Kaisar. Sounded very tired too. I don't know what I should do, Sundar.'

'Certainly Kaisar needs all the help he can get, but sometimes Nilu can be so stubborn and single-minded. Once an idea enters her head, she dives headlong. You know, she becomes obsessive. Now all she thinks is about saving Kaisar. But she needs a bit of saving too. Have you given the idea of marrying her some thought? That would really be the best thing for all concerned, Bhaio.'

'Yes, I've thought a lot about it. But somehow it doesn't sound right, especially after what has happened between Adela and me.'

'I thought something deep was going on between you two,' said Sundar.

'Yes, I think so.'

'So, it's not the same – is it?'

'No.'

'I hope you have raised the matter of the divorce with Adela.'

'Well. I meant to, Sundar, but when I got there – you know, what it's like – I just couldn't bring myself to ask for it. I hoped Adela would bring up the subject herself, but she didn't.'

'I don't know what's been playing around in your mind. You have to pull yourself together, Bhaio.'

'Yeah, Sundar.'

'How's your son?'

'He's beautiful. He just fixed his eyes on me for a long time.'

'He knows who you are, Bhaio. Happy – yeah?'

'Yeah. How's your father, Sundar?'

'He's very poorly. That's why I came to consult the Jinn. He's been asking about you, Bhaio.'

'I'd love to see him. Would you take me to see him?'

'Yeah, sure. I don't know when, though. I'll get back to you in a couple of days.'

Syed Kalam Noorpuri – the son of the Bringer – came out to the patio to tell them that his father was ready.

All had taken their places on the carpet facing the Bringer, who was also seated on the floor, against the rear wall. Stepping carefully, Tapan and Sundar made their way and sat next to Masuk Ali and Cook Bhai. There were pillows scattered on the carpet to lean on and blankets for covering feet. No food was allowed but you could chew paan, provided that the movement of the jaws was subtle enough to be almost inaudible – and there was certainly to be no expectoration. Everyone except the Doctor had a paan in his mouth. As the acolyte to the ceremony, the son of the Bringer took his place next to his father against the rear wall. Although not completely dark, the lighting was minimal: two candlesticks throwing small flames on either side of the Bringer and a few joysticks glowing lazily in the stillness of the room. At first, apart from musk from the bodies of the Bringer and his son, there was only the smell of sandalwood from the joss sticks. Then the son added the scent of roses by scattering water from a sprinkling jar. On the rear wall the Bringer and the son cast long shadows that thinned out on the ceiling.

Suddenly the Bringer started making strange sounds: indistinguishable syllables merging into one another, in a nasal flow, broken only by some guttural interruptions. No one recognised the sounds, let alone understood them. The shadows at the back were absolutely still.

Now the nasal flow, without the guttural interruptions, assumed the complex modulation of a symphony. First bees, swarms of them, humming among flowers, from around the hive, then from deep within their honeycombs. Would the Jinn listen to their summons? Wind rustled through the leaves of endless rows of bamboo, right up to the sky. Not yet.

Then there were waves so gentle, so regular that they seemed not to break at all, but slide over the scales of fish that gathered on the surface to look at the sun. After a hummingbird fluttered its wings, the rain began to fall, the interminable rain of monsoon. Not on tin roofs, but on the silk covering of an umbrella. Even the sitar held its breath and trembled for minutes to conclude a raga. Still the Jinn didn't come.

At last the Bringer gave his voice to the purring of sewing machines, like the ones Tapan had heard so often before; room after room, flat after flat throughout East London, Bangladeshi women driving their machines as they churned up endless collars, sleeves and button holes. It really surprised Tapan that the noise that had annoyed him so much previously, disturbed his sleep on so many occasions, could be so beautiful. Suddenly the candles fluttered abruptly and went out along with the joss sticks.

The room was full of cold air. Even with blankets wrapped around their shoulders, they couldn't stop shivering. Then they heard the mountain landing on the roof. It felt as if the house was about to cave in, but it didn't because the Jinn was a being of light, or air. And he had arrived.

Panting heavily, the Jinn said, 'Why'd you call me? I'm too old to be zooming around the world at a moment's notice. I was praying happily in Azmir, calling the name of Allah, then I hear this buzzing. Someone sending me secret codes and names. I don't like it but one is bound by the ancient order to respond to a summons. Ya, I had to come, but why assault my eardrums with that damn noise of sewing machines? Surely even in England you could find something better to call me with. Anyway, get on with it. Ask me what you need to ask, but be quick about it. I'm sure you want me to be a silly clairvoyant for you. I don't understand why you waste a Jinn's time with such nonsense. You should have called a gypsy woman for that.'

From the dark, the Bringer called out the names. First he called Abdul Ali, who stuttered and almost choked on his words.

Before he could articulate anything clearly, the Jinn said, 'Come on, man. Don't be a scary baby, I'm not going to eat you alive. But I know what you want to ask. No, you're not returning to Bangladesh as a big man. Forget about it. Your lot is in England now. So make the best of it.'

Then he called Masuk Ali.

He was also choking, but managed to say, 'Koh-i-noor.'

'What about it?' said the Jinn. 'If you want to rescue it like they do in the movies, then forget about it. But keep on digging, the stone will come to you.'

The Doctor was the third to be called out.

'Venerable Jinn, Hujur, I'm most desirous of knowing about my wife-bibi,' said the Doctor. 'Is she romantically involved with any other fellow? Will she come back to me?'

'How come *you're* here, Doc?' said the Jinn. 'I thought you didn't even believe that I exist. Anyway, don't be so vain, man. Who would fancy your old, ugly wife? No, she won't come back to you. But if you change your financial practices, then there's a slim chance.'

Then he called out Tapan.

Before Tapan could open his mouth, the Jinn said, 'You want to know whether you will fly – don't you?' Tapan didn't say anything, but the Jinn continued.

'Very strange notion. Don't you know that your kind don't fly. Only the winged creatures and us Jinns can fly.' Then, after pausing for a long time, the Jinn said, 'But wait a minute. I see something very odd indeed. A flying mole. Oh, no, it can't be true. Please, please I can't say any more. It will be a blasphemy against Allah's law.'

It took the Jinn a while to calm down. Finally the Bringer called out Sundar.

'How long does my father have? Should I take his dead body back to Bangladesh?'

'You know the rules,' said the Jinn. 'You shouldn't ask questions about life and death. Even we Jinns know nothing about these matters. But bury your father where you consider his home to be. You know, the place where he really belongs.'

The Jinn was in a hurry to leave; the Bringer thanked him for responding to his summons. Suddenly there was silence again, the mountain lifted from the roof, and the Jinn was gone. The son of the Bringer lit the candles.

On the road to their tower block, they spotted the guys who'd followed them earlier. Seeing them waiting they decided to split up. Cook Bhai walked to the front of the block, past the men. Tapan and Masuk Ali went around the back. There, Masuk Ali knocked on a door on the ground floor. A middle-aged Bangladeshi man let them in. From there, along a secret passageway, they arrived in the ground-floor flat underneath which the tunnel began.

Lifting the hatch, they went down the shaft, into the basement. For a while they stayed quiet in the dark. Above them they could hear the men in suits going through the ground-floor rooms, but never suspecting what lay under their feet. Soon they gave up and Masuk Ali lit the candles and both he and Tapan sank into the hammocks.

Swinging gently, Masuk Ali asked, 'What was all that about, Soul Brother? I don't dig that crazy stuff about flying.'

'I know it's crazy, Masuk. I can't describe it. It's a feeling that I sometimes get.'

'Don't you go and try it for real. Bloody dangerous, innit? If you don't kill yourself, they'll put you in a loony bin.'

Eyes half closed, Tapan looked at Masuk Ali's shadow undulating on the ceiling like a boat on gentle waves, but he didn't say anything. After a while Masuk Ali got up, put on his miner's helmet, and went down the tunnel to dig.

Tapan rocked in the hammock, thinking about Tipu. He must be asleep at this hour, or had he just woken up crying? Was Adela breastfeeding him to console him? But Nilufar – caring for Kaisar – wouldn't sleep through the night. Perhaps she would have slept, as he was about to do in the hammock, if she, too, had been enraptured by the passionate embrace of muscles, metal and earth as Masuk Ali dug the tunnel.

CHAPTER 19

The next day Tapan woke up late. As always it was dark in the basement, but he never thought he could have slept so soundly in a hammock. Masuk Ali had already left. Tapan stayed rocking in the hammock and lit a cigarette, but after a while, couldn't resist the call of the tunnel. Unlike Masuk Ali and Cook Bhai, he didn't need a helmet with a light on. His nose was more than enough to enable him to negotiate the dark tunnel. After randomly exploring some of the tributaries, he crawled along the main tunnel until he reached the face. He could sense that the Tower was only a short distance away. Perhaps a few more weeks of labour and Masuk Ali and Cook Bhai would take the tunnel right beneath the Tower. Then it would be simply a matter of boring upwards.

He rolled over and lay on his back on the damp earth. It felt so safe that he would have switched his mind off if he hadn't then begun thinking about Brother Josef K – the mole who showed him the secret passageways through East London. You see, even moles get lonely and want to connect with other moles.

One day during the summer of '78, as they were standing together on the picket line, Tapan had greeted Brother Josef K, and then, on the spur of the moment, as he looked into Brother Josef's solitary eyes, that as always were searching for somewhere to burrow, he'd invited him to have a tea with him. To Tapan's surprise, Brother Josef K nodded his head. On the way home, Tapan bought two bagels with salt beef from *Beygel Bake*. It took them only a few minutes to arrive at Sundar's flat, where Tapan was then living.

Tapan made a pot of tea, put the bagels on a plate. Taking a bite of one of the bagels, Brother Josef K shook his head but Tapan had to wait until he'd finished munching his mouthful, swallowed it, and taken a sip of the tea to find out what had prompted this movement.

'Uncanny. So uncanny, Comrade. I knew that certain patterns in history repeat themselves, but never thought that they could copy themselves.'

'What are you talking about, Brother Josef?'

'This thing in Brick Lane. You know, I've seen it before. Yes, comrade. Way back in '36, in Cable Street.'

From then on, whenever they got together, Brother Josef K took Tapan on long walks around East London. Even though Brother Josef K was much older and bulkier than Tapan, he walked so fast that Tapan had trouble keeping up with him. While on the road Brother Josef K never spoke. Only when they arrived at the door of his house in Hessel Street would he open his mouth. 'We've arrived then, Comrade,' he would say boldly, his voice crackling like deep frost at the unexpected arrival of the sun.

First they would go down through his repair shop on the ground floor to the basement, which was just as cluttered with broken radios, old clocks and watches and dismembered gramophones as the shop upstairs. No, it was more cluttered and cramped as books, newspapers and magazines competed with the mechanical junk to make the place their own. Brother Josef K appeared among them as if he were the stranger. But, that wasn't the place where he lived. Beyond the thick oak door, further down the stairs – low arched and crypt-like – was his place, as cluttered with printed pages and mechanical junk as the floor above. It was large enough, though, to accommodate a single bed, a small desk with a purple-shaded study lamp, an electric cooker, a small refrigerator and an ancient wardrobe. Adjacent to it was the bathroom with blue tiles and Don Quixote, skeletal and hunched up on his horse, facing the loo. The place was silent. Tapan had always imagined it to be like the bottom of the ocean, though he had no idea what the bottom of the ocean was really like.

Once the oak door was secured tightly behind him, Brother Josef K would say, 'All right, Comrade?' as if he were testing the acoustics and trying to find the right modulation. He would make coffee, light his pipe and go through the places they had walked by, as if it was only after the event, and in the ghostly simulation of words, that he was able to see them for the first time. Had Tapan noticed, for instance, Kingsley Hall in Bow, where Gandhi – dressed as a half-naked fakir – stayed in 1931? Did he know that Gandhi brought his own goat all the way from India and milked it himself each morning? Cockneys really loved him, Comrade, they really did. But they were rather alarmed by his uncompromising veggie style. Blimey, not even fried bacon!

You wouldn't have thought so but in Fulborne Street, yeah Comrade, the whole lot – Lenin, Stalin and Trotsky – were cooking up October '17. Way back in 1907. I hope you had a good look at Jubilee Street, where our old friend Kropotkin used to bore the pants off his young and rather edgy followers with his long-winded philosophising. Like Gandhi, his methods weren't that sound, eh Comrade?

About them Jewish places, what can I say? You didn't know that they existed here. Right? I grant it's hard to believe, but our places used to be as numerous as your Bangladeshi ones are now. You see – except for some old fellows like me – we moved on north. I heard that even Bloom is about to go. I bet you had no idea that once the Pavilion Theatre and the Grand Palais used to do full-house with Jewish entertainment along Whitechapel Road. You know, in those days, we Jews knew how to have fun. Yeah, Comrade, Rivoli Cinema was where you now see the new mosque. I could never forget, I was so scared, Comrade. If we had known, we never would have gone to see *The Cabinet of Dr. Caligari*. We were supposed to be at the synagogue but some of us boys, you know, sneaked out when the Rabbi was doing a long Talmudic number. We had no idea what kind of film it was. All them long fingers, elongated by the dark shadows gave me nightmares for years. When Mosley appeared on the scene, wearing all black, I thought I had seen him in that film. Isn't it funny, Comrade? Did I tell you about Artillery Passage? One of your fellows – damn it, what was his name? – you know, the one who shot Sir

Michael O'Dwyer? Yeah, Udham Singh. He used to hide in an attic there.

How could he not have remembered Udham Singh before? So many times Tapan had passed through Artillery Passage, but he'd never felt the presence of Udham Singh. Now it occurred to him that Udham Singh had been a mole long before him. He was glad that he'd been there.

It was strange that Udham Singh should follow the path already traced by Syed Ali – our first man and the first cook. If Tapan had believed in reincarnation how beautiful it would have been to imagine that Udham Singh was actually Syed Ali in a different body at a later time. Like Syed Ali, he'd grown with the memories of blood engraved on his soul by the colonial machine. Perhaps there were many others who also dreamt of avenging the Jalianwallahbag massacre of 1919, but he was the one who acted on it.

When he arrived in England in the summer of '33 no one had suspected him. Rather, he was thought of as a suave gentleman with more than a touch of anglophilia about him. Even Sir O'Dwyer, who had reason enough to be suspicious, trusted him as soon as he laid his eyes on him, and appointed him as his chauffeur without bothering with security clearance. In fact, O'Dwyer couldn't believe his luck when Udham Singh came along: he could finally put to rest the rumours that he hated all Indians. Sitting stiff and chin-up next to Udham Singh in the driving seat, O'Dwyer would go around London showing off his intimacy with brown fellows. These drives replayed documentary newsreels of his times in India when he played a colonial lord with a loyal Indian servant. Udham Singh was happy to go along with these archaic black and white scenes, because they allowed him to find the ideal location for shooting O'Dwyer. Often on their own, he had ample opportunities for killing O'Dwyer on the quiet and disappearing, but he decided he wanted to make it a public event. He disappeared from Devon where he was working with Sir O'Dwyer and began the life of a mole in East London. In 1940 he saw his opportunity when Sir O'Dwyer was appearing with other Empires types at a public meeting at Caxton Hall – where he shot O'Dwyer dead at point-blank range.

Apparently O'Dwyer looked moved as he saw Udham Singh approaching him. Perhaps he thought he was coming to greet him with the wild enthusiasm characteristic of the typical Oriental. Perhaps it was too late for him to realise that stereotypes could kill.

Although the events leading up to the shooting of O'Dwyer were momentous, Tapan was more interested in what happened to Udham Singh afterwards, why he had let himself be captured. He wondered whether Udham Singh knew that he would never return to India. Certainly if Udham Singh had become a mole, hiding and burrowing like Vatya Das, he might have evaded the long arms of British law. How Udham Singh would have loved to have spent time with Vatya Das – whispering in his ears so gently that even the walls of his burrow wouldn't have registered the slightest vibration – as Udham Singh was doing now to Tapan. Yes, yes, Tapan knew that if Udham Singh had been content to remain a mole, they never would have found him. It wasn't that he was unhappy being a mole. Indeed he spent some of his happiest hours in the attic in Artillery Passage, but he'd wanted to be a bird too.

Tapan had no idea how much time had passed. Enveloped in the moist earth, he felt so safe and comfortable that he could have stayed there for the rest of his life. But he had to go up. From the basement he climbed up the shaft to the ground floor, and then to the flat on the seventh floor.

Neither Masuk Ali nor Cook Bhai was in the flat. It was already night but he wasn't hungry. He went out onto the street. No matter how hard he tried he could never correct the illegal immigrant's stoop. His flat cap came right over his forehead and his chin was almost drowned in the lapel of his long coat. As he wandered the streets, he suddenly found himself in Adler Street. Looking at the bell-tower of St.Bonifatius Haus, he became – as always – overwhelmed by the memories of Altab Ali, who was murdered there on May 4, 1978.

At the end of Adler Street he turned around and headed for Brother Josef K's flat. Cold wind was cutting through his bones and the streets were empty, but at the turning of Fairclough Street Tapan had the distinct feeling that someone was following him.

He couldn't see anyone, couldn't hear a thing – not even a soft footfall on the pavement or the creak of a shoe. If a body – no matter how aerodynamically shaped – moved in the slightest he could pick up the vibration from the air. But there was nothing. If everything else failed he could always rely on his nose. God damn it! But how could he orientate his snout among such a smell of spices? But while crossing Christian Street he was able to pick up, beyond the spices, a distinctive smell. At first he thought he was confusing himself with someone else, because that other smell was exactly like his own. Perhaps there was no one there, perhaps it was only paranoia. So he eased himself for a while. Then it occurred to him that this could be a trap. Someone could be mimicking his odour to induce a false sense of security so that he could move against him at his most unguarded moment. He quickened his pace, almost ran through Burslem Street, and turned into Hessel Street. He looked around – still panting – and seeing that the street was empty, rang the bell. No response for a while. Tapan took his rizlas out and, his hands shaking, began to roll a fag. Suddenly Brother Josef K came from behind and said, 'Comrade.' Tapan was taken aback. Perhaps Brother Josef K had been watching his door from the outside as moles often do.

Breathless, shreds of tobacco dripping off the rizla, he told Brother Josef K that someone had been following him. Brother Josef K scratched his giant, bald head with curly fringes and smiled with a faint chuckle. He said he knew all about it, because it was he who had been following him since he turned into Fairclough Street. No wonder Tapan had smelt a familiar odour. Brother Josef K was a mole too. Cautiously, Brother Josef K opened the door and they went in together. First the shop, then the basement, through the thick oak door, until, descending the steep stairs, they arrived at Brother Josef K's place.

Tapan didn't have to explain anything. Brother Josef K knew his situation well from the way he flared his snout, from his gait and posture. He toasted some bagels and made tea. Brother Josef K sat on one side of the bed, Tapan on the other. For a long time there was silence in the dimly lit room. From time to time Brother Josef K got up to check the door, cocking his head to the left so that he could pick up any intruder in the vicinity, lowering his voice to a whisper to evade detection. But, he was more than willing to talk without holding anything back.

'You know, Comrade,' he began, 'for the most part of history we Jews have been hunted. Time has tied us to dreadful names such as Inquisition, Pogrom and Gas Chambers. We feel cornered and trapped. Have I told you my recurrent dream? I've had it as far back as I can remember and still do. It begins with an ordinary scene. When I was young, I could be kicking a football in the yard, or on my way to school. Now mostly I'm out shopping for fruits and vegetables, or cleaning the windows of my shop from the outside. You see, Comrade, irrespective of the initial setting, it always proceeds the same way. Oh yes, it is a sunny day and I'm in a very happy mood. For some reason, especially if I find myself cleaning the windows, I hum a Yiddish song. But I have never imagined myself as one of those "strange exotics in a land of prose" as Brother Zangwill had us painted. As you can see, Comrade, I'm prose myself – very ordinary. Anyway, it happens so suddenly that it takes time for me to realise what has happened.

'A mob, all worked up for Jewish blood, is after me. I run as fast as I can, try all sorts of tricks to lose them. Even if I lose them for a while, they always find me at the turning of the next street. Finally they corner me in a street with high walls and no way out. Sensing blood, the mob rushes in with everything they've got. I'm usually less scared of the ones with iron bars, knives and jagged stones in their hands. I fear most the ones who come empty handed. They have it all along in their minds to use their teeth on me. I know that they would tear open my belly with their teeth and go berserk on my intestines. But what can I do?

'In this situation one could do either of two things: go underground or take to the air, dig a burrow like a mole and hide under the earth, or fly away like an insect or a bird. The first option is easier and involves less risk. But it is less efficient because they can always smoke you out, or wait at the mouth of your burrow for you to surface. To be a flyer – either a gigantic insect or a bird – is very difficult. And also very risky. You can kill yourself in the process, but if you succeed, the rewards are greater.

'But I don't dare be a flyer even in my dreams. When the mob

224

is ready to pounce on me, I become a mole and dig a passage underground with my paws. But they don't give up and I dig deeper and twist and turn into more convoluted passages. I entertain the idea that if I can construct a labyrinth I will be safe. It is hard work but I do end up laying out a labyrinth. Yet, they are always about to get me in the end. That is when I get up to put on the light, listen for any unusual sound, and check my oak door. For the rest of the night I don't sleep. You see, Comrade, I'm just a mole.'

Between bagels and cups of tea they talked for few more hours. Brother Josef K told him that although he was a mole, he had never felt solitary in his dreams. Usually his father would be there, but not to punish him, or to tell him off for turning into a mole. No. His father licks his fur to clean it, washes his paws with his own bare hands, and rubs his snout against his. Before Tapan left, Brother Josef K told him not to attempt to become a bird. 'You do it as a last resort, Comrade,' he said. 'Only if you don't have any other option left.'

When he arrived back at his shelter he didn't see Masuk Ali or Cook Bhai. Perhaps they'd gone down to the basement and were digging the tunnel. He went to bed, but his mind was going over and over Brother Josef K's idea that the Battle of Brick Lane '78 was inseparable from the Battle of Cable Street '36. Soon, both Brother Josef K and Sundar were whispering in his ears. There was no competition between them as each awaited his turn: as soon as one had ended, the other began. They went on like this the whole night, whispering their memories of *Our City*. The only difference between October 4, 1936 and July 17, 1978 was the season: during the autumn, Josef, the Yiddish boy, listening to the low murmurs of the grown-ups in his father's repair shop in the Jew Market, the tick-tock of modern time moving fast to erase them from the face of the earth: Krakow, Auschwitz, Treblinka – nowhere was safe; Mosley marching in black; Josef singing *No Pasaran, No Pasaran* on the cobbles along the long length of Cable Street; forty-two years later, during the hot summer, Sundar, a young Bangladeshi waiter stumbles on Altab Ali dying between the beech trees singing from St. Mary's yard and the tall steeple of St. Bonifatius Haus; Sundar screaming a tunnel of wind down Brick Lane, no words, just a scream to exist; and Josef, his father screaming too, pouring out the dregs of pogroms and the dread of centuries. But there was joy too: Mosley didn't pass the clock tower at Gardiners; old orthodox Jews, looking like Polish noblemen, slipped through the autumnal chill, and danced in the street well into the night; little Josef was happy then, but *Kristallnacht* will be repeated forty-two years later in Brick Lane: there were Sundar's feet, keeping pace with Altab Ali's coffin, as they went tracing the memories of blood all the way to Downing Street. Yet it is their bodies pressing through the asphalt that really did it: so many of them surfaced on July 17, brown faces, their eyes cleansed of terror, so many of them sat unyielding on Bethnal Green Road, their separate bodies merging into one another. No one spoke a word, but Sundar, his eyes feeding on the sun, saw his father next to Brother Josef; he was wearing a white askan and chewing paan and digging his body deeper and deeper into the ground. At last Sundar knew that the National Front could not pass through Brick Lane any more.

CHAPTER 20

Nilufar was in bed with a book, not really reading, just looking and listening to the pages as they fluttered like moths' wings. She got up to check Kaisar who was sleeping on the floor of her sitting room. At first, in the partly darkened room, she hadn't noticed that he was sweating. A check on his temperature confirmed a fever; he hardly moved, only moaned slightly. She dabbed his head with a wet towel. At the door she stood for a while as if guarding the room against the intrusion of some evil spirit. If her mother had been there, she would have prayed loudly and sealed the room with divine words. Her own words had lost their aura a long time ago.

She got up and went to the bathroom. On the loo, she noticed the ivy, its leaves dry and yellowed. From the low ceiling a spider had spun its web to tangle its tendrils and the leaves. Spiders always knew best; it knew that the ivy was already dead. It must have been ages since she'd last watered it. Now she knew what the spider knew, but still she got up to water the plant. Muddy water dripped on the floor. There was no sight of the spider – laughing its head off, hiding in a cranny, or some dark corner, perhaps. She went back to the bedroom. At least she wasn't alone; she could hear Kaisar's disrupted, heavy breathing.

She turned sideways in the bed, looking at the long, thin triangle of light that spilled through the open door into the room. In the distance, an ambulance rushed on its way, sirening in the night. Apart from Kaisar's heavy breathing there was silence again. She knew, just as during the last few nights, she wouldn't be able to sleep.

The next morning her mother – accompanied by Shapna and Shahid – came to take Kaisar to see the Most Venerable Pir-Sahib. Before that her mother wanted them to have breakfast together. She had brought two canvas bags full of cooked food.

It really surprised Shapna that Nilufar hadn't created a big fuss about their mother's decision to take Kaisar to see the Most Venerable Pir-Sahib. Even a short while ago, Nilufar would have launched into a full-blown tirade against the Most Venerable one, calling him all sorts of names. Now she seemed prepared to go along with anything for Kaisar's sake.

As they made tea in the kitchen, Shapna told Nilufar that the day before they'd been to the airport to see their father off to Bangladesh. He'd been asking questions about Kaisar and they'd had a tough time evading him. At one point her mother nearly gave the game away by bursting out crying, but Shahid had been so thoughtful: he'd led Surat Ali to the restaurant upstairs for a tea, and kept him occupied with his anecdotes about the quality of in-flight lunches and the rudeness of air-hostesses.

Just before the final announcement of his flight, her mother told their father not to forget to light a candle at the village shrine for each of the children. Her father nodded his head, but her mother wanted to be sure. She said, 'Don't forget our Nilu. Promise me, you won't.' Her father became very still, his cigarette almost burning his fingers, and there was a hint of dampness in his eyes. He lifted his chin as if to squeeze the tap of his tears tightly shut behind his eyes. But her mother continued to look at him so directly that he had to open them. He wiped his eyes with his sleeve and set off abruptly through the passport control, without looking back, to the security check.

That morning, her mother had got up early to prepare khichuri, parata, boona lamb and fried deshi cheese. On the way to Nilufar's flat she made Shahid stop at Ambala to buy some meesty-sweet. She made sure that he got rashmallay for Nilufar and ladoo for Kaisar. Now she set the food on the table; Shapna and Nilufar brought fresh tea from the kitchen.

Everybody was at the table except Kaisar who, slumped on the sofa, was staring at the television. Shapna and Nilufar laughed at their mother's attempt, as in the old days, to hurry Kaisar along, but Shahid pulled a serious face. He said, 'If he'd had some discipline, he wouldn't have been so spoilt. All he needs is a strong hand.'

Shapna pretended she had heard nothing; Nilufar was about to say something cynical but stopped when she saw her mother coming back into the room.

As usual, everyone at the table was relishing Hasina Bibi's cooking, but Kaisar, after nibbling at a parata, was dozing off. Seeing this, Hasina Bibi started looking anxious again, and was about to say something, but Shahid coughed to draw attention to himself. He told them that he'd already exchanged contracts on their four-bedroomed semi-detached in Bromley, and they would be moving soon.

'Now that I've two restaurants and plenty of income coming in, it's time to move on to a better place. So many low-class people around here. You might think of me as an uppity/wuppity sahib, but one has to admit it, the ghetto is not a right place for my daughter to grow up. Where we are going, everything is decent. Only nice English people. No Country Brothers to spoil the place for you.'

Nilufar gritted her teeth, determined not to start a row. Suddenly Kaisar perked up and said, 'You're talking a load of crap, brother-in-law. I kinda knew that Thatcher Maggi was filling your head with shit. But you're... okay, you made few bobs, but you're still a Paki, innit? See how them posh places treat you.'

Her mother and Shapna had their heads down, pretending to be concentrating on their plates. Nilufar, although quietly pleased by Kaisar's outburst, said, 'Enough! Let's have some peace and quiet.'

But Shahid wasn't going to drop the matter without having the last word.

'You don't know what you talking about, Kaisar. Your head is not correct. You'd do well to listen to Misses T. She has no time for the lazy/uzzies, dole-mongering types. You must admit that some of our Country Brothers are... But she's a mighty friend of us business people. I think our people should stop moaning and listen to her. There would be plenty of profit for everyone.'

Kaisar threw his hands in the air and looked to be on the point of exploding when their mother slipped in to say, 'I hear that Maggi missus is very fond of colour prejudice. It's a very bothering matter for our Deshi people. Na?'

'A bit of colour prejudice doesn't harm anyone, Motherjan,' Shahid replied, picking at fragments of lamb stuck between his teeth. 'I don't mind their swamping/wumping talk as long as they don't do a runner after eating in my restaurant. I must say it has practically no effect on us business people. Besides, Maggi Begum likes nothing better than moneymaking activities. When you make plenty, she doesn't even see in what colour of skin you carry yourself. This is my policy, Motherjan. Make plenty money and stay above the colour line.'

Suddenly Shapna thumped the table and screamed, 'Stop it.' Nilufar was shocked by the bitterness in her sister's face as she turned away from Shahid. After this, the meal stuttered to an end in an embarrassed silence.

As they cleared the table her mother told Nilufar, 'Now that your father is away in Bangladesh, it is best that Kaisar moves in with me. Look at you. Oh Allah, how your health is getting ruined taking care of your little brother.'

'I'm fine, Amma. It's no trouble looking after Kaisar.'

'Also, you've your teaching-wuching and social work and what not to do. You can move in with me for a while too. I can feed you something decent. Oh Allah, you're getting so thin.'

'That wouldn't be a good idea, Amma.'

'Listen. Your father will never know. Even if he knows, who cares? I hope he comes back from Bangladesh with his head corrected. Come home, my first born; we will cook together like old days.'

Nilufar closed the subject by saying that she would think about it. She packed Kaisar's things, explained to her mother his medicines, and what to do in an emergency. Of course, she could always call on her.

After they had left, Nilufar took stock. She had disengaged from everything to look after Kaisar – even from Tapan. Now that her mother had taken him, what was she to do with so much free time? Perhaps she should take a holiday, perhaps go to one of those Greek islands that colleagues at work had been telling her so much about. It would have been so nice to go with Tapan, the two of them laughing their heads off watching the awkward antics of the English on the beach, or watching the sun go down in the Aegean, or getting drunk on Metaxa and losing all inhibitions to dance to a Rebetika on the floor of a cheap tourist restaurant. But Tapan couldn't go anywhere. She put the plates away in the kitchen and arranged the lounge back to its old order. She was hoping that Tapan would phone. She was feeling so alone.

CHAPTER 21

Tapan took the tube at Whitechapel to meet Nilufar in Soho. At Aldgate East Poltu Khan got on and sat beside him.

'Where you going, Tapan Ali, my man?'

Tapan mumbled the first place that came to his mind.

'Russell Square. I thought I'd check out the old SOAS library.'

'Would you believe, I'm heading that way myself. Strange, how we two always seem to be heading in the same direction. I'm not a sentimental man, Tapan Ali. If I were, I'd have said we're connected. You know, soul to soul.'

Now Tapan had no option but to go along with Poltu Khan. Once in SOAS, Poltu Khan suggested they had a tea in the canteen before entering the library.

They sat in a corner with a window to their back, away from the students, who were occupying the front and the middle tables. Stirring cubes of sugar into the polystyrene cup, Poltu Khan said: 'If you don't want to keep company with me... well, what can I say? Too bad but – seriously – I understand. I'm sure you've heard a load of losers bad-mouthing me. You see, unlike them, I have it sorted. I say, if you have to whinge like a sissy, why bloody bother to be an immigrant? I say this immigration thing is not for the faint hearted. You're an educated man, Tapan Ali – what do you think?'

'I don't know what you talking about, Mr. Khan.'

'Bloody losers always moaning about me not having the right method. Of course, they don't say it to my face. When they see me they get too busy licking my ass to open their bloody gobs. It doesn't please me to look at them kindly, but the thing is, I do help them.'

'You do whatever you like, Mr. Khan. It's none of my business.'

'You're damn right. But the thing is, I do help them. Have you wondered how many of them would've had it cushy as legals without my help? What the fuck they know about correct method? Anyway, damned if I give a fuck about that moral shit. Tell me, Tapan Ali, am I right to say that mushy stuff about good and evil has no place in the life of an immigrant? Yeah, yeah, I know you'll give me some liberal crap about upright conducts.'

'I'm not here to judge you either way, Mr. Khan. But surely you've some criteria to guide your actions.'

'I knew you were a reasonable man, Mr. Tapan. When I said I'd a soft spot for you – believe it or not – I really meant it. Yeah, certainly, I've my rules of conduct. But let me put it this way. What I amount to is no more and no less than an immigrant. I see you look a bit puzzled. Let me ask you a question: What has made us become immigrants in the first place? What, indeed, made us leave behind our friends and relatives, the land in which we grew up?'

'I suppose we wanted to better ourselves. Improve our life chances. Some of us simply wanted to eat. I don't have to remind you how things are back in Bangladesh.'

'Good, good, Tapan Ali. You're on the right track. But let me put it this way. It might sound crude, but the fact is, none of us came here for any morally compelling reason. We didn't become immigrants for some fancy idea – er, what do you call it? – yeah, utopia in our heads. We've betrayed so much – our neighbours, our friends, our parents, and our country – to come here simply to live some goody-goody lives. No, my friend. From top to bottom we had no other consideration than – as you put it – bettering ourselves. People less kinder than yourself would say: we've been purely and squarely a selfish lot.'

'That's a bit over the top, if I may say so, Mr. Khan.'

'May be, Tapan Ali, but I don't go around quarrelling with them. That's not my style. I say, yeah, fuck with that whole crap about good and bad. The less I care about them, the better it is. You see, I'm a pure immigrant. As such I'm beyond good and evil. But I've my criteria of action.'

'What are these, Mr. Khan?'

'Well. You see, at the end of the day I do take stock of things. I count the things that have increased my wealth, my power and my avenues of pleasure. The opinion of others doesn't concern me. Nor do I care about appropriate methods. I'm only interested in results. I would use any method – legal-illegal, legitimate-illegitimate, kind-cruel – to achieve them. Of course, one can't ignore the economy of method. For instance, I don't do drugs,' said Poltu Khan.

'So you draw a line somewhere?'

'Sure, but not for any moral crap. It's a free market, innit? If there's a demand, you supply it. But I don't go near drugs because it is a costly method for increasing your wealth and power. You know the authorities are very touchy about it. It reminds them that there's a big hole in the free market system. So they act rather irrationally and out of all proportion on this subject.'

'I thought the authorities had given you a blank cheque, Mr. Khan.'

'Come, come, Tapan Ali. Don't you listen to rumours. Anyway, I'm a successful immigrant. I've accumulated a lot of wealth, and in the arena where I operate, I've power. Some people would humiliate themselves like domestic dogs to gain my favour, and others fear me like they fear Shitladevi. You know, the queen of smallpox herself. As for pleasure – what can I say? Of course, I gain enormous pleasure in taking stock of my wealth and power. I eat in the best restaurants; beautiful women buzz around me to pluck my honey. I'm a successful immigrant, Mr. Tapan. I'm a happy man. So why should I spoil it all by worrying about nonsense like good and evil.'

'So you will sell anybody, Mr. Khan, as long as it increases your wealth and power?'

'As a rule, yes, of course. But in practice it depends who we're talking about and under what circumstances. It might give me pleasure to save someone too.'

'So you have some conscience after all.'

'You're not hearing me right, Tapan Ali. Can't you tell the difference between pleasure and that moral crap?'

'Okay, okay, Mr. Khan. You made your point.'

'Listen. Let's not beat about the bush – right? I know you're in a spot of bother right now. If you want, I can fix it for you. I told you before, and I'm telling you now, I'd like to help you. I don't know why I feel like that about you, but the fact is I do. It has nothing to do with kindness. By now you should know that I don't give a shit about that kind of nonsense. It would just please me enormously to do something for you. Don't worry if you can't come to my office. Leave your address, I'll get in touch with you. Otherwise, I'll just have to trace you – won't I?'

'I know you've been tracing me, Mr. Khan. But what I don't get, is why you haven't given me in already? I don't know what game you're playing with me?'

'Bloody hell, there you go again. Weren't you listening to me? You don't get what I'm saying – do you?'

Tapan stayed silent for a while and then he said he needed to go to the loo urgently.

'Of course, if you need to go, you need to go. But think over seriously what I said. It's not every day that I offer to help out someone for free.'

Tapan lifted his rucksack from the floor and left it on the chair to show that he wasn't planning a runner. He walked calmly to the stairs leading to the bar in the basement, which was packed with students and the smell of beer and cigarettes. As soon as he was sure Poltu Khan couldn't see him any more, he jumped down two or three steps at a time, snaked through the crowd in the bar, out through the side exit, then almost ran through the long corridor to the stairs up to the lobby. Apart from the porter and the security guards, the lobby it was empty.

At Russell Square station, he took the winding stairs down, becoming dizzy as he went round and round on the metallic steps, sounding like a tap dancer. On the platform he looked around to see if Poltu Khan was already there, waiting. He thought it odd that a wily old fox like Poltu Khan should fall for such a banal trick. Wouldn't he have deduced that he wasn't coming back the moment he saw him hesitate a second as he put the bag on his empty chair? Or, perhaps it just pleased him to let him go.

When Tapan finally reached Soho, Nilufar wasn't there. She

must have left thinking that he wasn't coming. He rang her number, then Sundar's. Neither was in. He wandered around Soho for a while, hoping that Nilufar was doing the same, that somehow he would bump into her. Then he returned to his shelter in East London. Neither Cook Bhai nor Masuk Ali was in.

Tapan was surprised to see the key to the ground floor flat hanging from a hook in the kitchen. Masuk Ali usually carried that key with him everywhere. He even slept with it. Tapan took the key, went down to the ground floor and into the flat. Lifting the hatch, down the shaft, and through the basement, he entered the tunnel. He groped through the tunnel, going as far as he could go, then took several of the tributaries. He began slowly, but speeded up after a few metres, breezing through the tributaries. By the time he ended he was tearing along at the velocity of a runaway train. He felt so happy that he didn't realise how tired he was.

He slumped in the hammock and swung himself gently. Was it Vatya Das, who was whispering in his ear? Yes, it was him, but he was flying, his ashes consorting with the thermal and he was telling him, 'Tapan Bapu, look, no one can catch me now. Isn't it wonderful to be a bird?' Yes, I know, Vatya Da, if I become a bird, no traitor can sell me out, no Immigration can catch me, but how can I become a bird? Please, tell me, Vatya Da, please. 'You know, I can't tell you that, Tapan Bapu. But my brother Mansur al-Hallaj, you know him, don't you? He can't tell you either, but, perhaps, he can show you.' How can a mystic be your brother, Vatya Da? Have you stopped being a materialist? 'Don't be silly, Tapan Bapu. A materialist is always a materialist – even when he becomes a bird. Anyway, listen, it's not the time to argue. Just follow Brother Mansur al-Hallaj.'

Tapan pricked his ears to listen to the wind from the tunnel and, as he swung in his hammock, he felt as if he was one of the crowd gathered on the banks of the Tigris. He couldn't tell if anyone else had noticed Huma – the bearded griffon and the mightiest of birds. Huma was hovering high above the minaret that kept an eye over the river. Even if no one else had noticed him, everyone knew that it was a grace indeed if Huma's shadow fell on them. In fact, that person would be raised to heaven immediately.

Perhaps the Vizier, Hamid ibn Abbas, had an inkling of it. Otherwise, why would he be mingling among the crowd, dressed as a beggar? More than anyone else it was Hamid ibn Abbas who needed to be touched by Huma's shadow. After all, he must have known that he was going straight to hell for the sins and abominations he had committed. For years he had plotted to get rid of al-Hallaj, had him arrested for blasphemy, and forced the judges to pass a death sentence on him. It was laughable, really, to think that such a rare lover of the divine – as al-Hallaj was – would claim himself to be divine when people heard him cry out in his moment of ecstasy: *ana'l-Haqq*. Even Hamid ibn Abbas, in his heart of hearts, knew that. He knew that al-Hallaj not only pursued the way of the *fana* – the annihilation of the self – but actually achieved *fana*. His love was *ishq* – that rare *jouissance* of the devout. But Hamid ibn Abbas was determined to get rid of al-Hallaj on charges of blasphemy.

It was Baghdad, 26 March 922.

First they whipped him a thousand times. Needless to say, a fraction of it would have killed most men, but al-Hallaj smiled through it as though he was the happiest man on earth. Silent, as they amputated his hands, then his legs, still he smiled. The only thing that worried al-Hallaj was the growing paleness of his face. He mustn't show a face drained of blood, as if the joy had left him, as if the ecstasy of love wasn't his any more. So he used the blood from the stumps of his amputated hands to redden his face. He looked radiant again. Seeing him like this, Hamid ibn Abbas became doubly worried and went up to the top of the minaret to see if he could spot Huma. But Huma had a way of evading unwanted eyes; it certainly hadn't come to take Hamid ibn Abbas to heaven.

Hands and legs amputated without anaesthetic and a thousand lashes on top, still al-Hallaj didn't die. As the night approached they hung his trunk from a scaffold with a hook, as the butchers did a piece of goat in a bazaar. It was a dark night and the guards prevented anyone approaching the scaffold with torches. Yet, in the dark, al-Hallaj shone like a full moon. From the distance, people could see a ray of love and ecstasy brightening the dark sky. In the morning, when the spring mist lifted and the dew slid down from the leaves of grass into the ground, they came to look for him. Surely, they thought, he would be dead by now, but he was still alive, glowing and smiling. Finally, with a single blow, the executioner cut al-Hallaj's head off, which was then exhibited from a long pole at the main bridge that crossed the Tigris. But it continued to glow and smile until...

The trunk was gathered in a reed basket and soaked in naphtha and burnt to ashes. From the minaret they scattered the ashes into the water of the Tigris. Just then Huma glided in to lift the ashes into the sky. No one, not even Hamid ibn Abbas, had the slightest inkling of it. Ho, ho, Brother al-Hallaj, you became a flyer. Didn't you, didn't you? Like Vatya Das, the materialist barber. What a fine sight you two are making, wings synchronised, flying together and taking the thermal. Yeah, beyond the clouds. Go brothers go. Higher, go beyond the blue. Would you take me, brothers, would you take me with you? Thank you, brothers, thank you. I can hear the swish of your wings. You are coming down for me, aren't you? Ah, I'm so happy, brothers, to be in your company. So happy.

CHAPTER 22

Tapan finally met Nilufar three days after their ill-fated appointment in Soho. He arrived early at the National Film Theatre on the South Bank. They didn't plan to see a film; it was the cafe they were coming for. He took a table and waited; she arrived within minutes.

While he kept the table, Nilufar queued at the self-service counter to buy sandwiches, muffins and cups of tea. She looked tired and a bit tense. He looked relaxed and exuberant. She looked at his eyes to see if they told her anything different. No. They were as transparent and as happy as the face.

'How are you?' she asked.

'Isn't it strange that I should be feeling so happy? But I really do, Nilu. Nothing worries me any more. Now I can even lift off the ground without even trying to do so. You want to see it, Nilu?'

Far from being reassured, Nilufar was even more worried. She could understand his anxiety, his disorientation. After all – given the stressful condition of his life on the run – it was natural for his moods to swing back and forth. But this obsession with flying was really scaring her. If he continued like this he might end up doing something catastrophic.

She was remembering a dream in which she finds herself ringing – over and over again – the same bell to a tall tower. She is desperate to reach the man on the roof. No one opens the door. It seems the man on the roof is suffering from the strange delusion of thinking that he is a bird. He is about to take off, but she can't do anything to stop him.

'How is Kaisar?' asked Tapan.

'He's doing well. Now that my father is away, he is staying with my mother.'

'How are you?'

'I'm fine. But you really scare me, Tapan. I can't fathom you any more. The things you say or do.'

'Don't worry about me, Nilu. I've never felt better. I feel so light. See.'

'Damn you. There you go again. I had this horrible dream the other day. Something terrible happened to you. If you stay like this you will end up... Shit! How do you expect me to wait for that moment? You don't understand what love does to you, do you?'

'But nothing will happen to me. You see, I feel so light and happy now.'

'Shit. Stop it. I can't take this nonsense any more.'

'Sorry, Nilu. I don't understand why you're getting so upset.'

Nilufar felt she wasn't getting through to him at all, so she decided to change the subject. 'Anyway, what did you want to talk to me about?'

'You know, I went to see Adela and Tipu.'

'Yeah. I suppose Tipu is your son. How is he?'

'He looks so beautiful. He has my grandfather's face. He kept staring at me with his green eyes.' Nilufar stayed silent, staring down at the table, picking up the muffin crumbs from the plate.

'That's nice. I'm happy for you.'

'Thanks, Nilu. I'm sure you'll like him.'

Nilufar felt she'd had enough of beating around the bush.

'Did you raise the divorce issue with Adela?'

'Well. As I told you before, it's a bit complicated.'

'Listen. I don't have time for your waffle. Give me a straight answer, will you?'

'I didn't raise the issue.'

'I don't understand, Tapan. What am I to make of it?'

'Look what that bloody marriage did to me and Adela. It destroyed what we had between us. I don't want this thing to happen again. Especially not with you.'

'We've gone over this ground before,' said Nilufar. 'But this is not the real reason why you didn't raise it with Adela. I wish you were a bit more honest with me, Tapan.'

'Yes, we have discussed it, but still I'm not sure. I don't want to make the same mistake twice. But I suppose...' Tapan hesitated as if he was about to confess to some shocking secret.

'What?'

'When I saw Adela I felt so sad. I suppose also guilty for abandoning her when she was having the child and all that. I suppose I just chickened out.'

'It's just typical of you. But what about your feelings for Adela?'

'We have a past together. I can't deny that, Nilufar. Now she is the mother of my child. I hope you understand that. But I only love you.'

'I don't know what to do with you, Tapan. Now we seem to be back to square one. And how long do you think you can keep up with this stupid mole business? And this nonsense about flying? I'm really scared, Tapan. These things have got to stop.'

'You worry about nothing, Nilu. I'm fine. I told you I've never felt happier and lighter.'

'Shit, there you go again. Okay, fuck the marriage idea, but if you love me, you have to promise me something.'

'You know I will do anything for you.'

'End this illegal immigrant thing right now and go back to Bangladesh.'

'I thought you wanted me to stay in England.'

'Of course I wanted you to stay. I didn't want to lose you. But now that you don't want to go through the only option left to us, I don't know what else to think.'

'I feel nothing will happen to me. Don't you worry, everything will turn out fine.'

'By what miracle? You can't go on being illegal any longer. If you do, I feel something terrible will happen to you. I just wouldn't be able to bear it, Tapan.'

'Look at me, Nilu. If I thought something bad was going to happen to me, wouldn't I be worried?'

Out on the embankment, they lit cigarettes. He held her around her waist as they walked, and from time to time –

241

whipping up sparks of elation – he sunk his nose into her thick black hair and kissed her cheek. She didn't respond, staying locked in herself. She walked rigidly, dragged quickly at her cigarette, and once or twice glanced at the brown gloom of the river. She had no time for the screaming sea gulls hovering overhead.

CHAPTER 23

'We gonna build a archway in Brick Lane for that bloody diamond. What do you think about it, Soul Brother?' asked Masuk Ali, as he put his helmet on. Today they had come down to the basement much earlier than usual, and brought Tapan along with them.

'Koh-i-noor is very precious, Masuk,' said Cook Bhai. 'We can't leave it in the open air. Thieves will nick it – na?'

'I never thought of it, Cook Bhai,' said Masuk Ali. Then he said to Tapan:

'Cook Bhai has a crafty brain. He always thinks super cool.' Then he turned to Cook Bhai:

'You think crafty, don't you, Cook Bhai?' Cook Bhai gave a shy smile and kept chewing his paan.

'Where should we put the bloody stone then, Cook Bhai?'

'There's plenty of time for that, Masuk. When we get the stone out of the Tower, we'll think about it.'

Masuk Ali again turned to Tapan and said: 'When the diamond comes to Brick Lane, we'll make a big splash, Soul Brother. No bloody wankers will be able to ignore our Bangla Town then. Innit, Soul Brother?'

Masuk Ali and Cook Bhai went inside the tunnel. They were so far from the mouth that Tapan could only hear the faint clicking of pickaxes as they worked at the tunnel face. He lay in the hammock, chewed paan, and rocked gently using his dangling legs. From time to time the green bucket on the pulley came creaking out of the tunnel full of rubble. As Tapan sensed the passional trialogue of muscle, metal and earth, he felt a surging desire to go into the tunnel himself, crawl its length, zigzag its tributaries and dig with his paws. He had to restrain himself because he needed to complete the remainder of his task for the second issue of the Doctor's *The Good News*.

But then he suddenly wanted to see Adela and Tipu, and to see them now. He shouted down the tunnel that he was leaving, though he wasn't sure whether Masuk Ali or Cook Bhai heard him, or whether it was only the echo of his own voice that trembled out of the tunnel. He climbed the shaft and hurried out onto the street. As soon as he turned the corner, Poltu Khan appeared from nowhere.

'What's wrong with you, man?' he said. 'Do you always lose your bag like this?' He handed to Tapan the rucksack that he'd left at the SOAS canteen.

'Thank you, Mr. Khan, for bringing my bag.'

'I see you really don't trust me, do you? As I said before, I'd like to help you. I don't like to see an educated man wasted.'

'Thank you Mr. Khan, it's very kind of you. But I'm really fine, and happy.'

'Good. But your little problem needs sorting, doesn't it? Let me do it, please.'

'Thanks, Mr. Khan. I'm really fine.'

'Okay. Well, what can I say? I don't know why but it will please me if you consider me as a friend.'

'Thank you, Mr. Khan.'

'Perhaps, you'll think of me differently if I let you in on a secret.'

'What's that?'

'Perhaps you've noticed that there've been a lot of immigration activities and police raids in the places you have taken shelter.'

'Yeah. I thought you were involved in all of them.'

'I was involved all right. I had to bust my ass to figure out where you were staying. But not for the reason you suspect.'

'What for then? It's your job – isn't it?'

'Yeah, it's my job. I know you won't believe me, but I was there

244

to protect you. You see, I've my sources. I knew that someone has been informing on you. So, when the Immigration and Police came to raid for you I was there. Creating a diversion. For this purpose, sometimes it was necessary to give away some other wretched illegals. All I wanted was to save you.'

'It doesn't make any sense to me. Why would you want to protect me? We're not relations, not friends. I'm sure you know my views about people like you.'

'I don't know why. But as I said, it pleases me to save you.'

'Come on, Mr. Khan, let's not play games any more. What's really going on?'

Poltu Khan stayed quiet; his brash confidence seemed to have deserted him for once. He looked fragile.

'Maybe you remind me of something.'

'Of what?'

'I don't know how to put it, Tapan. I suppose, you remind me of myself.'

'I don't follow you, Mr. Khan. What are you on about?'

'I wasn't born like this, you know. I suppose, the whole immigration thing went into my head. I was once foolish like you.'

'Now you're not. So, what's the problem? And, why bother with me?'

'I don't know, Tapan. Since I laid my eyes on you, something happened. But don't get me wrong. I'm happy with my life, and proud of what I've achieved.'

'So, let me alone, Mr. Khan. I don't need your help. Please.'

'Give me a chance. Please. If I'd taken another direction, I would have been like you.'

'I can't see you as an illegal immigrant, Mr. Khan.'

'Not that. But something I can't explain. Something inside, you know.'

'It doesn't suit you to talk like this, Mr. Khan. And, if you really want to help me, don't bug me any more.'

Tapan turned briskly, but looked back before moving away. Poltu Khan seemed forlorn, almost abject, his eyes looking at Tapan as if begging, 'Please, Brother. Please, give me a chance.'

Tapan took the tube from Whitechapel station and by 9.30 arrived at Manor House. The London traffic was finally slowing down and the twilight patches between orange pools of light were assuming their brief but eerie solitude. He wondered whether someone was still shadowing him, but he didn't care about it any more. He was getting fed up with being a mole and burrowing among dark places. Now he would rather have visibility, lightness and flight.

When he rang Adela's bell, she was already tucked up in her bed for the night. From under the blankets, she stirred with the wariness of someone who lived alone in a fearful city, wondering who it could be at this late hour, what danger might be visiting her. She left her bedroom with the caution of a nervous cat, tiptoed downstairs and stilled herself flat against the wall, hoping that the predatory caller had given up and moved on to other prey. But the bell rang again. Reluctantly, she put the corridor light on and shouted out to the caller to identify himself. She hurried to open the locks, the bolts and the chains as soon as he coughed to clear his throat.

He was about to apologise for turning up so late in the night, but she pre-empted him by saying how pleased she was that he had come. God only knew how worried she had been about him, and the worst of it all was not knowing what had happened to him. Before he could put his rucksack down she asked whether he was hungry, should she scramble an egg and make some toast, or would he prefer some rice? He said he wasn't hungry, but he would love a cup of tea. While Adela made tea, he went upstairs to see Tipu.

Breathing in rhythmic waves, and wrapped in a quilt, Tipu was asleep, his face streaked with the light from the corridor. Tapan sat quietly beside him on the bed and put his fingers through his hair, then kissed his forehead. He wasn't sure what prompted him, but he couldn't prevent his mind from conjuring up a vision of the future in which he saw Tipu ambling through the English landscape as if he had always belonged to it. For a moment this vision troubled him, especially seeing how easily Tipu shed the black of his hair, the brown of his eyes, and the dusky shadows that slightly clouded his skin. How pathetic, he told himself, to feel this way, for wishing his son to carry the load of his past like a wretched donkey. Yes, Tipu would be better off without the signatures of his father's body, his terrible memories; he would be free to live his life with all the privileges that went with being an Englishman. Rather than feeling sad about this vision of the future, he should be joyous. Yes, happy enough to be holding Tipu tightly against his chest and dancing around the room until all traces of the past had been erased.

Perhaps he was a bit abrupt, for as he was about to lift Tipu in his arms, his son woke up screaming. Adela came running. While she calmed Tipu down and put him back to sleep, Tapan stood in the dark corner, holding his breath like a toad. He felt choked among the ghosts of the past crawling down the shadows on the walls.

Adela brought him toasted crumpets spread with honey, and tea with two spoonfuls of sugar as usual. He left the crumpets untouched but took a sip from the cup. Adela, slightly conscious of herself, sat head down in front of him in her white, almost see-through voile nightdress. It surprised him that he should feel uneasy at seeing the outline of the breasts that he had seen and touched so many times. Even more surprising was the spark of desire that triggered a nervous tick in him. Sensing the situation, Adela got up with the excuse that she needed a cardigan; she was feeling rather cold. In the abrupt motion of getting up, she – without being aware of it and just for a split second – gave him her green eyes, not in their habitual impassivity but in their brightest emerald, as if a sea had caught fire. She went upstairs and he went out to the patio to smoke a cigarette.

Wrapped in a large, baggy jumper Adela came down and waited for Tapan. When he came in from the patio she asked him whether he would like a glass of wine. He said he would if she was having one.

On her second glass she said: 'Sorry Tapan, it's really my fault.'

'It's nobody's fault, Adela. So don't blame yourself – yeah?'

'Look at you. What's happened to you – are you ill or something?'

'I'm fine, Adela. Never felt better.'

'Seriously, Tapan. Have you seen a doctor?'

'Believe me, I feel really good. I could almost fly, you know.'

'Sorry. I'm so sorry, Tapan. What's going to happen to you now?'

'I don't know, but I feel happy.'

Tapan went out to the patio for another fag and Adela poured herself more wine. When he came back she said, staring into her glass: 'You know, it's not too late. We can put things right again.'

'I don't get it, Adela. What do you mean?'

'We can get together again. After all, we're still married.'

'What! Have you gone crazy or something?'

'No. I'm serious. Think about it; it makes sense.'

'It doesn't make any sense to me. It's daft.'

'You want to stay here, don't you?'

'Adela, please. We've travelled that way before.'

'We were silly then. Now we can make a better job of it. At least for Tipu's sake. Besides, I still have feelings for you.'

'No, Adela. We can't turn the clock back. And Tipu is better off without me. Anyway, thanks for the offer.'

'Sorry. I know I've made mistakes. It's my fault that you're in such a mess. But please, let me do something.'

'Don't feel guilty, Adela. I told you it's not your fault. Nobody's fault, really.'

'But what are you going to do?'

'I don't know, but I'm very happy.'

He finished his glass of wine, went upstairs and picked up Tipu – who this time didn't make a noise. He held him close, pressing his cheek against his, feeling a sensation of such rare joy that he almost broke into an ecstatic whirl. He had to check himself because he didn't want to do anything to disturb Tipu. He walked around the room several times, and finally came to the patch of light that slipped through the narrow opening of the door. He fixed his eyes on Tipu's face bathed in the light, then kissed his forehead. Breathing rhythmically, Tipu continued to sleep. Tapan put him back to bed.

Adela was still sitting in the same chair with the glass in her hand as he gathered his rucksack.

'I need to make a move. Otherwise I'll miss the last tube.'

Adela wanted to say that he could stay the night, but swallowed her thoughts with a gulp of wine as he put his rucksack behind his back.

He came close to her and said: 'Adela, thanks for everything. You're a good woman. Please never allow yourself to feel guilty. Take care of yourself.'

Then he bent down to give her a kiss on the cheek and left. Adela didn't move or say anything; she remained motionless with the glass in her hand, feeling what she should have felt when he left through the same door the first time.

CHAPTER 24

Hours had passed since his journey to Adela's, but the temper of the night hadn't altered much. As before, the fog clung to Green Lane as to the crest of a solitary upland. He walked briskly, vaguely aware of his surroundings, which seemed deserted except for the furtive movements of some well-wrapped figures in long coats. Everything seemed right for moles to be surfacing from their burrows. Perhaps to others, he himself looked like one of those furry creatures, hopelessly out of place on the overground – even under the cover of darkness. Strange to think how quickly the instinct of a mole had become an inseparable part of himself. Yes, as soon as he left Adela's, he had assumed the stoop and angular posture so typical of his kind. But now, he didn't want to be a mole any more.

Still on Green Lane, as he was passing Clissold Park, a fresh wind from the lake blowing between the darkened trees, a figure came in from a side road. Tapan moved up a gear, but the figure seemed determined to keep pace with him. Halfway through the park, near the orange of a lamppost, the figure called him out, 'It's you, Brother, innit?'

Halting in the oasis of light, Tapan turned around and waited for the figure to come through the mist. As ever in his duffel coat and round glasses, Kofi entered the oasis with a broad smile on his face. Kofi embraced him and said, 'Where you been, Brother? I've been looking for you everywhere. I go to East London but Sundar tells me nothing. Anyway, how you been?'

Tapan said that he was fine, that he had never felt so good.

'So I see, Brother. You've turned into a mighty fine mole. Wicked,' said Kofi. He asked Tapan whether he fancied a joint; they could always take a detour through the park. Tapan said he'd rather not, as he didn't want to miss the last train.

'No problem, Brother Mole. You can burrow at my place for the night.' Tapan said he would love to but he had to get back to East London.

Lighting fags, they walked together along Green Lane, towards Manor Park station. On the way Kofi asked him about his plans. Tapan said he didn't have any plans, but was fed up with dark places. If he had his way, he would only have light, so much that he would dazzle the eyes of his pursuers, leaving them blinded for good.

'Halleluiah, Brother, halleluiah,' Kofi said. 'Yeah, Brother Mole, the digger, he was a righteous soul. Didn't he serve us well? I'd be lying if I say he means nothing to me now. Underground still gives me sweet memories. But it's time for us to be leaving them dark places. Yeah, Brother, catch light and go surfacing.'

'Yes, I want to surface. From there I want to catch the thermal and go up and up,' said Tapan.

'Don't say it, Brother – you wanna be a flyer? That's mighty dangerous. Very few I know who can whistle with the true passion of a bird and be a flyer. I'm not saying you can't be one, but it's still very dangerous. If the flyer-passion doesn't fill your inside real good, it could kill you. Very risky, Brother, very risky.'

'I'm not planning on taking risks, Kofi. I just feel light, that's all.'

For a while they walked in silence, but as they passed the heavy mass of the pumping station, Tapan asked Kofi about his plans. Just as so many times before, Kofi said that he was going back home, that he really had a good plan this time: he would offer his services to restore the old slaving posts that littered the Gold Coast, and that would bring the tourists in – the rich diasporic types looking for roots or the white ones desperate for doing a really exotic number – and help the national economy. Then Kofi laughed and said, 'I'm serious, Brother. I'm really going back home this time.'

At Manor House station, Kofi waited with Tapan on the platform. When the sound of the train approached from the tunnel, Kofi suddenly took off his amulet and put it around Tapan's neck. As the train moved away, Tapan looked from behind the glass door at Kofi standing on the platform with a smile on his face, and he remembered the story of the amulet. From the platform, Kofi – even up to the last moment – didn't wave his hands to say goodbye, he just stood still, smiling as the train gathered speed and entered the dark tunnel.

At Finsbury Park, Tapan felt like touching the amulet but he cringed back into his seat as a suspicious looking guy got onto the train. Despite so many empty seats in the compartment, the guy – tall and slim – stayed standing with his gloved hand clutching the handrail. He swayed languidly as the tube turned the bends, but his eyes – hidden behind the broad brim of his hat – fixed their stare on Tapan's reflection in the opposite window. Or at least that's what Tapan thought. When Tapan saw the guy still standing in the same slouched posture beyond Holloway Road, he was convinced that he was keeping an eye on him. He was planning to get off at Caledonian Road, but the guy beat him to it. Now on his own, he eased himself in his seat thinking that his paranoia had turned an innocent passenger into a sinister pursuer. How difficult it would be to leave his mole's self behind.

At King's Cross, he got off to change platforms for the last Metropolitan line train to Whitechapel. As he was about to approach the tunnel to the platform, he spotted Poltu Khan.

Tapan went out of the station, walked a circuit around the neighbouring streets and came back through a side entrance. He looked around, listening to his own footsteps sliding up the tunnel, but there was no sign of Poltu Khan. Perhaps he had given up and gone home, or perhaps he was moving with the stealth of a perfect mimic, camouflaging himself in his, Tapan's shadow. For some reason he headed for the Northern line. Only when the tube went past Moorgate did he realise that he was on his way to see Bombay Bill. He got off at London Bridge.

Halfway across the Tower Bridge, on the western catwalk, Tapan saw, through the dense canopy of mist, a figure hunched against the railings. He edged up to him, coughed to draw his attention, but the figure didn't stir. Then he noticed that, unlike the bulk of Bombay Bill, this man had a thin, slight figure. He continued across the bridge. He heard footsteps. Was it Poltu Khan mimicking him so subtly that he had no way of telling when he lifted his foot and Poltu Khan dropped his? This was absurd, this mole's wariness. Tapan tried to straighten his neck. He stopped, leant against the railings and listened to the Sirens singing from the waves that he couldn't see in the dark. He wasn't sure whether they sang to caress his skin with the delicate fingers of a lover, or to drag him down into the darkness that flowed beneath the bridge. He was hearing footsteps again. Sniffing the mist with his snout and head slumped, he picked up Poltu Khan again. When Tapan turned, Poltu Khan was right in front of him, the cigarette between his lips trembling. Poltu Khan's hand shook as he pulled a Dunhill from the packet and offered it to Tapan.

'Let's at least share a smoke, Brother. Please.'

Tapan turned around and kept on walking. Poltu Khan followed him, whimpering like a dog. 'Please, Brother, Please. Do, as you please with me. Kick me, spit on me, but let me be with you.' Tapan ignored him, kept on walking. 'Just a smoke together, like brothers. Please. I promise I wouldn't bother you any more.' Tapan kept on walking, silent.

'Take care, Brother. God bless you.' Poltu Khan's voice was brittle and Tapan stopped and wanted to say, Okay, let me have one of your cigarettes, but Poltu Khan had already run into the dark. Tapan paused for a while, then continued across the bridge.

Once off the bridge on the north bank, he went through the low arch to the promenade facing the Tower. He sat down on the same bench where he had sat on the first day he had gone on the run. Behind him, in the Tower, Koh-i-noor was locked up in its cell of glass, but this time the ravens didn't stir. He got up from the bench and, crouching, pressed his ear against the paved ground. He could pick up rumblings from the bowels of the earth and from as far east as the Isle of Dogs. He was surprised that he couldn't hear Masuk Ali and Cook Bhai digging. At this hour of the night they should have been at the most passionate phase of their endeavour. Had they given up, or were they just resting?

He hadn't noticed that Bombay Bill, wearing an old sheepskin coat, was standing over him.

Bombay Bill gave a whistle and said: 'It's you, innit – my Cockney Hindustani friend? Fancy bumping into you here.'

'I was looking for you, Mr. Bill,' said Tapan as he lifted himself up from the ground.

'I hope not down there. Deep under the ground,' said Bombay Bill.

'I looked for you on the other bank. And, of course, on the bridge. But I never expected to find you on this side of the river.'

'Well, after closing time, I fancied a walk. It's so damn dark. You can't see the bloody river. Not like in Hindustan, malum?'

'I don't know about that. But how did you know it was me?'

'Ah, let me see. I usually don't cross the river. North of the river is a foreign country to me. Malum? I don't know why I came here. I suppose out of sheer fancy. You understand this, my Hindustani friend. Sorry, I should say my Cockney friend – no? Or you want me to call you English? Go ahead, ask me. Why not, even the damn Negroes are calling themselves English these days. Nowhere to hide even in my own country. Malum?'

'I thought you said you were Hindustani. Anyway, you haven't told me how you recognised me in the dark.'

'I saw a geezer coming down the stairs. I said, Who could that be? Not some bloody nig-nog, or mugger or something. So I hide behind a tree. While the geezer passes the lamp, I see his face. Oh no, not a bloody Paki. Damn scroungerwallah. Sorry. I should've said an English gentleman. Or a Cockney fellow. Or d'you prefer to call yourself Black? Very odd, very odd. Anyway, then it dawned on me that I knew that face. So I come over to say hello. But what were you looking for in the ground?'

'Never mind. Why do you hate us Blacks so much?'

'What's wrong with you, eh? First you want to be a Cockney and now a Black. Such confusion. Don't tell me you want to be a Chinaman too.'

'It's none of your business what I want to be. I bet if you had your way you would lynch me. Perhaps from one of the branches of this chestnut tree. Then come back with your baby daughter to enjoy the sight.'

'I'd be lying if I said the thought never crossed my mind. When I think of how the Pakis robbed me of my country. Sorry, sorry. I promise never to use that kind of language again. You see, it's a habit of many years. You know I was born in India.'

'I know. You told me before.'

'Yeah? Anyway, it makes me mad that India isn't my place any more. I must also admit that I used to get very angry when I saw coloured immigrants like yourself having it easy in England. You know, living in them nice council houses. Also getting them jobs. Malum, what am I saying?'

'It's a load of crap, Mr. Bill. But what I think won't make any difference to your views – will it?'

'Who knows? As it happens, I'd been thinking of getting to know a Paki to find out. Then you came along. You see, in Hindustan, I only knew the barracks. And of course the rivers, the land and the weather. People we didn't know much. My father used to say that India was ours. We English had made it. If only there weren't any dark people there. He thought you lot had really spoilt India. Now I'm old. I think of the rivers so much. Did I tell you that since our first meeting – yeah – I somehow felt that I was going to meet you again?'

'What made you feel that way?'

'Oh, call it a mole's intuition. You're in a spot of bother, aren't you? I've never met an illegal – though I've often thought about them. Sometimes even thought about hunting them down. You know, the way we moles hunt worms and tear them to pieces. True, I've never met an illegal, but I know one when I see one. After all, like them, I'm a creature of the underground.'

'I guessed as much when I first saw you.'

'Good,' said Bombay Bill. 'You should know that I meant what I said the first time I saw you. I really wanted to help you. Don't ask me why, but it's not everyday that one meets a fellow creature from down below. You know, you can't fool me. For instance, just now when I saw you pressing your ear against the ground, I knew that you were listening for things that go on deep underground. Malum – yes? We're never wrong on these things, are we?'

Bombay Bill lit a cigarette and set off briskly; Tapan followed, as if they had made an arrangement to go somewhere together. Bombay Bill asked where Tapan had his shelter and without any hesitation, Tapan told him of its exact location. 'So, you want us to surface in Shadwell, then.'

Of course, it would be risky to go down the sewers without the necessary precautions. It would be like walking blind in a mine-field. Yes, in an emergency, you had to make do with what was at hand, but it would be a dangerous task without a two-way radio, a safety lamp and breathing apparatus. All Bombay Bill had was a torch. Even with thirty years experience behind him as a ganger, during which he'd led a gang of flushers through many hazardous moments, Bombay Bill was hesitating to go down. He wouldn't mind taking risks himself, but it would be reckless to take someone else down without the right gear. But perhaps he was exaggerating the risk. After working fifty years down in the sewers – first twenty as a flusher, then as a ganger – he ought to be able to make a safe run without instruments. Yes, he knew the sewers beneath London like he knew the face of his father. Both were labyrinths, but his mastery over their convoluted secrets was as natural as downing a pint of bitter.

Bombay Bill lifted the manhole cover, but before taking a step down he said, 'You came back to see me because you knew, didn't you? You knew I was a creature of dark places.'

Flicking his cigarette into a pool of water, Tapan said, 'Yes. I just told you – didn't I? But I didn't look for you for that reason. I came back because you meant it. When you offered to help me, you meant it. Right?'

Bombay Bill spat and said, 'I can show you the sewers – them dark places – my son. It's up to you if you want to live in them places. For myself, I would go back to Hindustan. You get my point, my son? Don't tell me you Pakis have become junkies for dark places. Pardon my language. But it's very strange, the whole business. I never could figure out you Hindu people.'

Bombay Bill had entered the circular shaft, and ring by ring he was going down the cold metal. Tapan followed behind. After some twenty feet or so, on the landing at the end of the first shaft, Bombay Bill hesitated again. Even with his experience he had no way of knowing if dangerous gasses were forming at the second level. They could kill you instantly. How badly he needed a safety lamp now! Edging past Bombay Bill, Tapan crouched over the mouth of the second shaft and sniffed the air. Without getting up, he wheeled his body swiftly to take the first rung down. 'It's safe, Mr. Bill.'

Bombay Bill didn't doubt him for a moment, though he was amazed at what he had witnessed. He had acquired some rare intuition himself by working down in the sewers for fifty years. He could find his way through the labyrinth without a map, turn the bends without a light, and from down below he could pinpoint exactly what lay above ground. He'd also had the good fortune of working with some old flushers who could pick up any oncoming torrent of floodwater from several tunnels away. Yet to pick up the level of gases without a safety lamp was something else. For that, one had to become, like one of them bloody rats, a real native of the underground. Suddenly he was scared of Tapan, but he still followed him a further twenty feet down the shaft to the local man-entry sewer. It was oval and barely five feet high.

Tapan wanted Bombay Bill to lead, but Bombay Bill said he preferred to stay behind. He wasn't sure what Tapan might do to him: for all he knew he might lunge at him like a bloody animal and tear him to pieces. God, he didn't want to end up a corpse down here, amongst the shit. But there was no turning back; he had to see this thing through. Under his long coat he clutched the cold hilt of his knife.

In his working life Bombay Bill would have worn waders that went right up to his groin. Now he merely folded his trousers up and, crouching, waded through a foot of water and muck. So did Tapan. As they went through the tunnel, Bombay Bill kept his right hand tightly on the hilt of his knife, while with the left he held his torch. The light made a thin long shadow of Tapan on the wall. Silently through the dense mist, hot and cold – detergent mingling with shit – they moved on in a single file.

'Thank you, Mr. Bill, for bringing me down here. It's kind of nice – isn't it? But what are we looking for?'

'Stop fooling around. You don't need me to show you around this place. It's more like you brought me down here. What d'you plan to do with me?'

'What do you mean? I came to look for you. True. Because you meant it. You wanted to help me out. Remember?'

'I sussed your trouble, didn't I? I thought a fellow like you could do with a... you know, underground place. I don't like to brag. But I've some knowledge of the sewers. So I thought I could show you the ropes. If you need to make a quick getaway. You know, in an emergency like. Or take it quiet for a while until the whole thing blows over. But you're a natural to sewers – aren't you?'

'I don't know what you're talking about, Mr. Bill. I don't know any of the routes. I'm just following your light. If you asked me what lies over our heads, you know, overground, I haven't a clue.'

'Yeah, yeah. I wasn't born the other day, you know.'

Suddenly Tapan turned around and faced Bombay Bill. It was just as well that he was blinded by the torchlight, or he would have seen Bombay Bill tightening the muscles of his face, and pulling the knife out from under his coat.

'You don't believe me Mr. Bill. But it's true.'

'Yeah, I believe you. Get moving, will you.'

'Where are we going, Mr. Bill?'

'You want to get to Shadwell, don't you?'

The tunnel was so inhospitable that only the most abject of creatures could make its home here. Yet, Tapan was completely at ease, as if it was his natural habitat. He wasn't even worried when he smelt Bombay Bill's fearful and violent thoughts drowning the stench of the tunnel. He thought it was natural that Bombay Bill should feel that way. After all, he was alone with a sinister Hindu in the dark, at the mercy of the Hindu's slyness and thuggery, not to say of the Hindu's readiness to run amok.

Raising his torch to shoulder height, Bombay Bill pointed to a larger tunnel ahead. It was one of those medium-sized interceptory tunnels that an old toff named Bazalgette had built. Once they reached its broad opening, Bombay Bill rushed past Tapan to get into it, as if he would be much safer there. Up until now he had been following the exact line of Tapan's course; now the route was his. From behind, Tapan lunged to grab hold of Bombay Bill. Both of them fell sideways, rolling in the sewer-bed. Now the darkness was complete as the torch slipped out of Bombay Bill's hand and sank in the muck. But he had managed to pull his knife out and press its sharp edge against Tapan's throat. He screamed and the tunnel echoed his cry.

'What the fuck you doing – you damn Paki? I gonna slit your fucking throat. You think you're smart, eh? I knew all along what game you're playing. I ain't a fool, you know. Malum? How do you like it, eh? I'm gonna slit your throat. You fucking nigger. You drove us out of Hindustan. Now you come here to finish us off. I gonna slit your fucking throat. Bloody Paki.'

Tapan stayed quiet. Bombay Bill was breathing so heavily he thought the old man was about to die on him. The knife was making a nick on his throat.

'Are you all right, Mr. Bill?' Tapan asked at last.

'What the fuck are you trying to do to me? If you mess around with me again, honest, I'm gonna cut your fucking throat. Malum?'

'You were going the wrong way, Mr. Bill.'

'What do you mean – the wrong way?'

'I had to do it because you didn't see it.'

'What you talking about?'

'You were about to step into a pocket of gas. You know how dangerous that could have been. That's why I jumped on you.'

Bombay Bill knew that the sewer bed was full of pockets of gas and how deadly they were. Yes, in his eagerness to get into the larger tunnel he hadn't seen it. But even if he had been more cautious, he wouldn't have detected the dangerous pockets without a safety lamp. Tapan was clearly something else. Bombay Bill dropped his knife.

'Did I cut you, my son?'

'I'm fine Mr. Bill. It's nothing. Just a scratch.'

'Sorry, my son, sorry. It's my nerves, innit.'

'Why, Mr. Bill?'

'I really meant it, you know. I really wanted to help you. Don't ask me why. But I've never been with a dark fellow like you, you know, alone. And down here. Bloody sewers only made matters worse. Even though I've worked here for fifty years. But then I never came down with a dark fellow like you, did I? Let me own up to something. Way back, when I was a nipper, I heard things about you people. You know the kind of stuff your mum tells you.

Scary stuff to make you stop doing naughty things. How you fellows are sinister like. You know, doing bloodthirsty things. I better not repeat them. Sorry, those things were playing on my mind. I hope you'll forgive me. I promise you, that will never happen again. What should I call you?'

'I'm Tapan Ali. Obviously I don't like your views. But I don't hate you either. If I had an arrogant temper I would've pitied you. But I don't. Naturally you can't easily forget what you were taught. I can't ignore what you think and say about me either. But I came to see you because you meant it. I don't know why, but I believed you really wanted to do something for me. By the way, my place of departure was Bangladesh.'

'Ah, that's Babuland, innit? Let me come clean on it. Among all the people of the Raj, we thought your kind were the worst. Yeah, the most slimy and the most sinister. But my father had some mofussil postings there. If I'm not mistaken, most of my rivers, you know, the ones I miss so much, are from there. Let me see. Yeah, Padma, Brahm-aputra. Have I said their names correctly? Look son. I'm really sorry. What can I do for you?'

'You meant it, that's enough for me. Besides, you brought me here – didn't you? I thought if I could find a nice place below ground, I'd be safe. I'd be able to move around safely using the sewer system. Now I'm not sure.'

'I also thought you could use this. That's why I wanted to bring you down here. Show you the secrets of the sewers. But I see that you already sussed this place out. So what you going to do, Ali? Or should I call you Tapan?'

'I don't mind. If you like, call me Ali. I must admit I still have feelings for dark places. I can sense things down here. But I'm fed up with tunnels, underground, burrowing, hidings and dark places. I say to hell with moles. I want to surface. I want light, Mr. Bill. I want light.'

'How will you manage that?'

'I don't know, Mr. Bill.'

'If you like, you can move in with me. I have a spare room at the back of my house. Nobody will know. You know, I've no children. Never married. You can cook me curries. Real hot. We can eat together. How does it sound to you?'

'Like I said, Mr. Bill, no more hiding. Now all I want is surface and light.'

'You're not thinking of doing something dangerous, are you?'

'No, Mr. Bill. Nothing dangerous.'

Groping in the muck, Bombay Bill retrieved his torch. Then they climbed into the interceptory tunnel that lay less than a metre or so ahead. Now they could walk upright and had enough room to stay, if they wished, side by side. Tapan, though, didn't like the sewers any more; the mole in him had left: he felt out of breath and claustrophobic. Luckily the interceptory tunnels weren't as dangerously bedded with gas-traps as the local man-entry ones were. So, even though Tapan's snout-detector was switched off, they could make a safe passage. It was enough to rely on Bombay Bill's expertise. Unaware of how Tapan was feeling, Bombay Bill said, 'Let me show you something special, son.'

Bombay Bill led him – after the long stretch of the first interceptory and few more turnings – to an enormous tunnel. 'That's a large interceptory. Bazalgette's master work,' he said. 'Impressive, innit?'

With its high arches, pillars and buttresses, it was like a gothic cathedral turned upside down. But Tapan didn't care for this sort of place any more. Bombay Bill, on the other hand, was happy. He ran up the slope of the buttress, swung around the columns, and then slid down with his arms spread out. He asked Tapan whether he would like to go up. Tapan declined, but Bombay Bill's playfulness made him feel somewhat lighter. Putting a fag between his lips, Bombay Bill sat down against a wall, next to a shallow weir. His torchlight on the wet buttress conjured up what looked like the cascade of a waterfall. Tapan looked at it for a while, rolled a cigarette, and then sat down too. Now that Bombay Bill had turned his torch off, the tunnel – apart from the glow of their cigarettes – was dark once more. Tapan felt as though he was sitting beside Vatya Das, sharing a smoke with him, as he had done so many years ago by the lake in his grandmother's village. As he continued smoking, as he became more forgetful in the silence of the moment, he almost asked Bombay Bill, 'Tell me Vatya Da. How did you manage to fly?'

'Were you saying something, Tapan Ali?'

'No. Just thinking of old times.'

'Yeah, old times. I wish I was back in Hindustan. Especially seeing them rivers in old Bengal. But I know I'm not going back there again.'

'I'm not going back to Bangladesh either.'

'That's some crazy talk, innit. What you plan to do then?'

'I don't know yet, Mr. Bill.'

'I suppose you could stay hiding for a while. This place could have been ideal for you. But you don't want to do that any more – do you?'

'No, Mr. Bill.'

'You know, for me the sewers were heaven-sent. Down here I could forget the world. I could be anywhere, you know. We flushed the muck, evaded the gas traps, the rat bites, disease and the torrents after rain. The world above didn't suit me. England felt a strange country to me. Down here, in the dark, I could even be in Hindustan. In a way, it has been my home.'

Bombay Bill hadn't noticed that Tapan was fainting, but before he blacked out he managed to say, 'Take me out of here, Mr. Bill. I can't take underground places any more. It's so dark, it's going to kill me. Please, please, take me out.'

Bombay Bill lifted Tapan across his shoulder and made for the nearest exit. But the man-hole shaft was too small for him to carry a man up to the surface. He needed to revive Tapan sufficiently so that he could make it up on his own. Of course, Bombay Bill would need to help him, prop him up from behind and encourage him. How he wished he had some water he could give to Tapan, but he didn't have any. What to do?

Then he remembered, from way back in India, how his father massaged his mother's feet to revive her when she fainted in the heat of the dry season. As a boy, he had looked on panic stricken from the edge of the bed, thinking that his mother was dying, but she made a swift recovery. That afternoon he had gone for a walk with her by the river. He and his mother, both barefoot, walking at the edge of the water. Birds with long legs and beaks, whose names – like so many other things in India – he never knew, strutted ahead of them on the sand. He still remembered their grey and white colours, their funny steps, and their markings on the sand – like rows of stars in parallel lines. These images were still as vivid in his memory as the cool river water that touched his feet.

Often in the afternoons he would see an Indian boy bathing his herd of buffaloes in the river. It came naturally to him to wave his hand to the Indian boy and watch him. But on that occasion he felt the presence of the boy was spoiling the scene. He wanted to be alone with his mother and the birds and the river. He wanted to feel that it was his secret world, his alone, just as his mother was his, looking at him lovingly with her blue eyes beautifully fringed by blond curls. But the brown boy smiling stupidly from the river was spoiling it all. He wanted to go down there and smash that smile out of the brown boy's face, because the smile was so innocent and so stupid. But deep down he sensed that the brown boy was smug; he could see from the way the brown boy conducted himself that he knew that there was no difference between himself and the river, between himself and the sky. All these elements belonged to the brown boy and the brown boy belonged to them.

They walked briskly further along the river so that he didn't have to see the brown boy's stupid smile. Yet, as they walked, as the horizon darkened, as the birds flew out, he could sense that the brown boy was still smiling. In that moment, all he could think of – a little white boy marooned in a distant colonial outpost – was violence. How pleasurable it had been to imagine the most atrocious violence that he could inflict on the brown boy. Horror! Horror!

Yes, his father had massaged his mother's feet when she fainted – and she got better. Now Bombay Bill, feeling his way in the dark, took off Tapan's shoes, then his socks. They were full of muck. First he needed to clean Tapan's feet, but there was no clean water, so he took his handkerchief out and switched his torchlight on.

Up until now he hadn't seen Tapan's face closely. Now the torchlight fell on Tapan's face and he was squinting, as though the light had penetrated through his closed eyelids. Tilting his wrist upwards, Bombay Bill changed the angle of the light slightly. Tapan's face was more clearly visible now. It was a brown face like

263

the boy's who had smiled so stupidly from the river. If you looked closely – Jesus, would you believe it? – the face had the same smugness. What the fuck had he got to be so smug about? Did he have some crazy idea that the whole of London was his? Who did he think he was? How easy it would be to smash that smugness out of his face, right now in this very sewer. All he had to do was to wrap his white handkerchief around the damn Paki's neck and squeeze it tight. See what happens to his smugness when his fucking tongue comes out. Or should he hang him with his belt the way they used to do the niggers? Who does he think he is? The Lord Mayor of the City?

Bombay Bill laid Tapan's feet on his lap and used his handkerchief to clean them of muck. He massaged the ankles and the entire length of both feet – their toes, balls, insteps, heels and the soles. If only he had some oil, it would have been so much better – but what to do? Luckily his mother had taught him to put coconut oil in his hair – a custom she picked up, despite his father's objection, from her Indian ayah. After a moment's hesitation, Bombay Bill put both of his hands on his head, ran them through his hair to gather the oil in his finger pads and palms. Then he began massaging Tapan's ankles and feet again, rubbing them gently with his oily palms, and now and then applying pressure with his fingers. He continued to do so until Tapan groaned faintly. Bombay Bill asked, 'Are you okay, son?'

Tapan said he was still feeling a bit faint, but he was fine now. He thanked Bombay Bill for taking care of him.

'Don't mention it, son. I consider it a privilege.'

Still a bit shaky, Tapan climbed up the shaft, Bombay Bill propping him from behind, encouraging him, saying, 'Don't give up, son. I'm with ya – malum?'

Slowly they surfaced through the manhole onto the street. The outside was as clogged with mist as the sewers had been. Since they were near Shadwell, Tapan said that he could make his way from there. But Bombay Bill insisted on escorting him. After crossing only a few more streets, they arrived at the block where Tapan was staying.

'Promise me something, will you? No funny stuff. You can come and see me for anything. I really mean it – malum?'

'I know you mean it, Mr. Bill. As I said, I came to look for you because you meant it. Thanks for everything.'

'Come and see me any time. God bless ya, son. God bless ya.'

'Take care, Mr. Bill. Bye,' said Tapan as he turned to enter the porch.

He had no idea that at the moment he surfaced from the sewers Haji Falu Mia had died.

CHAPTER 25

'Do you remember what the Jinn said, Cook Bhai?' asked Masuk Ali.

'We have been hearing from the Jinn for a long time, Masuk. You don't expect me to remember everything. But if you specify the occasion I might be able to help you,' said Cook Bhai.

'You know, when Sundar Bhai asked him about where he should bury his father?'

'Ha, I remember that very clearly. The Jinn said he should bury his father where he belongs. You know, where his home is.'

'It's easy, innit?' said Masuk Ali. 'The old man wanted to be taken back to Bangladesh. So the home is there, innit?'

'I'm not so sure about that, Masuk.'

'What you saying, Cook Bhai? Bangladesh is not home then?'

'Bangladesh will always remain a kind of home. But in our minds only. Practically, England is home now. So, it's a double-wuble, either-mither situation. You know, like we have an eye at the back of our head. You understand me correctly, Masuk?'

'Where did you learn this fancy talk, Cook Bhai? I don't dig it right. You saying we monsters or something? Eye on the back! Sorry, Cook Bhai, it's kinda weird.'

Tapan laughed out loud; so did Cook Bhai. Masuk Ali put his burning cigarette into one of his nostrils, pressed a saucer to the back of his head, bugged his eyes out and grunted – his version of the hybrid monster. But then he sneezed so hard that the cigarette flew out of his nostril and the saucer broke on the floor.

Clearing up the broken pieces, Masuk Ali said, 'We must make a move, Soul Brother.'

'Why are you so keen to get rid of me, Masuk?'

'It's serious information, Soul Brother. The fuckers know you're here. They're coming to get you soon, innit.'

'I know, Masuk. But I don't want to run any more.'

'What you saying, Soul Brother? I don't dig it right.'

'I'm fed up with running, Masuk. I just want to stay put and have a nice cup of tea with my friends.'

'I don't want no wanker netting you, Soul Brother. Listen, one more cup of tea and we're moving.'

Tapan smiled and then rolled a cigarette. Taking a puff, he said, 'I thought you two would be down in the basement. You know, digging.'

'Funny you should ask that, Soul Brother. We're done with that kinda thing.'

'I thought you'd dig until you reached the Tower and get that diamond out.'

'That's right, Soul Brother.'

'So what's happened?'

'You know, we were resting a bit in the hammocks. It was then that Cook Bhai brought up the subject. Do you remember, Soul Brother, what the Jinn said?'

'Yeah. He said keep digging, the stone will come to you.'

'Right, Soul Brother. I couldn't make much sense of it, but Cook Bhai said something real crafty. It made a lot of sense.' He shouted to Cook Bhai who was in the kitchen. 'Aren't you, Cook Bhai? You real crafty – innit?'

Cook Bhai didn't say anything, but came back from the kitchen with a fresh pot of tea.

'So, what did you say, Cook Bhai?' asked Tapan.

'Nothing special. Just that it occurred to me that we were wasting our time digging underground. If we spent our efforts on the overground we would be in a better position to achieve our goal.'

'I still don't get it, Cook Bhai,' said Tapan. He was about to explain further when Masuk Ali – as usual – butted in.

'I also didn't get it the first time, Soul Brother. You know the scheme is real crafty.'

'I understand that you don't want to dig tunnels any more, and

267

that you want to spend your energies on activities on the surface. But how does it get you Koh-i-noor?'

'Yeah, Soul Brother. We gonna put our stuff out there. You know, on the overground. So that no bleeding sod can miss us. Even the fucking blinds couldn't go about without seeing us. If we carry on like this, the whole goddamn London would be our patch. Now you see the crafty bit, Soul Brother?'

'Sort of.'

'If London becomes ours, then everything in it is ours too. Including that bloody stone – innit? So why bother digging – right?'

It was about five in the morning when they went out into the street. It was still dark, and the fog – true to its mythical attachment to London – stayed so immobile that the early morning traffic looked as if it was passing through a solid object. Masuk Ali, a fag dangling like a firefly from his lips, looked back cautiously every so often, as if, just behind the shield of fog, someone was on their trail. Cook Bhai, too, was wary. Unusually, it was Tapan who didn't sense any danger, or feel any anxiety about being followed. Now the only thing that was bothering him was the fog, because it devoured the dawn in which he would have loved to walk at his ease, clearly visible to all, light and delicate, a man simply taking the streets that connected the landmarks of his city.

Masuk Ali stopped at a telephone booth to call Sundar. No, Sundar wasn't taking his father's body back to Bangladesh. Instead, he was having him buried in the Woodgrange Park cemetery in Upton Park. It was where both of Haji Falu Mia's wives were buried: Maureen to the right, at the front, Sundar's mother to the left, at the back. Two women, white and brown, under the same patch of land, hemmed in by housing estates on all sides. The only thing that distinguished the gravestones were the engravings that looked like hearts or leaves or cupolas. What set them apart weren't their shapes, sizes or colours, but the direction in which the tapering ends of their cones pointed. On Maureen's grave, the engravings pointed downwards, on Sundar's mother's, as on all the Muslim graves, they pointed upwards. But the roots of the oak and the ancient church that stood in the middle connected them – a white Irish woman and a brown Bengali woman – to a shared colonial past. And the man they had shared between them across continents would soon join them under the same patch of earth and the three of them together – without waiting to hear the chimes of the church bell, or to be covered with oak leaves – would add their bones to the pillars of our city.

Along the pavements, by the trunks of the naked trees, Tapan, Masuk Ali and Cook Bhai – wrapped in overcoats, mufflers, woolly caps and gloves – made their way to Spelman Street. Not many people had risen yet, and the concrete playing area – usually noisy with Bengali kids kicking footballs, skipping or lounging around – was silent.

Facing the playing area was the council block where Tapan would now stay. Promising to be back to see him soon, Masuk Ali and Cook Bhai left to visit Sundar in Brick Lane, which was close by.

On his own in the flat, Tapan slumped on the settee, smoked a cigarette and fell asleep. When he got up it was ten in the morning. He went around the flat, which was similar in decor and smell to the other Bangladeshi flats he had stayed in before: bright wall-papers and carpets with floral motifs, framed Arabic calligraphy, or the shrouded cube of the black stone of Mecca, and reproductions of photographs or paintings of a river or an idyllic village from Bangladesh – always identical in composition and colour – and the accumulated odour of spices mingling with the mustiness typical of damp slum dwellings. He unpacked his things, made his bed with the blue sheets and the covers that Nilufar had given him in Limehouse, and went to the kitchen to make a tea.

He was passing along the corridor when he was struck by how gloomy it was. It shouldn't have been so dark, especially not at ten in the morning. Perhaps he was a bit inattentive, but if his mole's instinct hadn't left him, he wouldn't have stumbled against the toy train and spilt his tea. Damn darkness: he couldn't stand it any more.

Room by room, window by window, he went around the flat opening the curtains. As it wasn't a bright day, the light didn't come pouring into the rooms. Yet, even the dull light was enough

269

to make him feel that he wasn't living in his burrow any more, hiding and making blind runs in the dark. Yet, he wanted more, so he slid open the door and went to stand on the balcony. Despite the murkiness, despite the damp chill, it felt so nice to be out in the open, to be using all the natural light to make himself visible, to roll a cigarette slow and easy. Simply then, and without a single wary glance, he lit it between the shields of his palms and blew the smoke like a man who was not only happy, but felt it the most natural thing in the world for him to be out there, on the balcony, harvesting each last particle of light.

Tapan paced the balcony, wishing there was a mirror there, so he could see – without the slightest distortion – the figure of a free man: no longer head bent, slouching, but erect and looking straight on. He felt like humming one of those Baul songs that he'd heard years ago at Pir-Baba's shrine with Bisu Bhai, on his way from his grandmother's to his grandfather's village. It would have been nice if he could sing, but that wasn't strictly necessary: all he had to do was to stomp his feet, swirl around and feel the music to catch the lightness – and then lift off without having to move an inch.

Although he wasn't quite there yet, he was sure that it was only a matter of time before he got it.

He looked down and saw some Bengali boys in the playing area, doing nothing in particular. Some of them were sitting on the wall, others leaning against it, and yet their postures seemed carefully choreographed. He wondered why, despite their seeming aimlessness, they had arranged their bodies so carefully. Perhaps it was not to mean anything in particular, but simply to be there, upon this land, as if it were their territory and they were like the trees that grew naturally on it. Moving slightly to his left, and letting his eyes travel along the short passage of Heneage Street, he could see the traffic of Brick Lane.

Everyone said how lucky Haji Falu Mia was in timing his death so perfectly that his janaza-funeral could take place on the most auspicious moment of the week, during the Friday Jumma-prayer. At that time the Brick Lane mosque, where Haji Falu Mia had been a regular, would be full of people. As he sat on the sofa and drank his tea, Tapan thought how easy it would be for him to attend the funeral. All he had to do was to go down into Brick Lane, no more than a minute's walk from the flat. Yet, he wondered whether this was the right thing to do. It wasn't that he was afraid of exposing himself, that illegal self that should remain hidden. He felt awkward about going to the mosque because, like a Baul, it wasn't his way.

He sat down in silence and concentrated his mind on Haji Falu Mia. His first thoughts were of regret: over not seeing the old man much recently, and over not impressing on Sundar that he should take his dead body back to Bangladesh, but then he decided that he didn't want to dwell on regrets.

And although he hadn't spoken to Sundar yet, Tapan felt he would understand his reasons for burying his father here. No one could take Haji Falu Mia's memories away, his bitter-sweet memories of Bangladesh, memories that had made him live out his life in a particular way in England, memories that helped him cope with the difficulties he faced, memories that often visited him like an intimate friend on whom he could always rely. Yet, if Haji Falu Mia had a home, it was surely England. So it was appropriate that he should be buried here.

So, not dwelling on regrets, he reflected on how glad he was to have known Haji Falu Mia. Truly, the two of them had some good times together: Haji telling his stories, and he listening – stories of the early days, of the sailors voyaging into the unknown, of founding the city of the immigrants. Haji was happy then, even proud, though he didn't say it, but you could tell by looking at his eyes, or at the corners of his lips – when you could see them behind his long, bushy beard. That is what Tapan wanted to remember, nothing else; just the way Haji was in those moments: happy as an architect of a new city.

Shahid wasn't happy. He should have been moving to his new house, but instead had to drive to the airport to meet Surat Mia, his father-in-law, who was returning from Bangladesh. Shapna, though, was glad that their move to Bromley was postponed, because she got to stay a bit longer in the place where she grew up with her family. She hadn't expected their father to be back so soon from Bangladesh, but he had arranged his return the moment he heard that Haji Falu Mia's condition was critical. He had already set off from his distant village to take the plane from Dhaka when they sent him the second telegram, telling him that Haji Falu Mia – his long time friend and his brother-in-law – was dead.

Nilufar's mother was busy cooking a feast. This was not for her husband's return, but because after the funeral everybody would gather in her house. She was expecting about fifty people. Shapna, Auntie Halim and Cousin Rima were helping her. Even Sofia, Sundar's half sister – Haji Falu Mia's daughter by Maureen – was trying to help, but Nilufar's mother wouldn't let her. She made Sofia sit by the table in the kitchen and gave her a cup of tea. Poor Sofia was in a state, sobbing for the father whom she loved, but whose world she hardly knew. About the Islamic rituals, her father's last rites, she hadn't a clue. From time to time Nilufar's mother would approach Sofia, pass her hand gently over her head, sob a little, and tell her some anecdotes about her father in Bengali, which Sofia did not understand at all. Curiously, neither Shapna nor Rima, who were perfectly bilingual, would volunteer to translate. This wasn't because they disliked Sofia, but because what Nilufar's mother said was really untranslatable – old ritual dirges and sentimental memories. They didn't carry much meaning, except that in the saying a grief had been expressed, and a relationship of care had been established.

Nilufar was alone in her flat. As soon as they knew that her father was coming back, it was decided that it would be best if Kaisar moved in with her again, though right now he was at a rehab clinic, somewhere in south London. It was expensive, but it had to be done; Kaisar needed to be de-toxed under expert supervision. They couldn't take any more chances, especially after he had disappeared a couple of nights before. To pay for the clinic, their mother hadn't hesitated over selling her jewellery, Nilufar had given up the little savings she had and Shapna had forced out of Shahid as much as she could.

Although it was eleven in the morning, Nilufar was still in bed. From time to time she looked at the phone, longing to hear a human voice, but she couldn't bear to look for long, because her gaze took in the photograph of her family on the picnic to Kew

Gardens, a time when the whole family was so close and happy.

Over the years Nilufar had got used to a solitary life, and at times even considered herself lucky to be alone, for being able to do whatever she wanted. Today, though, she wished she had been at her mother's, helping her with the cooking and all the other preparations. With her father coming back, she couldn't risk going home. How could she bear this terrible moment? She wasn't looking for a miracle, but if only Tapan could have been there to share this moment with her, she could have told him things that she had never told anyone before: of her loneliness, of how much she misses her father and how much it hurts, and that it makes her cry not to be there with her mother right now, and, of course, of her love for him, and how desperately she misses him – especially in a moment like this when she feels so alone.

Surat Mia arrived on time for Haji Falu Mia's janaza-prayer at the Brick Lane mosque. As on any other Friday, the mosque was full of people, and after the main Jumma-prayer, after they had prayed for Haji Falu Mia's soul, the black hearse – followed by black limos and many private cars – lead a long procession all the way to Woodgrange Park cemetery in Upton Park. Along the way, as the cortege passed, the Bangladeshis of East London – old and young alike – stood in silence and intoned their prayers for Haji Falu Mia. Even if they didn't know him, they felt an intimate kinship with him, because he was giving his bones to this land, bones that would be played as flutes, their harmony making this land less foreign, and more their own.

It was about half past twelve when Tapan left the flat. He didn't care who saw him; all he wanted was to reach Woodgrange Park cemetery before the funeral cortege arrived. He got a bus immediately, and within twenty minutes was there, in the cemetery, as he had hoped, before the cortege arrived. He wandered through the cemetery, which was largely deserted, except for a pocket of activity at the back. It felt desolate on this winter's day. He wished the oak that stood in front of the ancient church had been an evergreen tree, but it was leafless, its skeletal branches adding grey to an already dull sky. He went through rows of English and

273

Christian graves, mostly marked with simple headstones, except one or two with old and opulent structures.

Past the oak tree and the church, he found the Muslim graveyard. Since Tapan didn't know Sundar's mother's name, he couldn't locate her grave; it could have been any of the graves with names that ended with Begum. Finally, he reached the hub of activity. The grave had already been dug and the men, including the mullah, were waiting for the body to arrive. The mullah bid Tapan salaam and asked if the dead person was his relative. Tapan said he was a friend. He could see that the mullah was puzzled that he'd arrived ahead of the cortege, but he didn't ask him whether he had been to the janaza-prayer. Suddenly one of the men dropped his cigarette and said that the cortege was there.

Uncle Halim and Surat Mia at the front, Sundar and Shiraz at the back, carried the dead body. A large crowd followed: so many familiar faces – Masuk Ali and Cook Bhai, Doctor Karamat Ali, the Most Venerable Pir-Sahib and the Bringer of Jinn, Shahid – amongst others. When Masuk Ali spotted Tapan, he came running. 'What do you think you doing here, Soul Brother? Jesus, the place is full of fucking rats. Innit. You gone crazy or what? Let's get out of here fast.'

Tapan smiled and said that he wasn't going anywhere until the burial was over. Masuk Ali shook his head and said, 'I don't dig it right, Soul Brother. What's happened to you? Crazy, innit.'

Tapan told him that he was fine, but he had finished with running and hiding. He had been wondering what had happened to Poltu Khan since that encounter on Tower Bridge. How terrible Poltu Khan had sounded then! Tapan had even begun to wish that he hadn't walked away from him and he asked Masuk Ali if he had seen him.

'Why, Soul Brother, why you want to know about that nasty piece of work? I hear the fuckin' rat has gone underground.' Seeing Doctor Karamat Ali approach, Masuk Ali moved away but kept an eye on them from behind the oak tree.

Doctor Karamat Ali took Tapan by the arm and said, 'How's my staff reporter doing? Tip-top, yes? Good to see you surfacing, Mr. Tapan. But how about your troubles with that status business? You know, that il-legal nonsense.'

Tapan told him that he was fine. In fact, he'd never felt better, and didn't care about his legal status any more. The Doctor looked puzzled, but then said, 'What's happened to you, Mr. Tapan? Someone in your legal position can't afford, you know, to let your guards down. I heard the Immigration is very edgy. They're desperate for results. And I don't have to remind you about informers. Please do be cautious, Mr. Tapan. Any help, you can always count on me.'

Almost exasperated, Tapan told the Doctor that he was fine, only that he didn't care for hiding and dark places any more. Then he said, 'Have you ever observed how birds fly, Doctor Ali? Aren't they wonderful? I hope you won't mind me asking, but have you ever wondered about flying?'

Doctor Karamat Ali shook his head and said, 'Funny that you should ask me this question, Mr. Tapan. In fact, I did consider it, especially when my wife left me. But it's too risky Mr. Tapan. Too risky.'

'It's good to know that I'm not alone. If you have the right feelings, it's not dangerous. Not at all, Doctor Ali.'

'But please don't go around trying any crazy stuff. Promise?'

'You know me, Doctor Ali. I'm not into crazy stuff.'

'Glad to hear that, Mr. Tapan.'

'Thank you, Doctor Ali.'

'Oh yes, I was looking for you to discuss another matter really,' said the Doctor. 'You know, I was hoping to get some advertisements for *The Good News*. I'm afraid, no luck. It's seriously draining my finances. Not that I care about finances. You know, the paper was entirely philanthropic. But with this kind of loss I would be a total beggar soon.'

'I see.'

'So I thought my philanthropic concerns would be better served if I went into politics. You know, if I become a councillor. Perhaps, in time a Mayor. What do you think, Mr. Tapan? But sorry to say, I'm stopping the paper. You can help me around the grocery. Or you can be a helper with my doctory business. I need someone reliable. I'll pay you a bit more. How about forty pounds a week?'

Tapan shrugged his shoulders; he was glad that he didn't

have to correct and translate the Doctor's terrible writing any more.

Now they saw that people were shuffling around the grave as the body was about to be lowered into it. Swift and deft like a magician, the Doctor slipped five ten pound notes into Tapan's pocket and hurried along to be by the mouth of the grave.

From inside the grave, the mullah and the Bringer of Jinn received the body, as the Most Venerable Pir-Sahib, using the rich timbre of his voice, recited Koranic verses. Poor Shiraz, who seemed awkward and out of place in this congregation, broke into a sob. Sundar held his half-brother and comforted him. How similar they looked: they had the same curly hair, the same bone structure and the eyes of their father. Apart from their differing heights, the only thing that set them apart was the colour of their skin. Sundar was dark brown; Shiraz, like Maureen, was pale and white. Yet, at that moment, the two of them, locked in an embrace by the graveside of their father, couldn't have been anything else but brothers.

Once the body had been lowered into the grave and the mullah and the Bringer of Jinn had climbed up, the rest of the people formed a queue. One by one they threw earth into the grave until it was closed.

Then they stood in a circle around the grave, their palms in front of their faces, their eyes closed. Between reciting Arabic verses, the Most Venerable Pir-Sahib prayed for the personal salvation of Haji Falu Mia's soul. Tapan, though, was imagining Haji Falu Mia walking erect with his stick down Brick Lane, and becoming – between the mosque and Taz store – his beloved albatross.

Slowly people were drifting away, but Tapan remained, leaning against the naked oak. As the Bringer of Jinn passed, he paused and said, 'Remember. The Jinn's never wrong. Sundar Mia correctly buried his father where the home is. And you will be a flyer. Salamalikum. Peace be upon you.'

CHAPTER 26

After the funeral Tapan made his way back to his shelter. In the entrance lobby to the tower block he hesitated over whether to take the stairs, or give the rickety old lift a try. He did neither, and, instead, turned around and took to the street again. A short walk through Heneage Street brought him to Brick Lane. How nice it felt to be there, stopping to look at the Bangladeshi fishes and vegetables in the grocery shops, and, without meaning to, ending up in a magazine & music shop, listening to the latest Bollywood numbers, and somehow not being able to avoid the sari shops, Koranic stalls, and always chewing paan and exchanging gossip with friends. Today, though, he didn't see many familiar faces, as most of his friends and acquaintances were at Nilufar's mother's place.

And yet he couldn't walk past Brick Lane without stopping for a tea and a samosa. As soon as he popped into Spice-Land, Dulu Mia – the waiter on duty – came running to greet him.

'Long time, Country Brother. Where you been? We thought you had gone back home.'

Tapan was happy to see him. 'Where would I go, Dulu? Home is right here. No? Just been a bit tied up with things. Anyway, how you been?'

Dulu Mia brought him dahl pouries, gulapjam and tea. From the kitchen, Najbat Ali the chef, who was a village-brother of Cook Bhai, came to say hello. He asked Tapan why didn't he come by the restaurant after closing hour to share the staff meal with them. Nothing special, but there would be fried koi fish and ayer fish with fenugreek. Tapan thanked him and said that he might. He hadn't realised how hungry he was; he finished his dahl pouries and gulapjam in double quick time.

As Tapan was rolling a fag and taking sips of the tea, Fakir Abbas popped into Spice-Land and came to sit by him; he too asked him where he'd been lately. Tapan gave him the usual answer that he'd been a bit tied up with things but he was now ready to surface. Head down, in a low whisper – as if it was a highly sensitive secret – Fakir Abbas told him that there would be a gathering in the basement of his flat in Fashion Street. Many of the devotees of Baul from all over East London would be there. He told Tapan that he would be most welcome. Yes, said Tapan, he would love to come.

As Tapan was leaving Spice-Land, Makbul Chawdery, the community politician, was coming in with his entourage. Seeing Tapan he stopped and said, 'How's our philosopher doing? Why don't I see you in my office any more? We need people like you more than ever. You know my youth training project? Prince Charles himself is coming to open it. Come to my office, I can sort a job for you. Did I tell you that the Prime Minister herself phoned me?'

Then one of his entourage whispered something into Makbul Chawdery's ear. It must have been about Tapan's illegal status, because the community politician suddenly looked very uncomfortable, and walked past Tapan briskly – and without bidding goodbye.

It was now about four in the afternoon. The murky light on which the day had just about sustained itself faded completely; the play of darkness and neon had already begun. Tapan, not bent-head, not slouching, but erect like Haji Falu Mia, walked through Brick Lane.

At Henriques Street, he did something that he hadn't done before. He pressed the bell to Nilufar's flat. As soon as Nilufar heard his voice on the intercom, she let him into the building. Although he had never been there, it wasn't difficult to work out that to reach her flat he had to take the long corridor, then a flight of stairs, then another long corridor.

She looked at herself in the mirror. God, the way she looked, but what could she do about it? There was no time now to change into something nice or even wash her face, but she should at least put some kohl on her eyes. After she had let him in, Tapan made no apology for his unexpected arrival. All he said was that the flat was much bigger than he had imagined. Nilufar made tea and they sat facing each other across the small table and lit cigarettes.

But why had he come? Was it to say a final goodbye? Long, terrible seconds ticked by as Nilufar sat there, her bright, kohled eyes sunk into her teacup, smoke screening her face, but she couldn't bring herself to say any of the things she'd imagined saying to Tapan only a short while ago. Tapan, on the other hand, had no trouble saying what he wanted to say.

'I thought I should let you know I'm fed up with this bloody hiding and underground business. I've decided to surface.'

He wasn't sure how Nilufar would react: perhaps she would be cross at his stupidity, but she only smiled, as if relieved, and said, 'Oh, that's good. I'm glad you've decided this. So when are you going back to Bangladesh?'

'I didn't say I was going back to Bangladesh.'

'So, what are you going to do then?'

'I don't know, Nilu. But I know that I'm not hiding any more. And I'm not going back to Bangladesh.'

'That's daft. Real daft. You're not planning something crazy?'

'No. Nothing crazy. I promise you.'

'I hope so. But you scare me, Tapan. I really don't understand what you're on about.'

'Well, I don't either. But I feel strongly that I mustn't hide any more.'

'But don't forget that you're an illegal immigrant. So how do you plan to surface and avoid being sent back to Bangladesh?'

'Yeah, I'm surfacing, Nilu. But nobody's going to catch me and send me back.'

'Now you're really scaring me. Goddamn it, I wish I didn't care, but I do love you.'

'I do love you too, Nilu. I'll always love you. I've told you what I had to tell. I don't see the point of discussing it further. Let's stay with this moment only, the feeling that we love each other. No other times and nothing else should matter. Yeah?'

The Nilufar of old would never have accepted this fuzziness. Now, she was content to take him at his word, to let herself be held in the moment, be swept along by the feeling of love.

Perhaps they were tempted into feeling an impending sense of doom, as if, on their way down dangerous rapids, they would cling to each other, desperate to feel each other's proximity one last time. But that would have involved thinking about consequences, about events that lay in the future, and draining these moments now of their elusive substance. Anyway, what good would it do to think of doomed love, of saying a final goodbye, of imagining Tapan as ending up, God only knows, in what kind of self destructive madness? So they didn't let either memories of the past or the fatal anticipation of the future come between them. Only the moment: absolute now – and nothing less.

At last everything was right to give in to the play of pure sense, his body and hers trembling together as if plunging into the sacred, and each giving pleasure, just as much as receiving it, with the tenacity of fanatics. Sometimes it was with delicate touches – such as when a hand merely skimmed over the surface of a skin – that made them fold and unfold like the petals of shy mimosas at the merest breeze. At other times it was with a violence that seemed like mindless cruelty – almost strangling, biting and tearing each other apart. Each time there was a different configuration of pleasure, and they took all of it with the same absolute devotion. Yet there were times, especially during the lulls before they fanned the flame of the senses once more, when Nilufar would search in his eyes for a sign of sadness. Surely he couldn't hide his melancholy, his feeling that he was saying a final goodbye so completely. But Nilufar saw nothing but joy, so she became joyful herself as she inhaled the next breath. From the kitchen to the corridor, the bathroom, then to the sitting room, sometimes in the dark, at other times under bright lights, they continued to harvest senses – smells, looks, tastes and touches – as much from the surface of their skin as from the depths of their organs. Then the telephone rang. Nilufar was reluctant to answer, but Tapan said, 'Answer it Nilu. It could be urgent.'

She hadn't heard her father for such a long time that she didn't recognise his voice immediately. His voice was trembling, almost breaking into a sob. 'My big daughter, please come home.'

After that there was a long silence; she held on, stunned. Her father tried once or twice to say something, but choked on his words. Finally she said, 'Yes, Abba, I'm coming home.'

While he put his pants on, rolled a cigarette and made tea, Nilufar had a quick shower. Almost instinctively she went for her blue jeans, then she turned around to open her trunk. Although she hadn't worn a sari for a long time, she had quite a few – received over the years as gifts from parents and relatives – nicely ironed and folded, protected by naphthalene. She took out a green cotton sari and the matching blouse. As she put them on she smiled, remembering what Auntie Halim had said – years ago, in the inner courtyard, and among the women – that one never forgets how to wrap a sari, the way one never forgets how to swim. Had she had long hair she would have plaited it, but she couldn't go flaunting her bob, loose and defiant, so she swept back her hair, pinned it, and attached an artificial bun – a present from her mother when she first came home with the bob. Then she put kohl on her eyes again, and walked to the kitchen, where Tapan – with a smile on his face – was drinking tea between taking puffs at his cigarette.

She felt awkward, but Tapan said, 'You look so beautiful, Nilu.' There was no sarcasm in his voice; he really meant it. Yes, she looked so beautiful in her green that he felt like taking it off and rubbing his naked skin against hers once more. But that wasn't the moment for it. Since they couldn't be seen together in the street, they decided that he would leave first. Still a smile on his face, eyes full of joy, he kissed her gently on her lips and walked out. He didn't turn back because he didn't want to see her face turning sad, perhaps tears in her kohl-black eyes, dark streams on her cheeks. He wanted to leave with memories of joy.

Surat Mia's phone call had come after the end of the gathering to honour the memory of Haji Falu Mia. Most of the people had left Nilufar's parents' home in Brady Street. In the kitchen, Shapna, Auntie Halim and Cousin Rima were helping Nilufar's mother with the washing up; in the sitting room, chewing paan, Surat Mia had been telling Uncle Halim about his trip to Bangladesh. Shahid was hovering between the rooms, impatient to return to his place. He still had some more packing to do before the removal van came at nine in the morning to take them to their new four-bedroom, semi-detached in Bromley.

Surat Mia still hadn't yet greeted his wife properly since his return from Bangladesh. From the airport he had gone straight to Haji Falu Mia's janaza-prayer at the Brick Lane mosque, then to the burial. It wasn't the shortest route but Surat Mia passed by the kitchen on his way to the bathroom. Nilufar's mother of course noticed him and went to the bedroom to wait for him. When Surat Mia joined her, he said he would tell her about his experiences in Bangladesh later, after everyone had left, but he wanted to know about Kaisar.

Lying didn't come easily to her, but she said Kaisar was visiting a friend in Birmingham. Anyway, the good news was that Kaisar would be moving out of his bed-sit, away from the bad influences of his friends, and most importantly, he would share the flat with Nilufar. Hearing her name Surat Mia became misty eyed and looked beyond his wife, as if trying to remember something from the distant past. Nilufar's mother then asked whether he had lit the candles for their children at the village shrine. Surat Mia said he had. But did he light one for Nilufar? Of course, he had lit a special one for his Nilu, how could he not do it for Nilu – his first-born? Surat Mia was silent again, his lips quivering. He kept his jaws locked tight so that his face couldn't betray his emotion, his fragility. But when Nilufar's mother asked him what he was thinking, he broke down. She had to hold him, comfort him. He said that he was missing Nilufar so much, that he wanted to see her, and that he wanted her to come home.

But there was so much unresolved between her husband and Nilufar, so much about which they had never spoken openly, that Nilufar's mother had to voice her concerns. She asked Surat Mia what he was going to do about the issues that divided them. Surat Mia said, 'Truly, Nilufar's mother, I've been thinking. I can't lose my daughter over some silly-billy ideas. We belong to different generations, na? I may never appreciate her funny-wunny English ideas. You must agree, Nilufar's mother, they are most incorrect. But I can't lose my daughter over them. I suppose I just have to accept our differences. But if there is love, you can get on with all sorts of differences. Is it correct or not, Nilufar's mother? I want my Nilu home.'

Tapan was glad that the night, unlike the gloom of the day, was bright. Apart from the lifting of the mist, there was a near full moon, and the lampposts and the neon signs cast their light over wider spectrums than normal. Instead of choosing the dark shadows at their limits, he eased himself through their middle, as if he was out to feed on light. Now he wasn't at all worried by the eyes, all those shifty eyes, that went clicking along his path.

Even when a guy stayed behind him for four turnings – from Jamaica Street to Assembly Pass, crossing Mile End Road into Cleveland Way, and then crossing Cambridge Heath Road into Buckhurst Street – Tapan walked head up, slowly and at his ease. He stood under a particularly bright lamppost in Buckhurst Street. He rolled a fag and waited for the man to catch up with him. He'd decided he would say good evening to him and ask for a light, but for some reason the man didn't show up. He lit up and carried on walking, and the ground beneath his feet seemed to support him like a layer of air.

On Bethnal Green Road, he laughed to himself, thinking about his nervousness when he took this road the day he made his first run as an illegal, and his panic when Poltu Khan tapped his shoulder.

Had he thought about it, he would have been surprised to discover that he had walked non-stop for two hours, briskly, criss-crossing a large chunk of the middle body of Tower Hamlets, and yet he didn't feel tired. Rather, he felt elated, as though at each step he was drawing energy from this melting space, from his city. From Bethnal Green Road he entered Brick Lane. His timing was immaculate; he reached Spice-Land at the stroke of midnight.

When he arrived the last of the punters were leaving. In the dining area of the restaurant, Dulu Mia – with the help of two other waiting staff – was clearing up. At the till, Hamidullah, the owner, was counting the take. Seeing him enter, Dulu Mia shouted out 'Deshi Bhai' and Hamidullah stopped counting and said, 'Come in, come in. How come we don't get to see your face these days? You're rare as a dodo-bird. Come in, Tapan Ali, come in. Your presence is a blessing to my establishment.'

Najbat Ali the chef came up from the basement to say hello. He said everything was ready; once the staff had finished clearing up, they would sit down to eat. Hamidullah said, 'Chef, I hope you've prepared something special for our esteemed guest.'

When Najbat Ali said that it wasn't anything special, Hamidullah shook his head. He said the chef should take out some coke and meesty-sweet from the stock for their guest. He shared a cigarette and paan with Tapan as he counted the money. Before he left, he insisted that Tapan should visit his place one day for a proper dinner.

After Hamidullah had left, the staff – three waiters, the chef and two kitchen hands – sat down to eat together. Everybody was making a fuss over Tapan. Najbat Ali served him the largest koi fish and the best pieces of ayer fish, and Dulu Mia kept filling his glass with coke. What was wrong with being an illegal immigrant? As far as they were concerned he was simply one of the Deshi Bhais. Anyway, how can one of us be illegal in our own city? They talked, they gossiped, they laughed as they ate, and every so often one of them would tell Tapan that he could come there anytime to eat. Perhaps he needed a job; they could easily fix him up with one in any of the restaurants. All he had to do was ask. Serving him more coke, Dulu Mia said, 'You're Deshi Bhai, don't forget that. You're one of us.'

After the meal, as he was about to leave, Najbat Ali gave him a dozen cones of paan.

When he arrived at Fakir Abbas's place in Fashion Street, just a turning off Brick Lane, the Baul session had already begun. As he went down to the basement he came upon about twenty people – mostly sweat-shop and restaurant workers – who were circling the musical hub in the middle of the room. Tapan was pleased that Sundar, Masuk Ali and Cook Bhai were there. Surprisingly, there was no smell of ganja in the air.

Although the idea of a separation between musicians and nonmusicians was absurd in a gathering like this, there was an ensemble of four. Fakir Abbas was the singer and the melody-maker with his two-string dootara; his brother was the keeper of the base-line with his one-string ektara, and the other two were the percussionists – the players of doog-doogi drum and cymbals. Almost all of the rest were keeping rhythm by either banging tin cans or clapping their hands. Tapan remembered the meeting of the Bauls from years ago, at the shrine of Pir-Baba, on his way from his grandmother's to his grandfather's village with Bisu Bhai. It should have felt strange to be participating in a meeting of Bauls here, in London, but it didn't.

It didn't take long for Tapan to be drawn into the music. Soon he was clapping his hands, thumping his feet and shaking his head with the rest of them. As he continued, as the music conjugated with his organs, as he climbed the elusive ladder of the senses, as joy added to joy, he felt his feet were touching a secret rhythm from beneath the English crust, from the womb of the earth. He was becoming a mole, but in a different way. There was so much speed in his body – accelerated further as he touched the amulet that Kofi had given him – as he spun to lose his heaviness. The whole process was so smooth that it was ridiculous to think that it could be dangerous. For a moment he imagined he was seeing Brother Joseph K smiling at him as he unlocked his doors to receive him. Something amazing had happened; he felt so light that he could almost fly. Ah, at last, the flying mole!

It was about four in the morning when the Baul meeting ended. At the corner where Fashion Street meets Brick Lane, Masuk Ali and Cook Bhai took their leave, but Sundar insisted on accompanying Tapan to his flat. Moving between the kitchen and the sitting room, they lit cigarettes, had tea and paan. Although the funeral seemed ages ago, Tapan felt that he ought to say something about Sundar's father, but Sundar hushed him.

It had been a long day and Sundar was tired, but he couldn't go without saying what he had been meaning to say to Tapan for the last few days.

'Don't you forget that this is our city now, Bhaio. So stop acting like an illegal. You're a free dweller, Bhaio. Free.'

Tapan didn't pay Sundar much attention; he was still with the

Baul music. Sundar got up to go but came back from the door and hugged Tapan, and told him, 'Don't do anything rash, Bhaio. Promise me.'

After Sundar left, Tapan didn't go to bed. He didn't want to waste his feeling of lightness and joy on sleep. He danced and danced, and without even flapping his wings, he felt he could fly. So he who was once a mole became a bird.

CHAPTER 27

I'm Nilufar Mia.

Daughter of Surat Mia and my mother.

It's not that I don't know my mother's name but I have never heard anyone calling her by her name. If he wants to be distant, my father calls her Begum; in moments of tenderness she is Nilufar's mother. People who do not know her well call her Surat Mia's wife; people close to her call her Nilufar's mother. To me she is simply Amma. My mother calls me Nilu; so do my other relatives and friends. My mother says they called me Nilu not because I was born so dark as to be almost bluish, like Krishna, but because she liked the sound of my name; so did my father. She says the blue of indigo that her forefathers were made to grow by the British never crosses her mind when she calls me. Nor does she think of the blue of the sky under which she grew up, by the banks of the river Surma. For her, if that sky isn't full of black rain clouds, it is the open door for the heatwaves from hell. On some afternoons, though, she thinks of blue saris; she says she loves me like blue saris. She loves to eat blue berries; she says she loves me like blue berries.

My father isn't the kind of person to think about blue; he doesn't express his feelings much. I knew, though, that his mother's sister, who was a hunchback, whose husband never came back from the sea, who trapped bulbul birds with snares, and who spoiled him with duck eggs and thick milk, was called Nilufar. She was black like me. My father's eyes dream when he remembers her; he has the same eyes for me too.

287

I don't remember much of Bangladesh; for me it is mostly a memory through the memories of my mother. So many times I have pinched myself for feeling that things that really happened to my mother, happened to me. She has so many stories to tell, my mother, and when she tells me how they used to go, she and her sister, picking wild roots in the swamp so that they wouldn't starve, I feel I am listening to myself.

What can I say about my mother's music, the music she makes as she cooks and cleans – sometimes when alone but at other times among a house full of people? There was a time when I looked for memories in it, but in truth it is from London that I know it. Yet, often, I take dips into the music of my mother and stay drowned in it for a long time. In those moments I don't feel like looking at my watch.

I was six when my father brought us over here – my mother, Shapna and I. Kaisar was born in England. My own memories of Bangladesh are limited to the sound of a mortar husking rice, the pond in which I was nearly drowned, the rain in the morning – and in the afternoon, the flood water that came right under our bed, the little fig tree that I climbed, but like a kitten couldn't get down from, and the poor bear that was made to dance in the courtyard of our hut. Yet, how could I forget the journey, especially the way my mother's sister – that's Sundar's mother – wailed when we left. So alike those two sisters, both married to Londony immigrants. My mother was married much later than her sister, but she came to England much earlier. I also remember the bumpy ride in the bullock-cart over a dusty land. It took hours for us to get to the station where we caught the train to Dhaka; then to England in a plane.

Something strange happened as we approached the station in the purple of dusk. From nowhere, a man – everybody said he was mad – stopped our bullock-cart. He wouldn't let us go until we gave him something to eat. He kept on shouting. Even now, I can't forget what he said, 'Go England. Good eating. Plenty, plenty rice. Plenty, plenty meat. England, good eating.'

Uncle Halim always used to say that we came to England to eat. I sometimes like to think that it wasn't true, but it is hard to deny that it was our stomachs that drove us out of our ancestral land.

Indeed, growing up in England – though we never had any toys, hardly ever went out to see films, had no fancy clothes, and never a holiday – we ate well. Like a man obsessed, my father bought all the fish and meat he wanted to buy; my mother cooked them, and we ate. When my father saw starving black or brown people on television he would smoke furiously and shake his head, saying, 'Oh Allah, such misfortune. No food, no food.' Those nights he would eat so much that he couldn't sleep; and my mother would make juice out of zinger roots to soothe his stomach.

At school they called me Paki, spat in my face, but I didn't cry. I licked my face with my tongue and grew hard on poison. My father used to say, 'Why the girl so quiet. Is she feeding on anger?'

I was doing well at school and he was proud of me. I learnt the Koran too; fasted and prayed like most girls of my age in our community. We stayed among ourselves, visited each other's houses, and ate food. When we couldn't eat any more, we hovered like flies around food and talked food. In my teens I was so fed up with food that I stopped eating. Some doctor diagnosed me as anorexic. People said to my father, 'Surat Mia, your family is turning proper English. You must be proud of having a daughter with proper English disease.'

Even Doctor Karamat Ali said, 'Nothing to worry, Surat Mia. Your daughter is just turning Western.'

My father was proud of me then; he was proud of me until I came back a woman from the university. Then my ideas, and everything about me, and even the way I walked, became a source of shame for him. He stopped looking at me. Now he looks at me cautiously, keeps his distance, but gets very anxious if I'm not around.

Yes, I licked my face, and I had rage in me. But I also broke out of and broke the world in which, my father thought, a female like me should have been happy to live. He thought it was rage too. I never got to tell him that I simply wanted a different world. I do not have that kind of communication with my father. Now we are polite to each other and very cautious about what we say. But I love my father and I'm so glad to be coming home.

My mother hasn't asked me about marriage for a long while; it is a sour topic between us. I don't know whether she thinks of me as growing old into a lonely spinster, with a dry and bitter womb, but I can see that she feels sad for me. Yet, if Tapan had asked me I would gladly have married him. Who knows, we could have been happy together. Somehow, we never got the chance. I suppose, if I hadn't had that hang-up about marriage, if I hadn't seen it as such a betrayal of the kind of person I think I should be, I could have forced the issue. I know my suggestion of marriage was tentative; I didn't make Tapan feel that I wanted it, only that it was something that I could do to help him out. If he hadn't been so stubborn about it, I suppose we could have worked it out. I guess it had something to do with Adela.

I used to think that I knew him. Perhaps I thought of him as a bit indecisive, but he was mostly calm and collected. But since he turned illegal, and as time went by, as he became used to the subterranean world, I saw him beginning to lose all bearings. I think he even forgot why he'd become illegal in the first place. That thing, that illegal thing, had become an obsession with him; he seemed to be making all that effort, all that sacrifice, for the sake of being illegal. Everybody could see that it had become the sweetest thing to him. I could easily have become jealous of it, but I didn't – I think. What someone else would have thought of me in those moments is, of course, a different matter. I began to wonder whether he'd wanted to end up in a bad way from the very beginning. Perhaps he wanted to atone for the crimes of his grandfather, whose ill-gotten riches – gained for his collaboration with the British empire – had brought him to England. There was a time when he used to listen to me; now he lives in his own world.

I'm worried for him the way I was worried when my mother nearly died giving birth to Kaisar. In those days I could pray; now it would sound so false that it would make even the most compassionate God laugh. I could take his thing about being a mole – at least it helped him hide well. He was safe as a mole. But his recent talk of being so happy, so full of joy and light – and all that nonsense about flying – really scares me. I don't trust him not to end up doing something really crazy. Oh god, why the bloody informers don't sell him out soon? Yes, he would be deported, but he would be safe. I can't let him put himself at risk that way.

How could I face myself if something terrible happens to him? Yes, I will inform on him; and I will do it before something terrible happens to him. I know my own people will brand me a rat, a traitor; perhaps even Sundar will go along with them, but I don't care. I can't let something awful happen to him. Love is such a terrible thing. I wish I had never been so foolish as to be in love.

I need to be calm because there is so much to do. I suppose our place in England is not as difficult as it used to be. At least we have learnt how to defend ourselves and shout for what is due to us. We have built our own city and learnt to look after our own. We had to do it because England is all we have by way of a home. There is still so much to do, though. I have to bring Kaisar home tomorrow. He's already looking well; the shine on his beautiful face is coming back. I'll look after him, make sure that he doesn't do drugs again, and that he makes something of himself. I can't fail – we immigrants can't afford to fail. We will do anything to survive; we're going to survive.

I know you don't want me to be sad, Tapan. I promise you I won't be sad. I won't go near, even by accident, any part of the past that has a hint of sadness about it. We had some joy between us, didn't we? I will only remember that. And always those moments in Limehouse when we became sound and smell together. I know I was very silly then; I spoilt it all with my stupid jealousy of Adela. I promise you, never again will I remember that bit. Only the way we became sound and smell together, and how beautifully, like Nataraj, you danced in the circle of fire. I will never be sad again because I will be able to dip into those beautiful moments the way I dip into the music of my mother. And of course, I'll give you my word that I'll survive. Remember, I'm the daughter of an immigrant.

CHAPTER 28

First in the room in which he sleeps, then the room next to it, and finally in the sitting room, he opens the curtains, the windows. Sliding open the glass door he goes out onto the balcony that overlooks the east. He has a cotton lungi and a thin half-shirt on. Contrary to most days of this lingering winter, the sun is out. Already the morning mist has lifted. There is no one in the concrete playing area. All the balconies are empty too. Further to the front, just behind another block of houses, Brick Lane is getting ready for the punters: sweat-shop workers, restaurant workers on their day off, wholesale traders, and the tourists looking for the colour of the Orient in London. Everything looks light in the sun, even the heavy mass of the stolid council tower blocks, and the solitary stumps of the leafless trees.

Below his balcony, three floors down, a green plastic ball rolls out of the porch. A boy runs after it and hurries back, shivering. Seeing the boy, Tapan realises that it is cold out there, but he doesn't feel it. Today is the day when finally it will happen. Someone has just informed on him, and the Immigration is on its way. Yet, he doesn't feel anxious, not because he has given in to the inevitable, but because he has freed himself from feeling that way.

Sea gulls are a common sight further to the east, along the riverbank, but they are rare in this part of the city. He is not curious to know what has brought them here; he is simply happy to see them again. He hasn't seen one since he left his first shelter in the Isle of Dogs. Confining themselves to a narrow patch of the sky, between his balcony and Brick Lane, gulls are circling, catching light in their wings and gliding. He doesn't feel envious of the birds, nor does he flap his arms to lift off into the sky. He doesn't even need to touch Kofi's amulet to propel himself against gravity, because the motion that cuts the air is already well within him. He doesn't need to do anything stupid like imitating a bird. No, he is not going to jump off the balcony in the delusion that he is some winged creature who ought to be frolicking in the sky.

He goes inside the flat, not because he feels exposed on the balcony, or feels the need to hide. He comes in simply because he is desperate for a cup of tea and a fag – and, of course, a cone of paan. Besides, he needs to have a shower and put some decent clothes on before they come for him. He eats some chocolate cookies with his tea, then, lighting a cigarette, he thinks of Tipu. There were times when he used to worry about Tipu growing up without any memory of him, of his brown skin and of his culture. Indeed, he used to have dark fantasies in which his people, subjected to the cruellest of genocidal machines, faced a final solution. It could still happen, but now – between puffs at his cigarette and looking at the gulls through the glass door – he allows himself to think that in the world in which Tipu will grow up, these things, these little pegs of our ancient memories, will cease to matter. Perhaps it will be a garden where, at the cross-roads of so many forking paths, at the inter-mingling of so many species, odours and colours, a thousand flowers will bloom. How beautiful to think that Tipu could be any or all of these flowers, and it would not make a difference. Perhaps this is one of his absurd fantasies, but it will please him to take strolls through this garden because, even if he takes a wrong turn at any of its forking paths, there will always be something amazing to look at, to smell and touch.

Already the immigration officers, with a police escort, will have set off from their base. Smiling, he tells himself how disappointed they will be when they get here. He enters the cubicle to have his shower. He doesn't want to be smug, but if they think they can catch him, they'd better think twice about it.

He feels sorry for the poor informer because he or she is bound to get a hiding from the Immigration for their wasted journey. Especially today – on a rare, sunny Saturday after the long gloom of winter – when they should be going out to the park with their families. But what can he do about it?

He is not the kind of person who sings under the shower. He has always found this solitary ritual rather comical. Yet, at this moment, as the hot water plummets on him, he – as if responding to the baton of the most amiable of conductors – begins to hum. No lyric, not even a single word, but he hums twirling Kofi's amulet. Perhaps they are memories but he doesn't feel that way about them. As he hums under the shower he feels a torrent of names enveloping him with a symphony of sensations: names like Vatya Das, Syed Ali, Altab Ali, Haji Falu Mia, Udham Singh, Brother Josef K, al-Mansur, Sundar, Kofi, Doctor Karamat Ali, Poltu Khan, Masuk Ali, Cook Bhai, Comrade Moo Ya, Bombay Bill and the Bringer of Jinn among others. If some of them have shown him the pathways of moles, others have traced a line of flight for him in the sky. Some of them have been so kind to him that they taught him the secrets of both moles and flyers. He is so grateful to them that he would, if he had long hair, lay it on the ground for them to walk on. Ah, my brothers. Some of you have been the sculptors of our city with your bones. Surely, you don't want me to desert her now – turn my face and walk away. I'm giving you my word, I'm not going anywhere. Here, right here, in the belly of London, is my home too.

Still humming after the shower, he dries himself, and then puts on a soft cotton lungi and a long, silk punjabi-shirt. Suddenly he adds movement to his humming; he is whirling around and shaking his head. Adela, you have been so kind to me, my pale one. I know the history of our skin came between us, but as always, when you come to me in the night, I can't refuse you. How can I refuse you, my pale one? Nilufar, my Nilufar, there is nothing more to be said between us; I just speak your name and a road opens between tall trees, and I walk and walk, hoping to reach the orchid, perhaps just behind the valley. Nilu, I know you will survive. Because you are the guardian of our city of immigrants.

There is a commotion down in the block; people know that the immigration officials are on a fishing raid. They wonder whom they have come to catch today. Some people are banging pots and pans, others are hitting their ceilings with brooms, and everyone is ululating. More music to add to his music, and as he moves so delicately, as if he is standing still, he becomes a whirlpool of joy.

As usual the lift is not working. So they take the stairs. Step by step they are climbing: first floor, then the second floor, and climbing for the third floor where, in the flat next to the stairs, an illegal immigrant is hiding. To their surprise they find the door is open; and they hear someone humming inside. It is as irresistible as a Siren's song from the depths. First the police, then the immigration officials rush in.

Nilufar is just back from the clinic; Kaisar is sleeping next door. Folding her sari back into the trunk, she ambles through the kitchen, and opens the window at the back. She is not a bird watcher, but she can't keep her eyes off a solitary gull: it is hovering and circling, so full of joy.

ABOUT THE AUTHOR

Syed Manzurul (Manzu) Islam was born in 1953 in a small northeastern town in East Pakistan, (later Bangladesh). He came to Britain in 1975. He studied Philosophy and Sociology and then literature at the University of Essex between 1978-86. He has a doctorate and currently works as a lecturer in literary studies at The University of Gloucestershire, specialising in postcolonial literature and creative writing.

His writing grows out of his memories of Bangladesh and the experience of working as a racial harassment officer in East London at the height of the National Front provoked epidemic of 'Paki-bashing' which terrorised the lives of many Bangladeshis and other Asians in the area. Experiences from these years fed into the stories in his first book, *The Mapmakers of Spitalfields*, which reflect both the trauma of racism, but also the creativity and achievement of Bangladeshis remaking their lives in Britain. He is also the author of *The Ethics of Travel: from Marco Polo to Kafka* (Manchester University Press, 1996) which explores the question: how is it possible for us to encounter those who are different from us – racially, culturally and geographically – and what are the consequences of such encounters?

'There are many who date the day he took to walking as the beginning of his madness. But others mark it as the beginning of that other walk when, patiently, and bit by bit, he began tracing the secret blueprint of a new city...'

He is Brothero-Man, one of the pioneer jumping-ship men, who landed in the East End and lived by bending the English language to the umpteenth degree. He, 'the invisible surveyor of the city' must complete his walk before the mad-catchers in white coats intercept him and take him away.

These stories, set in London's Banglatown and Bangladesh, bring startlingly fresh insights to the experiences of exile and settlement. Written between realism and fantasy, acerbic humour and delicate grace, they explore the lives of exiles and settlers, traders and holy men, transvestite hemp-smoking actors and the leather-jacketed, pool-playing youths who defended Brick Lane from skinhead incursion. In the title story, Islam makes dazzling use of the metaphor of map-making as Brothero-Man, 'galloping the veins of your city', becomes the collective consciousness of all the settlers inscribing their realities on the parts of Britain they are claiming as their own.

praise for *The Mapmakers of Spitalfields*

'Monica Ali isn't the first person to write about the Bangladeshi communities who live in Brick Lane. (This is) an antsy, edgy collection of short stories, full of wit and fantasy, about Brothero-Man, one of the pioneering ship jumpers.'
Sukhdev Sandhu, *London Review of Books*

'a poignant and powerful eloquence. His book is a key text of our cities and their now-times, and should be read by all those who claim a part of their future.' Chris Searle, *Tribune*

'A new literary map for Spitalfields' Debjani Chatterjee, *Rising East*

www.peepaltreepress.com